Liz Fielding was born with itchy feet. She made it to Zambia before her twenty-first birthday and, gathering her own special hero and a couple of children on the way, lived in Botswana, Kenya and Bahrain—with pauses for sightseeing pretty much everywhere in between. She now lives in the west of England, close to the Regency grandeur of Bath and the ancient mystery of Stonehenge, and these days leaves her pen to do the travelling. For news of upcoming books visit Liz's website: lizfielding.com.

Kate Hardy has been a bookworm since she was a toddler. When she isn't writing Kate enjoys reading, theatre, live music, ballet and the gym. She lives with her husband, student children and their spaniel in Norwich, England. You can contact her via her website: katehardy.com.

REDEEMED BY HER MIDSUMMER KISS

LIZ FIELDING

ONE WEEK IN VENICE WITH THE CEO

KATE HARDY

MILLS & BOON

REDEEMED BY HER MIDSUMMER KISS

LIZ FIELDING

MILLS & BOON

Redeemed by Her Midsummer Kiss
would never have got beyond Chapter Three without
the constant encouragement and support of my
wonderful Zoomies: Louise Allen, Lesley Cookman,
Janet Gover, Joanna Maitland, Sarah Mallory
and Sophie Weston.

I am for ever in the debt of the Quayistas, and the
champagne is on me when we finally meet up for our
much-delayed writing retreat in the Lake District.

CHAPTER ONE

'With burdocks, hemlock, nettles, cuckoo flowers, Darnel, and all the weeds that grow.' —King Lear, William Shakespeare

'MURDERER!'

Lucien Grey's first reaction to the furious pounding on his front door was to ignore it. After a succession of village worthies, from the vicar to the chair of the parish council, had called to introduce themselves, invite him to open the summer fete or join the bridge, cricket and tennis clubs— all of which he'd politely declined—he'd found a screwdriver and removed the knocker.

And the village had finally got the message. This, however, was not the polite knock of someone hoping to involve him in some local good cause.

The hammering was hard enough to rattle the letterbox.

Concerned that there might have been an accident in the lane, that there might be casualties, he curled his fingers into fists to stop his hands from shaking and forced himself away from his desk. Confronted by a furious female thrusting a fistful of wilting vegetation in his face, it was too late to regret his decision. But he didn't have to stand there and take abuse from some crazy woman.

Wearing dungarees that had seen better days, her white-blonde hair escaping from a knotted scarf, and with pink, overheated cheeks, she looked like someone from a *Dig for Victory* poster circa 1942.

He took a step back, intending to close the door, but she had her boot on the sill faster than the thought could travel from his brain to his hand.

It was a substantial leather boot laced with green twine and, as he stared at it, a lump of dried mud broke off, shattering into dust and clouding the polished surface of the hall floor.

'Who are you?' he demanded. 'What do you want?'

The words were out of his mouth before he could stop them. He didn't care who she was or what she wanted.

Too late.

She was going to tell him. With her foot firmly in the door, there was no escape other than to walk away and leave her in possession of his doorstep. Tempting as the thought was, she was clearly riled enough to follow him inside to continue her verbal battery, so he stood his ground.

'I live in the cottage next door,' she replied, 'And you have sprayed my garden with poison.'

She was tall, but the lack of make-up and shining pinkness of her face made her look like a girl playing dress-up in her great-grandmother's—make that her great-grand-*father's*—clothes. Her expression, as murderous as her ridiculous accusation, eyes sparking with fury, suggested otherwise.

'Look at these!'

She shook the dying plants in his face, the bright yellow rubber gloves she wore adding to the bizarre image.

He looked at them then frowned.

'They're nettles.' This madwoman was berating him over nettles? 'Dead nettles.' Clearly not a disgruntled member of the gardening club... 'Whoever sprayed them did you favour, but it wasn't me.'

'Not dead. Dying,' she snapped back. 'Dead nettles are *lamium album*, a valuable nectar source for bumble bees. These are *urtica dioca*, the habitat and food source for red admiral, peacock and small tortoiseshell butterflies.'

'Madam, you may not have noticed, but there are hundreds of nettles—'

'If you look carefully,' she said, cutting him off mid-sentence, 'you will see where the caterpillars have woven silk tents around themselves while they pupate.' She pointed the tip of a grubby, yellow rubber finger at one of the wilted leaves. 'That is a red admiral,' she added. Then, in case he hadn't got the point, '*Would have* been a red admiral if the nettle patch hadn't been sprayed with weed killer.'

'I'm sorry, but if you'd witnessed some of the atrocities that I've seen you wouldn't be weeping over a few butterflies.'

'Sorry?' She looked up from the nettles. 'Such an easy word to say, and rendered meaningless the moment you followed it with "but".'

She was right, of course, but he wasn't about to indulge in semantics with the woman. He just wanted her gone and rescue came from an unexpected source.

'Isn't that a caterpillar?' he asked as he spotted a movement amongst the wilted leaves. 'It looks very much alive to me.'

'What?' She took a closer look. 'Oh my God, it's a small tortoiseshell. There'll be dozens of them.'

'And I have it on good authority that they'll be very hungry.'

She glared at him, not in the least bit amused.

'Very hungry. And you've just wiped out their food source with your chemical attack.'

Lucien felt his blood run ice-cold.

'How dare you?'

'Dare?'

She didn't back off. On the contrary, she took a step closer, dark blue eyes in his face. Large, long-lashed, very dark blue eyes that provoked explosion of memory, a flash-back to a burst of pain in another time, another place. He stepped back, throwing up his hand in a defensive gesture.

'Mr Grey?'

It was the burning sting of the nettles brushing against his arm that jolted him back to the doorstep and the present, to the woman who'd disturbed him.

Her free hand was on his arm, steadying him. She was so close that he caught the sharp scent of fresh herbs and the sweetness of lavender on her clothes, could feel her soft, earthy warmth stirring his numb body to life.

'Lucien?'

Her mouth, soft, pink, inviting, was millimetres from his own. She was pressed against him, supporting him with her body. As the stirring became more urgent, more noticeable, her lashes swept down...

He could not have said who moved, only that the gap closed in a hot lightning strike as their lips met in the kind of mindless kiss that sizzled like an electrical overload. *Light the blue touch paper...*

He was somewhere else. The ground was shaking, he was choking, and he knew, just knew, that he had to hold on to this woman, had to save her...

'Mr Grey...' She was holding him and for a moment everything was all right. 'Mr Grey!'

A shiver went through him as he dragged himself back to the silence of a Cotswold village where the only sound was the distant echo of a cuckoo.

'Are you okay?'

The mad nettle woman was regarding him with real concern. He'd just kissed her as if the world was about to end and she was asking him if he was okay? No outrage, no stinging slap...

Could it all have happened in his imagination? The flashbacks came out of the blue, but that was unlike anything he'd ever experienced...

'It's nothing,' he said, taking his cue from her. 'I was stung. My own fault.'

She didn't answer for a moment, those compelling eyes continuing to hold his gaze before dropping to the ugly scar on the inside of his arm, livid against the faded yellow of skin exposed to years of sun. His automatic reaction was to pull away and cover it but she tightened her grip on his arm, preventing him from touching it.

'Don't rub it!' she warned.

'It's nothing,' he repeated. 'An old wound.'

'Yes...'

She continued to hold his arm as if expecting something more but, when he didn't elaborate, she said, 'I was talking about the sting. If you rub the histamine and formic acid into your skin, it will make it much worse. Leave it for ten minutes, then run it under cold water and wash it with soap and water.'

'You don't carry emergency dock leaves?'

He invested the enquiry with all the sarcasm he could muster, desperate to escape, regain his composure and a sense of control. She let her hand drop, leaving behind a smear of dirt from her glove.

'I'm afraid they suffered the same fate as the nettles.'

'I am sorry,' he repeated, and this time he meant it.

He was sorry that he'd left his desk, sorry that he'd opened the door and sorry that he'd chosen Lower Haughton as a bolthole.

The Dower House, part of a great estate, was on the outskirts of the village, isolated but for what, according to the letting agent, had once been the gardener's cottage.

'I was told that the cottage next door was empty,' he said.

'The bees, the butterflies and the insects are always in

residence.' She shook her head again, this time impatiently, and a lock of fair hair made a bid for freedom, bouncing over her left eye. She grabbed it with huff of impatience and brushed it behind her ear. 'I would have done the neighbourly thing of calling to introduce myself when I arrived home, but I was warned that you didn't welcome callers.'

'I'm here to work,' he said. 'I don't have time to socialise.'

'I understand, and you have my word that I won't be knocking on the door to borrow a cup of sugar.'

'There would be no point. I don't use it.'

'Maybe you should give it a try.' Her mouth twitched, and for a moment he thought there might be a smile to take the sting out of her words, but she managed to restrain herself. 'It has a very dodgy history, and isn't great for your health, but it beats the hell out of weed killer.'

'From what I've seen of your garden, madam, weed killer should be at the top of your shopping list.'

'Excuse me?'

'You have to admit that your garden is a bit…'

Realising that he was being drawn into a conversation he hadn't asked for, didn't want, he stopped.

'A bit…?' she prompted and, when he refused to be tempted, a hint of a victory smile drew his gaze back to her mouth.

Sweet, yielding, tasting of strawberries…

'The word you're struggling for, Mr Grey, is *wild*,' she said, snapping him back to reality.

'Are you telling me that it's deliberate?'

She might smell like heaven and have come-to-bed eyes but she was a crazy woman who had the dress sense of a navvy and actively encouraged weeds.

She almost certainly had cats.

'And how does the rest of the village feel about that?' he asked. 'Because, when I arrived in Lower Haughton, I noticed a sign boasting that it had won a gold medal in the Best Kept Village competition last year. They didn't win that with weeds.'

'You'd be surprised.'

'Only if I gave a damn,' he said, determined to put an end this conversation. 'I don't know what happened to your nettles, but I will find out, and I'll make sure it doesn't happen again.'

He made a move to close the door, but the boot stayed put.

'I know exactly what happened,' she said, and clearly had no intention of moving until she'd shared the bad news. 'You've hired a couple of cowboys who cut the grass too short and whose answer to everything else—bugs or weeds—involved chemicals.'

'I've hired no one. The lease includes garden and cleaning services. The men who were here this morning were just doing their job.'

'Then it wasn't carelessness?' She was very still now. 'It was deliberate,' she pressed. 'A contract killing.'

'No!' The last thing he'd wanted was a chat with the garden crew. They'd called out to him about the weeds when he'd come back from his run, and he'd told them to do whatever they thought best. Finding himself on the defensive, he said, 'You can't deny that your garden is overrun with weeds which, according to the contractors, are encroaching on mine.'

'What constitutes a weed depends on your point of view, Mr Grey. Unlike your sterile acre, my great-aunt turned her garden into a wildlife haven, and I intend to keep her legacy alive.'

A wildlife haven?

The cottage backed onto the river where he forced himself to run every morning. A glimpse of thatch beyond what, in the days when it had been part of the Hartford estate, must have been a well-kept orchard. The trees were thick with blossom, but the grass and weeds grew thick and high with neglect. He'd been told that the cottage was empty.

Not any more, apparently, but how she kept her property was none of his business and he held up his hands in a gesture of surrender.

'I'd offer to buy you replacement nettles, but I doubt the local nursery would be able to supply them.'

'Not intentionally,' she agreed, an idea that appeared to amuse her. 'Don't worry about speaking to your so-called gardeners. I'll make sure that they don't repeat their offence.'

She finally stepped back but, free to shut the door and go back to his desk, he found himself reluctant to do either.

'Will you be able to save them?' he asked. 'The caterpillars?'

But, now that he was the one who wanted to talk, she was the one backing away. 'I'll do my best.'

And then she turned and strode away down the drive. Lucien stood for a moment, watching as her long legs covered the ground so fast that she was almost out of sight when he called after her.

'There are plenty of nettles on the path by the river.'

Stupid. She must know that. But she didn't hear. Or maybe she did, but she didn't look back, and a moment later she was out of sight, leaving him with only a powdering of dry mud on his hall floor and a burning itch in his arm to show that she'd been there.

His hand hovered over his arm as the urge to rub it intensified.

Don't touch it for ten minutes?

Really? It was that specific? Or was that the length of time she wanted him to suffer?

On the other hand, she'd sounded as if she knew what

she was talking about. With a garden overgrown with nettles, she had probably learned the hard way.

Honey was practically running by the time she reached the ancient oak near the gate of Lucien Grey's hideaway. Out of sight of the house, she leaned against its trunk to catch her breath.

She couldn't believe that she'd called the hero of Bouba al-Asad a murderer. Lectured him like a schoolboy.

Now that the rush of adrenaline-fuelled anger had receded, she felt a rush of shame. The man who had once courted danger in his flak jacket and helmet, veteran of a thousand reports to camera while under fire in the world's trouble spots, had the gaunt, hollowed-out look of a man who'd seen too much.

He was not the tanned, vigorous man whose shrapnel wound she had cleaned and dressed in a makeshift hospital while he'd continued to talk into the camera. She'd told him that he needed to be medevacked for proper attention, irritable that he'd been taking up her time when, unlike her other patients, he had a choice about being there.

Catching her tone, he'd looked back, and there had been a moment when he'd actually looked at her. Not just as some faceless person who'd patched him up, but really looked at her, as if searching for the person behind the mask and the disposable gloves.

He'd taken a step towards her as if to say something but, at that moment, an explosion had shaken the temporary hospital, filling the air with choking dust, and she'd had her hands full with the evacuation of the wounded.

By the time she'd had a moment to catch her breath, to think about him, he was gone.

She'd been astonished when she'd come home to discover that they were neighbours. The gossip in the village shop was that he had leased the Dower House in order to write a book about his experiences, but the excitement at having a celebrity amongst them had been swiftly quelled.

He was polite, she'd been told, but invitations to dinner, to give a talk to the WI and to open the village fete had been declined due to the pressure of a tight deadline, and she hadn't called to introduce herself and remind him that they'd met.

It should have been galling that he hadn't recognised her. But, after ranting at him like a fishwife, she was grateful that she'd been wearing a mask the first time and that he'd been too distracted to notice her, but for a rare moment of connection that had never left her. That for a split second had been there today...

According to Alma Lacey, who cleaned, shopped and cooked for him, he spent all his time locked away in his study—a room she had been forbidden to touch—and she rarely saw him.

Maybe he was working long hours, but that was more than screen pallor. A close-clipped beard did nothing to disguise the way the skin was stretched over the fine bones of his face. There was a glint of silver in the familiar thick mass of dark curls, and when she'd stepped up to face him she could feel him trembling.

He'd been angry but he hadn't been seeing her. He'd gone to some much darker place inside his head, and in a heartbeat she had been supporting him as the terror had gripped him, as it had morphed into raw need. A need that had found a shocking echo deep in her belly.

She knew that emptiness, that desperation. Feeling his unmistakable response to her closeness, she'd wanted the mindless oblivion of physical connection, and for a moment she'd been a little lost herself.

A shudder passed through her—an awareness that all it would have taken was a touch and they would have been ripping each other's clothes off right there on the doorstep.

Lucien Grey had been something of media heartthrob, a reason to switch on the evening news, and no one would blame her for grabbing a moment of meaningless lust.

No one but her.

He bore scars that went much deeper than the one on his arm. Invisible scars that were carried by men and women returning from the front line, having lost friends and having seen things that were burned for ever into their brain.

She knew enough, bore her own roster of mental scars, to understand that he'd had no idea where he was in that moment, no idea what he was doing. It had happened to her when she'd caught the chemical stench of the weed killer and it had felt as if the war had followed her home.

She would have to apologise, and under normal circumstances that would have had to be done face to face. Not this time.

While he really needed to get out and talk to people, he wouldn't want to see her again. She'd leave a note, a pot of honey and some early strawberries from the garden on his back porch where Alma Lacey would find them and take them in.

But not before she'd rehomed the infant caterpillars on the nettles on the towpath and done what she could for the red admiral larvae and the tortoiseshell eggs.

What she should have done instead of storming next door with her accusation of lepidopteral homicide.

CHAPTER TWO

'To be ignorant of what occurred before you were born is to remain perpetually a child. For what is the worth of a human life unless it is woven into the life of our ancestors by the records of history?' —Marcus Tullius Cicero

LUCIEN SHUT THE door and leaned back against it, rubbing his face hard with his hands in an effort to clear his head. Wipe away the disturbing encounter.

That was the most he'd spoken to anyone in the weeks since he'd been back in England, but her anger had made it easier. He hadn't stopped to think, he'd just reacted, but it had not been his finest moment, even if she had just called him a murderer.

And then there was a look that had sent him reeling back into the darkness. The choking dust, the certainty that he had to save her: where had that come from?

And that kiss…

Had that been real or part of the flashback? It had never happened before, and he could taste strawberries… Or had that been the smell of them on her lips?

He didn't even know her name and she'd been mad enough about the nettles. If he'd kissed her, she would certainly have beaten him with them, and with every justification.

He needed to get a grip, get back to work, but first he'd ask the housekeeper for the woman's name and write a note, apologising for his rudeness. And the damn nettles. He'd better email the letting agency too, to explain what had happened and ensure that her precious wilderness wasn't violated again. He could only hope that she'd keep her promise not to bother him.

Except that he was already bothered. He could still see her mouth within kissing distance of his own. Feel every point where her body had touched his: her hand on his arm, his shoulder. Her breasts against his chest. Her hip, her thigh...

And those eyes.

One minute they'd been flashing with anger, then something unreadable that had tapped into a fleeting memory, leaving him with a disturbing sense of *déjà vu*.

As if he could have forgotten meeting a woman with that much passion. He swore, turning to look out of one of the tall windows on either side of the front door, seeking a distraction from the fear that his brain was turning to mush.

He'd barely noticed the garden when he'd arrived and hadn't left the house since. His mother used to talk wistfully about the garden she'd had as a child and, little more than a child himself, he'd told her that one day he'd buy her a cottage in the country.

These days he owned a London flat that overlooked the Thames. It wasn't a home, just an investment sourced by his accountant when he'd been a thousand miles away. If he'd been there, he'd have been safe from annoying neighbours and their nettles. But the same careful accountant had arranged for it to be let while he'd been on an overseas assignment and he hadn't anticipated returning until early next year.

He turned as sounds from the kitchen warned him that Mrs Lacey had arrived. He did his best to stay out of her way, communicating via notes stuck to the fridge with a magnet. However, there were some things you could not put off, and an apology was one of them.

She was stocking the fridge and nearly dropped a pot of yogurt when he walked into the kitchen.

'Mr Grey, you startled me… Is there something I can get you?'

'No… That is, yes. I need the name of the woman who lives in the cottage next door.'

He didn't doubt that she knew it. Lower Haughton was that kind of place.

'Do you mean Honeysuckle?'

'Is that what it's called? Honeysuckle Cottage?'

'What? Oh, no. The cottage is Orchard End. Honeysuckle lives there. She inherited from her great-aunt a few months ago.'

'Honeysuckle?' Anyone less like a flower would be hard to imagine. 'Her name is Honeysuckle?'

Mrs Lacey smiled. 'Honeysuckle Rose. So sweet.'

That wasn't the word he would have chosen. Passionate, angry, alive… He tightened his hand into a fist, desperate to drive away the thought.

'Has she been here?' Mrs Lacey asked.

'She has. Apparently the garden people sprayed weed killer on her nettles.'

'Oh, dear. She won't have been happy about that.'

A prime example of English understatement.

According to Honeysuckle, he was a murderer, a contract killer, a purveyor of chemical warfare…

Images flashed through his mind of a reality she couldn't begin to imagine. The next thing he knew, he was sitting at the kitchen table and Mrs Lacey was placing a cup of tea in front of him.

'I've put some sugar in it. I know you don't normally take it, but you look as if you could do with it,' she said.

'Miss Rose said much the same thing.'

Was she *Miss* Rose?

Mrs Lacey didn't suggest otherwise. 'If that's what Honey said, Mr Grey, you should listen. Her family are a bit of a legend around here.'

He sipped the tea despite the sugar and she was right. It helped.

'A legend? In what way?'

'Well, Jack Rose went to China with Lord Hartford back in the nineteenth century. They brought back all sorts of plants no one had ever seen before. And James Rose was championing organic gardening when everyone else was rushing to chemicals.'

'I see.'

'James's daughter, Flora Rose, was Honey's great-aunt. Her passion was for re-wilding the countryside,' she continued. 'It's thanks to her that we have so many wildflowers and butterflies in the village.' And presumably nettles, he thought. 'They bring in the visitors.'

'The letting agent mentioned that the owner was abroad.'

'Honey flew home when Flora was taken poorly just before Christmas. Not in time, sadly.' She shook her head. 'The poor girl was in bits about that, but Flora didn't want her worried. In the end we decided to call and tell her that she needed to come home. I just wish we'd done it sooner.'

'She stayed on when she inherited the cottage?'

'No. She went back to work straight after the funeral, but she's home now. We're all hoping that she'll stay. There's always been a Rose at Orchard End but there's not a lot to keep a young woman in the village these days.'

'No. Well, thank you for the information. I'm sorry to have disturbed you while you're working. I'll take this upstairs with me.'

'It's a lovely day out there, Mr Grey. You should bring

your laptop down and work in the garden. If you go down by the boat house you might see—'

'Boat house? No one mentioned a boat house.' Or maybe they had. He hadn't paid much attention to the details.

'It's through the copse. Towards the big house. You wouldn't find it unless you were looking for it. No one will disturb you down there.'

Too late, Lucien thought.

He was already disturbed and would remain so until he'd apologised to his butterfly-loving neighbour. Once he'd done that, he would be able to put her out of his mind.

'It's a lovely spot. When I get back, I'll clean it out for you,' Mrs Lacey added when he didn't answer.

'Thank you,' he said, responding on automatic, then belatedly catching what the woman had said. 'Back? Are you going away?'

'It's my brother and sister-in-law's golden wedding anniversary this weekend. Jane and I started school on the same day and we've been best friends ever since. I met Mr Lacey when I was one of her bridesmaids. It'll be our golden next year.'

He managed a smile. 'Congratulations. Will you be away long?'

'We're driving over this afternoon so that I can help Jane get ready for the party, and then the four of us are going to spend a couple of weeks in a villa we've rented in Spain.'

Lucien had done everything he could to avoid Mrs Lacey in the months since he'd arrived at the Dower House, but her absence would leave a huge gap.

'The agency has arranged for someone else to come in while I'm away,' she assured him. 'Sarah doesn't cook, but I've filled your freezer. It's all labelled. I've stuck a list to the top of the freezer. Just take out what you want in the morning and follow the instructions on the lid. You won't know I'm gone.'

'You underestimate yourself, Mrs Lacey.' She had been unfailingly considerate, un-intrusive and, if he wasn't eating much, it had nothing to do with her cooking. 'I hope you have a wonderful time.'

The river that flowed at the bottom of the Orchard End garden wasn't grand. No more than twenty metres across, the Hart was little more than a stream, but it was sparkling in the morning light as Honey walked along the path. She planned to leave her peace offering in the back porch of the Dower House.

She hadn't walked this way since she'd come home, and was drawn by the glimpse of pink amongst the grass that could only be fritillaries. Having taken a photograph with her phone, she looked around. The trout were rising to snap at thousands of mayflies that had just hatched, a sign that the river was in good shape.

The same couldn't be said of the old boat house.

It was a substantial, two-storey timber building that had once been a pretty pale blue, the windows and balcony on the upper floor painted white. Now the faded paint was peeling off in strips and the glass in a couple of the windows was cracked. Shocked by the decay, she climbed the steps to the wide deck to take a better look.

There had been punts, rowing boats and a sleek slipper launch when she'd been a child but, through one of the cracked and filthy panes, she could see that the wet dock was empty. There was only an old punt, falling to pieces, its cushions shredded by mice, lying at the back.

She wondered if the present Lord Hartford—who'd handed the whole lot to an agent to manage, preferring to live in the south of France—hoped the same fate would befall the boat house.

Like Hartford Manor and the Dower House, it had been listed as a building of historical interest and could not be demolished without permission. But restoring it to its original status as a luxurious playhouse for the rich and entitled, under the watchful eye of Historic England and local planning authority would cost a great deal of money.

The only alternative was to let it rot until, eventually, it fell down. A sad ending that wouldn't matter much to anyone but for the fact that Lower Haughton was in a narrow valley. Should the boat house collapse into the river during one of the storms that were becoming increasingly common, the water would rapidly back up.

The Manor and Dower House were not in any danger, and the cottage was far enough back to be safe, but the village would be flooded...

'Miss Rose. To what new disaster do I owe this pleasure?'

Honey, absorbed in visualising exactly how flooding would play out—the evacuation of the cottages, the inundation of the shops on the lower part of the village—jumped half out of her skin.

'It hasn't happened yet,' she replied, spinning round to face Lucien Grey.

Too fast.

The world lurched a little and she threw out a hand to keep her balance. For a moment she had it, but then there was a crack as the board on which she was standing yielded to the sudden movement, and there was a shocked, slow-motion moment as her right foot disappeared through the deck.

Flailing wildly now, she lost her grip on the basket and strawberries rolled across the deck like blood spatter. Then there was a jolt through her entire body as her foot hit loose gravel and began to slide forward.

At that point she lost her fight with gravity and went down backwards in a bone-shaking fall. Her shoulders hit first, then her head whipped back and thumped against the deck. Winded, she thought it was over, but the weight of her body carried her forward on the gravel until her foot caught on something. She gasped with pain as it was wrenched sideways and her sandal fell off, probably never to be seen again.

For a moment she thought that was it, but then something jagged drove into her foot. She would have screamed if she'd had the breath. Warned Lucien Grey to stay back. But the deck shook beneath her, intensifying the pain, as he leapt to her rescue. He'd be no help if he ended up in the same position, but he was the one who was yelling, 'Don't move!' as he knelt beside her.

She closed her eyes, heard three urgent beeps as he dialled 999 and a moment later said, 'Ambulance.' There was a momentary pause. 'Oh, yes,' he said with a sigh that might have been regret, 'She's certainly breathing, but she's had a fall and hit her head…'

It's my foot!

'And she might have hurt her leg.'

Foot, foot, foot…

'Conscious?'

She opened her eyes.

'Yes, she's conscious. How old?' He looked at her for an answer, but she was shivering, light-headed… 'She dresses early nineteen-forties allotment, but I'd say she's about thirty.'

I'm wearing crops and my favourite linen shirt, and I'm twenty-nine…

'No, I won't move her.' He gave his address. 'Tell the crew to drive around to the back of the house and cut across the grass, then follow the footpath through the wood to the boat house.'

Having given the despatcher directions for the crew to find them, he took off his sweater, knelt down and tucked it around her, comfortingly warm from his body.

'They won't be long,' he said.

His hand lingered for a moment on her shoulder but, before she could summon up the breath to thank him, he stood up and walked away, each step causing a minute, agonising jar that seemed to go through every cell.

'Be careful...' Her mouth moved, but no sound emerged. *For heaven's sake...*

She dragged in some air and tried again, this time with more success, but there was no answer.

Had he gone to meet the ambulance? Gone to direct them to where she was lying before getting on with whatever kept him so busy at the Dower House?

What had she expected when she'd called him a murderer? Accused him of chemical warfare...?

Under the circumstances she should be grateful that he hadn't walked away and left her lying there. Grateful at the swiftness of his reaction, even if his description of her had been less than flattering.

She didn't need or want his flattery.

A hand to hold onto right now would be good, though. She had to clamp her lips tight against the temptation to call out and beg him to stay with her until the paramedics arrived.

Twenty minutes, she told herself. It would take twenty minutes for an ambulance to arrive from Maybridge. She needed to concentrate on relaxing her muscles and breathing through the pain. Concentrate on the scent of his sweater—fabric softener and leather where his back had rubbed against his chair. Something more personal. His soap, maybe...was that sandalwood?

Her attempt to identify the elusive scent was shattered by a hideous screeching sound. Muscles that she'd worked hard to relax immediately tensed and this time, as the pain ripped through her, she had enough breath to let the world know how it felt, letting out a long, agonised, 'Owww!'

'Hang on, I'll be right back.'

She remained very still for a moment, barely breathing until the pain subsided a little, just grateful that he was still within shouting distance.

She looked in the direction his voice had come from. There was no sign of Lucien Grey, but the boat house door, having been dragged on rusty hinges, stood open.

'This is so not the moment for exploring,' she muttered, but without conviction as, clammy and dizzy, she closed her eyes.

When she opened them, he was kneeling beside her, his hand on her forehead.

'You look terrible. Did you faint?'

'My blood pressure dropped.'

'You fainted.'

'Smartarse,' she muttered then, noticed that he was holding a hammer. 'Are you going to finish me off?'

He responded with a huff that wasn't quite a laugh, muttered something that might have been, 'Don't tempt me,' and removed his hand, leaving a chill where it had been.

'You had me worried for a moment,' he said, turning his attention to the boards above her leg, 'but your tongue is as sharp as ever.'

'I'm sorry about that but I'm having a bit of a bad morning.'

'For which you have no one but yourself to blame. I'm sure I don't need to remind you that you promised not to bother me again.'

'I'm not bothering you!'

He glanced at her. 'This is not bothering me?'

'No. Yes… I was going to the village to post a birthday card.'

'The village is in the opposite direction,' he pointed out.

'There's a public footpath through your woods, and I thought, why not take the scenic route and leave some strawberries and a pot of honey on your back porch? Something to sweeten you up.'

'I got the message. No need to hammer it home.'

'And then I noticed the fritillaries,' she continued, determined to finish.

'Fritillaries?'

'Do you have to repeat everything I say?' She would have shaken her head at his ignorance, but it hurt too much. 'Those pink flowers over there. Bees love them,' she added, but he didn't look. 'That was when I saw the state of the boat house.'

'And why would you care?'

'I'm a concerned citizen?' she managed, through teeth gritted against the pain.

'You are trespassing, Miss Rose. Causing even more damage.'

'Don't be such an ass, Mr Grey…' She'd gone for brisk but didn't make it much above a whisper. 'There's water… in my basket…' He raised an eyebrow.

'Is that wise?'

'My blood pressure…'

CHAPTER THREE

'Here's Thyme to give you courage and Rosemary for the past, Sweet Lavender for a loyal heart and Rose, a love to last; Sage for a life that is long and brave, Mint to quicken the brain, Violets to ward off evil ones and Basil to cure the pain.' —R B Lytton

LUCIEN GREY SET the basket straight and handed her the bottle of water without comment, but Honey's hand was shaking so much that she couldn't flip the spout.

He took it from her, opened it and then placed a hand beneath her neck to support her. Those long, cool fingers tangling in her hair were better than any painkiller but, afraid he was going to lift her head, she squeaked out a warning. 'No!'

'You think you've a back injury?' he asked.

She made a quick tour of her body, flexing muscles. 'No. Whiplash, probably...'

He nodded but didn't take his hand away as he placed the bottle to her lips. As she was flat on her back, most of it ran down her face and neck.

'Have you had enough?' he asked when she stopped to catch her breath.

'Yes...'

'Tell me if you want more.'

He put the bottle down, then undid all his good work by catching his watch strap in her hair.

She might have overdone the scream.

He muttered an expletive as he disentangled it. 'Sorry...'

She wasn't sure if he was apologising for swearing or for the hair but, heart hammering, she reminded herself that he was trying to help.

'It's okay... Ripping out my hair made me forget all about my foot.'

'So not all bad news, then.'

'My foot is the bad news,' she muttered, but he was now fully focussed on the boards that needed moving, testing the wood with his fingers.

'The wood is really soft here,' he said, looking up to where she could see the damage to the balcony, where water must have been coming through for years. 'You're lucky it's just your foot that went through.'

'I'm glad you think so,' she said, but he was already working at the spongy wood with the claw end of the hammer. 'You do realise that you're tearing apart a listed building?' she continued, more to keep herself focussed on something other than the pain than because she cared.

He tore up a sizeable chunk of the deck and threw it to one side. 'It's just an old boat house.'

'The operative word is "old". It has history.'

'It's an old and rotting boat house,' he said, moving on to the next plank. 'A health and safety nightmare that should be pulled down before it falls down.'

'I refer you to the word "listed". Pulling it down would get the owner into all sorts of trouble.'

That finally got his attention. 'You were serious? I know the house is listed, but what's so special about the boat house?'

'It was designed by some famous nineteenth-century architect who was a friend of the Hartfords. Their weekend parties were—' she dug her nails into her palms as a wave of pain hit her '—legendary.'

'There's a lot of that about,' he said.

'What?'

The word came out as little more than a squeak and he stopped what he was doing.

'Is there anything I can do?'

'Just get on with that,' she said through gritted teeth.

'I've heard that there's a legendary family of gardeners,' he prompted as he tore up another piece of the deck.

'Oh?' Alma had been talking. Which meant that he'd been asking... 'Maybe "notorious" is a better word for the boat house,' she said. 'Rumour has it that the titled and the famous used it to indulge in all kinds of extra-marital shenanigans. I've been told that the bedroom has a mirrored ceiling.'

'Only told?' He'd got to a point where the wood was still in good condition, and it splintered as he levered it up. 'Are you telling me that you haven't been up there to check it out?'

'The Hartford family were still in residence at the Manor when I left home. Trespassers were discouraged.'

'I'll go along with that.'

'It's probably just lurid gossip,' she continued, ignoring his interruption. 'About the mirror. The rest is true enough. Aunt Flora once saw the Prince of Wales swimming naked in front of the cottage.'

'What a pity she didn't have a camera with her. The tabloids would have paid well for that picture.'

'What? No! It was the one who abdicated. He was with Mrs Simpson, and she was naked too, but a photograph wouldn't have done Flora any good. The newspapers had been gagged.'

He stopped what he was doing and looked at her.

'You're talking about the mid-nineteen-thirties. How old was your aunt?'

'At the time? She must have been about ten. Her father had a word with his lordship and after that the guests stayed downstream.'

'I'm surprised they were bothered.'

'My great-great-grandfather was not a man to be trifled with.'

'He was one of the gardening legends?'

'Yes.' She swallowed. How long had it been since he'd called the ambulance? 'The previous Prince of Wales— King Edward the VII,' she added, to make sure he knew who she was talking about '—was a frequent visitor with his mistresses too. And in the sixties, there were parties with rock stars, designers, artists... Princess Margaret was a regular—'

'Hello?' A tall figure in a green paramedic uniform appeared by the deck. 'What's happened here?'

'I put my foot through a rotting board, went down hard on my back and hit my head,' Honey said before Lucien could put in his pennyworth.

The man turned to him anyway. 'Did you see it happen, sir?'

'Yes. I think it's just the one weak spot, but test before you put your weight on it. And don't slip on the strawberries.'

'Thank you, sir.' The man stepped carefully onto the deck, checking the board would take his weight before he moved on, then knelt down beside her. 'Hello, miss, I'm Raj, and this is my partner Jools. What would you like me to call you?'

Honey had had a lifetime of that moment of disbelief when people heard her name for the first time, but they'd need all her details, so she braced herself.

'My name is Honeysuckle Rose.'

The paramedic glanced at Lucien to check just how hard that the bang on her head had been.

'Rose is her surname,' he confirmed.

'Most people take the short option and call me Honey,' she said.

'Right then, Honey. Jools will take your blood pressure while I take some details. Do you live here?'

'No,' she said, quickly, holding out her arm for Jools to attach a cuff and fix a pulse oximeter to her finger. 'I live next door at Orchard End. I was on my way to deliver strawberries and a pot of honey from my aunt's bees… My bees…'

She was talking too much…

Jools took her temperature while Raj began to rattle through the standard questions: date of birth, medical history, allergies.

'Do you live alone, Honey?'

'Yes.'

Lucien raised an eyebrow. 'Really? No cats?'

She didn't miss the implication that she was a crazy cat lady who grew weeds and in the seventeenth century would probably have been ducked in the village pond as a witch.

'Raj isn't interested in four-footed companions, Mr Grey. He's concerned about how I'm going to manage.'

'Let's worry about that when we know the worst,' Jools said quickly, sensing an edge to the exchange. 'Can you tell us exactly what happened, Honey?'

She repeated what she'd said, then added, 'My foot caught on something as I went down, so there's a sprain. And I appear to have speared it on something. A nail, possibly. Or a piece of wood.'

Lucien muttered an expletive. 'Why the hell didn't you say?'

'You've seen enough first aid to know that there is nothing you could have done except remove the boards. Which you've done.' She turned back to Jools. 'And I've almost certainly got whiplash.'

Raj smiled. 'You seem to know what you're talking about, Honey.'

'I'm a nurse, Raj.'

'Oh. Right.' He frowned. 'I haven't seen you at Maybridge General.'

'I trained in London.'

'That's a bit of a long commute,' he said, taking a torch from the bag and peering beneath the deck.

'What have we got?' Jools asked.

'It looks like a piece of wood has broken off one of the piles holding up the deck. It's embedded in her heel. We need to get her out of here…'

They checked to make sure that there were no back injuries and then, using a backboard, lifted her out.

Lucien swore as he saw the long, jagged splinter of wood that was embedded in her foot.

'Are you going to leave it there?' he demanded.

'That's best left for the hospital to deal with, Mr Grey. Will you be coming with us in the ambulance?'

'No!' Honey said before he did. 'That's not necessary.'

Three hours later Honey, with her foot cleaned, stitched and booted in a brace to support the sprain, her neck in a collar, and clutching a bag containing a shedload of pills, dressings and holding a pair of crutches, was wheeled to the front entrance of the hospital.

'Shall I take you over to the phone so that you can call a taxi?' the porter asked.

'That won't be necessary.'

Honey's heart did a little up and down flutter as her reluctant neighbour lowered the newspaper he was reading and rose to his feet.

The up was relief. Her purse, along with her phone, was

in her basket, which was probably still on the boat house deck. She'd thought she would have to call and ask Alma or Brian to pick her up.

The down was guilt.

Lucien Grey had been stuck here for hours waiting for her, all because she'd been side-tracked by a glimpse of fritillaries.

'Mr Grey... I didn't expect you to follow me. To wait for me.'

'I realise that you have a very low opinion of me, Miss Rose—'

'No!'

The man was a hero. Front line reporters and photographers were supposed to keep their distance, report dispassionately, but while everyone else had been running for cover he'd risked his life digging a family out of their bombed home in the middle of a rocket attack.

His eyebrows rose in way that suggested he was not convinced by her denial.

'Really,' she insisted.

He shrugged. 'You may have forgotten your promise to stay away from my front door...'

'I was going to your back door,' she objected, 'And I wasn't going to knock. I was just going to leave the honey and strawberries with a note apologising for the way I spoke to you yesterday. On the bench. In the porch.'

'What a pity you didn't stick to the plan,' he muttered, folding the newspaper and handing it to someone who was patiently waiting for a loved one.

'When I saw the state...' She stopped. He didn't care about the boat house. Why would he? 'You're right. I should have posted the note and given the strawberries and honey to someone who deserved them.'

'I agree, but the accident happened in my garden. And,

since you had neither purse nor phone with you to call for assistance, I had little choice but to deliver them.'

Begrudging, but he'd made the effort, and that was what counted.

'I'm sorry you were put to so much trouble, but thank you. If you hand them over, I'll call a cab.'

'Don't be ridiculous. I'll drive you home.'

The porter, who'd been watching this exchange with interest, said, 'Excuse me, Mr Grey, but I just want to say what an honour…' He stopped at her touch and read her warning look. 'Well, I'm sure you've heard it all before. Let's get you on your feet, Honey, and you can be on your way.'

'Thank you,' she murmured to him as he settled her on her crutches.

He nodded. 'You take care now,' he said. 'Both of you.'

He whirled away the wheelchair before she could answer, and she turned reluctantly to face Lucien, who had retrieved her basket from beneath his seat.

'It was very kind of you to come and pass on my things. I really am sorry you've had such a long wait when I know that you're working on your book.'

'I've passed the time looking up fritillaries, nettles and some of the gossip about Hartford Manor on my phone,' he said.

'Oh? Did you learn anything useful?'

'That fritillaries like damp meadows, that you can make rope from nettles and that I have a very low tolerance of hospital waiting rooms.'

He relieved her of the bag containing antibiotics and painkillers, dropping them into her basket and leaving her with both hands free. It was, however, noticeable that he kept a safe distance between them as she carefully swung herself in the direction of the door.

Very wise.

The way things were going, she'd probably trip him up and lay him out cold on the waiting room floor.

It might even be an accident.

'So?' he asked. 'What's the damage?'

'A sprain and a foot packed with antibiotics.'

'Which means?'

'Ice packs at regular intervals, keeping my foot up as much as possible and time.'

'Those butterflies have got a lot to answer for.'

'Don't blame the butterflies!' she shot back, finally snapping. 'They're the victims here.' Honey's head was suddenly splitting, and she felt clammy. 'Can we get a move on? It's hot in here and I need some fresh air.'

Lucien took a sideways glance at her. Honeysuckle—such a ridiculous name—was much too pale and she was undoubtedly in pain.

All his instincts demanded that he offer her support, but he was rather afraid that her response would be to hit him with a crutch.

No doubt he deserved it.

He didn't want to be here, but he'd had a choice. She hadn't. Clearly, he was the last person she'd have asked for help, but when he'd picked up the honey to return it to the basket he'd discovered her purse and phone, and it had been too late to catch the ambulance.

And that, he told himself, was the only reason he'd followed her to the hospital. So that she would be able to call for help or pay for a taxi.

Of course, by the time he'd arrived, she'd been whisked away to have an X-ray and he'd had no choice but to wait.

Afraid he'd miss her if he went for a walk in the hospital grounds, he'd bought a sandwich and a newspaper to hide behind.

He'd read it from end to end and done both crosswords

before she had finally appeared. A time-wasting nuisance, but there was no denying that he had been partly responsible for her accident. He had no excuse for the way he'd spoken to her, yesterday or today.

He hadn't seen her note, but she would discover his in the letterbox by her gate when she got home, and hopefully accept that he wasn't entirely without manners.

Or pity.

There was a bench not far from the front door which, from the litter on the ground, and the smell, was clearly there for the benefit of smokers. At that moment it was unoccupied.

'It's a bit of a trek to the car,' he said. 'Why don't you wait here, and I'll bring it to the door?'

'It's a no-parking area.'

'It's a pick up, not parking—and to be frank, Miss Rose, you don't look that hot.'

'I wasn't actually aiming for hot. But I left my lipstick in my basket—'

'Dammit! That wasn't...' He stopped. She was in pain and he was being a jerk. 'Do you need your water bottle?'

'No.' Then, making a effort to be polite in the face of his irritation, 'Thank you. I just want to get home and have a cup of tea.' She found a smile from somewhere. It wasn't the real thing, but it was a brave effort. 'Since you feel so bad, I'll let you make it.'

Damn the woman. She didn't give an inch. But he was fighting down a smile of his own as he headed for the car park.

CHAPTER FOUR

'...dandelion wine is summer in a glass. Rich, golden and warming...' —Anonymous

IF SHE'D THOUGHT about it, Honey would have expected a famous and well-heeled bachelor to drive a sleek, fast two-seater. Or maybe one of those dashing sports cars that looked like something out of a wartime movie would have suited him better.

In both instances she would have been wrong. Lucien Grey was driving a four-wheel drive. Not a glossy new one, the kind with a fridge in the boot for picnics, but one that had been around the block more times than it could count. And might have run into it a time or two.

'Whoever sold you that saw you coming,' she said.

'A friend who finds sheep more relaxing than shell fire loaned it to me.'

Honey swallowed. She was feeling better after a few minutes in the fresh air and had no excuse for her snippiness. There was just something about Lucien Grey. It had been there in the heat of a hospital tent set up in a refugee camp. It had been there yesterday on his doorstep.

If she were a cat, she'd say he was rubbing her fur the wrong way. Which was ridiculous. She wasn't a cat, and he wasn't stroking her, although the idea was a lot more appealing that it should be. The memory of that kiss had left an undeniable impression. The taste of him had lingered all the while she'd been rehoming the caterpillars. And when he'd draped his sweater over her, laid cool fingers against her neck...

'Well,' she said with sham brightness, 'that was very kind of him.'

'Her. Jenny Logan?'

'Oh...yes.' She was one of the few women reporting from trouble spots. 'Sheep?'

'The last I saw of her she was up to her neck in newborn lambs with a film crew in tow.'

'A film crew?'

'Are you going to repeat everything I say?'

'I'm sorry,' she said. 'It must be infectious.'

'You are...'

She tilted her head to one side...or would have done if the collar hadn't been holding her neck rigid.

'I am?'

'Causing an obstruction.'

'I told you this was a no-parking area,' she reminded him, handing him her crutches. Then, realising just how high it was, she looked for something to hang onto so that she could pull herself up into the seat.

There was nothing.

The kind of people who drove around in four-by-fours were, it seemed, expected to be fit enough to climb aboard under their own steam.

'This isn't going to work,' she said. 'Give me my basket and I'll call a taxi.'

'Don't be ridiculous.' He put the basket and the crutches on the back seat, then turned to her. 'Put your arms around my neck and I'll lift you in.'

'What? No!' she protested. 'I may have a flower fairy

name but I'm a fully grown woman. You'll throw your
back out.'

'Leave me to worry about my back and just do as you're
told.'

'Excuse me?'

'We're blocking the hospital entrance. Close your eyes
and think of your weeds if getting that close to me bothers
you. I promise it will be over in a minute.'

As if to confirm what he was saying, the driver of one
of the buses that stopped at the hospital hooted impatiently.

Honey, left with no choice, threw her arms around his
neck and once again found herself up close and very personal with Lucien Grey.

Her eyes were on a level with his mouth, her body touching every part of him from breast to knees.

His skin was warm and her fingers tangled in the wild
mop of dark hair that curled over his neck. Place, pain and
the presence of an irritable bus driver faded out and she
found herself fighting the urge to purr.

Even as the thought sent a whisper of heat through her
veins, his hands were on her waist and she was airborne.

As she held on for dear life she could feel his bones
through the thin cotton of his shirt and the increase of his
heartbeat as he took her weight, could hear the faint huff
of effort before he dumped her unceremoniously on the
passenger seat.

'That wasn't so painful, was it?' he asked.

'More painful for you than me,' she assured him, easing herself carefully round to face the front as he shut the
door and climbed in beside her.

It was a long time since she'd been in such close contact
with a man and now it had happened twice in two days.

She could still feel the warm skin of Lucien Grey's neck,
the tickle of his hair, the hard bones of his chest as he lifted

her. She was reliving the touch, the taste, of a sensuous lower lip indelibly imprinted on her memory.

And there was his sweater, a comfort as she'd lain on the deck, in the ambulance, while she'd been waiting for the X-ray, knotted around her neck. His scent, the knowledge that he'd been wearing it against his skin, lent a deeper intimacy.

Her head seemed to be spinning a little and there was a distinct shortness of breath as long-forgotten sensations were jarred into life.

The only sensation she wasn't feeling was pain.

'How's your back?' she asked, desperate for a distraction.

'Telling me that you were right. You are no flower fairy. Can you manage the seat belt?' he asked.

She quickly fumbled for it, stabbing at the slot before he took it into his head to lean across and do it for her, finally making the connection on her third attempt.

'Done.'

He pulled down his own and, with a wave of apology to the bus driver, started the engine, pressed play on the CD player and pulled away.

The music was something classical. The clearest signal that he was done with answering her questions.

She mentally zipped her mouth and J S Bach remained uninterrupted while Lucien negotiated his way out of Maybridge.

'Why was Jenny Logan up to her neck in lambs?' she asked, once they were on the main road. 'And why was she being filmed?'

'She bought a smallholding on the border of Wales and Gloucestershire as a country bolthole a few years ago. Now she's decided to turn it into a rural skills centre and our production company is making a television series about her journey.'

'You have a production company?'

He glanced at her, clearly irritated, but said, 'We set it up a while back when she wanted to leave front line broadcasting. She had plenty of ideas but needed a partner with ready cash, a long credit line and the contacts she needed.'

'Is that what you're going to do when you've finished your book?' she asked. 'Or will you go back to front line news reporting?' Bearing in mind the obvious signs that he was suffering from PSTD, that would clearly not be a good idea.

'It's time for a change,' he said. 'Jenny's done a good job, but it's time for me to step up so that we can expand our range of programmes.'

'Is that why you were staying with her?' There had been rumours of a romance, but that had been a while ago.

He glanced at her, clearly exasperated. 'I was staying with her because my flat is let until October.'

'It sounds like the perfect set-up,' she said, 'So why are you dodging the locals in Lower Haughton when you could be down on the farm?'

'It was not the peaceful retreat I'd anticipated. In either location,' he added pointedly, and they covered the rest of the journey in silence.

'Turn down the lane,' she said once they were through the village. 'And keep going for about fifty yards. You can pull in and park in front of the stables.'

'You have stables?' Lucien glanced at her with a look that suggested she was not the only one who could ask irritating questions. 'Isn't that a bit fancy for a gardener's cottage?'

'Head gardener,' she reminded him. 'But they were for the work horses used for pulling the mower in the days before the estate was mechanised, and hauling the trees felled in the wood. Now it's home to Aunt Flora's ancient car and her still room.' Catching his look, she said, 'That's where the lady of the house bottled fruit and made potions and cordials. And, in Aunt Flora's case, wine.'

'Dandelion?' he suggested as they passed a gash of vivid yellow fringing the long stone wall that fronted the cottage.

'First pick a gallon of dandelion petals…'

It was so much easier when Lucien Grey was rude, Honey decided. Stroking fantasies were blown away, along with guilt about her own sharp tongue.

'A gallon? That's an awful lot of dandelion petals.'

'It takes effort to make summer in a glass. Elderflower champagne is less work.'

She and her aunt had made that together every year when she'd been growing up. 'I was going to pick the flowers tomorrow.'

It had been such a special thing to do together until she had turned into a stroppy teenager, moaning about having to spend a precious Saturday sterilising the equipment and picking the flowers, when all she'd wanted to do was go into Maybridge and meet up with school friends.

Tomorrow had been about trying to hold on to something precious, and she blinked back the tears blurring the heavy cream blossoms in the hedgerow.

'There's always next year,' he replied. 'If you're still here. Village opinion is that there's not a lot to keep a young woman in a place like Lower Haughton.'

She fought down the lump in her throat. 'For such a recluse, Mr Grey, you seem to pick up all the gossip.'

He didn't answer as he drove through the wide gap where the gate had been leaning drunkenly open for as long as she could remember. The stable block had been built at a ninety-degree angle, sheltering the cottage from winter winds sweeping down the valley, and Lucien pulled up in the courtyard that fronted it.

'You only get a glimpse of the cottage from the towpath,' he said, looking up at the deep thatch of the roof as he walked around the vehicle, retrieved her crutches and opened the door. 'It's much bigger than I realised.'

'It was originally three cottages, but there was always someone eager to entice Jack Rose away. Lord Hartford went to great lengths to make sure he was never tempted.'

'Jack was your great-grandfather?'

'Great-great-great-great…' She made a vague gesture, not up to counting exactly how many greats. 'He travelled all over the world on plant gathering expeditions with his lordship. His sons trained under him and all but one of them went to work for other great houses.'

'While the one left behind succeeded his father as head gardener.'

Honey nodded. 'There's always been a Rose at Orchard End.'

'And now that's you? Mrs Lacey said you inherited it, but surely it was part of the estate?'

'It was, but one of the Hartfords had a gambling habit and he sold off the estate cottages and the village properties to his tenants about fifty years ago. That way he had the cash to pay his debts, with the added bonus that he no longer had the expense of maintaining them.'

'So your great-grandfather bought it?'

'He thought it was a scandal, and refused to have anything to do with it, but Aunt Flora borrowed the money to make sure her father could stay in his home.'

'He had no sons?'

'Their names are on the village war memorial.'

'I'm sorry.'

'Yes…' They had both seen what war could do. 'And I'm sorry if you were hoping that I had a lease that was about to expire so that you'd be rid of your annoying neighbour.'

'I'm the one with a short-term lease,' he replied, 'and your aunt made a good investment.'

'She did it for love, not profit,' Honey said, taking advantage of his distraction to slide down unaided from her seat.

The drop was further than she expected. She landed on her uninjured foot, but the jar of it went right through her body, and she was unable to stifle the squeak of pain.

Lucien turned as she reached out for something to hang onto and, before she could grab the door, he caught her, supporting her while she struggled to catch her breath.

So much for avoiding another of those heart-pounding close-ups.

'Idiot,' he said, clearly irritated by her unwillingness to rely on anyone. 'Is your key in the basket?'

'No, I've got it. If you'd just…'

He eased his hold so that she could reach her key pocket but did not let go when she had them in hand.

'Hang on,' he said as, without warning, he bent to hook his arm beneath her knees, lifting her so that she once again had to throw her hands around his neck.

'No! Stupid man! Put me down!'

He ignored her, although his knees noticeably buckled as he carried her along the path to the front door.

She fumbled to find the rarely used front door key on her key ring and slid it into the lock. As she turned it, Lucien shouldered his way in through the hall, dumping her, with every appearance of relief, on the sofa, and startling the cat, who shot behind the nearest armchair.

'Now who's the idiot?' she asked as he bent over, his hands on his knees while he recovered. 'Acting like some macho Galahad. We'd have been in a right pickle if you'd collapsed under my weight.'

Unexpectedly, Lucien began to laugh.

'What's so funny?' she demanded.

'You really do have a cat.'

'That's not how it works,' she said. 'Joseph Banks believes that this is his cottage. I'm only tolerated because I provide meaty chunks twice a day.' Then she began to laugh too. 'The cat has me. Alma and Brian took him in when Aunt Flora died,' she added, 'but he was sitting on the doorstep waiting for me on the day I arrived home.'

'Are you suggesting that he knew you were coming?'

'I'd love to think it was some feline extrasensory super power but it's more likely that he followed Alma when she came over to stock up the fridge.'

'Dogs are friendlier.'

'Is that so? Maybe you should get one,' she suggested, easing herself into a sitting position. 'For goodness' sake sit down and get your breath back.'

'I'm fine.' He straightened, hand to his back, stretching out the kinks. 'I'll make that tea. '

'That would be most welcome, but could you fetch my crutches first? I really need the bathroom.'

'Will that be upstairs or downstairs?'

'Don't even think about carrying me upstairs.'

He grimaced. 'I'm trying not to.'

'Just fetch the crutches. I can take it from there.'

The minute he was gone, Honey used the arm of the chair and her good leg to haul herself upright. She was sweating by the time he returned, but he handed her the crutches without comment and placed her basket beside the sofa.

'Don't lock the door,' he called after her as she shrugged off his sweater and swung herself in the direction of the downstairs suite that had been installed for her great-grandfather in his final years.

It had since been modernised by Flora when she had made the decision to move her bedroom downstairs. Not because she couldn't manage the stairs, she'd insisted, but to stop Honey worrying that she'd fall.

'You'll find the tea in a caddy marked "Tea",' she threw back at him, 'and the teapot in the cupboard above the kettle.'

Lucien filled the kettle and took a couple of mugs that hung from a china-laden dresser that took up half the wall of the heavily beamed kitchen. He set them on a small tray and opened the tea caddy.

A ceiling rack over the farmhouse table was hung with dried herbs, and he feared the tea would be some weird mixture created by Great-Aunt Flora. But, while the tea was loose-leaf, it had the reassuringly familiar scent of Earl Grey.

The teapot was glass with an inbuilt strainer. A teabag-in-a-mug man, he'd never made tea in a pot or used loose tea. He put in one scoop, then added another just in case. There was a bottle of milk in the fridge, and he poured some into a small matching milk jug.

The cat, a large ginger creature with a white bib and paws and impressive whiskers, had recovered from its fright and began to weave itself around his ankles, looking up and mewing pathetically.

'Sorry, Joe, feeding the cat is above my pay grade.'

'He responds, when it suits him, to Banks, and he was fed this morning. He's just trying it on.'

He turned to find his endlessly annoying neighbour watching him from the doorway. 'I didn't see any sugar.'

'I don't take it and I know you don't. There are biscuits in the tin.'

'I can't see one marked "biscuits".'

'Try the one with a botanical drawing of *rosa canina*. The dog rose,' she translated.

'Are you hungry, Miss Rose?' He'd only had a mouthful of the sandwich he'd bought since breakfast, and she'd had nothing. 'Can I get you something?'

'I don't know, Mr Grey. Can you cook?'

'I can make a sandwich. Or I could call out for something?'

'So could I, but all I want right now is a cup of tea.'

Unconvinced, he opened the biscuit tin, added some shortbread to a plate and followed her as she made her way carefully back to the sofa.

He put the tray on a low table before pulling an ancient, much-patched leather pouffe in her direction.

'It's your foot you have to keep raised, not your eyebrows,' he said, catching her look. 'Here...' He put a hand beneath her calf and lifted her foot into place. 'Have you got a bag of frozen peas for the ice pack?'

'Probably,' she said. 'Are you offering to apply it?' She didn't give him time to come up with an excuse. 'It's okay, I was just kidding, but I'll let you be Mother.'

'Milk first or second?' he asked without comment.

'Neither. I've spent too much time in parts of the world where milk is a risky option.'

'Mrs Lacey said you'd been working abroad.'

'When I should have been here. Aunt Flora insisted she was managing, had all the help she needed, but she was too old to be on her own.'

'There was no one else?'

'A couple of world wars and the Spanish flu wiped out most of the Rose family. Those that are left are far flung. Brian was doing the heavy work in the garden, and Alma did her shopping and the cleaning, but it wasn't enough.'

'It's never enough,' he said, thinking of his own mother dying of cancer while he'd been thousands of miles away reporting on the agony of strangers.

She'd hidden it from him and had kept up a cheerful front when he'd managed a moment to call. She'd been a strong, stubborn woman who didn't want to be a bother, protecting him from the worry.

And here was another one. Despite the snappy retorts, Honey was pale. 'You may not take sugar, Miss Rose, but maybe you should have a spot of honey in your tea.'

'I was bringing the last pot to you. I hope it wasn't broken.'

'No, it's safe in your basket.'

'In that case, let's both have a restorative spoonful and then you can take it home with you. And there will be more strawberries, although you'll have to come and pick them yourself,' she said as he bent to retrieve the honey from her basket. 'I don't suppose you found my missing sandal?'

He glanced at the strappy sandal she was wearing on her uninjured foot. She'd have been a lot safer sticking to the boot she'd jammed into his door.

'It will be under the deck,' he said, tearing his gaze from the elegant ankle exposed by the calf-length trousers that clung to her legs.

'Wet and muddy.' She sighed. 'If it hasn't rolled down into the river and been washed away.'

He stirred a little honey into each of the mugs. 'I'll look for it when I get back.'

'Thanks. If you give it to Alma, she'll drop it in when she's passing.' He must have looked blank because she said, 'Alma Lacey. Your housekeeper?'

'Oh, right. I didn't know that was her name.'

'You know mine.'

'Yes,' he admitted unenthusiastically. 'It's a bit of a mouthful.'

'It could have been worse. My grandmother was called Hyacinth. Can you imagine? Every time someone shouted, "Hi!" in the street, you'd turn around thinking it was you.'

'You can take the horticultural theme too far,' he agreed.

'It's family tradition. Every girl born into the Rose family is given the name of a flower or shrub doing its thing that month.'

'They're all there.' She made a vague gesture at a stand on which rested a large family bible. 'I'm the last entry.'

'Honeysuckle.'

Her smile was worth the effort. 'Bravo, Mr Grey.'

'Rose suits you better.'

'Because of the thorns, no doubt.' Large blue eyes glinted back at him with a look he couldn't quite decipher. A look tugging at an elusive memory…

'If we're sticking with horticulture, surely "Nettle" would be more appropriate?' he suggested.

For a moment he thought he'd gone too far, but after a pause, when it might have gone either way, she laughed.

'You have to be the rudest man I've ever met. But if you'll drop the "miss", I can live with Rose.'

'Which means that I lose any right to object if you choose to call me Grey.'

The smile widened. 'That's the way the cookie crumbles, Mr Grey. You have to make your decision and live with it.'

CHAPTER FIVE

'Life is like a rose garden—watch for the thorns and keep the pest spray handy.' —Anonymous

LUCIEN GRITTED HIS TEETH.

Thorns...

Honeysuckle Rose had been a thorn in his flesh since the moment he'd made the mistake of answering her furious hammering on his front door. And yet, despite the nettles, her quick tongue and the hours wasted at the hospital, it was the taste of strawberries that he couldn't shake off.

Had he kissed her? The memory seemed more real every time he thought about it and yet it seemed unlikely. She wasn't a woman to hold back...

He picked up a mug and offered it to her.

'Your tea, Honey.'

He'd anticipated a smile, amusement or triumph. But, instead of taking the mug, she placed her hand around his.

'It's a bit hot for the moment, but thank you, Lucien. For the tea. And for everything you did today.'

Her touch was gentle, disturbingly intimate, and for a moment he was in danger of spilling hot tea over her hand and her sofa.

'What was I going to do? Leave you with your leg stuck in a hole?'

Now she smiled. 'Are you saying that you weren't tempted? Not even for a moment?'

'I'll plead the fifth on that one,' he said, returning the mug to the tray. 'Do you need your painkillers?'

She glanced at a tall casement clock in the corner. 'Not for another hour.'

'In that case, why don't you lie down for a while?'

Wonder of wonders she didn't argue when he pulled down a large soft cushion and propped it against the arm of the sofa for her to lie back against. Didn't object when he lifted both her legs so that she could turn around and stretch out.

There was nothing but a barely discernible shiver, but the walls of the cottage were thick and, despite the fact that it was a warm day, it was cool inside.

'Are you cold?' he asked.

'Just a bit. There's an Afghan on the armchair.'

Banks had taken up residence and hissed his disapproval at being disturbed. Lucien gave him back a hard stare, jerked the colourful knitted blanket from under him and spread it over Honey's long legs.

He took her painkillers from her basket, programmed his number into her phone and then placed everything within easy reach on the table.

'Call me if you need anything.'

She responded with a wry smile, no doubt hearing the difference between the invitation and the hope that she would do no such thing.

'I've taken up enough of your time, Lucien. I won't keep you from your book.'

'It's not going anywhere.' In every meaning of the word.

'It must be difficult,' she said. 'Having to relive what you've seen.'

He lifted his shoulders, shrugging it off, because what could he say?

'Did you keep a diary?' she asked.

'An audio diary…' Listening to it, hearing the background soundtrack of explosions, crying children and men and women wailing in grief, was tearing lumps out of him. 'When you're constantly on the move, notebooks get lost. It's safer to download it to the cloud every night.'

'Our smart phones…what would we do without them.' It was a statement rather than a question and didn't require a response. 'It's important. What you're doing.'

'Is it? I sometimes wonder.' For a moment their eyes locked and there was a repeat of that *déjà vu* moment, the feeling that it had happened before.

'You've done more than enough, Lucien.'

He should have seized on her dismissal with relief, gratitude, at being released from any further obligation. Instead, he found himself wishing that he'd been less abrasive. Was welcome in this peaceful room instead of someone she clearly wished she'd never set eyes on.

'Are you ready to risk the tea now?' he asked.

'Please.' He placed the mug in her hands and she wrapped her fingers around it, welcoming the warmth, taking a sip and sighing with pleasure. 'You really don't have to stay, you know. I'll be fine.'

'I was rather hoping to finish my tea before you kicked me out. And have a piece of what looks like home-made shortbread,' he said when common sense, and every other kind of sense, was urging him to grab the chance to escape.

'Help yourself,' she said. 'But do sit down. I'm getting a crick in my neck looking up at you.'

He took a piece of the shortbread and bit into it as he crossed to the armchair vacated by Banks, who'd followed the Afghan to the sofa and settled in the corner near Honey's feet.

The soft leather was aged with wear, and as he sank into it it wrapped around him like a hug. It felt familiar, like coming home—something he hadn't experienced in a very long time.

'This is very good,' he said, distracting himself from the thought with the shortbread. 'Did you make it?'

'Aunt Flora used to bake it for Brian to have with his tea when he was working in the garden. Making it helps to keep her spirit alive.'

'Like the elderflower champagne?'

She pulled a face. 'It's stupid, I know. She's gone…' she murmured, doing her best to brush off what was clearly a painful loss.

'It's what we do when we lose someone,' he said. 'A way of keeping them with us. My mother loved custard creams. I can't stand them, but I always seem to have a packet around somewhere.'

'How long since you lost her?'

'Five years. Cancer. My father took off when I was a baby,' he added without thinking. It was a rejection that he never talked about. Not even Jenny knew…

'That must have been tough for both of you.'

'It's a common enough story. What about your parents?' he asked in an effort to deflect any more questions. 'Are they close enough to come and take care of you?'

'They died in a road accident more than twenty years ago. I've lived here ever since.'

'I'm so sorry to hear that. It was good of your aunt to take you in. It feels like a refuge,' he said. 'This room…'

Oak beams, a deep inglenook fireplace, and rich dark green velvet curtains that in winter would shut out the draughts.

He could see the rear garden through a pair of French windows that opened onto a terrace and beyond it the meadow lawn. From this distance the blossom in the orchard looked like an Impressionist painting and the only sound was the ticking of the casement clock.

Realising that Honey was watching him, waiting, he said, 'It would be easy to believe that I've slipped back a century.'

'It's the beams. Aunt Flora used to say that oak doesn't know it's dead, that it continues to breathe.'

'Your Aunt Flora sounds…'

'A bit potty?' she suggested, when he hesitated. 'I know, it's mad, but close your eyes and listen. Breathe with it.'

Aware that he was putting off the moment when he had to return to his desk and a world filled with pain, he closed his eyes.

In her fury, Honey had missed the chance to introduce herself and remind Lucien that they had met before, and now it was too late. Against all inclination he'd been kind today, and she had no wish to embarrass him with the news that he'd failed to recognise the nurse who'd cleaned his wound and stitched him up in the chaos of a refugee camp.

In that heightened atmosphere, with the sound of fighting getting nearer, that heart-jolting connection had felt important, but it had been no more than a fleeting moment. It would barely have registered in Lucien Grey's hectic life. That it had stayed with her only demonstrated the emptiness in hers.

She watched as the tension left his shoulders, his breathing changed, and he slipped into what she could see was much-needed sleep.

It was a kind of magic.

It was how her aunt had soothed her, helped her to sleep, when she had first come to Orchard End, too young to understand the finality of death. All she'd wanted was for her mother to come back and give her a hug, for her father to swing her up into the air.

She'd learned to use the technique herself when stressed about exams and her brain wouldn't stop whirling.

And during that awful time when, six days after Nicholas had put his ring on her finger, promising to be back to marry her in six months, she'd heard about his death on the ten o'clock news and her world had collapsed for the second time.

And after Flora's death when her body—held together for so long by little more than sheer willpower—was no longer able to keep up the lie that everything was all right and Honey had become a medical evacuee.

Sleep…'nature's sweet restorer'…was a gift that she gladly gave Lucien Grey. Gratefully accepted as she closed her own eyes and listened to the ancient oak breathe.

When Lucien opened his eyes, it took a moment for the room, the garden and the ticking clock to come into focus and for him to realise where he was. A moment for it all to come rushing back.

How long had he been asleep? The mug beside him was cold. He looked at the sofa, certain that Honey would be watching him, amused, but she too had fallen asleep.

The only watcher was the cat, who blinked lazily, yawned and stretched. He held his breath as it stood up, turned around, then settled back down, but Honey didn't stir.

The temptation was to close his own eyes and sink back into the rare oblivion of a dreamless sleep. Instead, he forced himself to his feet and very quietly carried everything out to the kitchen, put the milk away in the fridge and rinsed the mugs and plates, leaving them to drain.

He filled a glass with water and placed it on the table beside the painkillers, hesitating for a moment, uncertain whether he should wake her. And found himself looking down into her open eyes.

'Is there anything you need before I leave?' he asked.

'No…' There was a hesitation, as if she had thought of something but it was too much effort to summon it up.

'I haven't forgotten your shoe,' he assured her, but her lids were drooping and, even before he'd finished speaking, she was asleep again. He doubted that she'd been truly awake.

He closed the front door as quietly as he could, checking that it was locked. Then stood for a moment, gathering himself.

His neighbour was an unsettling mix of sweet and sharp and he'd been off-balance ever since he'd opened his front door yesterday. She'd left, but her presence had remained, prickling over him like the faint burn of the nettles that still tingled beneath the skin.

As he stepped out of the shelter of the porch, he was assailed by the scent of the rose scrambling over the thatch. It was covered with a mass of fat little buds, but a few small, semi-double flowers had opened in the warm May sunshine, and they showered him with pale pink petals as he brushed passed.

With his arms full of woman, he'd barely noticed the garden. Now he could see that it was crammed with spring colour. Not just the conventional flowers, but familiar tall pink spikes of something he only knew as fire weed, the first plant to colonise bomb sites. And the frothy white stuff that grew along the hedgerows. Both were weeds, but the bees and butterflies clearly appreciated them.

And scrambling through the trees were the flowers that were on the biscuit tin. *Rosa canina*. And honeysuckle. So, May was her birthday month. Wasn't that a flower too?

Not that it mattered. He wasn't about to send her a bunch of roses—or honeysuckle, come to that.

Nettles, now. He could definitely be tempted…

He ducked as a swallow nearly scalped him before disappearing under the cottage eaves. Orchard End was teeming with life, with renewal, and his own senses seemed sharper, more aware, as he breathed in the scent.

It was easy to see why Honey thought his own garden was sterile. Why she'd been so angry that he'd put hers at risk. A dower house, he knew, was a place for a widow to move into when her son married and her daughter-in-law took her title, her place. A home for a woman who had all the time in the world to lavish on her garden.

Until now, he hadn't noticed anything wrong. Hadn't noticed anything much if he was honest with himself. He was noticing now as he walked down to the boat house in search of Honey's missing shoe.

When you took the trouble to look, it was easy to spot the slightly darker green shapes where flower beds had been cleared, flattened and reseeded in order to reduce the maintenance costs.

No pruning, no weeding, just an unobstructed lawn to be kept in check with a ride-on mower. But where was the colour, the scent, the movement of insects? He understood the practicalities, but the reality was depressing. Even weeds, he thought, had to be better than this.

He reached the boat house and looked round. Honey was right. It was in a dangerous condition, which was perhaps why no one had mentioned it. He'd contact the agent and warn Mrs Lacey to stay clear. He didn't want any more accidents.

He took rather more care crossing the decking and groped under the deck until he found Honey's shoe. It was, as she'd feared, wet and muddy but, once he'd cleaned it, he'd leave it for Mrs Lacey…

Which was when he let slip an expletive.

Honey was half asleep when the phone rang. She reached for it, planning to switch it off, then blinked as she saw the caller's name.

'Lucien…?'

'Honey. How are you?'

'I've just woken up. Is there a problem?'

'Well, the good news is that I have your shoe.'

'The bad news, I take it, is that it's ruined.'

'No. I've cleaned it up and it'll be fine once it's dry.'

'Great. So what's the bad news?'

'You said that I'd done enough, which suggests you had someone else in mind to call if you needed anything. If it was Mrs Lacey, I have to tell you that she's on the other side of the county, baking for a party before heading for sand and sangria in Spain. She's going to be away for the next two weeks.'

'The party is this weekend? Brian mentioned it when he came round last week with some plants. Brian's her husband,' she explained. 'He must have told me when they were away, but I couldn't have been paying attention. But it's not a problem.'

'No, it isn't. I'll bring the sandal round myself.'

'There's no need. Honestly. I won't be wearing it for the next couple of weeks.'

'I know, but you did mention calling out for something to eat.'

'Did I?' She frowned. 'I don't believe I actually said that. Only that I was capable of it. I'll probably just scramble some eggs.'

'I imagine you could do that by looking at them,' he assured her.

'That would be a useful skill, but sadly I need heat and a saucepan like everyone else.'

'You're going to have to work on your spells.'

'Are you suggesting that I'm a witch, Lucien?'

'There's definitely something a little bit…'

'A little bit what?'

'It'll come to me,' he said. 'But forget the eggs. I have

a very generous lasagne left by Mrs Lacey. Far more than I'll be able to manage.'

Was he offering to share?

'It would be a pity to waste it,' he prompted, when Honey, for once lost for words, said nothing. 'I'll bring it when I drop off your shoe.'

Her stomach rumbled. She hadn't eaten anything since breakfast and Alma's cooking was always a treat.

'You could make it last for two days,' she pointed out.

Because it was a fact.

And she was an idiot.

'I could,' he acknowledged, 'but she's filled the freezer and there's a curry with tomorrow's date on it. I'd hate to mess up her system.'

Lucien Grey didn't have the look of a man who would be dictated to by a date written on a freezer pack, but her ankle was swollen inside the boot and her foot was throbbing painfully. The thought of standing while she made even the simplest of suppers was not appealing.

'Would that be one of Alma's legendary chicken curries?' she asked.

'Can I hear you drooling?'

Having given him every opportunity to get out of his guilty obligation to be a good neighbour, Honey finally conceded to hunger. 'Possibly.'

'Then you know that you would be doing me an enormous favour by saving me from tomorrow's leftovers,' he said, seriously heavy on the sarcasm.

'A big enough favour for a share of the curry?' Afraid she might have pushed him too far—that lasagne was calling her name—she quickly added, 'Just kidding. Did you lock the front door when you left?'

'I did,' he assured her.

'Not a problem. Only strangers come to the front in the country, and it'll be quicker if you come along the towpath.

You'll find the back door key under a stone frog.' Then, as an afterthought, 'You could pop into the glasshouse as you pass and pick some salad leaves.'

'I have never "popped" anywhere in my life,'

'Hop, step, jump…' she suggested, at which point she discovered that she was talking to herself.

'That was bad, Banks.' The cat blinked at her. 'No, really. He feels guilty about the butterflies,' she continued as she rubbed behind his ear. 'Which he should. But, while he's wishing me to the devil, and I suspect a gnat's whisker from calling me a witch, it seems that he's determined to do his duty as a good neighbour. So I really ought to stop…'

Stop what?

Stop pricking him, teasing him? Smile and say thank you nicely…? Too late for that. He would think she was faking it even if she wasn't.

She'd fled the kindness of people when she'd arrived home too late to hold Flora's hand as she slipped away, staying only long enough to bury her and make arrangements with Alma and Brian to look after the cottage and take care of Banks. That done, she'd rushed back to the refugee camp where she could hide her self-pitying tears in the misery around her. Bury her guilt in helping strangers.

And it had worked until the moment she'd hit an emotional wall and the ground had come up to meet her. She'd been home a couple of months but, while she hadn't removed her door knocker like Lucien, she had found excuses to turn down invitations to village coffee mornings and to join the book club or the village fete committee. She'd shielded herself from what she felt to be the undeserved sympathy of people who had known her most of her life.

Unlike Lucien, however, who had a tenant in his flat and a film crew at the retreat offered by Jenny Logan, she'd returned to the healing peace of her childhood home, the welcome of the bees and a garden that needed her. Even a cat who grudgingly offered a pretence at affection in return for food and a favourite chair.

Lucien Grey might be an antisocial grouch, but she knew enough of what he'd seen and been through to have been kinder.

'Bugger…' she muttered, grabbing her crutches and heading for the bathroom. 'Must try harder.'

CHAPTER SIX

'Remember me when I am gone away, Gone far away into the silent land; When you can no more hold me by the hand, Nor I half turn to go yet turning stay.' —Christina Rossetti

HONEY PULLED A face at her reflection. The make-up she'd applied before leaving the cottage that morning had been minimal, and now it was history. Despite the long doze on the sofa, there were dark smudges under her eyes, and the surgical collar had to be the least flattering accessory known to man.

Lipstick might help, but the only one to hand was bright red, which would make her look like a clown.

As if it mattered.

Lucien Grey would neither notice nor care what she looked like. He'd leave the shoe, the lasagne, and possibly some salad leaves if she was lucky, before retreating to the safety of the Dower House.

The fact that she had even thought about wearing it made her put it down. She simply washed her face, brushed her hair and tied it back with a clip, then raided her aunt's wardrobe for a clean long-sleeved black top that hung down to her hips.

Damn the woman!

Lucien cut the connection before he said something he'd regret.

Not that it would bother her. She'd come right back with some smart reply. Honeysuckle Rose… The most inappropriate name ever.

In a moment of weakness, he'd offered to share his supper, and in return she'd teased him, laughed at him and given him orders…

When he'd spotted her heading towards the boat house he should have turned round and gone back to the peace and quiet of his study.

Except that it wasn't quiet, not in his head. And there was no peace. At least when he was trading insults with her he could forget about the horrors in his head for a few minutes.

Annoying as she was, he found himself saying stuff to her that he'd never told anyone. Normally that would have had him running for the hills, but it was refreshing to be with someone who wasn't walking around him as if treading on eggshells…

He picked up the lasagne, collected the damp shoe from the porch and headed down the garden towards the towpath.

He'd always been running down here before, driving himself to move, not seeing anything but the empty space in front of him and hearing only the thud of his feet and the occasional irritable quack and flutter of wings as a duck flapped out of his way.

He set off briskly enough—he couldn't run with the dish in his hand—until frantic cheeping caught his attention. He slowed, looked round and saw a flotilla of newly hatched ducklings, tiny balls of fluff, scurrying through the water to keep up with their mother.

He watched until they disappeared beneath the overhanging branches of a willow and, pushing open the back gate of Orchard End, he realised that for the first time in months he was smiling.

Not forcing it in order to be polite, or because people were being kind, but without having to think about it.

The large stone frog by the back door doubled as a flowerpot, and as he lifted it to retrieve the key it released the pungent, pine-like scent of rosemary.

It was likely that the whole village knew where the key was kept, but he'd learned a little about country living while staying at Jenny's and, having unlocked the door, he returned it to its hiding place.

'Hello?'

Getting no answer, he left the shoe on the rack in the mud room and uncovered the lasagne and slid it into the hottest part of the Aga before glancing into the living room. It was empty, so he returned to the garden in search of the glasshouse.

Long, with a sloping roof and clearly very old, it had been built against the rear of the stables. It was filled with small plants in seed trays, larger plants in pots and plants growing in a border against the wall. And there were salad leaves on the bench.

By the time Honey made it through to the kitchen, Lucien was rinsing the leaves he'd picked under the cold tap.

'I've left your shoe in the mud room and I've put the lasagne in the oven,' he said.

'As long as it's not the other way around.'

'I don't know. The shoe would keep your foot company in your mouth,' he said, finally turning round, eyebrow raised, inviting an answer.

'It's certainly big enough,' she admitted, remembering her determination to be kinder.

His gaze dropped to her mouth.

He had eyes the colour of bitter chocolate, emphasised by a fan of pale lines where they had been screwed up against sun too bright for sunglasses to offer total protection. A mop of dark curls that hadn't seen a barber in months and a close-cropped beard that was little more than stubble. Pretty much the way he'd looked the day he had stumbled into the medical centre with his arm in a mess. Only the dust was missing.

Now, with dark shadows not only around but in his eyes, the image was dramatically heightened.

It was all Honey could do to stop herself from putting her arms around him, doing whatever it took to ease the pain she saw in his face. Or maybe it was her own pain she hoped to forget, if only briefly. Maybe if he'd remembered her...

As if reading her thoughts, he turned abruptly and began opening drawers until he found mats and cutlery.

She watched for a moment until she realised that he was laying two places. 'You're staying?'

'It seemed more eco-friendly to use one oven.' He looked up. 'I thought you'd appreciate that.'

'I... Yes...'

'Go on, say it. You know you want to.'

She started, dragged back from the thought of how his skin would feel beneath her fingers, the way his stomach would tighten in anticipation beneath her palm...

'Wh-what?'

'That if I'm staying, I'll have to wash up.'

'Heaven forbid!' she exclaimed, relieved that he couldn't actually read her mind. Then, in case he thought she was going soft, because, like smiling and saying thank you nicely, he'd think anything else was fake, 'Just load the dishwasher before you go.'

He shook his head. 'Tell me, Honey. How have you lived so long?'

'It's a mystery,' she admitted, conscious of him watching her as she eased her way across to one of the cupboards, keeping the maximum distance between them.

'What are you doing?'

'I'm going to make a salad dressing.'

'You're lucky to have it. The salad. The plants were flagging in the heat of the glasshouse.'

'Oh…sugar! I watered when I opened up this morning, but it has been very warm today. I'll go out later—'

'No need. I've sprayed the trays, watered the salad pots and left the hose running on the bed to give them a soak. I think everything will survive.'

'Lucien…'

'I've never had a garden, but I do know that plants need water.'

'Never?'

'There's nowhere to dig in an inner-city tower block. Did you manage to rescue the caterpillars?' he asked, abruptly changing the subject.

'Well, I rehomed them on the towpath nettles. And the red admirals are in an old aquarium in the mud room. Some of them might survive.'

'I'm glad to hear it.' Then, 'Have you forgotten that you're supposed to keep your foot up as much as possible?'

'No, but…'

'That would be the "but" that negates everything that goes before it?' he asked.

'I hoped you might have forgotten that.'

Forgotten the words, remembered her…

'Why? You meant every word.'

She gave an awkward little shrug and would have nodded but for the collar. Hating the restriction, she ripped it off and flung it away.

'Should you have done that?'

'Probably not,' she admitted. 'But it was annoying me.'

'And we both know how that goes,' he said, pulling out a chair for her. 'In your own time.'

'This feels all wrong,' she said, sitting down.

'Because you're the one usually taking care of people?'

She held her breath. He had remembered...

'You told the paramedic that you're a nurse,' he said, pulling out a second chair for her foot. 'Have you done the ice pack thing?'

'Not yet,' she said, swallowing down her disappointment. 'I'll do it after supper.'

'It's true, then. Doctors and nurses really do make the worst patients.'

'No. I'll do it after supper and then go to bed. Right now, I need to make the salad dressing, which I can do perfectly well sitting down.'

'And how will you do that?'

'By asking you to pass me the ingredients,' she said. And smiled with all the insincerity she could muster, because that was what he'd expect.

He shook his head. 'Tell me what you need.'

'Olive oil, Dijon mustard, white wine vinegar, salt... Top left-hand corner cupboard.'

'Bowl?' he prompted when he'd found everything.

'In the dresser. And a small jug.' When he'd found them, she pointed up at the rack hanging over the table from which hung not only dried plants but kitchen gadgets. 'And that whisk.'

'What would you like to drink, with the lasagne?'

'A glass of something dark red and Italian but, since I'm on painkillers and antibiotics, I'll stick to water.'

'Was it very bad?' he asked. 'The injury?'

'Was it very bad? Let me think,' she said, finger to cheek in mock deliberation. 'Filthy wood rammed into my heel, massive infection risk, anti-tetanus jab, grade two sprain...' She paused as he muttered an expletive. 'Quite,' she agreed. 'But on the plus side I only partially tore a ligament and didn't break any bones. It could have been a lot worse.'

'It sounds horrendous. How long will you be on crutches?'

'As long as it takes.' About to tell him to help himself to wine or beer, it occurred to her that, if he was suffering from PTSD, he shouldn't have alcohol or caffeine.

He checked in the fridge, then looked at her. 'Where will I find the water?'

'In the tap?'

She was concentrating on the dressing when he knelt beside her and set about pulling free the Velcro strips holding the boot on her foot.

'What are you doing!'

'Applying an ice pack.' He stopped as he saw the compression bandage. 'Your toes are bruised...'

'That will happen.'

'I'm surprised you didn't scream the place down.'

'I was in enough trouble...' She gasped and grabbed his arm as he placed something ice-cold over her ankle.

'Did that hurt?'

'Do you care?' His face was level with hers and she saw the muscle tighten in his jaw. 'I'm sorry. I didn't mean that...'

'It's okay,' he said. 'I recognise a defence mechanism when I hear it.'

'I'm not—'

'It's why I left the farm and rented the Dower House,' he said, cutting off her denial. 'There came a point when Jenny, realising that if I had to force one more smile my face would crack in half, took pity on me and found this place.'

'You don't have to smile at me.'

'No...' He looked up and met her gaze head on. 'You are without doubt the neighbour from hell, but I don't have to pretend with you.'

'You're welcome.'

And there it was. A smile. Not one of those big, all-singing, all-dancing smiles that was all for show. It was no more than a shift of muscles. The deepening of a crease carved into his cheek at the corner of his eyes. Hardly noticeable at all unless you were conscious of every movement.

Realising that she was still clutching his arm, she let go, but as she'd reached out to grab him her cuff had ridden up and now he was staring at her wrist.

'Would you turn off the hose before the glasshouse floods, Lucien?' she asked, self-consciously tugging her sleeve down.

'What…? Oh, yes.'

'And close it up while you're out there?'

He nodded and, when he had gone, Honey sat for a moment, her hand wrapped tightly round her wrist covering the narrow circle of forget-me-nots that was usually hidden by the wide strap of her smart watch.

She'd removed it at some point in the hospital and forgotten it.

Lucien paused at the kitchen door to gather his thoughts. Honey had a tattoo?

That wasn't unusual, but he knew he'd seen it before somewhere. So it followed that he must have seen her. The odd moments he'd been experiencing ever since she'd appeared on his doorstep were not his subconscious playing tricks with his mind. They were real memories.

But why hadn't he recognised her? And why hadn't she said anything?

While he'd never heard her name before—who would ever forget it?—they had somehow been close enough for him to have got a close look at her wrist. Had they shaken hands at some event? Most women would have said something. Reminded him that they'd met before.

But Honey wasn't most women. Maybe when he hadn't

immediately recognised her she'd let it go rather than make him feel awkward...

The thought made him smile. As if. This was a woman who never thought before she spoke.

He rubbed at the scar on his arm, still itching from the nettle sting, and in that instant it all came rushing back. The reason her eyes had sparked a flashback, the remembered pain sending him reeling back from the doorstep...

He'd been told that the woman who'd inherited the cottage had been working abroad but he hadn't cared enough to ask where, or what she was doing.

Even when she'd told the paramedics that she was a nurse he hadn't made the connection that the woman with the English country garden name had been there, in the middle of the horror when a refugee camp had become the front line and he'd become one of the casualties.

Honeysuckle Rose was the nurse who'd cleaned and stitched his wound while he'd continued talking into the camera, sending in a report of the bombing.

She'd been anonymous in scrubs, her hair covered, most of her face hidden by a surgical mask, and he'd been on his feet even while she'd been trotting out the standard warnings about the danger of infection, septicaemia. Telling him that he needed to be medevacked for further treatment and plastic surgery, all the while knowing that he'd do nothing of the kind.

She'd pulled off the gloves she'd been wearing with a snap, binning them and reaching for a fresh pair ready for the next patient when, remembering his manners, he'd turned to thank her. That was when he'd seen the circle of small flowers tattooed around her wrist like a memory bracelet. One worn by someone who in her everyday life couldn't wear jewellery.

It had been a jolt, a reminder that this was about the injured crowded outside waiting for help but with none of his privileges. Angry at the horror around him, instead of thanking her he'd been going to ask if she'd be giving the rest of the injured the same advice and had found himself looking into a pair of dark blue eyes flashing back at him, her anger equal to his own.

She'd understood…had felt the same outrage…

At that moment he'd found himself looking at a different story but, before he'd been able to speak, a shell had landed close enough to shake the makeshift medical centre. His cameraman had caught the moment when the air had filled with dust and screams. That film, with him filthy and bandaged as he'd described the scene, had led the news bulletin that night, and later that year had won them both an award.

But after that he'd been unable to keep the distance between him and the story. And now she was here. Living next door to him. It felt like fate…

He turned off the hose, closed the windows, shut the door and returned to the kitchen.

'All done,' he said.

'Thanks. That was above and beyond.'

'Hardly. Honey—'

'From the smell coming from the oven, I think the lasagne is done. If you could get rid of the ice pack before I freeze to death?'

He removed the pack of peas, then knelt beside her to refasten the boot.

'Why didn't you mention that we'd crossed paths before?' he asked, concentrating on tightening the straps.

'When would I have done that?' she asked. 'While I was having a go at you over the nettles?' She managed a wry smile. 'I think I said more than enough. For which I apologised in my note.'

'I wrote a note too. Apologising for anything I might have done. I have moments when things get away from me…' He looked up then, waiting for her to tell him exactly what he'd done in that moment when things had slipped out of kilter.

'Why don't we just draw a line under yesterday,' she suggested, 'and enjoy our supper?'

No. There could be only one reason why his lips had tasted of strawberries…

'It's hazy, but afterwards my lips tasted of strawberries. I kissed you…'

'Heightened emotions,' she said. 'Anger. We were carried away by the moment. I understood what happened to you, Lucien.' She gave an awkward little shrug. 'I had no such excuse.'

'You didn't say anything.'

'I thought it was something you'd rather not be reminded of.'

'I'm an idiot, but not that much of an idiot. It's your eyes,' he said, unable to let it go. 'I knew there was something. It was there, just on the edge of my memory.'

'I was masked up. And you were too busy talking into the camera while I cleaned you up to notice me.'

'I did more than notice you.'

He stood up abruptly, walked across to the stove, moved the lasagne to the table, filled a couple of glasses with water, then sat down opposite her.

'I came back to look for you when things had calmed down, but you'd been evacuated.'

She frowned. 'Why would you do that?'

'Because when I asked if anyone else would be medevacked out of there, your anger singed me. And I got it, Honey. You thought I was some entitled jerk who was wasting your time when there were women, children, whole families, with no means of escape.'

'No. You were doing an important job, but you were angry too.'

'At that moment I was angry with the world.'

They exchanged a look that acknowledged their mutual horror of the situation in which they'd found themselves.

'We did what we could with what we had,' she said.

'I know.' He cut into the pasta, dividing it between two plates. 'I was going to ask if I could shadow you for a while, so that I could show the world what you were doing. I believed it was a story that people at home should see.'

'You didn't need me for that, Lucien. There are people in refugee camps all over the world doing the same thing every day of their lives. Any one of them would have given you your story.'

'Maybe.' He offered her a plate, but did not let go when she took it, forcing her to look up and meet his gaze. 'But with you it was personal.'

'That's ridiculous. We scarcely exchanged a word. You didn't even know my name.'

'Sometimes,' he said, 'a look is all it takes.'

CHAPTER SEVEN

Honeysuckle, covered in clusters of scented tubular flowers from late spring, signifies happiness, devotion and everlasting bonds.

HONEY DIDN'T DENY IT. She had never forgotten that moment, the look they'd exchanged. The realisation that his anger at the futility of war matched her own. For a moment if had felt as if she'd found a kindred spirit.

And yesterday there had been another of those looks as they'd faced one another down on his doorstep. A look that, for a moment, had sent him spinning back into a very dark place, ending with a kiss that had left them both confused and shaken.

She knew that place, had woken screaming from dreams in which she couldn't hold onto people who were slipping from her grasp, overcome with loss. If her expression had been as raw with need as his, that crazy doorstep kiss had been inevitable.

She shook off the darkness.

'When will the book be finished?' she asked, as she dressed the salad.

He raised an eyebrow at her abrupt change of subject, but let it go.

'The publisher is set to release it in the autumn. The

cover is done, blurbs written, but I've gone stale on it. It feels like the same old book that every front line journalist has ever written.'

'Looking in from the outside? Detached? Keeping their distance?'

'It has to be that way. You're there to record the story, not become part of it,' he said.

'So, what happened at Bouba al-Asad?' she asked.

'I mislaid my detachment in a field hospital when I came face to face with a nurse who shared my anger.'

'I'm sorry.'

'I'm not. But what I did that day was unprofessional. The building could have come down at any time. I had no one to miss me, but I put my cameraman in danger, and his wife did not hold back when I met her at the awards later that year.'

'That wasn't anger, Lucien, that was fear.'

'And she was right to be afraid. I thought she was going to hit me with that damn trophy.'

Honey frowned. 'Surely he was well clear, filming you as you dug that family out of the rubble?'

He shook his head. 'Dave gave up yelling at me to stay back and got stuck in beside me. Some of it was filmed on a mobile phone by a kid who sold it to the networks.'

She reached across the table and turned over one of his hands, stroking her fingers over the dark lines where concrete dust had become embedded.

'When I was training,' she said, 'there was an old man on the ward who'd been a miner. He'd been caught in a tunnel collapse as a young man and had marks very like these on his back.'

For a moment he let his hand lie there, warm against her palm, then shook his head.

'I lost my head for a moment,' he said, retrieving his hand to pick up his fork. 'You were the human dimension in that conflict, Honey. Hands on, helping every day. Your story is the one that people should read, not mine. How long were you working for the aid agency?'

She didn't answer and he looked up, assuming that she had a mouthful of food, but her grip on the fork had tightened.

'My first tour was in West Africa…' She swallowed. 'It was just over six years ago.'

He frowned. 'The Ebola crisis?' She nodded and he let slip an expletive. No wonder she didn't want to talk about it. 'That was a tough posting.'

'I was needed.'

'I can't begin to imagine how bad it must have been.'

For a moment all she could manage was a nod while she caught her breath and took a sip of water.

'I'm sorry. You don't have to talk about it.'

'The worst of the major outbreak was over by the time I got there,' she said. 'Since then, it's been refugee camps. What about you?' she asked, turning the conversation back to him.

It was obvious that she didn't want to talk about her involvement in disaster response, and he didn't want to talk about the things he'd seen. So gradually, between mouthfuls, they shared details about a few days grabbed on a beach in Turkey, his visit to Petra and hers to the Valley of the Kings.

Similar interests, similar pleasures…

'And now you're home in the peace of Lower Haughton, taking care of the weeds,' he said.

Honey startled herself with a laugh. The evening had passed in what felt like a flash. It had been an age since she'd talked to someone—really talked…

'A weed,' she informed him, 'is only a flower growing in the wrong place, and even those need help. It's not that easy to grow a wildflower meadow. Grass is a bit of a thug.

Its roots have to be kept in check if anything but daisies and dandelions are to grow.'

'I know nothing about gardening,' he admitted, 'but when I walked down to the boat house to find your shoe I could see where there had once been flower beds.'

'What they did there was nothing short of vandalism.' She shook her head. 'There's fruit, or some ice-cream in the freezer, if you'd like some?'

'No, I'm done. I could make some coffee, if I haven't outstayed my welcome?'

'It's a little late.'

'Of course,' he said, getting to his feet. 'You've had a stressful day. I'll clear up and leave you in peace.'

'It's a little late for coffee,' she said. 'And I'm sure you've been advised to cut down on caffeine. But, since you're of-fering, I'll take a camomile tea. You should try it. It's re-laxing and aids sleep.'

'Do I have to go out and pick it?' he asked.

Oh, the temptation...

She gave herself a mental slap on the wrist and said, 'Not this time. You'll find a box of bags in the cupboard above the kettle, and I vote we take it outside. Now the sun's gone down, we might be lucky enough to see some bats.'

'Bats?'

'Pipistrelles. Don't worry, they're small, and they'll be more interested in feeding on insects than building a nest in your hair.'

'Are you suggesting that I need a haircut?' The light caught on the glint of silver as he raked his fingers through the mass of dark curls.

'Not for me,' she said, then blushed a little. 'Or the bats.'

'Most women I've met are scared witless by them,' he said. 'But then you are an original.'

'Thank you.'

'I'm glad you took it as a compliment.'

'A woman whose next birthday begins with three, and dresses early nineteen-forties allotment, has to take them wherever she finds them.'

Lucien looked as if he was going to say more but clearly thought better of it. Having put on the kettle, he cleared the table and stacked everything in the dishwasher. He might be tactless, if not downright rude, but he hadn't had to bring her supper or clear up afterwards. And he had watered her drooping plants.

You could forgive a man who saw a need and, unasked, stepped in to fill it pretty much anything.

Ten minutes later they were sitting outside on a bench beneath a honeysuckle-draped pergola, mugs in hand.

'I missed this so much when I was overseas,' Honey said. 'The long, soft English dusk. The small sounds of birds settling.' And to tease him a little. 'The scent of honeysuckle.'

He closed his eyes and leaned back. 'If I'd had this, I don't think I'd have ever left.' He glanced across at her. 'You obviously love it here, so why did you leave?'

'My mother was a nurse. I have a picture of her in her uniform.' She looked at him. 'I barely remembered her, Lucien, and I thought if I could do what she did it would bring her closer.'

'Did it?'

'I don't know. I did the things she did, took my nursing degree at the same place she did. I fell in love at the same age she met my father. But I'll never know how she felt about anything.'

'You told the paramedic that you trained in London.'

'At King's. It offered a chance to work in Africa and east Asia but I don't know if that's why my mother chose it. There are so many things I'll never know.'

He understood that loss. Who was his father? Where was he now? There were so many gaps...

'You always wanted to travel?' he asked.

She shrugged. 'I'm a Rose. It's in the genes. What did you leave behind, Lucien?'

'Concrete, diesel fumes… No honeysuckle.' He turned to look at her. 'Why didn't your family call you May? After the blossom,' he added, when she raised her eyebrows at the abrupt change of subject. 'It's not a common name these days. Or maybe in your family it is. You probably have generations of relations called May.'

She took a sip of tea, appearing to think about it.

'There is a first cousin twice removed living in New Zealand, but I don't know of another. People don't have as many children these days. And, since you were listening when I was being interrogated by the paramedics, you must know that I was born in June.'

'I tuned out when they started asking for medical details.'

'Such a gentleman.'

'Such sarcasm.' He gestured at the pergola. 'Besides, the honeysuckle is out now.'

'We've had a warm spring and this one is a bit ahead of itself. It will still be flowering on my birthday. As will the roses. We all have two birth month flowers. When were you born, Lucien?'

'You're going to match me to a flower?'

'It's an old country tradition.'

He rolled his eyes but said, 'September.'

She thought about it for a moment. 'St John's Wort is in flower then.'

'I don't need to ask which of those names you'd choose for me.'

'Don't mock. It's traditionally used for mild depression, poor appetite and trouble sleeping.'

He shifted a little as she touched a sensitive spot. 'You said two flowers.'

'And for September they are the aster—faith, achievement wisdom—also known as Michaelmas daisies.'

'I'll take Michael,' he said with relief.

'And *convolvulus arvensis*. Affection, patience, intimate love.' She paused for a heartbeat. Maybe two. 'Also known as Morning Glory.'

Lucien, mid-gulp, spluttered and coughed. 'Dammit, woman, this God-awful tea just came down my nose!'

He glared at her, but she was pressing her lips tightly together in an effort not to laugh as he mopped his face with the hem of his T-shirt. And then he was laughing too.

'You are something else.'

'And what would that be?'

Before he could answer, she grabbed his arm, pointing at a small, dark shape flitting across the garden against the fading lavender sky.

'Is that…?'

'It is. Be very quiet,' she whispered, 'and you'll hear them clicking.'

They watched in silence as the little bats skimmed the garden using echo location in their hunt for insects and moths.

'Have there been a lot of women?' she asked after a while. 'Who are afraid of bats?'

'A few. One…' He shrugged. 'I have no idea if Charlotte was afraid of bats, but I do know that she was scared of my job and hated the fact that I was away more than at home. When it came to a choice—'

'She made you choose?'

'She wanted a family, a partner who was there. It's difficult to be in any kind of serious relationship when you're constantly on the move. Women get hurt.'

'Everyone gets hurt when a relationship ends.'

'That's true, but if I wasn't prepared to give up what I was doing for her I had to accept that I wasn't ready for commitment. In the end, you have to live with yourself, so you keep it casual.'

'But now you're home. Out of danger.'

'Out of danger but a mess. I punched some idiot who was mouthing off racist filth in a bar.'

'That didn't make the ten o'clock news. Or social media,' she added.

'He was smart enough to realise that he was the one who'd look bad, and my friends covered for me, but there comes a time when you know it's over.'

'That's it? There's no going back?'

'I've been seeing a counsellor, but the truth is that I've seen too much and I'm not in any shape to inflict myself on anyone. What about you?' he asked.

'No women.' He didn't laugh. 'One man. A long time ago,' she said, as if the words had been dragged from her. 'When he died in a plane crash, something inside me died too.'

He couldn't think of a thing to say. *I'm sorry* would be meaningless. To his relief, Banks appeared out of the bushes and stood in front of the bench, staring up at him.

'Your cat hates me.'

'He's not that emotional,' Honey explained, clearly as relieved as he was to be back on safe ground. 'He's just letting you know that you're sitting in his spot and expects you to move.'

'Dogs have much better manners, but Banks can have his bench. I have a chapter to kick into shape,' he said, standing up and offering her his hand. 'I'll see you safely inside.'

Honey would have stayed out longer to watch the stars light up, but she knew that if she didn't go in Lucien would insist on staying, or fret about her tripping over the uneven paving and lying injured until she was discovered in the early hours by the milkman.

A small sound escaped her, something between a groan and a sigh.

'Did you say something?'

'No. I was just thinking about my aunt here on her own with no one to see her safely inside. She always seemed indestructible, but I wasn't looking hard enough, and she never said a word…'

'My mother hid her cancer from me. It was a neighbour who found my number and called to tell me I had to get home.'

'Did you make it in time?'

'I had a few days with her. Time to say the things that had to be said. You?'

'Transport was difficult…' She looked up at him. 'Does it ever go away? The guilt?'

'No, but it helps a little if you keep telling yourself that they took pride in our achievements. That it was what they wanted for us. And they knew they were loved,' he said, as he helped her to her feet. He continued to hold her until he was sure she had her balance.

'But it's what we do that matters.'

'I'm sure she knew that what you were doing was important, Honey.'

He handed her the crutches, then put a steadying hand on her back as they headed slowly towards the door, ready to catch her if she tripped on the uneven paving.

It should have been irritating. She was perfectly capable of walking a few yards without falling on her face. No one had ever treated her as if she was fragile, even when it felt as if she were shattering into a million tiny pieces…

Lucien added the mugs to the dishwasher, then glanced at her.

'The tabs are under the sink.'

He found them and turned it on. 'Do you need a hand with the stairs?'

'There's an *en suite* bedroom on the ground floor.'

'For your aunt?'

'She had it installed for her father but gave it a very classy makeover when she decided to move downstairs. I'll be very comfortable.'

'You've got your painkillers where you can find them?' She nodded.

'What about another ice pack?'

'Don't fuss, Lucien. I can manage.'

'Of course you can,' he said, but he didn't move, and she suspected that it was less about concern for her than reluctance to go back to the dark and empty Dower House, where the echoes of a war that haunted him were waiting. 'Thanks for...'

'The bats?' she offered when he hesitated.

'The bats were special,' he agreed, grabbing at something impersonal. 'But I've got five thousand words to write, and you need to sleep.'

'You're going to work now?'

'I'm going to try,' he said, finally making it to the door. 'Lucien...'

He stopped and half turned, his expression so intense that her words remained unsaid in her throat.

For long seconds they were frozen in that moment, before he spun round and walked swiftly back to her, taking her face between his hands.

She could feel the roughness of his scarred palms against her cheeks, smell the warmth coming off his body, musky, masculine, overlain with the head-clearing scent of the rosemary growing in the frog by the door.

But her senses were overridden, consumed by the intensity of his gaze, and when he breathed her name, every syllable of Honeysuckle Rose a question, she forgot what she had been going to say and closed her eyes.

Her pulse beat once, twice, before, with a raw, desperate groan, his mouth came down on hers with a fierceness that carried her back until she was stopped by the curved door of the vintage fridge with only his body, the bones and the heat of him holding her upright.

Her crutches hit the floor with a crash, her fingers digging into his shoulders as he leaned into her, drinking in his kiss like water in a desert.

It took her breath, stopped her heart, turned her centre to liquid heat, and she gave it back with all the passion she'd been hoarding for years.

Lucien was the first to recover his senses, leaning his forehead against hers while he caught his breath.

'Honey…'

He was holding her so close that there was no disguising his physical response. He was going to apologise for that, or the kiss. She heard it in the agonised way he'd said her name, and she couldn't bear it.

'Don't!' He lifted his head, searching her face. 'It's been a strange day,' she said before he said it, or something very like it. The kind of excuses men made when they'd done something that they immediately regretted and were desperate to escape. 'And those words won't write themselves.'

He continued to look at her for what felt like a lifetime, then took a step back.

Without his body to hold her against the fridge door, she was in danger of sliding into a crumpled heap at his feet, and she grabbed for the handle the second he bent to pick up her crutches.

'Honey,' he began, but she cut him off.

'I know. Casual.'

'The word I had in mind was "unforgettable",' he said, handing her the crutches before he turned and left without looking back.

Honey, released from the effort of appearing to be completely in control, from the effects of that mind-blowing kiss, was finally able to sink onto the nearest chair. That was when she discovered that it wasn't only her legs that were trembling but her entire body.

Exhilarated. Afraid...

She drew in a long, shuddering breath, laid her head on her arms and waited for her heartbeat to settle back into its normal steady rhythm.

She was still struggling with that when her phone, lying beside her bleeped to let her know she had a text.

Lucien was all but running by the time he reached Honey's gate, only slowing once he'd heard the catch snap into place.

A safety barrier.

It had been there from the moment he'd spotted her on the boat house deck. The insults and the banter were a kind of foreplay, a disguise for the sexual tension, there from that moment on his doorstep when anger could so easily have spilled over into hot, mindless sex.

Casual...

That kiss hadn't felt like any casual encounter he'd ever known. And now he knew for certain that it had happened before. That he hadn't been dreaming or imagining that he'd kissed her on his doorstep.

He'd felt it, known it somewhere deep in his gut, but had been controlling it until she'd said his name in a way that had bypassed his brain and gone straight to his...

He stopped and cursed himself for an idiot.

He'd been on the point of leaving when she'd thought of something she needed and called him back. The rest was all in his head. What he wanted to hear...

He took out his phone but, reluctant to risk the intimacy of her voice in his ear until he'd had a long, cold shower, he opted for the safety of a text.

Honey, I'm sorry...

He deleted that. Told himself to keep it brief and to the point.

You called me back just as I was leaving, Honey. Was there something else you needed? L

He contemplated adding a kiss. Rejected the idea immediately and deleted the 'else', which might just come across as a little passive aggressive. 'Else' would imply that she'd asked for the kiss. She hadn't, but he could still feel where her fingers had dug into his shoulders as she'd clung on, her mouth hot silk and fully engaged.

And he deleted the 'Honey', which sounded far too much like an endearment.

He clicked 'send' then paced the bank, anticipating a swift reply. He waited long minutes and was about to give up, hoping that she was getting ready for bed rather than ignoring his message, when a beep alerted him to an incoming text.

I just wanted to say that I'll return your sweater when I've washed it. H

Matter-of-fact to the point of brusqueness.

He could hear her saying it in the same calm voice with which she'd reminded him that he had five thousand words to write. As she'd dismissed him with her cool, 'I know.'

For a moment he felt oddly deflated. He didn't know what he'd expected. The spirit, the sharpness of their usual exchanges? The soft, velvet voice that had made his name sound like a sin?

He swore at his own stupidity.

That hadn't been the voice of a woman thinking about

laundry. A woman who, despite the composure with which she'd sent him back to his desk, had clutched at the fridge door handle for support, barely able to stand after the kind of mind-blowing kiss that should only ever have ended up in one place.

She hadn't ignored his text. It had taken her that long to think of a convincing answer to the question...

Forget the cold shower.

He stripped off, waded out into the river and dived beneath the surface before he was the one hammering on her door and calling out her lie.

CHAPTER EIGHT

'...rosemary, growing by the door, allows only love to enter.' —Traditional

IT HAD TAKEN Honey frantic minutes to come up with a convincing answer to Lucien's text.

For most of that time she'd been kidding herself that she hadn't known what she'd wanted when she'd said his name.

He'd seemed so reluctant to leave and the thought had come to her that she should ask him to stay. Not because she needed help, but because he looked as if he did. There was plenty of room...

Still lying to herself.

Her body had been tingling ever since that moment on his front doorstep. Craving attention. The touch of a man's hand. His hand...

He'd said there were no serious relationships, but Jenny Logan had given him the keys to her four-by-four for just one reason. She wasn't down on the farm counting sheep. She was counting the days until he drove it back to her. It might be a forlorn hope that he was ready to settle down, but they had history. He'd feel safe with her.

Not that she'd been thinking of Jenny when Lucien's tongue had been blazing the way to a deeper intimacy, the soft ache of desire stoked to fever pitch but left unsatisfied.

She re-read his text.

You called me back just as I was leaving. Was there something you needed? L

Not answering was out of the question. He'd think there was a problem and within minutes he'd be back, fishing the key from beneath the frog to let himself in. All it would take was one look and he'd know how much she wanted him.

This was new, terrifying, a risk that she wasn't ready to take. She fastened her hand around her forget-me-not tattoo, digging her nails in to keep herself grounded.

The flower was supposed to alleviate grief, but it had become a reminder that everyone she had ever loved had been taken from her, and there was only so much pain one person could take.

She had to answer him...

He'd kept it impersonal and she must do the same.

Casting around for something, anything, she thought of the lasagne dish that she'd have to return, then saw his sweater lying on the arm of the sofa.

She thumbed in a brisk text that matched his matter-of-fact tone and hit send.

She'd wash the sweater and give it to the postman to drop in at the Dower House, along with Alma's dish. No more dicing with her dangerously attractive neighbour.

Unfortunately, her body wasn't on the same wavelength as her head and was still jangling with frustrated desire. Knowing that she wouldn't sleep, she went back outside to watch the moon rise against the darkening sky. And, because it had become chilly, she picked up Lucien's sweater to drape around her shoulders. She breathed in his scent one last time.

She had just reached the bench when she heard a splash.

Brian had told her that a pair of otters had been spotted on the Hart and, confident on her crutches now, she swung quickly down the garden to the gate.

There was something in the water swimming beneath the surface, and she held her breath, wishing she'd had the sense to bring her phone with her so that she could take a photograph when it broke the surface.

Which was when history repeated itself.

Except that, unlike her aunt, she wasn't ten years old, and the naked man rising from the depths of the river wasn't a royal prince who was about to cause a constitutional crisis.

Lucien was facing downriver towards the boat house, and, by the time he turned to step up onto the bank she had backed deep into the bushes. She was hidden from view but unable to move without betraying her presence, although her heart was hammering so hard it was a miracle that he didn't hear it.

He stood on the bank for what felt like an age, his wet skin silvered by the moon, the shadows highlighting bone and muscle.

Honey froze as he glanced towards the gate, then smiled and said, 'Rosemary.'

What?

The man barely knew a daisy from a buttercup, but the air was filled with the scent of the rosemary that had been growing by the garden gate for as long as she could remember. He must have brushed against it as he left. Or maybe she had as she'd taken cover.

He shook the water from his hair, then scooped up his discarded clothes. She was forced to watch as, with shoes dangling from the fingers of one hand, clothes in the other, he walked barefoot and buck naked along the path until he was out of sight.

It was the sun lighting up the corner of the room as it rose above the trees that made Lucien look up.

He blinked, rubbed his face and sat back, astonished to discover that it was nearly six o'clock and he'd been writing all night.

He stood up, stretched out limbs that had barely moved since he'd showered off his plunge in the river, pulled on fresh running gear and, as he and sleep were not on speaking terms, headed for his desk.

He'd told Honey that he had five thousand words to write. He'd done that and more and, for the first time since he'd yielded to pressure from his agent to write a book about his experiences.

He picked up his phone, checking in case Honey had sent a text, but there was nothing.

Which should have been a relief.

Was a relief…

There was something unsettling in the way she managed to tease things out of him and made him confront things that he'd hidden from both his counsellor and Jenny. His father's desertion, the memory lapses…

He grabbed a bottle of water and set off for a run. He took a detour via the boat house to take some photographs of the damage to send to the letting agent, along with a report of the accident and a demand that it was made safe.

That done, he began to walk rather than run along the towpath. He stopped to look at the fritillaries that had caught Honey's attention, drank some water then carried on at the same pace, keeping an eye out for the ducklings.

As he approached Honey's gate, he became aware of the clack of shears being wielded with vigour and the occasional expletive muttered in a familiar voice. He paused to brush his hand over the soft new growth of the rosemary bush that he'd noticed the night before.

It released a head-clearing rush of scent and Honey immediately stopped what she was doing.

She was half hidden behind a tall shrub that was bearing the brunt of her shears but, if she was hoping to remain unnoticed, she was about to be disappointed.

Her dress—a green print that was the same colour as the grass—might be long enough to cover her to her feet but the neckline scooped low to reveal an enticing hint of the treasure beneath. And it fastened all the way down the front with large cream buttons that had been designed to give a man ideas.

'Rosemary,' he said. 'According to Shakespeare, it's for remembrance. '

'According to Delia Smith,' she replied, 'it's for roast lamb.'

He frowned. There was a distinct edge to her voice. Honey was clearly annoyed at having been discovered being a very bad patient. Or was it embarrassment at her response to last night's kiss?

'I prefer mint with lamb,' he said.

'"Plant mint for virtue, marjoram for joy, sage for wisdom, thyme for courage and myrtle…"'

She began to hack viciously at the bush.

'Myrtle?'

'I can't remember the rest of it.'

'That bang on the head, probably,' he sympathised, but not believing her for a minute. 'You're up early.'

'I'm a lark. What's your excuse?'

That was better. More like the Honey he found so very… stimulating.

'I haven't been to bed. Does that make me an owl?'

She lowered the shears and finally turned to look at him. From the shadows beneath her eyes, he rather thought the early start was due to a poor night's sleep.

'That's a bit extreme, even for an owl,' she said with what sounded very like concern. 'Those five thousand words must have been highly stimulating.'

'It was a different five thousand words that kept me

awake. I decided to junk everything I'd written so far and start again.'

'And you've still got the energy for a run?'

'I feel a lot better now I'm on the right track. It must have been the camomile tea. But it's probably going to be a walk today.'

'Good decision. Take care not to nod off and fall in.'

He would have sworn that Honeysuckle Rose didn't know how to blush, but a tinge of pink flushed her neck as she turned away, taking a little more care with her clipping.

'Should you be doing that?'

'Forsythia has to be cut back after flowering or it gets leggy.'

'I'm not interested in the plant life. It's your foot that concerns me. How is it today?'

'Ice pack applied, pain killers and antibiotics taken.'

'But not propped up.' He opened the gate and held out a hand for the shears. 'Hand them over.'

'Lucien!' He waited. 'If I don't do it now, it will still look twiggy on open day.'

'Then tell me what to do and I'll finish it.'

'Oh, but—'

'I'm not a gardener, but you're cutting back a bush with outsize scissors while balanced on one foot. How hard can it be?'

A little huff of outrage escaped her lips, but she finally surrendered the shears. 'I've done most of it, but I can't put enough weight on my foot to reach the top.'

'How much would you like me to chop off?'

'Half a metre?'

'I think I can manage that.' He nodded at a wheelbarrow waiting for the clippings that were piled up around her feet. 'And the debris?'

'Follow the path beside the glasshouse and you'll come to a yard with a row of compost bins.'

He nodded, hefted the shears to get the balance and then began to chop away the top growth.

Honey didn't move and he stopped. 'I'm doing this so that you can go and put your foot up, Honey. I'll come and make you whatever concoction you desire when this is done.'

He didn't wait for her to argue but carried on cutting, and the next time he glanced back he was alone.

He made short work of the job, gathered up the mound of clippings and headed for the yard where he tipped them into a half-empty compost bin.

Then he took out his phone and put as much as he could remember of that quote about herbs into the search engine. Nothing came up, but a second check on "myrtle" informed him that it was an evergreen shrub with glossy, aromatic foliage and white flowers, that they were always used in royal wedding bouquets and meant good luck and love in marriage.

He frowned. Why would Honey hesitate to say that? She'd said there had been a man a long time ago, who'd been killed. Had they been married.?

Was it myrtle tattooed around her wrist?

He looked again at the picture. No. Those flowers had a much simpler shape and were blue. There were some very like it growing in the amongst the long grass.

'Honey?' There was a tap on the back door. 'Jack saw the ambulance leaving the Dower House yesterday, and of course we were all agog, but then we discovered that it wasn't Lucien Grey but you…'

Honey blinked, struggling to focus. 'Oh, hi, Diana. I must have dropped off for a moment. Come in.'

The invitation was unnecessary. Her visitor had already plumped herself down on the pouffe.

'Who told you I'd had an accident?' she asked.

'Sally Wickes. Do you know her? Her husband opened the bakery a couple of years ago.'

'We've met.'

'Well, they found your watch in the X-ray department after you'd left yesterday, and Sally's mother works in the office at the hospital, so she offered to return it to you.'

'So why didn't she?'

'She had the grandchildren last night, so she left it with Sally. When I called in this morning and heard you were laid up, I offered to bring it over.' She grinned as she produced it from her bag. 'The village grapevine is in full working order. I brought you a loaf too. And a couple of blueberry muffins, as the croissants were still too hot. They're on the kitchen table.'

'That's really thoughtful. Exactly what I need. My purse is in my basket.'

'Don't be silly. I didn't want to come empty-handed to the sick bed, but bringing you flowers is like shipping sand to the Sahara.'

'Well, thank you.' She glanced at her phone. 'I appear to have quite a few missed calls.'

'You know how it is. So? What happened?'

'It was just a stupid accident. I was on the path by the river when I noticed that the boat house is in a really bad state so, like an idiot, I went to take a closer look.'

'And?'

'And my foot went through a rotten board. There's a bit of damage to my heel from some rotten wood and I've sprained my ankle rather badly.'

'Ouch! Thank goodness for mobile phones, or who knows how long you'd have been lying there? It's not as if your neighbour ever leaves the house, and Alma's away...' Torn between defending Lucien and preserving his privacy, Honey decided that he'd much prefer the latter and said nothing. 'How are you managing?'

'I've got the crutches under control, but I'm supposed to keep my foot elevated for a day or two, which is why you find me lying on the sofa on such a lovely morning instead of in the garden, getting things ready for the open day.'

'Oh, Lord, that's quite soon, isn't it?'

'The third weekend.'

'We were actually wondering if you were going ahead with it this year. We've seen so little of you since you came home.'

'I needed some time, Diana.'

'We all understand. Flora's death, and Alma said you haven't been well… Now this. Will you have to cancel?'

'Cancel?'

Diana blinked at the sound of a man's voice and then her jaw sagged as she saw Lucien, in his shorts and a running vest, filling the doorway. While he'd clearly lost weight, every bit of softness from his body, there was no missing his wide, sinewy shoulders or the ropey muscles on his upper arms and thighs.

'Mr Grey.'

'The summer fete lady…' He frowned, clearly searching for a name. 'Mrs Marks?' he hazarded.

'Mrs Markham chairs the village fete committee,' Honey said, as Diana, uncharacteristically, seemed to have lost the power of speech. 'And she runs the antique shop in the village with her sister.'

'Of course. You left a card.' He came forward, hand outstretched but saw it was smeared with green sap from the new young leaves of the bush he'd been cutting back. 'Perhaps not,' he said, wiping it down his vest.

'Mr Grey saw me struggling with a pair of shears when he was on his morning run on the towpath, Diana,' Honey explained. 'And came to my rescue.'

'Did he?' It came out as a squeak. 'How kind.'

'One good turn. Honey stitched me up when I had a close encounter with some shrapnel in Syria.'

'Oh, but that's such a coincidence,' she said. And then clearly wondered if it was. 'But how naughty of you to be working in the garden when you should be resting your foot, Honey. You know you only have to ask and we'd all help.'

'That's exactly what I told her, Mrs Markham,' Lucien said, his face poker-straight. 'I'm about to make us both a drink. Will you join us? Tea, coffee?'

Honey rolled her eyes in exasperation at him. She'd been doing her best to keep their acquaintance to the level of a good turn from a passing neighbour...

Honey saw Diana struggle between wanting to stay and her desperation to get back to the village with the news that Lucien Grey was out of hibernation and the *You'll never guess where he's making himself at home* gossip...

'Thank you, Mr Grey, but I can't stay,' she said, gossip trumping coffee. 'It's my day to open the shop, but I called in to return Honey's watch and, since I was in the bakery, bring her some sustaining carbs.'

'Village life,' Lucien said. 'So supportive.'

'We like to think so,' Diana replied, never taking her eyes off him as she backed towards the door. 'We've missed you, Honey. If you need anything...'

'I'll call you. And thanks again for the bread and muffins.'

Neither of them spoke until they heard her footsteps speeding across the gravel drive.

'Is she actually running?' Lucien asked.

'With phone in hand, I imagine. You're going to have to hammer boards across your front door now that you've been spotted in the wild.'

'I'm more worried that there'll be a back door key hidden under a flowerpot.'

'Do you have a bolt?' Honey lifted her shoulders in an apologetic shrug. 'I'm sorry, but you only have yourself to blame. I made no mention of nettles, your part in the accident or your gallant three hours in the hospital waiting room. Then you ruined it all by offering her a drink.'

'I was hoping she'd ask for coffee so that I could join her, rather than have some herbal concoction foisted on me. And you appear to have forgotten that I brought you dinner,' he said. 'And rescued your plants.'

'I haven't forgotten a thing…' Feeling her cheeks heat up, she shook her head, realising that it was a conversation heading for trouble. 'I'm just sorry that your kind gesture has exposed you to speculation.'

'I doubt you fell through that rotten board with the sole purpose of making my life difficult, so stop apologising.'

'Only *doubt*?' she asked because, while her head was full of remorse for having laid him open to village gossip, her mouth hadn't caught up. 'You're not certain?'

'The only things in life I'm certain of are death and taxes. And the fact that you are trouble. Now, if it's okay with you, I'm going to clean up and then I'll put the kettle on.'

CHAPTER NINE

'Rest is not idleness, and to lie sometimes on the grass under trees on a summer's day, listening to the murmur of the water, or watching the clouds float across the sky, is by no means a waste of time.' —The Use of Life, John Lubbock

LUCIEN SPENT RATHER longer washing his hands than was strictly necessary, but he needed a minute after that exchange to compose himself.

The reflection looking back at him suggested it was going to take a lot longer than that, but when he couldn't put it off any longer he found Honey standing in front of the fridge, examining its contents.

'I can't take my eyes off you for a minute!'

Unabashed, she continued to survey the contents of the fridge. 'Was it Mark Twain who said that nothing improves the view like ham and eggs? Or in this case, the more portable option of a bacon sandwich.'

'Portable?' he repeated as she removed a pack of bacon and a butter dish from the fridge.

'I thought we might have breakfast in the orchard.' She nudged the door closed with her shoulder. 'Unless, of course, you had breakfast at some unearthly hour, in which case it would be a mid-morning snack.'

'It's nowhere near mid-morning.'

'That rather depends on when you started your day. In your case it could be any meal you care to name. Shall we settle on breakfast?'

'Whatever you say.'

'My three favourite words,' she said, rewarding him with a smile. 'Remember them. In the meantime, you know where to find the kettle, and you'll find a couple of mugs in the cupboard.'

'Honey…'

But she was already at the stove, laying slices of bacon into a pan, and he didn't waste his breath telling her to go back to the sofa and leave it to him. She was the nurse. Presumably she knew what her foot could take.

He filled the kettle, found the mugs and put some coffee in the cafetière. Honey raised an eyebrow, but she didn't say anything.

'Is there something else I can do?' he asked.

'Cut the bread?'

He located the breadboard, found a knife that suited him, sharpened it on a steel and cut four slices from the warm loaf.

'Oh, you're a keeper,' Honey said as he spread the butter without tearing it 'I just mean that I'd have ended up with mess of crumbs,' she added, all uncharacteristic blushing confusion.

'You need a sharp knife,' he said, doing his best to keep a straight face. Having found some tomatoes, he sliced them, then went out to the glasshouse to pick salad leaves.

The door and roof lights were open; everything smelled fresh and green. It was a calm space and he could easily spend a day in there working. All he needed was the right chair and his laptop…

Casual, he decided, could become his least favourite word. He pushed the thought away—he was in no state to offer anything more—and back in the kitchen he concentrated on rinsing and drying the leaves.

'Is the bacon ready?' he asked.

'It is.'

'Then I'll leave you to fill the mugs while I construct the sandwiches.'

'Only a man would treat a sandwich as a construction project.'

'Only a woman would suggest it was anything else,' he said, then smiled at her, so she'd know that he wasn't being serious.

Whatever smart remark she'd been about to come back with died in her throat and long seconds passed as they just looked at one another. Sandwiches were the last thing on either of their minds.

Damn, this was a mistake. He should have kept walking…

'Bacon,' she said, passing him the pan, before turning away to fill the mugs, giving them both a moment to catch their breath.

'Your BLT, ma'am,' he said.

'You're a bit of a ham yourself,' she shot back, putting lids on the mugs, taking a clean tea cloth from a drawer and wrapping the sandwiches. 'Can you carry everything?'

He caught the handles of the two mugs in one hand and picked up the sandwiches while Honey scribbled a note to stick on the door.

'"With the bees"?'

'Now you've been spotted looking very much at home here, I'm going to get more visitors. If I don't answer, they'll let themselves in, using the excuse that they're checking to make sure I haven't fallen and done myself more damage. And, if they don't find me, they'll come looking.'

'But not if you're with your bees.'

'Would you?'

'I might sit on the bench and wait for you.'

'In your case it would be guilt, not gossip.'

'I have nothing to feel guilty about,' he protested.

'So why are you here? Helping in the garden. Making coffee and sandwiches.'

He had no answer to that, at least not one that he wanted to think about. 'As I said to Mrs Summer Fete, village life is supportive. I fear it may be catching.'

'Unavoidable. She'll have you in her sights now, Lucien. You should get back to London before she has you signed up for the tombola.'

'London. Where nobody knows your name.' Why had that ever seemed such an attractive idea? 'I had planned to rent somewhere until my flat became vacant, but I wasn't in a great place when I arrived back in England. People were worried about me being on my own.'

'Because of the flashbacks? The panic attacks?'

He stopped. For a moment everything had felt calm, comfortable, and now he felt exposed, vulnerable, wanting to drop everything and run...

As if she sensed it, she let go of a crutch and put her hand on his arm, as if to hold him still. It was nothing, no more than a touch, and yet it felt like everything...

'You know.' He shook his head. 'Stupid. Of course you know. You've been there, you've seen it. You saw what happened to me when you came to the door brandishing those nettles and I did recognise you. I don't mean that I knew who you were, just that on some subconscious level I knew we'd met. That it had been important.' He looked down at her hand on his arm. It was small, but exuded strength... 'You held my arm then too. You're always there, holding my arm when I need it.'

'I should have done more, and afterwards I was ashamed that I hadn't, but I was so angry...' She gave a little hiccupping sob, and in a heartbeat she was the one needing the prop. 'I've been angry for so long...'

He knew how she felt—the rage, the utter helplessness—and, although his hands were full, he put his arms around her. For a moment she resisted, but then she gave it up, laying her head against his shoulder as he gathered her close.

For a while they stood there, drenched in the scent of apple blossom, while above them a blackbird sang his heart out.

'You need to talk about it, Honey.'

She lifted her head and looked at him. 'Is that what you were told?' she asked, answering a question with a question. She did a lot of that, but he needed to earn her trust. He picked up the fallen crutch and handed it to her.

'I was told that writing is useful,' he said, as they continued to make their way slowly through the trees.

'Writing, maybe, but I don't think you should be listening to your diaries, reliving your experiences every waking moment.'

'No?' He glanced at her. 'What would you prescribe, Sister Rose?'

'I understand that servicemen suffering from PTSD find being out in the open air, doing practical things with their hands, helpful.'

'Gardening?'

'It heals the heart.'

They were deep in the orchard now. The blackbird had followed them, keeping up his challenge. There was a soft buzz from bees working amongst the blossom but the rest was silence.

'Practical help in return for restoration of the soul. It sounds like a good deal to me.'

'Then consider yourself welcome to come and spend time in the garden whenever you like,' she said, heading for the trunk of a fallen tree that had been smoothed to provide a seat. 'I can always find you something to do.'

He handed her one of the mugs, then sat down beside her, unwrapped the sandwiches and offered them to her.

She took one and for a moment they both ate in silence.

'It's so peaceful here.'

'It's my favourite place in the entire world. When things were really tough,' she said, 'I would imagine myself sitting here. The scent, the hum of the bees...'

'The butterflies?' he suggested as one settled on the sleeve of her dress. 'What was Diana Markham talking about when she said you'd have to cancel?'

'The National Garden Open Day. Hundreds of people all over the country open their gardens to visitors for one or two days in the summer.'

'Like stately homes?'

'They don't have to be grand. Most are quite small, even allotments. Some people open their homes so that people can see their houseplants.'

'You just open your gate—metaphorically in your case—and allow people to wander around?'

'It's a more organised than that. It's for charity so there's a five-pound entry fee. And the WI serves afternoon tea.'

'Cucumber sandwiches and scones with clotted cream and home-made jam?'

'There's a little more choice of sandwiches, and wonderful cakes. With elderflower champagne as an optional extra.'

'Which you have yet to make.'

'I'm sure I can find a teenager to help for a small fee.'

'The way that you used to help your aunt?'

'I didn't expect her to pay me.' Aware that she sounded a little defensive, she added, 'Brian sells plants to visitors and this year, for the first time, I'm going to be the one leading a tour of the pond, the beehives and the meadow.

Doing my best to answer their questions. Any children who come along can take part in a bug hunt and pond dipping, and they get a plant to take home and nurture.'

'It sounds very special, but a lot of work.'

'The special makes it worth it.'

'And that's why, instead of keeping your foot up, you were cutting back the forsythia. Because otherwise it would still look twiggy on open day.'

She smiled. 'And now it won't, thanks to you.'

'So, what else will you be hacking down the minute my back is turned?'

'Nothing.'

'I don't believe you.'

'That is so rude.'

'Possibly, but I'm right.' She didn't answer. 'Tell me what I can do to help.'

'You have a book to write, Lucien.'

'One that you don't think I should be writing.'

'It doesn't seem like the best idea right now.'

'Maybe,' he said, 'but I felt I had to get it down on paper. That people had to know. The reality is that I was just spewing my guts on paper. Hoping to get it out of my head.'

Lucien was looking into a distance that no one else could see, and Honey grasped his wrist, anchoring him on the log beside her, safe in the peace of the orchard.

He didn't look at her, but he covered her hand with his own, acknowledging her awareness of his black moment. Reassuring her that he was okay.

'I've decided to take a different angle,' he said. 'One that tells the stories of the men, women and children I've met while I've been reporting from war zones. Their courage, the spirit of endurance. And the people who, in the midst of danger, are doing what they can to help. If the publisher doesn't like it...'

'He will,' she assured him.

'Maybe.' He looked at her then. 'But, if he doesn't, I'll return his advance.'

'You haven't spent it?'

'I've found a use for it, but thanks to Jenny's talent and hard work the production company has done very well. I can cover it.'

Jenny...

Honey extracted her hand from beneath Lucien's and took a bite of a sandwich she was no longer tasting, and she needed a swig of coffee to get down her throat.

'How is the project on her farm going?' she asked.

'Nearly there. One of the networks has bought it and it's lined up for next spring. After that, I'll be taking over,' he said, tossing a small piece of bacon to a tame robin.

'Jenny doesn't mind surrendering the lead after all her hard work?' Honey asked.

'She is taking a much-deserved break. She'll have to put herself out there, do the chat shows when the time comes, but with a baby on the way—'

'A baby?'

Honey felt the colour drain from her face and then Lucien put a hand to her back, steadying her.

'Put your head between your knees. There's no water. Will coffee do?'

'I'm okay...'

'And I'm Dick Robinson. Are you in pain?'

'No,' she snapped. Not the kind of pain that a pill could fix. How dared he kiss her? Not that first time—he'd had no idea what he was doing then—but last night had been different.

She'd wanted it so badly and if she hadn't been running scared...

And today he was back, playing house, and she had been loving it, wanting it, pushing Jenny to the back of her mind.

She shook him off, holding up her hand palm out, to keep him away.

'Don't…'

'Don't what?' he demanded and then, as the penny dropped, 'Dammit, Honey, you can't think…' He took a breath and drew back. 'Clearly you do.'

'She's your partner.'

'Jenny is my *business* partner. It's Saffy, Jenny's wife, who's having the baby.'

'Wife?'

'Their wedding was all over the media last year. I assumed you knew.'

It took a moment for what he was saying to fully sink in and then, overcome with embarrassment, she finally allowed her head sink to her knees.

'I don't know what to say.'

'A win, then,' he said.

Rude, but she was in no position to complain. On the foot-in-mouth scale, this was up to her patella.

'I'm so sorry…'

'Why don't you sit up, look me in the face and tell me that?' he suggested.

Right at that moment all she wanted was for the ground to open and swallow her. That wasn't about to happen, and mumbling an apology into her skirt wasn't going to fix this. She doubted anything could fix it, but she took a breath, lifted her head, squared her shoulders and turned to him, hoping for the smallest hint of forgiveness.

His face was, apparently, set in stone.

'There are no words…' No reaction. She swallowed. *Keep it brief, keep it simple…* 'I am so sorry, Lucien.'

Nothing changed in his expression for what felt like a lifetime, but then he reached out and cradled her cheeks between his hands.

'I'm not.'

It took a moment for what he was saying to sink in.

She had insulted him, suggesting that he'd be capable of betraying a mother of his baby with meaningless sex. Because sex with any man who could do that had to be meaningless...

And in doing so she had discovered—and betrayed—exactly how meaningful it would have been to her.

He leaned forward and touched his lips to hers in a *Did that actually happen?* kiss.

She had betrayed her feelings and he wasn't sorry. Wasn't he going to run a mile?

'There were rumours,' she said, searching his face, desperate for a hint of what he was feeling. 'Of a romance.'

'And of course you believe everything you read in the red-tops.'

It was her turn to let slip an expletive.

'I'm an idiot.'

He didn't contradict her, just put his arm around her, and somehow her head was on his shoulder.

'Lucien?'

'What?'

'Who's Dick Robinson?'

She felt the rumble of laughter. 'No one. It's just an expression my mother used when I told her something she thought was improbable.'

'Such as?'

'That I'd cleaned my shoes, done my homework, tidied my room.'

'Aunt Flora didn't have to say a word. She'd just look at me over the top of her glasses and I was gone.' She sighed. 'At the time, you're all moody teenage "it's not fair". You only learn to value those moments when they're just a memory.'

'What are you going to do, Honey?' His gesture took in the garden, the orchard and the cottage. 'Once I've written the book,' he said, 'I'll be commissioning and producing television series. Will you stay here and pick up the flag of conservation? Or will you be going back overseas?'

She shook her head.

'No.' She began to break pieces of bread off her sandwich, tossing them to the sparrows. 'After Aunt Flora died I wasn't sleeping, wasn't eating. In truth, my breakdown had probably been creeping up on me for a long time before that, but I finally cracked at the end of February. You think I was angry over the caterpillars? Believe me, it was nothing to how I reacted when a water pump froze.'

She'd known it for weeks but had been in denial. Saying it out loud made it a fact.

'But that doesn't rule out nursing here at home, does it?'

'I've lost my confidence, Lucien. The thought of being responsible for anyone's life fills me with terror. All I have ahead of me is a great big void with nothing to fill it with but making elderflower champagne.'

'Don't forget the dandelions,' he said in an effort to make her smile.

'You have to pick an awful lot of dandelions…' Her voice was shaking as the reality hit and he caught her hand, holding it steady. Holding her steady, as a few minutes ago she had held him…

'A whole gallon of petals, so I've heard.'

'You remembered.'

'When you talked about making it with your aunt,' he said, 'it sounded as if it really mattered to you.'

'It did. It does. But it's hardly a career.'

He was looking at her and it was there again. A repeat of that split second in the cottage before he'd kissed her. A life-changing moment when anything might happen.

Not now.

If he kissed her now it would be out of pity and she turned away.

'You have a beautiful home, a garden you're clearly passionate about. Maybe that should be your starting point?' he suggested.

'It's not mine.' She pulled her hand away. 'None of this is mine. This is Flora's garden and I don't know nearly enough.'

'You can learn if it matters to you,' he said. 'But she wouldn't have wanted her legacy to make you unhappy.'

'Then she shouldn't have left me.'

She waved the words away before he could offer her comfort. Or counselling. Who was the one with a problem now?

'Oh, wait… I get it,' she rattled on before he could say anything. 'You think I should set up as the local hedge witch, doling out potions made from the herbs in Aunt Flora's…sorry, *my*…garden?'

'Well, that's one option…and she clearly had a very good life.'

CHAPTER TEN

'Yet soon fair Spring shall give another scene. And yellow cowslips gild the level green.' —Anne E Bleecher

THE MINUTE THE words were out of his mouth, Lucien knew he'd made a mistake. Honey had been back on the defensive, blanking out a future that seemed to offer her nothing, and he'd fallen into the trap.

Having experienced an up close and personal experience of her blowing her top, he prepared to duck. For long seconds they both held their breath and then she swallowed hard and began taking the slow, measured breaths that he recognised from his own sessions with a therapist.

'Professor Flora Rose,' she said, when she was sufficiently in control to speak, 'was a botanist who travelled the world until she found herself saddled with a six-year-old orphan at an age when most women would be retiring. Not that she ever retired.'

'Professor…?'

He'd thought he was in trouble. This was trouble tripled…

'Alma didn't mention that when you were having your little *tête-à-tête* about the crazy woman next door?' she asked with that edge of sarcasm that made any conversation with Honey such a dangerously enticing game.

'I asked her for your name so that I could send a note, apologising for the way I spoke to you. Nothing else.'

'Oh, dear…' She shook her head but, as quickly as it had come, the tension seeped from her body, her voice. 'Poor Lucien. You asked a simple question and got a history lesson.'

'Pretty much.' At the time he'd wanted to escape. Now he wished he'd taken more notice. 'She told me that your aunt was responsible for all the wildflowers and butterflies in the village.'

'Her re-wilding project didn't meet with universal approval, but it's become something of a model for other places, and now it brings visitors to study, as well as enjoy, what has been done here. And that, of course, has proved beneficial for the local economy.'

'Like Diana Markham's antique shop?'

'Like the antique shop, the book shop and the boutique that sells locally made crafts and New Agey stuff,' she confirmed. 'And the Hartford Arms does a roaring trade in lunches.'

'Creating jobs,' he said. 'Keeping young people in the village.'

'All that,' she agreed.

'She sounds like quite a woman.'

She gave a little sigh and he wanted to hold her, as he had when they'd walked into the orchard, but he sensed that this was the wrong moment to do anything but listen.

'Your arrival was clearly a life-changing moment for her,' he prompted. 'How did she cope with a grieving six-year-old?'

'With kindness and the peaceful aura that touched everything she did. But, while my arrival might have kept her at home, it didn't slow her down. She continued to write books and articles, lectured to students who adored her and was honoured for her work. The present Prince of Wales was an admirer, and she ended her days as Emeritus Professor in Biodiversity at Melchester University.'

'I had no idea. The wilding, the stillroom, the herbs…' He stopped making excuses and was rewarded with a smile. The kind that came with a kicker. 'What?'

'She was an academic, Lucien, but you're right. She may also have been just a little bit of a hedge witch.'

He laughed out loud at that. 'You're the witch, Honeysuckle Rose, but you've got a lot to live up to.'

'I'd have had to be a second Florence Nightingale to get even close.'

'You've done more than most. You told me that you always wanted to be a nurse, like your mother, but you need to be thinking about the future. What did your father do?'

'He was a Rose,' she said, as if that was answer enough. 'He was working as a consultant on the restoration of a "lost garden". They made a television series about it. I have it on an old VHS tape that has been viewed so often that I'm afraid to play it any more in case it snaps.'

'If you'll trust me with it,' he said. 'I'll get it transferred onto digital for you.'

Her face was transformed by a smile. 'Can you do that?'

'Yes, but clearly it's very precious, so I'll give it to a professional.'

'Thank you.'

He picked up his coffee and for a while they sat in silence while the bolder sparrows came close enough to grab crumbs.

'You come from a family who cherished the earth, Honey,' he said, after a while. 'There's a huge need for that and, sad though it is, you are now the Rose at Orchard End. Perhaps this is the moment to accept your heritage.'

'I am not going to agricultural college.'

'No?' He grinned. 'I can so see you in your dungarees and headscarf, driving a tractor.'

'Stick around. There's a vintage tractor in the stables that comes out for hayrides at the village fete. Say you'll open it, and I'll let you drive it.'

'Tempting as that is…'

'I could call Diana right now. It would do wonders for the fundraising, especially if we offered selfies with the famous Lucien Grey for a small consideration?'

Her wide grin and those warm, sweet lips were the only things tempting him.

'Thanks, but I'll pass. Nice try at changing the subject, though.'

Her look suggested that she hadn't given up hope, but he refused to play.

'You have a science background,' he persisted. 'There must be a wide range of post-grad conservation and bio-diversity courses available. And rewilding is big news these days. With your knowledge, your background…' He didn't push it. 'Or, if you can't work face to face with patients, you could teach.'

She pulled a face.

'Honey, sweetheart, you've tried being your mother and been brilliant. Maybe it's time to start from scratch, go back to the hopes and dreams of that little girl before her life was changed by a traffic accident. It's time to find yourself,' he said, getting to his feet and tossing away the dregs of his coffee. 'But not right now. Right now there's a more pressing problem.'

She looked up at him, a frown creasing the space between eyes that had been all he'd seen of her that first time: dark blue eyes that had stayed in his memory.

'You were going to pick elderflowers today. For the champagne.'

'Now who's changing the subject?' she asked, those eyes huge and dark in the shade of the apple trees.

Tempting, tempting…

'Not at all. Just giving you time to think.'

'While I pick elderflowers? Was that an offer of help, Mr Grey?'

'It was but, unlike the village teenagers, I'll expect my payment in kind, Miss Rose. Two bottles?' he suggested, before there was any chance of a misunderstanding.

'You mean it?' she asked and, as she searched his face, he realised how important it was to her.

'Outside in the fresh air. Doing something practical with my hands. Sister Rose's orders, and right now I think she could do with a little of her own medicine.'

'I…' She shook her head. 'You're undoubtedly right, but not today. You haven't slept for twenty-four hours, and I need to sterilise everything and stock up on lemons and sugar before we start.'

We…

How long had it been since he'd used that word? With Jenny, but that had been business. This was something else. Something that was definitely not casual. It had only been a couple of days, but she had been there in his head for a long time.

'You're not planning on walking to the village, I hope?'

'If I said yes, would you insist on going for me?'

He wanted to tell her to stop. That she didn't have to wear a mask with him.

'There's a limit to my altruism,' he replied, following her lead and keeping it light, a little mocking. 'But I'm sure that if you phone the shop with your smallest need right now, you'll be inundated with offers to deliver.'

Her laughter was his reward.

'You are too smart, Lucien. And just a touch cynical.'

'Smart enough to accept that I need a couple of hours' sleep or I'm going to fall over. As for cynical, right now I'd bet my right arm that texts are flying all over the village and we're the subject of hot gossip in the Post Office queue.'

'Do you mind?'

'Do you?' he asked, realising that he hadn't thought of her, only himself. 'When I realised you had company, I should have made a discreet exit. I'm sorry if I've embarrassed you.'

'You were being kind, Lucien. If people choose to make something of it, that's their problem. Don't give it another thought,' she said. 'Go and catch up on your sleep.'

'If I leave, can I trust you to go inside and rest your foot?'

'I'll certainly rest my foot. Take this and put it on your pillow,' she said, leaning down to pick a flower, a cluster of small yellow bells, and offering it to him. ' "*Where the bee sucks, there suck I. In a cowslip's bell I lie...*" They are said to have a sedative quality.'

She picked another, held it to her nose for a moment and then held out a hand for a lift up.

'I'll walk you back to the cottage.'

'No need. I'm going to lie under that tree and count blossoms until the cowslip and the hum of the bees send me to sleep.'

' "*Merrily, merrily shall I live now",*' he said, continuing her quote, still holding her hand as he supported her to the tree. ' "*Under the blossom that hangs on the bough.*" '

She smiled. 'You know your Shakespeare.'

'Who knew that English Lit A level would ever be useful?'

'Handy for crosswords.'

He tightened his grip to support her as she lowered herself carefully, her dress blending in with the grass as she settled her skirt around her ankles, one booted, one so slender that he could have circled it with his thumb and forefinger.

'Lucien?' Honey was looking up at him. 'You're going

to have to let go of my hand,' she prompted, once she had his attention.

'Or I could take the grass option…?'

He was asking the question. Wanting to stay here with Honey.

'It is so much nicer out in the fresh air than in a stuffy bedroom on a warm, sunny day,' she agreed.

Out in the fresh air, doing something practical with his hands…

He shut down the thought, just grateful to be here as she began to count the blossoms.

'One, two, three…'

The grass was long, soft and threaded with wildflowers. As he stretched out beside her and sank into it, all he could hear was Honey's voice counting slower and slower, 'Twelve…thirteen…' and the soft hum of bees.

Honey was woken by something tickling her cheek. She brushed it away only to discover that it wasn't an insect, but Lucien, with a buttercup, propped on one elbow and watching her.

They were lying outside in the grass, a foot of space between them, and yet the moment had the rare intimacy of that first time waking with a lover.

'You sleep like a baby,' he said. 'Completely open, with no sense of how vulnerable you are, or that the world is full of dangers.'

'The cowslips did their job, then. Did you sleep?' she asked.

'I did, thank you, and for once without dreaming. But now I'm going to take a shower. Are you on for chicken curry tonight?'

'Your place or mine?'

'This is the healing garden,' he replied, leaning across to kiss her cheek. It was no more than a brush of his lips, but it set up the down on her cheeks in a mini-tsunami. 'Do you want a hand up?' he asked, standing up. 'Or are you staying there?'

'Staying,' she managed through what felt like cobwebs. 'No, wait…a hand…'

He grasped both of her hands in his and, once she had her good foot firmly planted, he pulled her upright, taking a step forward and catching her round the waist so that they were touching close.

'Shall I walk you to your door, Honey?'

She sucked in her breath. How could he make such an innocent sentence sound so seductive? How could she be seduced by the sound of his voice?

'N-no… I have to go and talk to the bees.'

That appeared to amuse him. 'Are they good conversationalists?'

'They don't say much, but you have to tell them everything important that's happening in the family.' She discovered that she had to swallow. 'Or they will desert you.'

'When you say everything…'

Lucien had not moved, yet somehow they were closer. So close that he must surely be able to feel how her heart was pounding?

She lifted her hand to place it over his and found an answering echo. If Lucien had not been holding her, she would have melted at his feet.

Her head was filled with the herby scent of crushed grass and warm skin where he had lain beside her and all she could see was his mouth, the enticing dip of his lower lip just inches from her own…

'When you say *everything*, Honey, will you tell them that I kissed you?'

'I…'

'And will you tell them that you kissed me back?'

Kissed him back, a fully engaged participant, for a moment lost to sense…

'Yes.'

Her mouth formed the word; no sound emerged. It wasn't an answer to his question—not that question, anyway—and Lucien took his time, searching her face for the slightest hint of hesitation.

It was only when she thought she might simply dissolve with longing, beg him for mercy, that his mouth descended agonisingly slowly with a touch that sent heat whispering through her body.

This was not like the first kiss when the fuse had been lit by anger, a mindless response to recognition on some subliminal level that had set them both on fire.

Nor was it like the second time he'd kissed her. That had been a different kind of recognition, a shocked acknowledgement of mutual desire. It had been a kiss like the first one that would have had only one conclusion, but for the fact that she'd been thinking of another woman—a woman whom she imagined was waiting for just that moment.

This time, when he touched his lips to hers, he was not a male imprinting himself on her, staking a claim like some jungle beast. This was a man offering himself as a lover. Waiting to be accepted.

It was unexpected, enchanting, rare…and her lips opened in welcome.

Lucien responded with a slow, sensually devasting kiss that eliminated coherent thought and had her crumbling against him, wanting more, wanting everything.

'Honey…'

He eased away, looking at her for a moment, then there was clear air between.

'The bees are waiting,' he said.

'I've got a lot to tell them,' she said, unable to still the betraying shake in her voice. *A lot to ask them.*

'Have you got your phone?'

'It's in my pocket.'

'Call me if you need anything. And make a list of the jobs that you want done in the garden.'

'There's no need.'

'I'm the one in need, but you'll have to tell me what to do. You wouldn't want me pulling up precious weeds by mistake. What is the opposite of weeding? Flowering…?'

'You are being ridiculous.'

'Really? How wonderful. I thought I'd forgotten how.'

He kissed her again, a touch-and-go kiss, a promise that he'd be back, then he picked up her crutches and handed them to her. 'I'll do a couple of hours every evening. Fresh air, useful hands…'

And then she was watching his back as he walked away through the orchard.

'Lucien!'

'It's therapy,' he called back, not stopping, not turning round, and she didn't know what she'd have said if he had. 'I'll see you at five o'clock.'

'Wear work clothes!'

He raised a hand and then he was gone.

The first thing Lucien did when he arrived back at the Dower House, even before he'd showered, was to pick up the phone and call Jenny.

'Lucien…' He heard the uncertainty in her voice, a combination of relief that he'd called, but concern that he'd called. 'How are you?'

'Actually, I'm fine,' he said. 'Thanks for the emails. I'm sorry I haven't returned them.'

'I guessed you were busy with the book.'

'That's no excuse. How are you? How's Saffy?'

'Good. Blooming, in fact… She had her second scan

last week. All good, and you're the first to know that we're going to have a little girl.'

'That's wonderful news. I'm really happy for you.'

'Thanks. You sound…more yourself.'

'I've been getting out into the fresh air. Meeting the neighbours.'

'Oh?'

'I discovered that the nurse who stitched up my arm a couple of years ago lives next door.'

'The one you tried to find?'

'Isn't there a proverb about searching the world for something only to find it next door? In the prettiest thatched cottage.'

'Possibly…'

'She hammered on my door, accused me of murder and now—'

'Murder?'

'It's a long story.'

'Well, it's certainly bucked you up. You had an idea for a documentary about her, I seem to remember.'

'Not just her. Something much wider.'

'Is it still a goer?'

'It might link to the book.'

'Oh, well, that would be perfect. And it's wonderful to hear you sounding so positive.'

There was no mistaking her relief. She had obviously been worrying about him. Or maybe their partnership.

'We need to meet up and talk about what other projects you've got in the pipeline.'

'We've got a meeting with the accountants pencilled in for tomorrow. I thought I'd have to do it on my own, but if you could come up to London we could fit something in afterwards.'

It was too soon but, conscious that he'd left the heavy lifting to her for longer than either of them had intended, he agreed. Then, aware that she was now well into the countryside, he asked if she was familiar with re-wilding.

'Saffy has mentioned it.'

'Ask her if she's heard of a Professor Flora Rose.'

After that he called the village bookshop to ask if they had any of her books in stock. They did and Laura, the owner, offered to deliver them if he would rather not come into the village to collect them.

Then he had a shower.

The back door of the cottage was open when Lucien arrived a few minutes before five.

He tapped and called out, 'Honey?'

There was no reply, but when he went inside there was a note along with a photocopied map of the garden fixed to the fridge door.

The note said:

I'm down by the pond. H

The pond? Of course there would be a pond.

He dropped his backpack on a chair, put the curry in the fridge and took the map from the fridge door.

It was beautifully illustrated with little sketches of small creatures, flowers and insects, presumably for visitors to the garden.

He headed towards the far side of the orchard where the ground dipped into a hollow and, a few minutes later, spotted Honey on the far side of a large pond.

She was standing on a picturesque bridge spanning the small stream that trickled over boulders to feed the pond. Sandpaper in hand, totally focussed on rubbing down the hand rail, she hadn't noticed him.

Her hair was tied up and pinned to the top of her head and, as she bent with the push of the sandpaper, her dress gaped slightly, offering an enticing glimpse of curves that made his palms itch.

He stood very quietly, enjoying the intimacy of the moment. So much had changed since their first explosive encounter. Things had been said, there had been a world-changing kiss…

'Are you going to stand there and watch, Mr Grey?' she asked without looking up. 'Or have you come to work?'

He grinned. Some things had changed…

'Just admiring the view,' he replied, joining her on the bridge. 'But I'm entirely at your disposal. Just tell me what you want, Honey.'

She glanced up, clearly about to come back with some quip, but no words came. As her gaze swept over his ancient T-shirt and lingered on his jeans, he felt his skin tighten. And she didn't have to say a word.

The answer was right there in her eyes.

CHAPTER ELEVEN

'Next time a sunrise or a meadow of flowers steals your breath, be silent and listen...' —Anonymous

HONEY SWALLOWED. Never had the bridge felt so small. Lucien was very close, and he wasn't looking at the water lilies or the flower-strewn meadow that rose along the valley, but at her.

'You'd like me to give everything a thorough rubdown?' he offered, and neither of them were under any illusion that he was talking about the handrails of the bridge.

'Um...' was the best she could manage through a throat that felt as if it were stuffed with hot rocks.

He took the sandpaper from her, dropped it in the work box at her side and took a step closer, leaving her in no doubt that do-it-yourself was the last thing on his mind.

'Lucien...' It could have been a protest or a plea—maybe it was a little of both. But even while her head was yelling at her to take a breath, take a step back and think about this, his T-shirt was bunched in her fists and her heart wanted him closer. To be touching him...

And then, blissfully, his hands were at her waist, drawing her into his body, and she was lost in a slow, sensual kiss—a promise that Lucien Grey was a man who knew how to take his time. To give pleasure as well as receive it.

'Hang on,' he said, catching her behind the knees and sweeping her off her feet to carry her from the sunlit bridge into the shadows of the orchard. He put her down on the long, soft grass. She was still catching her breath as he stretched out beside her.

'What are you doing?'

Stupid question. Having unfastened the first of her buttons, he discovered that there was also a hook, and his fingers were tickling her breasts as he searched for it.

'I'm doing something practical with my hands. In the open air. As prescribed,' he said, looking up as the top finally surrendered. 'I can stop any time. Just say the word.'

He waited. And it was there. The word that would stop this so that they could go back to rubbing down the handrails on the bridge.

Her brain was holding it up like a red card at a football match, but it remained firmly stuck in her throat as her body, with every nerve end reaching for his touch, gave the referee the finger.

Two more buttons bit the dust with agonising slowness.

'What's this? No bra, Miss Rose?'

'Upstairs, out of reach. Get on with it, Mr Grey!'

Lucien obliged, parting more buttons, cupping a breast in his palm and holding it for a moment before brushing the tip of his thumb across a taut nipple.

Honey's entire body jolted as what felt like an electric shock reached parts of her body that hadn't been disturbed for a very long time and there was only one word hammering to escape.

'Yes!'

His mouth followed his thumb and for a moment she lay back, lost in the bliss of his tongue while his hand continued to work on the buttons until her dress fell apart and a rush of cool air on her belly woke her to the madness...

This had to stop. She had to tell him to stop. But the lace

of her panties was no barrier and, as he touched the heart of her, she was clinging to him.

'Honey, sweetheart.' He kissed a tear away from her cheek. 'If this isn't what you want…'

Sensing that he was about to stop what he was doing, she grabbed his hand, holding it where it was, raising her hips to push hard against it and saying over and over what she wanted and couldn't have.

'We've no protection.' She slumped back to the ground, tears of frustration streaming down her face.

'Are you telling me that you didn't call the village shop the minute I left this morning and ask them to rush over an emergency pack of three?' He was looking at her with amusement now and she wanted to hit him. 'Are those the tears of a sexually frustrated woman?'

Her graphic response to that left him in no doubt how she was feeling.

'Hush… I've got you, Honey,' he whispered, his mouth at her ear. 'You'll find what you need in my back pocket.'

'You came prepared?'

'Would you rather I hadn't?' he asked, doing something indescribably wicked with the clever finger that left her nearly fainting with pleasure. 'Do you still want to do it yourself?'

'This morning, when I was sleeping like a baby in the grass, I was dreaming that I was naked and you were making love to me,' she told him, reaching for the button at his waist and making short work of his zip, her mouth promising heaven in a smile. 'All I want right now, Lucien Grey, is for you to make my dreams come true.'

'I'm sorry about the bridge,' Lucien said.

They had spent a long time over supper while she'd encouraged Lucien to talk. He'd told her about his mother and his childhood. At first, he'd been slow to yield the details of his childhood—how rejected he'd felt when his father had left—but he'd gradually opened up about school, university and the girls he'd known.

When they had reached the time when he'd begun reporting from the front line, he'd switched the questions to her, which was her cue to suggest they make a drink and take it outside.

Grateful that he'd taken the hint, Honey leaned back against the bench, stretching out limbs to which the life had been returned and looking up the stars.

'I'm not,' she said.

He laughed, recognising the words he'd said to her that morning.

'Nevertheless, I promised I would give you a hand in the garden.'

'And you totally delivered,' she said, smiling dreamily as she remembered every luscious moment. 'In the garden, in the shower, on the bed…'

'Honey?'

She turned to look at him, saw the question hovering, saw that he wanted her to tell him why she'd been alone for so long. But she was saved by Banks, who leapt onto the bench with a little growl then stepped onto Lucien's lap, where he began to turn around, plucking with his claws to make it more comfortable.

'What the…!'

Honey laughed, but mostly with relief. 'You're sitting in his seat, Lucien, so he's treating you as a cushion.'

'He's digging his claws in me,' he said helplessly.

'He's making himself comfortable.' Banks, finally satisfied, settled down and began to purr. 'Congratulations. You've been accepted.'

'Only because our scent is now combined.'

Startled by this unexpected perceptiveness, she said, 'That will happen if you share a shower, use the same soap…'

'It's a lot more than that, Honey.'

His expression was so intense that she shivered a little at the enormity of what had happened to her.

'You're getting cold.'

It wasn't cold. It was a goose-walking-over-her-grave shiver.

Lucien lifted the cat. 'I'm sorry about this, Banks, but Honey needs to go inside.' He stood up and returned the cat to the warm place on the bench where he had been sitting, then offered Honey a hand up, putting his arm round her as they walked back to the cottage.

'Would you like me to stay, Honey?' he asked when they were inside.

Honey had no doubt that Lucien was sincere, wanting her to know that he wasn't a man to have his fun and run. But they had gone a long way very fast, and they were both a bit emotionally bent out of shape.

The sex had been hot, and perhaps they both needed that kind of physical distraction as part of the healing process. Sleeping together was something else. That moment when you first woke, before the barriers were up, left you totally defenceless...

'For some reason I'm bone-achingly tired,' she replied, 'and I have no doubt that you're desperate to pull another all-nighter on your book.'

'With no better offers...' He picked up his backpack and slung it over his shoulder. 'I feel the need to say something.'

'Goodnight?' she suggested before he did something crass like thanking her.

'Goodnight, Honeysuckle Rose.' His kiss was lingering, and she found it much too hard to pull away. 'It's been special. Dream some more, and I'll do my best to make them come true.'

'Go!' she said, laughing now. 'And no midnight dipping on the way home. It's dangerous to swim on your own at night.'

'You saw me?'

'I thought you were an otter.'

'What a disappointment.'

'No…'

It was ridiculous to blush, but she did.

Lucien laid his knuckles briefly against her warm cheek, then seconds later she heard the back door click shut.

Honey slept and she dreamed—tangled, mixed-up dreams filled with shadows and people who couldn't see her, didn't respond to her desperate cries. There were taps without water, endless empty corridors with locked doors and someone screaming in pain.

She woke in a panic, sweating and shivering, her throat raw, not knowing where she was. It took her a minute to fight her way through the fog and realise that she was in Flora's room, and that she had been the one screaming.

It was still dark but she rolled out of bed, afraid to go back to sleep, knowing from experience that it would start up again the minute she closed her eyes and stood for a long time under a hot shower, desperate to wash the nightmare away.

When the shaking had stopped, she put a fresh dressing on her foot. The simple task, done a thousand times, gave her back a sense of control. By the time she'd made tea and opened the back door, the sky was tinged with pink and the dawn chorus was in full throat.

It looked as if it was going to be another perfect day, but she checked the weather then clicked through her emails and texts. There were some from colleagues asking how she was, what she was doing. Quite a few from people in the village, urging her to call if she needed anything. The vicar, bless him, said that it was good to see that Lucien Grey was getting out and about and making himself useful.

She spluttered tea down her nose as she read that.

Useful!

The vicar's reason for texting was to add an autumn date for the wedding diary, which dealt with the laughter. September was a long way off and she didn't know where she'd be or what she'd be doing by then.

She'd never sell the cottage, but unless she could get a job locally she'd have to let it rather than leave it stand empty, and there was no guarantee that a tenant would allow strangers to have wedding pictures taken in their garden.

There was a text from Laura Wells, owner of the bookshop, inviting her to fill Flora's vacant seat in her pub quiz team. The chair of the WI was trying to fill her programme for the coming year and was asking if she'd consider giving a talk about her experiences nursing overseas.

A bleep warned her that she had a new text.

Did you dream, Honeysuckle Rose?

Nothing that I'd want you to make come true...

She thumbed in her reply, then stopped.

Lucien would be concerned, would want to know what had been so bad, but she didn't want to think about her nightmare, let alone talk about it.

She deleted her response and instead typed:

I believe it's your turn to expose your fantasies.

Living dangerously, Honey? I have meetings in London today, but I have tomorrow marked down for bridge-painting and elderflower-picking. It's sausage casserole on the menu tonight, but I could mess with the system and swap it for prawns in a chilli sauce if you'd prefer?

Honey caught her breath as reality hit.

It wasn't the choice of supper that had her fingers curling back from the keypad. Anything that Alma had made would be a pleasure to eat.

It was the betraying heart-stop when Lucien's text had dropped into her inbox that stopped her from sending back a wicked text that would make him forget all about his meetings and come running...

She'd been sitting on the bench fooling herself that she was catching up on messages while in reality she had been waiting, like some desperate teenager, to hear from a man who had lit her up like Times Square.

The sexual tension had been off the scale three mornings ago when she'd been accusing him of murdering her butterflies. The sex had certainly been off the scale and she was fine with that. More than fine.

Great sex between two consenting adults was fun. Her friends and colleagues managed it and, even when things had gone wrong and they'd been hurt, they'd picked themselves up and got back in the game.

She'd had that once, as a student, but then she'd met Nicholas and it had just been the two of them, in a 'till death us do part' ring on her finger, 'see you in six months to plan the wedding', happy-ever-after relationship.

She'd waved him off at the airport six years ago and six days later he'd been dead.

She'd been in an emotional stasis ever since; all her energy, all her passion, focussed on her job. All her love had been reserved for the one remaining person in the world who'd always been there.

And then Flora was gone too, before she'd been able

to get home to tell her all the things that she'd now never get to say...

The loss, the guilt, had ripped the heart out of her. She'd felt nothing but anger until a burning rage had sent her to Lucien's doorstep where, lost in his own world of hurt, he'd thawed her out with a kiss that for a while he hadn't remembered.

Then with kisses that she would never forget.

They both had huge gaps in their lives—family gone, jobs they loved but could no longer do. It would be so easy to fill the void by falling into an emotional attachment.

But Lucien didn't need that kind of complication right now. The garden would help him heal. Talking, being with other people, a lot of great, uncomplicated sex... If she kept what they had light, physical, fun, she might be a conduit to his healing. But she had to keep it front and centre of her mind that this was going to be temporary. Casual. A summer fling that Lucien could walk away from, renewed, ready for the big life waiting for him once his book was written.

He'd asked her what she was going to do with her future. Next time he brought it up, she'd better have an answer.

She thumbed in her message quickly.

Have a good day but don't rush back. It's quiz night at the Hartford Arms so I'll be having supper there this evening—they do a very good steak with triple-cooked chips. If you fancy coming along and boosting the chances of the Butterfly Belles you'll be very welcome, but it's not compulsory.

She hit 'send' and then she texted Laura Wells to tell her that she'd be honoured to join the Belles.

Lucien read Honey's message, trying to read between the lines. She hadn't mentioned the quiz team. In fact, he'd had the distinct impression, from something Diana Markham had said that, like him, Honey had been avoiding the social life of the village.

He understood. She'd had some kind of breakdown and it took confidence to get back out there. But, despite their rocky start, she'd opened up the healing power of her home, of her garden, to him. Although it was her wit and her intelligence, and he'd be kidding himself if he didn't admit that it was also her sex appeal, that kept him going back for more.

Honey's demons were much harder to read. She'd opened up physically, no holds barred, and she'd talked about her grief at the loss of the aunt who'd raised her, but there was a lot more that she wasn't ready to share.

When they'd been lying in the orchard, drenched in the scent of crushed grass and the sharpness of some herb, catching their breath and laughing at the madness of what they'd just done, she'd let slip the words, 'I'd forgotten...'

Something in her voice, her words, had tugged at him. He'd reached for her hand as if to reassure her, though of what he couldn't have said, but the way she'd grasped it told him that his instincts had been right.

'Forgotten?' he'd prompted.

That catch in her voice had him braced for tears and her eyes had glittered over-brightly in the shadow of the trees. But she'd been smiling as she'd said, 'Excellent job on delivering the dream, Lucien. Can we do it again?'

He was hard just remembering that smile. Had been shallow enough to ignore the hovering question and missed the moment when, vulnerable, she might have let it all out...

This text was like that smile. A distraction. A step back from closeness, from the spilling out of secrets that followed an intensely intimate connection.

They had talked later over supper. Or rather, he had talked. She was a good listener, ever ready with a prompt.

Forget gardening. She would make a brilliant counsellor. And, like a good counsellor, she had kept it all about him. He should be feeling great about that. No emotional commitment, just great sex and counselling thrown in.

But he wanted more. He wanted her to trust him enough to share all her pain as he had shared his, having opened up to her in a way that he'd never done in counselling sessions.

She'd barely touched on the loss of her parents, of the man she had been going to marry, only opened up about her aunt. But it must have felt like a series of hammer blows. You got up from one and then there was another, and then the final one that tipped you over the edge...

He looked again at the text, shaking his head at the inclusion of the team's name, Butterfly Belles. Was she hoping to frighten him off?

He regretted agreeing to meet Jenny today, but he couldn't let her down now.

While a night in a crowded bar held no appeal, it was good that Honey was getting out into the community, but she needed support. He called her and, before she could speak, said, 'You had me at steak, Honey. I'll pick you up at seven.'

CHAPTER TWELVE

'...*nothing can bring back the hour Of splendour in the grass...*' —William Wordsworth

HONEY FOUND HERSELF listening to nothing. Lucien, having delivered his message, cut the connection, leaving her quivering with a confused mixture of feelings.

The Hartford Arms would be packed on quiz night. His arrival would cause a stir and all those people he'd been avoiding would be there.

On the other hand, if she was on her own, she would be inundated with questions about him. His presence would take the pressure off her, and if he was prepared for that it could be a good outcome. If it went wrong...

That didn't bear thinking about. She considered texting Laura and asking her to warn everyone. But if everyone tiptoed around him, treating him like an invalid, he'd know and that would be far worse.

And she could be worrying about nothing. He might yet decide to drop her at the door and beat a hasty retreat. She wouldn't blame him if he did. She would certainly give him that option.

Honey was upstairs, still drying her hair, when she heard the four-by-four crunching over the gravel a few minutes before seven.

There was no time for anything fancy. She ran a brush through her hair, added a touch of lipstick to her face and then, hanging onto the handrail, hopped one-footed down the stairs, hoping to make it before Lucien discovered what she'd been up to.

Too late.

She had a split second to enjoy the knee-melting sight of his long legs in clinging jeans worn soft with age, a loose-fitting white linen shirt, the sleeves rolled up to the elbow exposing muscled forearms and his scar before he exploded.

'I leave you for one day…!'

'My aunt was a stylish lady, Lucien, but I needed my own underwear.'

'And you've painted the bridge,' he said, ignoring the chance to make some outrageous comment. He really was mad.

'Do you want to go and walk round the garden while you cool off, then come back and try that again?' Honey suggested, taking the last few steps and, when he didn't move, stepping into arms held out to catch her in case she stumbled.

'Dammit, Honey, I told you I'd do it.'

'I've saved the second coat for you,' she said, putting a hand to his cheek where the stress lines were cutting deep. 'Did you have a bad day?'

He took a moment, a long breath, a shake of the head and then gave a smile of sorts. A contraction of the lines fanning out from his eyes softened his face and then moved to his mouth, slow, wide and heart-stoppingly seductive.

'Hello, Honey,' he said, and kissed her cheek. 'I love the way your sweater falls off your shoulder.' He kissed that too, taking his time until he reached the point where it curved into her neck. Then he kissed her other cheek. 'As for my day, I had to turn down lunch at The Ivy with my agent because I had a meeting with Jenny, the sandwich I bought had a severe case of depression—'

'That is rough.'

'And the train was running so slowly that I thought I would be late for our date.'

'This is a date?'

'I have to admit that it's been a while, but I've called to pick you up and take you out for the evening. What else would you call it?' he asked as he drew her closer, kissing her with sufficient ardour to demonstrate intention but with enough care not to mess her hair or smudge her lipstick.

She sighed a little, because it had been perfect. Too perfect.

'That level of flirtation is so practised that it deserves a slap,' she said.

'I'm glad that you appreciate the effort,' he replied with a grin.

She shook her head but was laughing as she reached for the crutches propped up at the bottom of the stairs. 'Don't feel you have to stop.'

'I meant it about the top. It's very sexy. But you're wearing a bra,' he said, running his finger under the strap in a way that sent a shiver ripping through her. 'And your skirt is too long. Those ankles were meant to be seen.'

'But not the technicolour bruises.' She lifted her skirt a few inches so that he could see.

'You're not wearing the brace?'

'My ankle needs movement, exercise,' she explained and, forcing herself to put a little distance between them, she headed for the door.

'I guess you know what you're doing.'

'I guess I do,' she agreed, swinging herself swiftly across the courtyard and leaving him to bang the door shut behind him.

'Even so. I'm sorry about today. It was stuff that I've

been putting off for too long. That because of you I finally felt able to face.'

'I'm glad...' She paused to snap the seed heads off a couple of tulips. 'I put the first coat on the bridge because the forecast said there was the possibility of rain.'

He held out a hand and looked up at the clear blue sky. 'What forecast was that? The nearest we've been to rain for the last two weeks is somewhere south of the Azores.'

'I might have been a little over-cautious,' she admitted. 'But with the wedding this weekend—'

'Wedding?' he repeated, startled out of his amusement at her inability to read a weather forecast.

Honey rolled her eyes. 'What is it about the wedding word that brings grown men out in a cold sweat?'

'I'm looking at you, Honey, and I promise you I'm not in the least bit cold. Are you sure you want to go to this quiz thing? It's not too late for prawns and an early night.'

Given the way that Lucien was looking at her, just getting to the car would be a win.

'I have to do this.' And she put on a sprint over the final few yards. 'Apart from anything else, I want to talk to the chair of the Parish Council about the state of the boat house.'

'The letting agent took some rousing to action. I was reduced to suggesting that you were considering asking for damages.'

'But I was trespassing!'

'I told him you were visiting me,' he said, 'Which was true. You were. They are going to send a surveyor to take a look.'

'That is brilliant. Thank you.'

'I live to serve. Meanwhile, since the Butterfly Belles' need is clearly greater than mine...'

'You've had a rough day, what with the depressed

sandwich and delayed train. You really don't have to do this, Lucien.'

'I've been in a pub before,' he said, opening the door for her. But his voice had lost that teasing note and a muscle tightened in his jaw.

'A pub where half the patrons want something from you? It's going to be noisy, and there will be no escape from the Diana Markhams of the village,' she warned. 'Just drop me off at the pub. I can get a lift home.'

'My face has appeared twice nightly in half the houses in the country, Honey,' he said. 'I'm used to total strangers acting as if they know me. But I'm not the only one here who's been avoiding the neighbours. And I'm not the only one in their sights. Your aunt's death has left a gap in the village and they're hoping that you are going to fill it.'

'Is that why you're tagging along? To run interference for me?'

'I'm tagging along because it's only the thought of spending the evening with you that has kept me going through the day.'

'That's a lovely thing to say, but next time take me with you. I can at least ensure your sandwich is edible.'

'I might take you up on that,' he said. 'But right now I'm going to pick you up and put you in the car, or we won't be going anywhere.'

She held up a hand to stop him. 'I've got this,' she said as, grabbing hold of the seat and boosting herself up with her good foot, she turned and dropped into the passenger seat.

'Spoilsport.'

'I'm attempting to dispel this notion you seem to have of me as a pathetic female who needs a man on hand to get her through the day.'

'I've seen you in tiger mode, protecting your infant caterpillars. You are many things, Honey—annoying, pig-headed, much too sexy for my peace of mind and the least pathetic woman I have ever met.'

He shut the door before she could think of a smart reply, and by the time he'd walked round the car and climbed into the seat beside her she was past it.

Lucien reached over and clicked open the glove box. 'I remembered that it's your birthday soon, although I don't know the date.'

'The tenth.'

'Well, if you look in there, you'll find an early present. It's not much, just a little something I saw in London that made me think of you.'

While he started the engine and pulled out into the lane Honey looked, and saw the iconic glossy green and gold gift bag in its depths.

'What is it?'

Scent? A silk scarf?

'None of the things that men buy women that are always the wrong colour or a scent she'd never wear,' he said, almost as if he could read her mind. 'I bought practical gifts that you won't stick in a drawer and forget. Something that you'll use. Plus, a memory to keep.'

She loved a scarf no matter what the colour.

'Practical is good,' she assured him as she parted the green and gold tissue paper and discovered a pair of soft leather gardening gloves nestling in it.

'Lucien! They are perfect! And some truly luscious hand cream…' She looked at him. 'Are you hinting that my hands are a little rough?'

'No complaints from me,' he assured her, glancing at her then concentrating as he turned onto the road into the village. 'Keep looking.'

The bag felt very light, but further inspection produced a memory stick.

'I looked up the series your father was in, and called in

a favour from a friend who transferred it onto digital from the master tape.'

'Lucien... I don't know what to say.'

'Wait until you've reached the bottom of the bag.'

'There's more?' She reached down into the bottom of the bag and, sure enough, found a package wrapped in green tissue and tied with a gold bow. 'What is this?'

'Reassurance.'

Puzzled, she pulled on the bow, unwrapped the package and then gave a hoot of laughter as she found herself holding a box of condoms.

'Something practical that I'll use?'

'How and when is entirely up to you.'

'Thank you, Lucien. A precious memory and three very useful gifts,' she said, and then was overcome with the giggles.

'Well, I'm glad that was a hit.' She shook her head, unable to speak. 'Are you going to tell me about this wedding and what it's got to do with your bridge?'

It took her a moment to find a tissue and wipe her eyes. 'I'm sorry...' She made an effort to pull herself together. 'It's just something the vicar said about the fact that you were making yourself useful.'

'In your own time,' Lucien said when she lost it again.

She took several deep breaths. 'Okay. I've got it. Weddings... Village newlyweds come straight from the church to have photographs taken, in the orchard when the blossom is out, or on the bridge with the water lilies and the meadow behind them in the summer.'

'The water lilies... Of course. That was the clue.'

'It was?'

'The paint is the same colour as the bridge at Giverny. Nice touch.'

'If it works for Monet...'

'Maybe you should start offering the whole package,'

he said. 'You're looking for a new career. "Weddings at Orchard End" has a nice ring to it. '

'No. This isn't a business, it's…' She stopped, wondering how she could explain it to a man who had lived his entire life in a city.

'It's a country thing?'

'More than that. It's a village thing. An Orchard End thing. Long before there were cameras, wedding celebrations took place in the Orchard End meadow. Everyone pitched in, brought food, someone played the fiddle, they danced, made love…'

'And more weddings followed as the night follows day. It's like something from *Cider with Rosie*.'

'We're in the right part of the country,' she pointed out. 'There's an old painting of a family wedding hanging in the study. His lordship provided a pig for the hog roast and a barrel of ale.'

'It sounds a lot more fun than any wedding I've ever been to.'

'Only if the sun is shining… Don't go in the car park,' she warned as they skirted the village green. 'Pull over here. If it all becomes a bit too much and we have to leave, you won't be blocked in.'

'I'll be fine,' he said, but did as she said and parked in the street.

'Ready?' he asked.

'Ready,' she confirmed. 'You?'

'Let's do it.'

It was a warm evening. The pub doors were fastened open and they could hear noise from beyond the bar door.

Honey was suddenly struck by a thought. 'Lucien…?'

About to push open the door, he said, 'Honey? Are you okay? There's still time to make a run for it.'

'Yes… No…' She waved away the suggestion. 'You were late getting back from town so how did you know I'd been painting the bridge? And that it's the same green as the bridge at Giverny?'

'Do you really want to know?'

She groaned. 'I've missed some paint, haven't I? Where is it?'

'Just here.'

He took his hand from the door and lifted a strand of her hair at the exact moment that the door was opened from the other side and they were caught standing so close that they might have been about to kiss.

The surge of noise that billowed out as the door was opened died away.

'Have you ever been in the Sunday papers, Honey?' Lucien murmured, his mouth close to her ear.

Her response, little more than breath, was scatological. Then, 'Do we run?' she asked. 'Or do we stay?'

'Lucien! How unexpected. How kind.'

Lucien lifted an apologetic eyebrow, then turned to face the woman who had greeted him.

'It's not entirely altruistic, Laura. Honey bribed me with the promise of a steak, but apparently I have to have to sing for my supper.'

'You're staying for the quiz?' She beamed. 'That's wonderful. Our table is just inside. I've forgotten my reading glasses, but I'll be right back. Honey will introduce you to everyone.'

The noise level had risen to normal and several people called out to Honey as they entered. But the Belles' table was near the door and there was no opportunity for people to detain her or engage them in conversation.

And no opportunity to ask Lucien how he knew Laura Wells before they were at their table and introductions had to be made.

'Lucien, this is Philly Wells, Laura's daughter, Josie

Harper, who runs the post office, and Elaine Masters, who was one of Aunt Flora's oldest friends.'

'In every sense of the word,' Elaine said as he shook hands with everyone. 'I hope you're good on sport, Lucien, because this lot are useless, and I only know about motor sport, which never seems to come up.'

'I'll do my best,' he said, taking the menu that Josie handed him and offering it to Honey. 'But no guarantees.'

'I'll have the rib-eye steak, medium rare,' she said without looking.

'Make that for two,' he said.

'And drinks?' Josie asked.

'Elderflower pressé for me,' Honey said. 'I'm on antibiotics.'

'And I'm driving, so I'll stick with water. Let me give you a hand, Josie.'

He started to rise but she put a hand on his shoulder, keeping him in his seat.

'There are at least three people lying in wait for you at the bar.'

'Maybe I should go and put Diana out of her misery now,' he said. 'If I agree to open the fete, we can all relax.'

'Oh, the sweet innocence of the man... Contemplate the words "inch" and "mile", Lucien, while Philly gives me a hand.'

'At least take my cash card.'

'No need. We run a table tab and divide the bill up equally at the end of the evening.'

Laura returned with her glasses and one of her shop's carrier bags, which she handed to Lucien. 'The last of the books you wanted arrived this afternoon. This saves me a trip.'

'Thanks, Laura.'

He handed the bag to Honey. 'Curiosity satisfied?' he murmured.

She put the bag at her feet without looking inside. 'Elaine was an international rally driver,' she said, curiosity under severe restraint.

Lucien, interested, asked all the right questions and Elaine, rising ninety, regaled them in her whisky voice with wicked, behind-the-scenes stories that had them all laughing until their food arrived.

The evening was relaxed and a lot more fun than she'd anticipated.

No one bothered Lucien while they were eating, other than a nod and, 'Good to see you here,' as they passed. Maybe Josie had issued a warning when she'd been at the bar. No one wanted to get on the wrong side of the woman who ran the village post office.

And the quiz was going pretty well, everyone head down and concentrating—the rivalry was intense.

And then someone dropped a tray of cutlery onto the flagstone floor.

CHAPTER THIRTEEN

'Let me not pray to be sheltered from dangers, but to be fearless in facing them. Let me not beg for the stilling of my pain, but for the heart to conquer it.' —Rabindranath Tagore

SOMEONE SHOUTED OUT a comment that made everyone laugh, adding to the noise and confusion, but Lucien was oblivious.

Before Honey could put out a hand to anchor him in place, he was on the floor, ducking, his arm held protectively over his head, knocking over his chair as he crawled for the door, desperate to escape.

His eyes were blank. He clearly had no idea where he was, only that he had to get away. Honey made a desperate bid to hold onto him, reassure him.

He shook her off and she clambered over the fallen chair to open the door so that he could escape. He saw the open front door ahead of him and he was on his feet and running before she could reach him.

He was fast, and too strong for her to restrain, even when she caught up with him. There was no hope of getting him into the car until he came out of it. All she could do was grab hold of a handful of shirt as he stumbled into the darkness of the village green, talking to him, saying his name over and over, spilling out a stream of the soothing words you would murmur to a distressed child. Telling him that he was safe.

Finally, he slowed, sank to his knees and fell sideways into a foetal position. They were far from the lights of the pub and the houses surrounding the green, out of sight in the middle of the cricket pitch. The grass was short, the ground hard and unforgiving, but Honey spooned herself around him as his body shook with sobs, holding him, keeping him safe, and all the time using soft, soothing words to bring him back from the nightmare.

Slowly he quietened and then, exhausted by the trauma, fell asleep.

Honey took a moment to text Laura and reassure her that they were both safe and that she'd settled up with her tomorrow. A little later, in the distance she could hear cars starting up and people calling out goodnight to one another, all no doubt wondering what had happened.

Tomorrow she'd call the chair of the WI and accept the invitation to talk about nursing in a war zone and the long-term damage to the men and women who had been under fire.

She felt Lucien stir and said his name, reassuring him that he was not alone.

'Where am I?' His voice was hoarse, cracked.

'You're safe, love. I'm here.'

'Honey…?' He looked around and when he saw her he groaned, pushing himself up into a sitting position. 'What happened?'

'You had a panic attack.'

He swore. 'I'm sorry. It hasn't been like that for a long time. If I'd thought for one moment…'

'No drama,' she said, quickly. 'But, if you're up to it, I think we should go home. Give me your keys. I'll drive.'

'I'll be fine.'

'They're not attached to your balls, Lucien. Give me your keys or I'll let your tyres down and we'll both be walking home.'

He looked, for a moment, as if he was going to argue, but then there was just the hint of a smile as he dug the keys out of his jeans pocket and handed them over. 'You don't mince your words, do you?'

'Parla come mangi...'

He frowned. 'Speak as you eat?'

'My last post was at a refugee camp on an island off the coast of Italy. It's what they say when you're struggling to get something off your chest.'

'Not something, I imagine, that's ever troubled you.'

'Or you, it would seem.'

'It's better to be straight,' he said, getting to his feet and offering her a hand, for which she was deeply grateful. While she'd been running she hadn't felt her ankle, but now it was throbbing painfully, and without his help she wasn't sure that she could stand.

'Let's go somewhere where the grass is more comfortable,' he said. She hung onto his arm, leaning against him, hoping that he'd think she was supporting him rather than the other way round. 'Did I make a scene?'

'Not much of one. You were out of there like a scalded rabbit while most people were looking at the poor girl who dropped the tray of cutlery. Don't worry. The Belles will have covered it.'

'I don't matter. I'm just sorry that I embarrassed you.'

'Believe me, I didn't have time to be embarrassed. The truth is that you'd had a long and tiring day in London.' She clicked the key to unlock the car door. 'If you hadn't distracted me, I would have noticed.'

'I wanted to be with you, Honey. I was having a good time.'

'I know, but we don't always know what's best for us,' she said. And she wasn't just talking about Lucien.

Despite not being fully recovered, he insisted on giving her a hand up into the driving seat, but she had to remind him to fasten his seat belt before she started the engine and took in a long, slow breath.

Her ankle was hurting like hell. It was a good job it was late and there were few cars on the road, because driving this thing was not going to be fun.

Elaine found her the following morning with her foot packed in ice.

'Josie said you looked rough,' she said, settling on the pouffe. 'But you look older than I feel.'

'I feel older than you look,' Honey admitted ruefully, but then Elaine drove a vintage sports car and had a partner thirty years younger than herself.

'How is your man? His car is parked in your courtyard, so I imagine he stayed here.'

Hadn't Josie mentioned it? The woman was discretion personified.

'I couldn't let him go home in that state and I've left him to sleep for as long as he can. Were there any comments after our somewhat abrupt departure?'

Stupid question. Of course there would have been comments…

'A couple of people asked if Lucien had been taken ill. I mentioned that he'd been to London and maybe he'd eaten something that disagreed with him.'

Honey laughed. 'He was complaining about a sandwich he bought for lunch but, seriously, thank you for covering for him. He's suffering from PTSD. The bombing…'

'I've seen it before, my dear. Back in the war, when it was called shell shock. And in drivers who've been in a crash. But what about you, Honey? You reacted too.'

'I jumped a bit, but then we all did.'

'British understatement is safe in your hands. Are you seeing anyone? You need to look after yourself.'

'I'm not suffering from PTSD, Elaine, but we've both been through similar experiences. Aunt Flora's death was the last straw, and I had a breakdown. I've had counselling, but mostly I'm soaking in the peace of the garden and drinking a lot of camomile tea.'

'That will help, but don't isolate yourself. I haven't bothered you, because it was obvious that you needed time to grieve, but I have been thinking about you.'

'That's what last night was about. Getting back into the community. I didn't intend to bring Lucien along, but he insisted.'

'He seems like a decent man.'

She told Elaine about the incident with the weedkiller—most of it—making her laugh. And the boat house. 'So, yes, he's a very good man. And now, by way of physical therapy, he's helping me out in the garden.'

Elaine raised an eyebrow. 'Is that what they're calling it these days?'

She didn't bother to deny it. 'It's nothing serious. He's just here for the summer while he writes it book.'

Casual...

'I'm glad to hear it. You need to get back on your feet and think about your future, but in the meantime a little fun is just what the doctor ordered.'

'Really? Who are you registered with?'

Elaine laughed. 'You're only young once. Make the most of it. But I wanted to see you to reassure you about Flora. You mustn't think that she was alone. She had her friends around her...someone was with her all the time, and she only allowed us to send for you because she knew you'd feel guilty if you weren't there.'

Honey swallowed down a lump in her throat and Elaine patted her arm.

'It was obvious how upset you were, and I was going to

come and tell you how sorry we were that we didn't override her and call you sooner,' she said. 'But you were gone before any of us could catch our breath after the funeral. Obviously you were needed.'

'Yes...' Not a lie. Every hand was needed, but she should have stayed for a few more days. 'I need to see everyone. Thank them properly. Maybe we could have a memorial lunch?'

'She would approve of that. June—asparagus from my garden, trout from the river, strawberries and lashings of champagne,' she said, then laughed. 'Leave it to me.'

'That would be wonderful. And, Elaine, you didn't leave it too late to call me. There were storms. I couldn't get off the island for three days.'

'It was an act of God, then. Out of our hands.' She nodded. 'The Parish Council will be in touch about putting a memorial on the village green. Steve Evans was all for commissioning some lump of stone with her name on it.' She rolled her eyes at the absurdity of the idea. 'Can you imagine what she would have thought of that?'

'I take it you shot the idea down in flames?'

'Not just me. Flora was growing oak trees from acorns she gathered in the Hartford woods. Brian has them safe and we're going to plant one of them on the green in her memory. With care it will provide a habitat for hundreds of living things until the next millennium.' She got to her feet. 'Is there anything I can do before I go?'

'Look in on Lucien? See if he's still asleep.'

Lucien emerged from sleep in slow stages, with an awareness of his face pressed into a pillow. Light filtering through sheer curtains. The sound of voices somewhere in the distance. He turned over and saw the space where someone had been sleeping beside him and then it began to come back to him.

Honey laughing. Laura bringing him a book. Eating, talking. The quiz…

His body jerked at the memory of the crash and, as he sat up, he realised that he was in Honey's bed.

He'd told her that he was going home but she'd driven him to the cottage, insisting that he shouldn't be alone. She'd put him in her bed and lain beside him, watching over him until he fell asleep.

He threw back the covers, and as he stood up the door opened.

'You're awake. Honey asked me to check.' The old lady was grinning and, realising that he was wearing nothing but his underwear, he pulled the bed cover around him.

'Where is she?'

'Lying down on the sofa with her ankle packed in ice.'

'Her ankle was better…' He knew he'd met this woman last night… 'Sorry, but I can't remember your name…'

'Don't apologise, young man. Not all war wounds are visible. I'm Elaine.'

'Elaine Masters. The rally driver,' he said, as that and a lot more came back to him.

'Honey took care of you last night, but she did more damage to her ankle when she ran after you, so if you're up to it she could do with a little TLC.'

'I'm on it.'

'Good. I hope to see you at the quiz next month. I'll make sure there's no more bother with the cutlery.'

'Maybe… Thank you, Elaine!' he called to her retreating back.

He looked round and found his grass-stained clothes where they'd fallen as he'd flung them off.

Or had he? As he picked up his shirt, he had a vague memory of Honey looking up at him, making some kind of joke as she unfastened the buttons.

It had been a while since he'd had such a bad incident.

He sat on the edge of the bed, his head in his hands, trying to fill in the blanks before he had to face her.

All he could remember was the need to get away, running into the darkness and then Honey holding him... He'd felt as if he'd turned a corner in the last week here, in the garden with Honey. He'd sworn, after the break up with Charlotte, that he'd never hurt another woman. But he'd made a commitment to help Honey get the garden ready for the open day and now, because of him, her injury was worse. He had to fulfil that promise. That was the easy part. The hard part would be easing back from a relationship that had lit him up, given him a glimpse of a future.

But he had no right to inflict the mess in his head on her.

'Honey?'

Lucien, deliciously grass-stained and rumpled, appeared in the doorway.

'Elaine said you were awake. How are you feeling?' she asked. 'Do you have a headache?'

'Forget about me,' he said as he saw how swollen her ankle had become. 'I did that to you. I'm so sorry.'

Honey lowered the book she'd been reading, the one that he'd ordered from the bookshop about a re-wilding project in Scotland.

'I'm beginning to really hate that word,' she said.

'I know. It's meaningless, but you're in pain and I'm to blame.'

'No, dammit, you're not. If I hadn't decided to go to the quiz night, none of this would have happened.'

'And if I'd listened to you and stayed at home, you wouldn't be in pain.'

'I have pills for that. You're a more difficult case. Here's a test. Josie brought over some *pain au chocolat* this morning when she returned my stuff, so go through to the kitchen and have some breakfast.'

Instead of heading for the kitchen, he crossed to the sofa and folded himself up beside her.

'I haven't had an attack that bad for a while,' he said. 'But then I haven't been anywhere.'

'Failed!'

'I heard you, Honey, but you took care of me. Now it's my turn to take care of you. What can I do?'

He looked so desperate that she took pity on him.

'I suppose you could try kissing it better.'

'I'd love to,' he said after a barely discernible hesitation. 'But I haven't got a toothbrush with me.'

'I don't think my ankle will notice.'

'Kiss your *ankle*… Right… Got it…'

That he was not quite himself, that he had lost the sharp edge that always made their encounters so heart-poundingingly edgy, was understandable. But that had sounded very like relief…

Even as the thought flickered across her mind, Lucien knelt at her feet and very gently kissed each of her bruised toes. He kissed the swollen, black and blue instep. Kissed her ankle so tenderly that Honey, who had foreseen breast-beating guilt and been determined to shrug it off as just a minor setback, closed her lids over the hot sting of threatened tears.

'Is it working?' he asked after a while. 'Honey?'

'Absolutely,' she said, blinking hard. 'It's the endorphins. They offer a temporary distraction from pain.'

'I can stay here all day if it will help,' he offered, but without the slow, thoughtful smile that never failed to send her imagination spinning.

'I have to admit that the idea of a man at my feet does have a certain appeal,' she said, making a determined effort to lighten the atmosphere. 'However, it would be hell on your knees, and there's a bride depending on you, so your future is breakfast followed by a couple of hours with a paintbrush.'

Lucien frowned. He'd no doubt anticipated being sent away to get on with his book, and had no doubt hoped for that escape, but the last thing he needed after last night was to be cooped up indoors reliving the events that had caused his problems in the first place.

'This is the outside-in-the-fresh-air, doing-something-practical-with-my-hands cure?' he asked.

'That's it,' she said, aware that he had avoided the word *useful*. And there had been no attempt to pick up her admittedly feeble attempt to raise a smile. Not that she was in any state for a repeat of their romp in the long grass.

He nodded. 'I'll see to it. What about you? Have you had anything to eat? Can I get you some coffee? Camomile tea?' Then he added without a hint of sarcasm, 'Can I carry you to the bathroom?'

'I've had a pastry and tea and a bathroom break, thanks to Josie, but you could take away the ice packs and put them back in the freezer.'

'She should have come and woken me.'

'She wanted to, but you needed the sleep more than I needed you fussing around me.'

'Fussing?'

Was that a touch of outrage? Better…

'Like a mother hen,' she said. 'And, while you're clucking around asking me what I want, you're still failing the listening test.'

'Okay,' he conceded, hands raised in surrender as he got to his feet. 'What I need most is a shower and a change of clothes, but I'll take the pastry with me, and I will eat it.' He crossed a finger over his heart. 'I'll have to deal with the inevitable emails after yesterday's meetings, but then I'm all yours.'

'Better. I'll give an hour,' she said, checking her watch as he gathered up the ice packs. It needed recharging. 'You'll find your keys on the kitchen table and the paint on a shelf in the stables. I wrapped the brushes in clingfilm when I finished yesterday, so you can use them as they are.'

'Yes, ma'am.'

'I'm afraid you're going to be on your own picking the elderflowers. I prepped everything yesterday,' she continued quickly before he could object. 'And this afternoon I'm going to introduce you to the art of making elderflower champagne.'

'You think you've got this all worked out, don't you?'

'If you don't think you can manage it, I'll send out a distress call.'

He shook his head. 'You are a piece of work.'

'And you are wasting your hour. You've already had three minutes.'

'I didn't think the clock started until I left.'

'Big mistake.'

'Seriously, Honey, you need to stay off your foot—and I don't care if that's "clucking".'

She smiled. 'No worries. I'll be the one lying back on an old cane lounger that's somewhere in the back of the stables. Behind the tractor. You'll be the one doing the work.'

Finally, a smile. 'I live to serve. Any special request for supper?'

'The sausage casserole will be perfect.' She looked at her watch. It wasn't showing anything, but she said, 'Five minutes.'

'I'm out of here Nurse Bossy Boots, but text me if you need anything before then.'

'You can count on it.'

Honey watched him as he walked away and heard the freezer door being opened and closed. She heard the clink of his keys as he picked them up. Small, everyday sounds, but the click of the back door as he shut it behind him had a finality about it.

He thought he'd blown it. It had been in every awkward move, every smile missed. This had been one setback, one bad incident, but he clearly believed that he was too messed up for even the most casual fling.

But, unless those birthday condoms were going to wither with age, she was going to have to convince him otherwise.

CHAPTER FOURTEEN

Take as many elderflower heads as you need, picked on a warm, sunny day, when they are fully open...

LUCIEN FOUND THE ancient cane chair, the kind of thing that might once have sat on the veranda of a rubber planter in the far east. He wiped off the cobwebs and added a couple of pillows, one for Honey's back and another for her foot.

A place had been created in one of the wide arms for a glass, and when the chair had first been used, it would probably have contained a glass of something exotic like a Singapore Sling. Today it was a useful home for her water bottle.

'Thanks, Lucien,' she said, easing herself into the pillow and allowing him to prop up her ankle. 'I haven't been in this room since Aunt Flora died, but cleaning it up yesterday, making it ready... I felt as if she was here with me.'

'And now?'

'Now it's mine, and I'm going to enjoy just sitting here, reading this lovely book you bought from Laura.'

But not nearly as much as she would have enjoyed being down in the meadow cutting the flowers herself, he knew. Although he didn't say that because she was trying desperately hard to prevent him from feeling guilty.

As if that were possible.

He picked up an oversized bucket and the secateurs. 'Fresh, frothy-looking blossoms from as high as I can reach,' he said, repeating his orders. 'And don't take more than a third from any one tree.'

'You've got it.'

'I won't be long.'

'Don't rush it, Lucien.' She smiled up at him and put a hand on his arm, and for a moment the temptation to lean in and kiss her almost overwhelmed him. 'Breathe in the warm air. Listen to the birds. Talk to the bees.'

'I seem to recall that they don't say much,' he said, forcing himself to move.

'But they listen,' she reminded him. 'Most of the time, that's enough.'

Honey watched Lucien go, aware that he was making a heroic effort to act as if nothing had changed, but the PTSD incident had undoubtedly shaken him.

Yesterday he would have kissed her before going off to forage.

Yesterday, they would have been doing it together. Laughing a lot. Maybe having their own *Cider with Rosie* moment...

Today, apart from being very tender with her poorly foot, he hadn't touched her, for which she had no one to blame but herself. If she hadn't been running scared of feelings that were spiralling out of control, they would have been safely at home in her kitchen last night. In her bed, putting his reassuring and very useful gift to good use. They'd still have been putting up barriers against the outside world, but they would have been doing it together. Those barriers had come crashing down for her. The world had been beating a path to her door all morning, in person, on the phone and by email.

They had all been very tactful.

People were happy to see that she'd managed to bring their reclusive neighbour to the pub. No one had mentioned their early exit, or the fact that they must have seen that his car had still been parked by the green when they'd left at the end of the evening. She was just grateful that no one had come looking for them.

But the upshot was that she was now signed up for all the things she'd been avoiding since she arrived home. There was no way she was going to be allowed to slip back into hiding.

Lucien, however, might take it into his head to disappear, find somewhere remote and sink deeper into himself. Jenny had tried to help, but she'd had her hands full with the farm and filming, with a baby on the way.

It was down to her to keep him on station, and she would do whatever it took to make that happen, even if it seriously annoyed him.

'Is that it?' Lucien asked.

The elderflowers were prepared for the champagne and were now weighted down, waiting for the magic to happen. The cordial was bottled and ready for the open day.

'The rest is time,' Honey said. 'I'll be okay by the time it's ready to be bottled, but thanks for today. I wouldn't have been able to do this without you.'

'I was glad to help. And it slipped my mind earlier, but Jenny asked if you'd mind sending her the recipe.'

Had he told Jenny about her?

'You could tell her yourself now that you're an expert,' she pointed out.

'I'd get the quantities wrong, and besides, you have the recipe on your phone. I'll send you her email.' He looked up from his phone. 'Unless it's some big family secret?'

'Hardly. She could find a recipe online, but of course

I'll send her Aunt Flora's just as soon as I've had a bathroom break. If you'll give me a hand up…'

He took both her hands and held them while she got to her good foot and steadied herself.

They were so close. Lucien smelled of warm fresh air, the scent of blossom, the oranges and lemons he'd squeezed. So delicious that she could have eaten him by the spoonful.

For a moment while she found her balance, while he looked at her, the world seemed to stand still.

Then a shiver seemed to go through him and the spell was broken.

'Okay?' he asked.

'Fine,' she snapped as she let go of his support and grabbed her crutches. She was very far from okay. She wanted to scream with frustration, but instead she took a deep breath. 'Honestly… Just give me a bit of room.' He looked doubtful, but he took a step back. 'Will you make sure the windows and door are all fastened tight, or the sugar will attract insects.'

She didn't wait to see if he did as she asked but took off on her crutches. When she emerged from the bathroom, he was in the study, looking at the painting of the wedding in the meadow.

'Is your bride doing this?' he asked, glancing at her.

'I believe the wedding reception is being held in the castle, but thank you for reminding me that I need a path cut through the lawn so that she can arrive at the bridge without the hem of her very expensive dress turning green.'

'And that's my task for tomorrow?'

'Brian normally does it. Under other circumstances, I'd do it myself. If you think I'm taking advantage, please say.'

'I know exactly what you're doing, Honey, but of course I'll do it.'

'Great. That's a weight off my mind.' She turned to head for the sofa, then stopped. 'Did you happen to notice any dragonflies while you were painting the bridge? Metallic blue-green insects with two pairs of transparent wings?' she prompted when he didn't answer.

'I know what they are,' he said, a muscle in his jaw working overtime as his careful mask slipped a little. 'I wasn't looking at anything but the paintwork.'

'Could you do that tomorrow?' she asked. 'Count how many you see and maybe take a photograph? Flora kept a diary entry of these things, although she painted what she saw. That's one of her water colours,' she said, turning to a small watercolour sketch of a water vole on the river bank. 'And the garden map is all her work. I'd like to carry on with that for as long as I can.'

'Why?' He didn't wait for an answer. 'She had a passion for what she was doing but you're just going through the motions. Trying to do what you think your aunt would want.'

He turned from the watercolour. 'From everything I've heard about her, she'd be telling you to think hard about where you go from here—because if you are anything like her you're going to be doing it for the next sixty years.'

'Right now, all I can think about is getting through the summer. Doing what has to be done. Count the dragonflies, cut a path through the grass to the pond for a bride...'

Help a man she was falling stupidly in love with to find a way into the future.

'I'm sorry, Lucien. Forget it. You've done more than enough—'

'I thought the "sorry" word had been banned.'

'It's a "do as I say, not as I do" rule.'

'Why doesn't that surprise me?'

'Because I'm the neighbour from hell? The one that you don't have to pretend with,' she reminded him. 'But that's what you've been doing all day.'

'No...'

'Pretending you're okay when all you want to do is run back to the Dower House, pull down the shutters and refuse to answer your door. You don't have to run away from me. I understand what you're going through.'

'And you think you can cure me?'

'No, Lucien. Only you can do that. I doubt you'll ever be truly free of the panic attacks, but they will get less intense if you give yourself a chance.'

'And what about you, Honey? Have you been thinking about the hopes and dreams of your six-year-old self? It's time for you to stop dodging the question and think about what you're going to do for the rest of your life.'

'I can't remember. All I can remember is wanting my mother. It blocked out every other thing and that's the truth. So run away if you must,' she said, 'but don't bother about the ice pack. I'm going to take a nap.'

'Another one?'

'Excuse me?'

'You were asleep when I came back with the elderflowers. I could hear you from the courtyard.'

'Hear me?'

'Little piglet snorts,' he said. 'But then I don't imagine you had much sleep last night. Your ankle must have been agony.'

'I had pain killers.' She had them, but hadn't taken them, afraid that Lucien might wake up not knowing where he was and have another panic attack. 'But you're right. I didn't sleep until I was sure you were okay.'

'And I am, thanks to you. While I'm being an ungrateful jerk.'

'Just a bit,' she agreed.

'Dammit, Honey, you've seen what happens. I'm not fit to be with anyone right now.'

'We're both a little bent out of shape,' she said, lowering herself into an old and saggy sofa that had been in the study for as long as she could remember. She'd slept on it as a child while Flora had worked. 'Why don't you just tell me what's been eating a hole in you all day?'

'*Parla come mangi?*'

'Well remembered, but I can't talk to you if you're standing up.'

Lucien glanced at the leather chair in front of the desk, but she said, 'That's too far away. I want to see the whites of your eyes while you lie to me.'

He pulled the chair closer to the sofa and sat down in front of her. It jolted down to its lowest setting.

'You knew it would do that,' he said, glaring at her.

'It's old,' Honey said. 'And you're a lot heavier that Aunt Flora.'

'Okay, you've got me, but I'm not going to lie to you.'

'You've been doing it all day. Not consciously,' she said, 'but it's there in everything you do. You want to touch me, but you're keeping your distance. You want to stay, and at the same time believe you should leave.'

He didn't deny it.

'You said that you didn't have to pretend with me, because you didn't care if what you said hurt me—'

'Because I didn't know you,' he protested.

'And now you know me, it's okay?'

He swore, apologised, and swore again. Dragged fingers through his hair as he sought the words to explain how he was feeling.

'Meeting you has been like a blast of fresh air blowing through my head, Honey. I thought I'd turned a corner but last night proved just how wrong I was. If we carry on with this, you are going to get hurt. Not like your ankle. I'm talking about the bits that never quite knit true.'

'Life is forever twisting us into something new. You've had a bad panic attack. They will happen, but if you take care of yourself they will become less frequent, less frightening. I'm not suffering from PTSD,' she said. 'I haven't been in a good way for a very long time, and it finally caught up with me, but things are getting better.'

'Fresh air and doing something practical with your hands?'

'It was helping,' she said. 'The only thing I lacked was the courage to put it to the test. Then your cowboy gardeners knocked down my nettles.'

'I owe them a drink for that.'

'For heaven's sake don't tell them why!'

'You think they'd be shocked?'

'I'm afraid they'd think it's okay to spray nettles.'

He laughed and she didn't think she'd ever heard a better sound. 'Heaven help them if they ever see you coming out of your corner fighting for something that can't defend itself.'

'It wasn't anger that saved me.'

She removed her watch, exposing the tattoo that the strap usually kept covered, and held her wrist out to him.

He took her hand. 'This is what jogged my memory that first evening,' he said. 'I remembered it from when you worked on my arm.'

She frowned. 'How? I was wearing gloves.'

'You'd finished with me and you were pulling them off when I looked back.' He ran his thumb over the tattoo. 'What are these flowers?'

'Forget-me-nots. They've self-seeded all over the garden. Little splashes of bright blue.' She turned her hand so that he could see the way it circled her wrist, then looked up. 'They are said to alleviate grief.'

'And do they?'

She shook her head and he folded her hand into his. 'Tell me about Nicholas. How did you meet?'

'Nicholas Furneval was a junior doctor. Six feet tall, a mass of light brown hair, green eyes. He was running along a corridor in answer to an emergency and, as he turned a corner, he sent me flying.'

'Don't tell me…he stopped to pick you up and got a mouthful of abuse for his pains.'

She laughed. 'You know me so well.'

'Well enough to know how that would go.'

'Not this time. He shouted an apology but didn't stop. He was waiting for me when I came off duty, insisted on taking me for a drink to apologise properly, which turned into dinner, then he insisted on walking me home, came in for coffee and never left.'

'You seem to have that effect.'

'You didn't stay.'

'You didn't want me to.'

'I was afraid,' she admitted. 'It was too fast.' Too everything. 'It's why I decided to go to the quiz night.'

'And why I insisted on joining you.'

'You knew?'

'It was the Butterfly Belles in your text. They were clearly meant to frighten me off.'

'You are too smart, Mr Grey.'

'I recognised the technique of a fellow bolter, Miss Rose.'

'I'm not bolting now, and neither should you.'

'No.' They just looked at one another until the clock chimed the hour and they both blinked. 'What happened, Honey? To your Nicholas. I know he died, but where, how?'

'Um…' It took her a moment to drag herself back to the story. 'He'd already applied to work for a medical charity and we'd only been together for a few months when he got the call.'

'He asked you to go with him?'

She shook her head. 'It was too late for that, but he produced a ring at the airport, said he wished I was going with him then went down on one knee in the airport terminal and asked me to marry him as soon as he came back. But he never did come back.'

'When was this?'

'He left London six years, eight months and three days ago. He died six days later, when the small plane in which he was travelling with a pilot and two nurses went down in a storm. It was in heavy forest, and they didn't find them for months.'

'So you decided to follow in his footsteps.'

'He'd wished I was going with him, Lucien. So I went. To be where he was. It was the only thing that made sense.'

He nodded. 'I can understand that.'

'Because you are a special kind of person. But I haven't told you this to make you feel sorry for me. I'm telling you because you think you're doing all the taking, and I want you know how much you've given me. It was finally making that physical connection. Feeling alive when you touched me.'

He frowned. 'There's been no one since Nicholas?'

'No.'

'You're beautiful, funny… What's the matter with the men out there?'

'Nothing. I was the problem. Some people react to loss with endless hook-ups, one-night stands, in an effort to rec-reate that feeling of being touched by someone you love. I turned inwards, because I knew there would never be any-one else. I put all my passion into my work. That worked until Aunt Flora died.'

She was aware that Lucien was barely breathing, so afraid that she'd stop talking, but that wouldn't be right. He'd told her everything that had ever happened to him, and if they were to be partners in this he had a right to know why she was the way she was.

'I carried on for a few weeks but the guilt about not being there for her when she needed me, when she'd been there all my life, finally broke me. I was found raging at a frozen water pump. Kicking it, swearing at it, completely out of control. I had to be sedated before they could ship me back to London. I had a week in hospital, counselling sessions and then home to Lower Haughton where, like you, I had been avoiding all unnecessary contact. People put it down to grief and they gave me the space they thought I needed. And then your cowboys sprayed my nettles.'

He lifted her hand to his lips. He kissed the back of her fingers, kissed her palm, as if paying homage to her.

'What can I do for you, Honeysuckle Rose?'

'Nothing. I know I will never be quite whole again, not the way I was before Nicholas died. I'll never be able to love anyone the way I loved him, and I'm not looking for that kind of relationship. But I can feel, I can laugh, Lucien. You've given me that. Given me back my life.'

'That's—'

'Too much responsibility. I know, and it's okay. This is just for the summer with no pressure to do anything but enjoy each other while we let the garden heal us.'

'And afterwards? What happens when the summer ends?'

'You have an important life waiting for you, Lucien. And while you were picking elderflowers I phoned Melchester University to ask about postgraduate courses. It's late, but Professor Flora Rose's name still has some pulling power. It may not be the answer, but I'm going to talk to someone there next week.'

'You make it sound so simple.'

'It is,' she said. 'Listen to the oak breathe, count the dragonflies, lie in the long grass and make love until the swallows depart. Then we can both start our new lives. No looking back.'

'Have you any idea what you'll do?'

'I'm interested in counselling,' she said.

'You'll be wonderful.'

'Thank you,' she said. 'And, now we've sorted that out, you can go and cut that path.'

He stood up but, instead of leaving, he joined her on the sofa. As the cushion sagged beneath him, she fell against him and he put his arm around her, drawing her closer so that her head was on his shoulder.

'That chair you were using today,' he said. 'The one in the still room.'

'What about it?'

'Can I put it in the glass house? If I put a plank across the arms for my laptop, I can write in there.'

'Is this because you feel obliged to stay and keep an eye on me?'

'Perhaps I want you to keep an eye on me.'

She turned to look at him. 'Maybe you should move in so that we can keep an eye on each other.'

'A *summer's lease*?'

'More Shakespeare?'

'He has the right quote for every occasion.'

'A no-commitment relationship with the end date pencilled in? A summer's lease,' she said. 'Although I should probably warn you that you won't be on your own in the glass house. I've an awful lot of plants to pot on for the open day.'

'I'll move the chair in later.'

'And now?'

'Now we'll just sit here and listen to the oak breathe. Maybe we'll fall asleep.' He turned to look at her with that slow smile that melted her bones. 'And maybe we won't.'

CHAPTER FIFTEEN

'The night is darkening round me, The wild winds coldly blow;' —Emily Brontë

IT WAS THE National Garden Open Day and Honey was at the pond with a group of children when her phone vibrated in her pocket. It was Alma, back from Spain with a fabulous tan and full of energy.

'Get back to the cottage asap! You have a very important visitor. Lucien is holding the fort, but he can't stay long—the visitor,' she added. 'You might want to run a comb through your hair.'

'What?' She had to be joking. At least one of the children always fell in the pond, usually on purpose, and she couldn't take her eyes off this bunch who were more of a handful than usual. 'Unless it's George Clooney, Lucien is on his own,' she said, just managing to grab the back of a boy's sweatshirt before he toppled in. 'What have you got there, Amil?'

He held up his jar to show her an eft but, as she gathered the children round to tell them about the life cycle of a newt, there was a scuffle and a small boy—one of the few who hadn't been hell-bent on a dip of his own—went in with a splash.

'Robert pushed me!' he yelled, floundering in the water, his feet slipping on the muddy bottom as he tried to stand.

'Back!' she thundered, in a voice learned from a former sergeant major turned nurse she'd worked with.

Parents were supposed to remain close by, and some did grab hold of their offspring, but no one came forward to offer her a hand as she waded in and grabbed the boy.

'Pond dipping is more exciting than I imagined,' Lucien said, appearing exactly when needed.

'My hero. Can you take him?'

Lucien caught hold of the boy, getting thoroughly smeared with mud and water weeds as he delivered him into the safe hands of one of the helpers that he'd brought with him.

'I'm sorry I couldn't drop everything and come. Has the very important visitor left?' she asked.

'Not yet. Sir, may I introduce Professor Rose's niece, Miss Honeysuckle Rose?'

Sir...?

Honey threw Lucien a puzzled look and then turned to find herself face to face with royalty.

'I appear to have caught you at an awkward moment, Miss Rose,' he said, grinning broadly.

Standing knee-deep in the pond, and wondering whether she should curtsey, Honey thought the Prince had the situation pretty well nailed.

'Children and water...' she replied, deciding that it wasn't the moment for formality. Under normal circumstances she would have climbed out without assistance, but she wasn't about to risk slipping on the muddy bottom and going under, so held out a hand for assistance.

'Like iron filings to a magnet,' the Prince agreed as Lucien, who was trying very hard not to laugh, grasped it firmly. She gave him an *I'll talk to you later* look, then turned to her visitor.

'My apologies for not coming to meet you, Your Royal Highness,' she said, drying her hands on the hem of her T-shirt. 'But, as you can see, we've been pond-dipping.'

'Have you found anything interesting?'

'We have.' She looked around at the group of parents who were staring, open-mouthed. 'Amil, come and show His Highness your eft.'

Lucien brought Amil forward and the newt tadpole was admired while a dozen mobile phone cameras snapped frantically.

'My apologies for arriving without warning, Miss Rose, but I was a great admirer of both Professor Rose and her father. They were visionaries in their field, and when Lucien sent an invitation to the open day, I asked my staff to find half an hour when I could come and see the garden for myself.'

Lucien had done this…without warning her?

'You are very welcome, sir. I hope the WI ladies offered you tea?'

'They did, thank you. It gave Lucien a chance to tell me what a special place this is. Not just the conservation and re-wilding work of your aunt, but about the healing atmosphere of Orchard End and how you have helped his recovery.'

'Not for the first time, sir,' Lucien said. 'Miss Rose is the nurse who took care of me when I was wounded.'

'You have known one another for a while, then.' He turned to her. 'Can I prevail upon you to give me the garden tour, Miss Rose?'

Nearly an hour later, their distinguished visitor, who'd seemed more interested in the healing aspect of the garden than the re-wilding, was ready to leave.

'Thank you so much, Miss Rose. Your aunt had such knowledge and vision. You must miss her a great deal.'

'Yes.' The word caught in her throat.

'The garden is delightful, but it's your experience with mental health that I'd like to tap into for a counselling scheme for young people that is being set up by a charity I am patron of. The way you're using nature to heal… My office will be in touch to arrange a meeting to discuss the role I have in mind.'

He didn't wait for a reply—obviously no one had ever said no to a personal invitation to meet him—but climbed behind the wheel of his car and, with his protection officer at his side, drove away.

'Lucien?' Honey said faintly.

'Yes?'

'Did His Royal Highness just offer me a job?'

'That's what it sounded like to me.'

'But he doesn't know me.'

'You are Miss Rose of Orchard End. Clearly that's enough.'

She shook her head. 'You're on first-name terms with him?'

'He's on first-name terms with me, which is not the same thing. We've met a couple of times at charity functions.'

'You knew him well enough to invite him to the open day.' She rounded on him. 'Did you know he was coming?'

'No idea, I promise!' he assured her, holding up his hands in surrender. 'Or I would have warned you. But he lives practically within shouting distance, and when I discovered that he'd written a foreword to your aunt's last book I wrote to him, hoping he might be able to spare half an hour to see Orchard End for himself.'

'Did he reply?'

'I had an acknowledgement from a member of his staff explaining that His Royal Highness had a very full diary and I assumed that was that. I was as surprised as you were when he walked in from the courtyard.'

'That must have given Brian a start. Did he ask him to pay the entrance fee?'

'I think the protection officer had that more than covered. And Alma was brilliant, completely unfazed. You have stacked up a lifetime of Brownie points with her.'

'That's a relief. She's been a bit disapproving since she came back from Spain and discovered that you've more or less moved in here.'

'I think you'll find that's concern rather than disapproval.'

'Why? Has she said something?'

'She had a little chat with me about how much the people of this village care for you. A suggestion that hurting you would be a bad idea.' He grinned. 'There was just the barest whiff of the stocks...'

'Oh, Lord, I'm sorry. When you've gone, I'll tell her about our "summer's lease" agreement.'

'The whole line is "...and summer's lease hath all too short a date..." Did we decide which summer?'

'Lucien...'

'Alma didn't have to warn me, Honey. I know exactly how the people of Lower Haughton feel about you. I wanted to give something back, to show you and the village how much you mean to me.'

'A result, then,' she said quickly, afraid that this was going in a direction she couldn't handle, that he wanted more than she had offered, could deliver. 'Although, I would have preferred not to have been in mud up to my knees when he arrived.'

'I hadn't foreseen that possibility,' he admitted, 'but you can wear your best dungarees when you visit Highgrove.'

She elbowed him in the ribs then, relieved to have skirted a difficult conversation, and looked up. The afternoon had grown heavy and still, the sky had an ominous brassy tinge and there was a distant rumble that might have been a farm lorry passing at the end of the lane. Or might just be thunder.

'Did you hear that?'

'It's a long way off. It might pass.'

'I hope so. Once it gets trapped in the valley, it just goes round and round,' she said as a raindrop hit her cheek.

The rain was bucketing down by the time they'd got the tables and chairs under cover. Normally they'd take a walk, or sit outside for a while after supper, which would have been the perfect moment to talk to Honey about the future, to confess that he was falling in love with her and that he was looking for more than a short-term lease.

He'd tried earlier, but she'd shied away and he hadn't pressed it. Now she curled up on the sofa and pointed the remote at the television. 'Just checking the weather,' she said. 'Are you going to work this evening?'

'No, I'm going to sit here with you on the sofa and watch some rubbish television with you, just like an old married couple,' he said.

'Don't…'

'Honey, I know it's only been a few weeks, but I don't want it to end.'

'Please, Lucien. I've told you why that's not possible. What time are you leaving in the morning?'

He wanted to tell her to let go of the past, to give herself a chance and give him a chance to make her happy. But she'd shut him down, afraid to take that risk, and he took her hand and kissed it, wanting her to know that he understood her reticence to commit.

'I'm catching the seven-thirty-five train from Maybridge.'

'It's an early night, then.'

'An early night,' he agreed, taking what she was prepared to offer, prepared to wait for her to stop looking back and instead turn to face a new future.

Lucien stepped outside as the taxi crunched over the gravel. The path round the front porch was littered with pink petals and everything seemed to be sagging a little.

'The roses have taken a battering in the rain.' It had finally stopped some time around dawn, but the air was still heavy.

'We haven't seen the last of it,' Honey said, and he put down his laptop holdall and wrapped his arms around her.

'You said you'd come with me the next time I had to go to London.'

'I'm sorry, but you're going to be in meetings all day, and I can't leave Alma and Brian to clear up after the open day.' She cradled his face in her hands. 'Just stay away from coffee and alcohol, eat a proper lunch and, if it all gets too much, find a quiet spot to sit and breathe. Or you can call me any time.'

'I'll call you anyway. And I'll let you know what train I'm on.'

'Don't rush back. If your meetings drag on or you feel tired, stay in London.'

'I will,' he promised. 'If you'll promise to stay out of the garden today? Everything is soaking and your ankle is still weak. Read, knit, watch old movies…'

'No gardening. Got it. Now, go,' she said, picking up his bag and handing it to him. 'Or you'll miss your train.'

He kissed her again then, because he had no choice, he got into the taxi.

'Lovely old place,' the driver said as they set off. 'My mum and dad had their wedding party in the meadow.'

Honey, not a knitter and anxious about the weather, turned on the news at lunch time. There were yellow flood warnings in other parts of the county, but nothing for the Hart. Even so, she took a walk down the garden to take a look at the river. It was higher than usual and running fast, but nothing she hadn't seen before when there had been heavy rain.

Lucien rang. 'We've broken for lunch. How are things down there? There are flood warnings on the news.'

'That's further north. I walked down to the river and I've seen much worse.'

'Stay inside, Honey.'

'I don't knit. '

'Then read a book, play patience, cook shortbread. Please, sweetheart… I'll get back as soon as I can.'

'Calm down, Lucien. Everything is fine. Go and have something to eat. Do what you have to do, and I'll see you when I see you.'

'That's your bossy nurse voice.'

'And are you listening?'

'Okay, okay. Lunch, quiet place, breathe…'

There was a moment when neither of them said anything, because it was enough to hear one another breathe, then she heard someone call his name.

'I've got to go. I'll see you later.'

'Yes.'

After he'd hung up, she held the phone to her breast, listening to the rain rattling like hail against the window.

She'd been so certain that her capacity for love had died along with her family, with Nicholas. Yesterday she'd stopped Lucien from saying anything that would change their relationship. But he'd made love to her with such heartbreaking tenderness last night and the thought of the autumn, just a few short weeks away, when Lucien would leave, was tearing a hole in her heart.

She hated that he was a hundred miles away in London, that she couldn't look in his eyes…read in them what he was feeling…

Half an hour later she received a text.

Baked sea bass, steamed baby new potatoes, broccoli with roast almonds for lunch, and a glass of delicious tap water. Now do you wish you'd come with me?

He'd said something like that before he'd left.

'You said you would come with me...'

The words send a shiver through her, but she sent back a rude emoji, made a couple of phone calls and checked her emails. She discovered that there was already an invitation from an aide at Highgrove, with a document laying out plans for the mental health initiative and her possible role.

Excited at the prospect, she spent a couple of hours looking at mental health websites until, just after four, the sky went black, the thunder that had been rolling up and down the valley all day settled overhead and she lost the Internet.

She put on Aunt Flora's aged mac, donned rubber boots and went down for another look at the river. It was still within the banks but higher and running much faster, and low-hanging branches that had been torn off trees were being tossed around in the fast-flowing current.

She went inside and checked the weather warnings. There was localised flooding but no warning for Lower Haughton.

She called Steve Evans, the chair of the Parish Council and Chief Flood Warden.

'Steve, the river is running very high, and there's quite a bit of debris in the water.'

'I'm on it, Honey. We've set up a command centre in the pub and we're keeping a watch on the foot bridge in case of blockages. If you can keep an eye on the river level where you are, that will be really useful.'

She texted Lucien.

The weather is foul. The trains are going to be all over the place. Stay in London.

A minute later her phone rang. 'The trains are delayed so I've taken a car. We've just passed Maidenhead and the driver reckons I'll be home in a couple of hours. Go to the pub. You'll be safe there.'

'I will, as soon as I've checked the river level, but it's going to be really dangerous on the motorway after such a long dry spell,' she said, trying to keep calm and not say or do anything to cause him stress. The thunder and lightning would already be doing that. 'Pull off at the next exit and stay in an hotel.'

'Honey…' There was a crackle and the signal began to break up. 'I love you…'

What? No. He mustn't say that…

'Please, Lucien, get off the motorway. Stay safe!' she said, losing it, but the signal had gone.

Mind in a turmoil, her hands were shaking so much that she struggled to hit the call-back button, but when she finally managed it, it went straight to voicemail.

'Lucien, you remember how important it is to listen to me. I am telling you to get off the motorway and find somewhere safe.' Her voice was shaking as much as her hands. 'Please, dear man, do it for me.'

Do it because I love you too. I love you…

The three most dangerous words in the world. Words she couldn't say, shouldn't even think.

'Call me and tell me you've done that as soon as you get a signal.'

She switched on the drive-time programme on the radio for the traffic news. There were accidents everywhere, delays, hold-ups…

She tried his number half a dozen times over the next three hours with the same result. Clearly he hadn't picked up her message or he'd be safe and dry in a hotel where he could have called her from a landline…

Unable to settle, she made constant trips to the river. The low cloud cover and constant rain meant that it was dark much earlier than usual. By seven o'clock, using the torch on her phone, she could see that water was spilling over the bank.

She called Steve.

'There's a report of a blockage at the footbridge. It looks as if someone's shed has been washed away. It must have been pretty substantial, or it would have broken up, but everything is catching on it. A team is on its way to clear it now.'

'It could be the boat house. I'm going to check.'

'Be careful, Honey. Don't take any risks.'

The continuous lightning followed by cracks of thunder was like a night-time rocket attack and it took all of Lucien's concentration and careful breathing to remain focussed on where he was. On Honey. His need to know that she was safe.

It got worse as he neared Lower Haughton after delays caused by accidents, breakdowns and endless detours. It had been nearly five hours since he'd been able to get a signal.

It was lashing with rain when they finally drew up outside The Hartford Arms. Inside it was buzzing with activity but he could see at a glance that Honey wasn't there.

'Lucien…' Josie looked up from filling a flask with soup. 'Thank goodness. Honey's been frantic with worry.'

'I couldn't get a signal. A lightning strike somewhere… Where is she?'

'Monitoring the river level.'

Of course she was.

'I'll send my driver back. His name's Marek and he's been an absolute hero. He needs food and a bed for the night.' He took out his wallet, offering a card.

'I'll sort it. You can settle up later. Go and find Honey.'

Ten minutes later they were at the cottage. 'Go back to

the pub, Marek. Call your family to let them know you're safe. Josie will take care of you.'

He checked the cottage, desperately hoping that Honey would be safe in the warm and dry. As if…

The light was on in the kitchen, but there was no one home. He dumped his laptop bag and ran down the garden towards the river. He was ten metres from the gate when water began to fill his shoes.

'Honey!'

He'd hoped to find her by the gate, but there was a glow of light and noise from further along the path in the direction of the boat house.

A lurching sense of dread sent him racing through water over his ankles. Rounding the bend, he could see that one of the supporting pillars had given way, that what was left of the deck was slewed at a drunken angle, half in the water.

He sought out Honey amongst shadowy figures working under an arc light to free the deck from the remaining support so that it could be winched out of the water.

'Honey!' His shout was blown away by the wind, drowned out by the whining of a chain saw and the continuous rumble of thunder.

And then she was there, her pale hair blowing about her face as she moved closer to the light, completely absorbed in thumbing a message into her phone.

'Honey!' he called again, just as a flash of lightning, so close that his hair crackled with static, struck the boat house, sending up a volley of sparks and freezing the scene so that it seemed as if he was the only one still moving, running through treacle as he heard an ominous ripping that overrode every other noise. Although he was shouting, it was like a nightmare where there was no sound.

And then he was diving towards her as the balcony parted company with the upper floor of the boat house.

CHAPTER SIXTEEN

'I sing of brooks, of blossoms, birds, and bowers; Of April, May, of June, and July flowers. I sing of Maypoles, Hock-carts, wassails, wakes, Of bride-grooms, brides, and of their bridal cakes.' —Robert Herrick

HONEY HIT THE ground with a thump that shook her bones. For a moment she just lay there, winded, trying to work out what had happened.

The light had gone out, there was a smell of burning and someone was lying on top of her. For a moment it was as if a bomb had gone off, but she was lying in mud, and someone was flashing a torch in her direction and she saw Lucien's face beside her. Blood, mingled with rain and mud, was running from his temple and he was utterly still.

Someone shouted, 'Paramedic!'

The next few minutes were like something out of a nightmare as she lay there while they tried to assess exactly what the situation was.

A groan reassured them and then Lucien opened his eyes.

'You were right about the motorway,' he muttered. 'Bad decision.' And then he closed them again.

'Is he making sense, miss?'

'Yes…' The word stuck in her throat.

'Can you tell me exactly what happened?' the paramedic asked once they'd got him into the ambulance.

'He saved my life.'

Lucien had been unconscious for what felt like the longest couple of minutes in her life.

The paramedic smiled at her, but didn't pause in his practised attachment of electrodes to Lucien's chest. 'I was thinking more about how Mr Grey was injured. No one else was near enough to see exactly what happened.'

She shook her head. 'He came out of nowhere and pushed me clear...' She'd heard a shout, had a momentary glimpse of the balcony disintegrating and pieces falling and then he'd barrelled into her, knocking her clear...

'It's looks as if something caught him on the side of the head.'

'A piece of wood.' She wanted to push the paramedic aside and examine him herself. 'Is there a depression in his skull?'

'I'll leave the poking about to the doctors. They'll stick him in the scanner and that will tell them everything they need to know.'

'I thought he was dead. He could have died...' She looked at Lucien, lying on the gurney in the ambulance, the whiteness of his face accentuated by a smear of blood from a cut on his forehead. His neck was in a brace...

'He's had a knock on the head but his breathing and blood pressure are okay. Just as well someone had the foresight to ask for an ambulance to be on standby.'

'Ambulance, fire service with a winch... I should be there. I'm supposed to be sending back reports to the flood warden.'

A hand grabbed her arm. 'You are going nowhere.'

'Don't move!' she said as Lucien tried to sit up.

He groaned, and lifted his hand to his head. 'I feel as if I've been hit by a truck. What happened?'

'You were playing the damn hero as usual,' she said, leaning over him so that he could see her.

'You're hurt!'

'No.' Just scared witless that his mad act of bravery had come close to killing him.

'Your face… Sweetheart, you're bleeding…'

'It's nothing. A scratch where I hit the ground. I'm not hurt, and neither would you have been if you'd listened to me and stayed in London.'

'Failed again. You'll have to write "must try harder" on my end-of-term report.'

'Idiot!' But she put a hand to her mouth and shook her head. She'd been determined to remain professional, calm. How dared he lie there, the colour of chalk, and make a joke of it? She'd so nearly lost him. Might still lose him…

'Don't cry, Honey.' His hand slipped down her arm to take her hand. 'It's not every day a man gets to save the life of the woman he loves.'

'They're not tears. It's raining…'

'And I'm Dick Robinson.'

'Then it's time to change your name by deed poll,' she said, smearing the tears and blood away with her palms.

'Mrs Grey or Mrs Robinson…' He caught his breath. 'Your choice.'

'Don't!'

'What?'

'You scarcely know me.'

'I knew you from that first moment, and if that bomb hadn't hit…' He stopped for a moment. 'I've been searching for you ever since, Honey. I just didn't know it. I love you, Honeysuckle Rose—'

'No.' She'd been shaking ever since he'd swept her from under the path of the balcony, but now her legs gave way and she sat down very suddenly. 'Don't! Don't say that.'

'That I love you?'

'You were so still… I thought you were d-dead, and it would have been my fault. If I'd done what you asked and gone to the pub…'

'You wouldn't have been my Honeysuckle Rose. Protector of caterpillars, healer of broken souls…'

The paramedic frowned, clearly concerned that he was rambling.

'We're ready to leave, Honey, so you need to be strapped in. '

She didn't want to take her eyes off Lucien, desperately afraid that he might have a fractured skull, that even now pressure might be building in his brain, that he'd slip into a coma and never wake up. Because that was what happened to the people she loved. They died.

But the ambulance couldn't move until she was properly seated, and she turned to face the front, fastening herself in while the ambulance doors were secured. Focussing on steady beats from the monitor, listening for the slightest warning of collapse.

The paramedic made some notes then looked up. 'Are you all right, miss? You've had a shock. Let me check your blood pressure.'

She was shaking and her teeth were chattering, but she surrendered her arm without argument, allowing nothing to distract her from Lucien.

'A bit low. Not surprising after such a shock. I'll mention it when we get to the hospital,' he said, offering her a box of tissues and a bottle of water.

'The rain,' he said kindly. 'It's run through the mud.'

'What? Oh, yes, the rain.' She mopped her face. 'Thank you.'

'He'll be okay.'

She wanted to tell him that she was a nurse and knew every possible outcome of a head trauma. How sometimes someone who seemed beyond saving made a recovery against all the odds. How sometimes what seemed to be a minor injury felled the strongest man.

But he was being kind, so she forced a smile and kept listening to the monitor.

Lucien woke with a splitting head, limbs that felt like lead and a moment of blinding panic when he was fighting to get away and escape before the familiar monotonous beeps and the unmistakable hospital smell brought the night rushing back in all its horror.

The rain, the river, the boat house and Honey…

'Honey!'

'Lo, the hero wakes.'

He turned. 'Jenny? What the hell are you doing here?'

'Hello, Jenny, how kind of you to drop everything and drive through storm and flood to bring me comfort. Are those grapes?' She plucked one from a bunch on the night stand. 'Just what the doctor ordered,' she said, popping it into her mouth.

'Where's Honey?' he asked, ignoring her sarcasm. 'How is she?'

'She was on the far side of stressed last night when she called me, demanding that I get here "though hell should bar the way". Or perhaps that's her normal state?'

'Not even close. She didn't actually say that?'

'Quote Noyes? She might as well have. If that's not her usual state of mind, I'll put it down to her brush with the Grim Reaper. Or maybe it was your close call that reduced her to a gibbering wreck.'

'For pity's sake…'

'Sorry, but it's hard not to tease a man so completely in the throes. I have to admit that she did look pretty grim. Mud, dried blood—that might have been yours—and a face whiter than the cliffs at Dover. The doc pulled up her records and, once I arrived to keep watch, she let him give her a sedative and find her a bed.'

'Where is she?' he demanded, tossing aside the blanket. 'Whoa! That gown is way too short!'

He pulled the blanket off the bed, tucked it round him and disconnected the drip attached to his arm.

'You're going to get into so much trouble with Sister,' she warned as the bleeping went into overdrive. 'Although, since the hospital is buzzing with rumours that you asked Honey to marry you in the ambulance—so romantic, but sadly too late to make today's headline—I guess you already are.'

'Mr Grey! What do you think you're doing?' Sister demanded, coming into the room.

'I'm going to find the woman I love.'

'Miss Rose is asleep.'

'Then I'll sit by her bed until she wakes up and answers my question. Or I could just discharge myself!'

'I'd listen to him,' Jenny advised. 'He's not in a joking mood.'

'He's had a bang on the head. That will knock the humour out of most people.'

'What's the damage?' Jenny asked.

'I believe the radiographer was overheard to say that he'd never seen a harder head. The doctor will be round to see you in an hour or so, and he'll probably discharge you if you've got someone to keep an eye on you.' Sister looked at Jenny. 'Would that be you?'

'No, it's not,' Lucien said before she could answer.

'Are you sure? It's the reason Honey summoned me,' she said. 'She wants me to take you home with me.'

'I am home.'

'Then I'll get back to my sheep.' She gave him a hug. 'Take care, partner. The network said yes to the idea you pitched to them yesterday, so you're going to have your hands full.'

'I'm fine.'

'Go and find your Honey, foolish man. And let me know if she says yes. I'll need to go hat shopping.'

Honey ached, her mouth was dry and she had to force her gritty eyes to open. It took a moment for her brain to catch up with the curtains around her bed and remember where she was.

Instantly awake, alert, she flung back the bedclothes. 'Lucien…'

'Here, miss.'

She swung round and, as if she'd conjured him up, there he was, wrapped in a blanket and sitting in the chair beside her.

'What on earth are you doing here? You should be in bed!'

'Absolutely.' He stood up. 'Move over. You look in need desperate need of a hug.'

'What? Lucien, you can't!' But he eased himself in beside her and pulled up the covers.

'A bit snug,' he said, putting his arm around her. 'Turn on your side and hang onto to me, or I might fall out and hurt myself.'

'You'll get us thrown out,' she said, but shifted onto her side so that she was pressed up against him, her head on his shoulder, her hand against his heart.

'Checking it's still ticking?'

She started, and pulled back, but he caught her hand and held it there.

'I thought you were dead. Then I was afraid you'd die because that's what happens to the people I love.'

'I know, sweetheart. While I've been sitting here, waiting for you to wake up, I've worked it out.'

'I don't know what you're talking about.'

'Yes, you do. You change the subject whenever the word "love" gets mentioned.'

'I can't…'

'You can't say it, Honey, but never tell me that you don't feel it.' Her hair was stiff with dried mud but he kissed the top of her head. 'Don't cry, sweetheart. It doesn't matter. They are just words.'

'I'm not crying,' she said, ignoring the hot tears running down her cheeks and into his gown. 'I never cry.'

'It's going to be Mrs Robinson, then.'

She shook her head and pulled away. 'It's not a joke,' she said. 'You think you understand, but you don't. Those three words have been the last thing I've said to everyone I've ever loved. My parents, Nicholas, Aunt Flora…'

'Your parents? You were only six years old.'

'I didn't understand why they were going away without me. I thought I'd done something wrong, and I ran down the drive, chasing the car, shouting, "I'm sorry, I love you", hoping that they'd hear and come back for me.'

'But they never did,' he said, thumbing the tears from her cheeks. Then he drew her close so that her face was pressed into his neck and the comfort of his steady pulse.

'I told you that they died in a traffic accident, but it was a motorway pile-up in bad weather. Twenty-odd cars, half a dozen fatalities.'

'I'm so sorry. If I'd known… And days after you saw him off, no doubt saying those same words, Nicholas died in a plane crash. I can see why you'd link the two incidents in your mind.'

'And the last time I saw Aunt Flora she said the kind of things you'd say to someone you don't expect to see again.'

'She was ninety-four…'

'I thought she'd last for ever, that we'd celebrate her one hundredth birthday with a party on the village green. But she knew she wouldn't see me again, and if I'd been paying attention I'd have known too. But I was busy packing, my head full of where I was going, what I'd need...'

He hitched himself onto his side so that he was facing her. 'Look at me, Honey.'

She lifted her gaze from his neck.

'She said everything she wanted you to know. You respect her best by living your best life and paying that love forward.' He wrapped his arms around her. 'You told me that I'd given you back your life. In the vanishingly small possibility that I get wiped out by a freak accident, do you really want to waste a minute of whatever time we have running from the risk that I might not survive until I'm ninety-four?'

'Ninety-four?'

'At a conservative estimate.' He waited. 'Unless, having got your life back, you're all set to start swiping right and making up for lost time?'

She didn't answer.

'Honey?'

'I'm thinking about it,' she said.

'I guess I deserve that.'

'I guess you do.'

'I'll make it easy for you. I don't want you to love me the way you loved Nicholas. I want you to love me because I'm someone who knows you and loves you for the woman you are now. And that's the last time I'll say it. Forget the words. They can join "sorry" in the "banned" dustbin. Love is what you do, not some empty phrase on a million Valentine cards.'

'Okay.'

'Is that your answer?'

She lifted her face from his chest and looked at him. 'To the Mrs Grey or Mrs Robinson question?'

'That's the one.'

'That's a lot bigger than the online dating question. Lucien, I need longer to think about it. Ask me again when you open the fete.'

Lower Haughton was packed for the annual summer fete. Everywhere was decorated with bunting. There were stalls selling everything, fairground rides, a 'scruffiest dog' show, pony rides. Rosie, the ice-cream van which appeared in a television soap opera filmed in Upper Haughton was there, and so was Honey, sitting at the wheel of her tractor and trailer.

The vicar tapped the microphone, deafening everyone. Certain that it was working, he said, 'Good afternoon, ladies and gentlemen. Welcome to the Lower Haughton Summer Fete. It's been a difficult few weeks but, thanks to the heroic efforts of everyone involved in clearing the river of the debris from the boat house, floods didn't reach the village. The footbridge was badly damaged, but the good news is that the Hartford estate have agreed to pay for the repairs. So the money raised today will go towards essential repairs for the village hall.'

A cheer went up from the crowd.

'I'm glad you all approve. But now, since I know that you're all itching to get out there and spend your money, I'm going to hand you over to Mr Lucien Grey, who you will all know from his news broadcasts from trouble spots and his own heroic efforts in rescuing civilians from their bombed house at Bouba al-Asad. And who saved our Honey...'

Lucien stepped up to the mike and waited for the applause to die down.

'A hero,' he began, 'is not someone out of the ordinary or gifted with special powers. A hero is a man or woman who, faced with a difficult situation, steps up and does what's necessary.

'There are heroes in this valley, in this village,' he went on. 'Men and women who manned phones, who risked their lives in appalling conditions to save their neighbours, their friends and their loved ones from threatened floods.'

He looked across the green to where Honey was sitting on her tractor, her hair tied up in a scarf nineteen-forties-style, wearing the same dungarees as she had the day she'd arrived at his door.

'There is one woman here,' he continued, 'who has risked her life many times for strangers—people who she will see for a few minutes, maybe an hour at the most, working in intolerable conditions. You all know Honeysuckle Rose.'

Another cheer went up, and applause.

Honey shook her head, but she'd asked for this.

'I came to Lower Haughton seeking refuge, a place to deal with the kind of wounds that are not visible. But Honey saw them, saw me, and made me part of this community. And if Miss Honeysuckle Rose will do me the enormous honour of marrying me, this is going to be my forever home.'

He looked across the green, where the heads of the expectant crowd faced her, and it was as if it was just the two of them as he said, 'Honey? What's it to be?'

As one, the entire crowd turned to look at her, holding its breath.

And Honey—after the kind of pause more usually associated with announcing the winner of television baking show—tugged on a rope and unfurled a banner above her head that read: *The future Mrs Grey.*

A huge cheer went up from the crowd. Honey was off the tractor and Lucien was off the podium and they were racing towards each other.

The crowd parted for them, clapping and chanting, 'Kiss, kiss, kiss…!' And then she was there in front of him, and she was in his arms, and he was kissing her. Everything in his world was about as right as it could be.

She pulled back, laughing. 'Nicely done, Mr Grey, but you still haven't opened the fete.'

'I declare this fete open!' he shouted.

More cheers then, having seen the show, everyone moved off to enjoy the fun, leaving them alone.

'I have something for you,' he said, producing a small velvet box and opening it to reveal a rather spectacular half-hoop of diamonds. 'Not useful this time, but it is for ever.'

Honey and Lucien's wedding day began on a fine day in early September with a simple ceremony in a quiet corner of the village green, where all Flora's friends had gathered to plant an oak sapling in her memory.

Later, they made their vows in the age-old ceremony in the church, paused for photographs on the bridge and then the meadow was the venue for the kind of old-fashioned wedding party that Honey's great-grandfather would have recognised.

There was a marquee for the buffet, a dance floor laid down on the turf for dancing and a traditional hog roast for the evening, when all the guests sat out under the stars. There was a barrel of ale from the local brewery, elder-flower cordial for the children and champagne for the adults, which all the village women had pitched in to make.

There was a fiddler and a local rock group for the dancing, and it was the group that was going to play for their first dance.

Lucien took Honey by the hand and they stood there for a moment, smiling at one another, barely able to believe how lucky they were to have found each other.

They hadn't had to think twice about the song they'd chosen. It wasn't something smoochy. They hadn't had that kind of relationship. It was a song to remind them of special moments, something to make them laugh.

'Shall we dance, Mrs Robinson...?' Lucien invited, 'Shall we dance, Mrs Robinson...' as the two guitarists in the band launched into the song, and he began to spin her into their new life together.

* * * * *

ONE WEEK IN VENICE WITH THE CEO

KATE HARDY

MILLS & BOON

For Gerard—one day we'll go back to Venice…

CHAPTER ONE

'If I could have a superpower,' Serafina said, 'I'd go back in time and visit every single Conte Ardizzone and persuade them to actually *fix* the problem instead of shutting off a room whenever there was a problem. And also,' she added wryly, 'stop them selling off the family silver when funds got low and then spending the proceeds on partying instead of sorting out the palazzo.'

Alessia winced. 'It's that bad?'

'It's that bad,' Serafina confirmed.

'Perhaps I should be giving you gin instead of coffee,' Alessia said.

Serafina shook her head. 'There aren't any real answers in the bottom of a gin glass, especially at ten o'clock in the morning. But coffee and a sugar rush would be wonderful.'

'Now *that* I can do. Sit down.' Alessia waved to the kitchen table, then busied herself with the expensive bean-to-cup machine Serafina usually teased her best friend about but was seriously grateful for right now.

Since her father's death, six months ago, Serafina had had to sort out the funeral and the endless admin, and then there had been the shock of finding out that the family trust fund was empty. And she was still having trouble getting her head round the reason *why* it was empty.

This morning's meeting at the bank had made it just that little bit worse.

While the coffee was brewing, Alessia took the lid off the jar containing *bussolai*, the ring-shaped lemon cookies that were a local speciality. 'Not another word until you've eaten three.'

The first cookie helped a bit. As did the second. By the third, Serafina could feel the sugar firing her up. 'You definitely have the magic touch, Lessi,' she said with a smile. 'Thank you.'

'Nonna's recipe never fails,' Alessia said. 'I'm assuming the bank isn't going to help?'

'No income equals no loan. And they've made it clear that even a solid business plan with projected income isn't good enough,' Serafina said. 'Bottom line: I still owe a chunk of the inheritance tax, and the only real asset I have right now is the palazzo itself. Which I can't sell, because it's entailed.' And now she was officially Contessa Serafina Ardizzone, the entailment meant that the palazzo was *her* problem. 'I can't rent it out or use it for any kind of business, because right now I'm pretty sure it'd fail every single health and safety directive going; but I can't afford to fix the problems, either.' She shook her head in mingled sadness and exasperation. 'If I'd had any idea about the state of the palazzo and our family finances when I was eighteen, I would've read law or economics instead of History of Art and picked a career that could support the palazzo. Or even become apprenticed to a builder who specialised in restoration, so I could all spend my spare time repairing the damage. Ten years of working on the place might've made enough of a difference.' She grimaced. 'But instead I thought the family money meant I didn't have to worry and I could study what I loved. Which makes me as bad as all the great-whatever-grandparents partying.'

In her case the partying had been with movie stars in

Hollywood rather than with rich nobles in Venice; but it had ended with a broken heart. Hers.

And now the rest of her life had fractured, too.

Strictly speaking, she could walk away and let whoever inherited the palazzo from her deal with the problems, uncaring that the mouldering and neglect would get worse with every year. But that wasn't who Serafina was. She didn't dump her problems on other people, and she wasn't a quitter.

Plus she loved her house.

Which meant she was the one who needed to fix things.

'You're being unfair on yourself. You make it sound as if you've idled away the last decade, and that's not true. You've worked at the Museum of Women's Art as a volunteer ever since you did your Master's, and you've spent two years on the board. You have transferable skills,' Alessia said. 'You can look at something, see the business opportunity, persuade others to make changes, and write a grant application that actually gets mon—' She stopped mid-sentence. 'Can you apply for a grant to restore the palazzo?'

'Sadly not. You need something special to make a case for getting a restoration grant,' Serafina said. 'There are dozens of crumbling fifteenth-century palazzos in Venice, and Ca' d'Ardizzone doesn't have amazing architectural features, frescos or anything else to make it stand out from the others.'

'What about the Canaletto in your drawing room? If you put it up for auction, surely it would go for enough to pay for the repairs?'

'It would,' Serafina agreed, 'if it wasn't a copy.'

Alessia's eyes widened in shock. 'It's a *copy*?'

Serafina nodded. 'Apparently my great-great-great-grandfather sold the original. The same goes for the family jewellery: the originals were sold off over the years, and what we have now are paste copies that are practically worthless. I could try putting the porcelain up for auction, but what it would raise would barely make a dent in the debts.' She frowned. 'Maybe my dad was right. Maybe there really is a curse on the family. If my great-however-many-times-aunt Marianna had been allowed to marry the man she loved, three centuries ago, she wouldn't have tried to elope, fallen down the stairs and broken her neck—and he wouldn't have cursed the family.'

Alessia shivered. 'That's so sad. But of course there isn't a curse. Curses aren't real.'

Intellectually, Serafina knew that was true; but deep down she wondered if there was something in the story. Apparently Marianna's lover had declared, 'No Conte Ardizzone will have a happy marriage.' And, from what Serafina could see, that was precisely what had happened over the centuries. In her own lifetime, her grandparents had lived in different wings of the palazzo and refused to see each other. Her mother had turned into a bundle of nerves who only ever saw doom and gloom, and her father had become a gambling addict. Further back, the rumours were that her great-grandparents and great-great-grandparents had had difficult marriages: all the partying meant they hadn't had to spend time together.

And then there was her own near miss: she was relieved she'd discovered Tom in bed with another woman before she'd been foolish enough to marry him. Particularly as she'd learned later that it hadn't even been the first time he'd cheated on her. It seemed her movie star fiancé had wanted the cachet of marrying a Venetian countess; he'd been a good enough actor for Serafina to believe that he'd loved her for herself, when he'd only wanted her for her social position.

She'd fallen for his charm. Let him sweep her off her feet. Thought she'd be the first one in her family for decades to get her happy-ever-after with the man she loved...

Though she'd never make that mistake again. Not now she knew Tom hadn't really loved her.

She shook herself. 'I know you're right. There's been a long line of people who lived in the glory of the past and either didn't notice the present changing round them or refused to see it.' She took another gulp of coffee. 'But I wish my dad had said something to me years ago instead of struggling on his own. I wish I'd known we were broke. I wish I'd explored all the shut-off rooms properly and realised that "economising on the heating bills" was a euphemism for ignoring the real problems.'

'Maybe your dad didn't want to burden you,' Alessia suggested.

'But I'm his only child, Lessi. If he couldn't lean on me, who else could he have leaned on?' Not her mother, obviously. Francesca Ardizzone would've gone straight into catastrophe mode. But why hadn't he trusted her? That stung. Badly. 'If I'd known how bad things were, if I'd had any idea he was gambling with serious money and not just for centimes and a laugh with his friends, I could've—well, at least have tried to stop him. And then he wouldn't have had that last enormous loss and that heart attack.' And then he'd still be alive…

'Serafina, your dad's heart attack wasn't your fault,' Alessia said gently. 'It wasn't anyone's fault. Even if your dad hadn't lost that money, he might still have had a heart attack. You know how it is: stubborn middle-aged men who like their pastries a little too much, don't do any exercise and won't listen to any advice. My dad's the same. And every single one of my uncles. It's the way that generation is.'

Serafina knew it was true, but it didn't stop her feeling guilty. Or alone. Or mixed up: angry that her dad had been reckless and left her to clean up his mess, and hurt that he'd kept it all from her. He'd moved investments from

the trust fund, hoping to beat the market, and got it wrong:
and then he'd borrowed money from the fund to win back
his losses. Except he'd lost again. And again. And again.
The trust fund was empty, so Serafina and her mum had
been living off her savings for the last six months. And the
money was running out.

She squared her shoulders. There was no time for mop-
ing. She needed to act. 'I need to make some money to fix
the palazzo—or at least to fix enough of it to let me start
making money from it, and the profits from that can go to
fixing the next bit.' She raked a hand over her hair. 'The
problems go back decades. They can't be fixed overnight,
but I don't have to do everything at once. The first stage is
to sort out some rooms to offer bed and breakfast, even if
it's only a single suite to begin with. But what makes Ca'
d'Ardizzone stand out from all the other ancient palazzos
offering tourist accommodation? What's my USP?'

'You, of course,' Alessia said with a smile. 'How many
other palazzos can offer *colazione con la contessa*?'

'Love the alliteration.' Serafina smiled back. 'And
breakfast with a countess is definitely going to attract one
particular segment of the market. But most guests are going
to want more than that.'

'Painting lessons? You could run a retreat for painters,
or for people who want to learn to paint. And where better
to paint than overlooking the Grand Canal?'

'The view from my balcony's perfect,' Serafina agreed,
'but I've never taught anyone to paint.'

'But you could. Your watercolours are beautiful.'

'I paint for fun. For me,' Serafina said. 'Looking at it
practically, I can't earn enough from art to pay the bills.
And I need to keep something in my life that's just for
me. Something to keep me sane.' Not that she'd ever
admit it, even to her best friend, but something to fill
up the empty spaces.

'OK. You've spent years working in an art museum and you know Venice like the back of your hand,' Alessia said. 'Maybe instead of art weekends, you can offer history of art weekends. Take your guests on a tour, and teach them about Venice and art.'

'That could work,' Serafina agreed. 'But first I need to get enough of the building up to standard, so people can actually stay at the palazzo. At the very least they'll want an en-suite bathroom, and renovations like that will cost money I don't have. The fact I need to take in paying guests at all makes it very clear I don't have any money. Nobody will agree to do the work on credit.' She sighed and took another biscuit. 'I almost wish I'd married Tom after all.'

'What?' Alessia looked shocked. 'But he cheated on you, Serafina. You would've been miserable with him.'

With a man who loved her title rather than her. 'I know. But Celebrity Life offered us a small fortune to run an exclusive on our wedding photos. I could've used money that to finance the ren—' Serafina stopped and snapped her fingers. 'That's it. You're right. *I*'m the USP.' She stood up and paced round Alessia's tiny kitchen. 'I know Tom was the movie star, but a Venetian countess would draw in the magazine's readers, too. The whole romance of Venice and an ancient palazzo—which, if we window-dress it and shoot in soft light, will look chic instead of shabby—and a society bride. If I marry someone who wants a society bride and we do an exclusive deal with the magazine over the wedding photos, I can use that money to restore the palazzo.'

Alessia shook her head. 'That's crazy, Serafina. It means marrying someone you don't love.'

No Conte Ardizzone will have a happy marriage.

Serafina shook herself. It was a myth, she reminded herself. Even if there was an awful lot of evidence in the unhappy marriages of her forebears to suggest it might be true. 'It won't be a permanent marriage. It'll be a marriage of convenience to suit us both, with a quiet divorce a year later. We both get what we want, nobody's hurt, and everybody's happy.' They didn't even have to live together: just make enough of a nuptial show to get the money for the photographs.

'Money—even if you're going to use that money to restore the palazzo rather than finance a lifestyle of partying—is *completely* the wrong reason to get married,' Alessia said. 'How about setting up a crowdfunding thing where people "buy a brick" or something and get a certificate for it saying that they've helped in the restoration of a Venetian palazzo? Bigger donors get something extra— once you've sorted out the accommodation, they can come and stay for a weekend of luxury.'

'That sort of thing works for public buildings,' Serafina said, 'but not for private homes. If I sell one brick at a time, it could take years to raise the money. In the meantime, the palazzo will decay that little bit more every day, and the renovation costs will grow—and probably at a faster rate than the donations come in.'

'Or maybe you could find a building company that would agree to staged payments in arrears, plus a discount, in return for publicity,' Alessia said. 'I did that feature for the Sunday supplement of La *Cronaca* last summer—the guy in Rome who took over his dad's construction company a couple of years back. He was looking at moving away from new builds and increasing their restoration work.' She looked thoughtful. 'Gianni Leto. I liked him. He was a bit intense, but he struck me as the reliable sort. Maybe you could talk to him. Working on a project like your palazzo would be good publicity for him. That puts you in a good bargaining position, because we can place features on the palazzo and its restoration. We can definitely get something in the lifestyle and travel magazines. If we're clever, we might be able to get a documentary out of it, too.'

They were more much practical ideas than her marriage of convenience, Serafina thought. Because who would want a temporary marriage to a penniless aristocrat who owned a money pit of a palazzo? And she had nothing to lose by asking Gianni Leto if he'd let her make staged payments. The worst-case scenario was that he'd say no, which left her in the same position as she was in now.

In the meantime, she needed to find a job with enough of a salary to pay the bills; working at the museum and giving all her time for nothing wasn't something she could afford to do any more. Not now the trust fund was empty. Though leaving the museum she loved so much was going to hurt. Badly. 'OK. Can you text me his details?'

'Sure. I'll do that now. And I'll email you the final press cutting and my notes, to give you his full background,' Alessia said.

Serafina hugged her. 'Thank you. And thank you for feeding me *bussolai* and listening to me whinge.'

'You're welcome to the cookies, and you weren't whinging. You're in a tough position and you need to bounce ideas off someone,' Alessia said. 'I still reckon you should set up a gin palazzo. It'd be perfect. You could have one of your pen-and-ink sketches of the palazzo on the label. Offer different flavours. For special editions, you could have bottles with Murano glass stoppers. You could do a deal with one of the glassmakers to offer exclusive hand-blown gin glasses. And the *pezzo forte*,' she said, flourishing one hand in the air, 'you can combine it with your B&B to offer gin-tasting weekends. Even gin-making weekends.'

'I love the idea,' Serafina said. 'Years ago, the ground floor of the palazzo would've been used as a warehouse. We have enough space for manufacture and storage. But gin-making means a distillery.'

'Not if you make bathtub gin,' Alessia said.

Serafina grinned. 'Now, who was it who did that feature on gin, made me go taste-testing with her and complained all the way through about the colour and taste of bathtub gin?' She sobered. 'To make a good, high-end gin, I'll need to buy equipment and employ a good distiller. Which means spending money, not to mention all the regulations about working environments—which *also* means spending money. And money's the thing I don't have.' She spread her hands. 'Until the palazzo's fixed, everything's a pipe dream. My ancestors' living in a dream world instead of facing reality is why I'm in trouble now, and it's my job to fix it. I'll start by talking to your builder.' She swallowed hard. 'And getting a paid job. I know Madi can't afford to pay me a salary, so I'm going to have to resign. But I'll sign up with all the employment agencies and contact everyone I know who might be able to offer me a job.' She wasn't going to let the situation defeat her. It felt daunting, but she intended to rise to the challenge.

And she was going to win.

Later that afternoon, Serafina read the interview and notes from Alessia. Gianni Leto came across as a man who wasn't afraid of hard work, and who saw traditions as something to be cherished but also to be questioned. He didn't seem to be the sort who pushed change for change's sake: but he definitely came across as one who would consider a different approach if it would give a better result, rather than being hidebound by the way things had always been done.

She could work with that.

And maybe, as her best friend had suggested, she could talk him into giving her a discount and letting her make staged payments in exchange for helping him with publicity.

The next page was a portrait of him. The moody lighting made him look like a film star. Dark hair, cut short, dark, intense eyes and the most beautiful mouth she'd ever seen.

She shook herself. What Gianni Leto looked like was completely irrelevant. She was more interested in his professional abilities. She'd been licking her wounds since Tom's betrayal, but sorting out things following her father's death and shouldering the burden of the palazzo meant that she didn't have time in her life for relationships in any case. Plus, for all she knew, he was already involved with someone.

Half an hour's searching on the internet told her that Gianni was definitely taking the family business in a new direction. His late father had done a lot of work with concrete, which had a massive carbon footprint; Gianni was looking to turn the company fully carbon neutral. And he was working on restoring properties rather than building new ones, using traditional materials where he could and new technology where it was appropriate. That boded well for him being interested in restoring the palazzo.

The company, under Gianni's direction, had paid for the restoration of the town hall in Bardicello two years ago. It seemed his father had built the hall from steel and concrete twenty years before; when part of the hall collapsed, there had been a massive scandal. Given the new direction of the firm, Gianni was clearly still trying to live that down. And perhaps, she thought, he was trying to restore his family's good name. Just as she needed to do—not that her dad had had a bad name, but if anyone learned about what he'd done with the family money then the gossip pages would have a field day.

Serafina had been focusing on Gianni Leto's professional life, but her search had also thrown up the fact that he was single. And he was focused entirely on his business, the same way she was focused on hers.

And maybe, just maybe, they could help each other by the plan that had horrified her best friend.

Marriage to a Venetian countess would give Gianni Leto social cachet and help to bury the scandal in his family's past. Marriage to him—provided she could persuade him into the photograph deal—would give her the funds she needed. He could restore the palazzo, giving him professional kudos. And she could pay for it, using the photograph money to start with and then doing the rest with money from the business.

They'd be able to give each other what they needed.

And then they could quietly part ways. Nobody got hurt. Everybody won.

Though this was a deal she wanted to suggest in person rather than on paper. First, she needed to set up a meeting.

Smiling, she switched into her email programme and began to write.

A business proposition from Contessa Serafina Ardizzone?

Gianni frowned. Didn't people of her class usually have someone to handle their business affairs, rather than doing it themselves?

But then he scrolled down to the first photograph and caught his breath.

The snap had clearly been taken from either the water or the opposite side of the canal, and showed a gorgeous four-storey Venetian palazzo. Fifteenth-century, he judged, a mix of gothic and Byzantine architecture. The stucco was painted deep pink; the white windows had stunning ogee arches; and there was a balcony running across the middle two storeys. He'd bet that the interior had amazing glass chandeliers and traditional Venetian terrazzo marble flooring. And the ceilings—at the very least there would be beautiful beams. There might also be frescos or intricate decorative plasterwork, things he itched to work with.

The next photograph showed the interior of one of the rooms. Exactly as he'd expected: traditional terrazzo flooring, flexible enough to move with the building. High ceilings. It looked as if they were wooden, rather than painted, but they were still gorgeous. Antique glass chandeliers. And damask wall-coverings—he zoomed in closer—that definitely showed signs of damp around the windows; it was obvious there were leaks. The rest of the interior photographs showed more of the same. Some of the floors appeared to be parquet; it was possible they'd been laid to cover up problems with the flooring beneath it.

The palazzo was the kind of building Gianni would give his eye teeth to work on: one that clearly hadn't been touched for decades, apart from the installation of electricity and maybe some plumbing, and even that had probably been decades ago.

But why was the Contessa asking someone from Rome to do the restoration, rather than someone local?

He scrolled down past the rest of the photographs to her short email.

I've recently inherited Ca' d'Ardizzone and it needs some restoration work. My best friend, Alessia da Campo, interviewed you last year for La Cronaca, and she suggested that this might be your area of expertise. If you'd be interested in tendering for the job, perhaps we could meet at your office in Rome to discuss options.

Gianni remembered the interview very well. The journalist had done her research beforehand, asked intelligent questions, and written a fair and balanced piece. If Serafina Ardizzone was her best friend, then he was happy to listen to what she had to say.

But it still nagged at him that the countess hadn't turned to a local firm. In his experience, that usually meant a

lack of trust somewhere. Either she'd been ripped off before and wanted a personal recommendation, or her family
were known locally for not paying their bills on time—if
at all—and nobody would advance her credit.

Wondering which it was, he flicked into the internet
and looked her up.

Contessa Serafina Ardizzone was the only child of the
late Conte Marco Ardizzone and Contessa Francesca Ardizzone. There were photographs of her parents: her mother
glittering in diamonds and designer dresses and her father
in old-fashioned evening dress, attending opening nights
at the opera and gallery previews. Since the palazzo bore
her family name, they'd obviously lived in Venice for centuries. It was clear that she came from an aristocratic and
cultured background: the complete opposite of his own. He
preferred rock to opera, loathed the pretentious squiggles
that people called modern art, and his family had been
desperately poor when he was young and his father had
been out of work.

Another story reported that her father had died six
months ago from a heart attack. He knew how it felt to
lose a parent that way; though whether Serafina had had
as tempestuous a relationship with her father as he'd had
with his own, he had no idea.

There were more photographs of Serafina in her role as
a board member of the Museum of Women's Art, wearing a designer suit and incredibly cute specs. He added
'bright' to his list; no charitable foundation could afford
to have a board member who didn't pull their weight, however pretty she might be. And Serafina Ardizzone was extremely pretty. Dark hair that framed her heart-shaped face
in ringlets, huge dark eyes, and a wide smile that would
have any man falling to his knees at her feet. She looked
like a movie star.

Which wasn't far from the truth, as the next story

showed Serafina with her arms wrapped round Tom Burford, one of the most popular action movie heroes. Tom's blond hair was a perfect foil to her dark beauty. It seemed they were Hollywood's golden couple and the photo had been taken at their engagement party a year ago. Though, even if Serafina been single, Gianni didn't have the time for a relationship. Or the inclination, since his break-up with Elena. In her family's view, his money had made up for the fact he came from a lower-class background and worked in a trade, and they'd just about been able to tolerate an engagement. But when the problems with the town hall came to light they'd been very quick to distance themselves from him. Elena herself had dumped him a couple of days later, and her lack of faith in him had broken something inside him. Maybe his heart; maybe his faith in himself, too. He'd thought she'd loved him, though clearly he'd deluded himself.

He'd learned from Elena that posh women were trouble: and a *contessa* was beyond posh.

He shook himself. This wasn't about him. This was about a job. Restoring a palazzo. To be part of the Hollywood elite meant that you had money; funding the restoration obviously wouldn't be a problem. And he knew he'd love the work. Part of him itched to email back and say straight away that he'd do it.

But.

Could he work with her? Would she trust his professional judgement and let him get on with his job? Or would she be forever asking questions and irritating him? The Hollywood photos and her aristocratic background suggested she might be a little snobby; but that story about her work with the art museum and the fact she was best friends with a journalist he'd liked suggested that maybe she'd be good to work with.

There was only one way to find out.

The best way.

Face to face. Where nobody could hide.

He replied to her email, suggesting three dates for a meeting the following week.

And then he'd find out exactly what her proposition entailed.

'Serafina!' Maddalena, the museum director, greeted her with a warm hug. 'I'm glad you're in today. You're the person I want to see most in the entire world, right now.'

She wouldn't be, once Serafina gave her the news.

But, before Serafina could tell her, Maddalena said, 'I've never thought of myself as a violent person, but I could cheerfully strangle Beppe Russo.' Beppe was the CEO of the company that had bought the building housing the museum.

'What's he done now?' Serafina asked.

'The lease renewal,' Maddalena said. 'I've nagged and nagged and *nagged* him for the paperwork.' She banged a hand on her desk. 'I finally got it this morning. No wonder he dragged his feet about handing it over. He's quadrupling the cost of the lease.'

'What?' Serafina stared at her in shock.

'We can't cover the extra costs. We can't even begin to cover them. And he knows it.'

'He can't quadruple the rent, Madi.'

'Oh, yes, he can. He owns the building. Our lease runs out in three months. He can do what the hell he likes, and he knows it.' Maddalena's hands balled into fists. 'Either we suck up the extra costs—which he knows we can't do— or we find somewhere else. And it's obvious he's banking on the latter, so he can gut the building and turn this place into a hotel.' She shook her head. 'But finding a new home within our budget… I'm definitely going to need you and your skills.'

How could Serafina possibly resign now?

And yet—how could she not?

Maddalena looked at her. 'Say something, *carissima*. You're the one with all the great ideas.'

If her palazzo hadn't been crumbling away, Serafina would've known exactly where the museum could move to.

Or maybe…

'Madi, can I tell you something in strictest confidence?' Serafina asked.

'Of course.'

'I was coming to see you to resign.'

'Resign? Oh, no.' Maddalena frowned. 'Why, *carissima*? You love it here—and we love you. Has someone upset you? If it's Beppe, I'll go and rearrange his—'

'Not Beppe,' Serafina cut in hastily. 'The problem is, the palazzo's falling to bits and it needs a lot of work doing to it—which costs money—plus I still owe a chunk of the inheritance tax.' Her father's gambling habit had done even more damage to their finances, but nobody else needed to know that. 'I love it here, but I need a job that pays the bills, and I know you can't afford to pay me.'

'I don't want to lose you. If that weasel Beppe hadn't dumped this on me, I would've found the money from *somewhere* to pay you a salary,' Maddalena said, scowling. 'Which is another good reason to strangle him.'

'If my palazzo didn't need renovating, you could've moved the museum to the ground floor and not had to worry about paying rent,' Serafina said. 'It's not as big as the space we have here, but we could maybe have temporary extra exhibitions in the ballroom, or in the *portego* on the *piano nobile*.'

The women looked at each other.

'I think we could solve each other's problems, *carissima*,' Maddalena said. 'We could pay you the same rent as we pay here. That would help you with the bills, wouldn't it?'

'I can't ta—' Serafina began, horrified at the idea of taking money from the museum she wanted to support.

'Rent is a running cost,' Maddalena cut in. 'And I'd much rather pay the rent to you than to someone like Beppe.'

Serafina thought about it. The rent would help her pay the bills. Having the museum on the ground floor meant that the house would be used properly again, full of people instead of ghosts. And she wouldn't have to resign from the job she loved.

But, given the situation with the museum's lease, it also meant she'd need to get the ground floor fixed within three months. She didn't have the money to pay for it, and the museum couldn't afford to pay her a year's rent in advance.

'Please don't resign,' Maddalena said. 'Let the museum rent your ground floor. It works for both of us. And we'll all come and help do whatever we can with the restoration in our spare time—paint walls, grout tiles, clean, fetch and carry, whatever.'

A team effort.

Saving the museum, saving the palazzo, and making life better for all of them.

Could they do it?

'I'll speak to the guy I'm hoping will assess the palazzo,' Serafina said. 'If he says the ground floor can be fixed in three months, then it's yours.'

And for the first time in months she felt a flicker of hope.

CHAPTER TWO

ROME. THE ETERNAL CITY. Serafina had loved her three years studying in the city, the way that you could turn the corner of a busy modern street and suddenly there would be ancient buildings right in front of you. She'd got used to the traffic rushing around instead of gondolas and motor boats and the water bus, and on days when she'd missed the canals of home she'd walked alongside the broad, fast-flowing Tiber, soothed by the water.

She walked past the Colosseum simply because it was her favourite building in the city and even the sight of it made her smile, and then she headed for Gianni Leto's office.

Surprisingly, it was all steel and glass. How could someone who was changing his firm's focus to the restoration of old buildings work in something that was the complete opposite?

But criticising him would only put his back up. And she needed to do a charm offensive to get him on her side—for the museum's sake as well as her own. Mentally preparing herself for the encounter, she walked up the stone steps, took the lift to the top floor and found the reception area for Leto Construction.

'Good afternoon,' she said to the receptionist with a

smile. 'I'm Serafina Ardizzone, and I have a meeting scheduled with Signor Leto at two.'

'He's expecting you.' The receptionist smiled back. 'Let me show you through to his office.'

Gianni Leto's office was small but very neat. It was minimally furnished with a desk, a chair, a chair for visitors and a filing cabinet. The surface of his desk was clear except for a laptop and a mobile phone. The walls that weren't glass were painted magnolia, and a series of large photographs in black frames hung at intervals. Serafina presumed that the buildings in the photographs had either been constructed or restored by Leto Construction.

The man himself stood up as the receptionist ushered her in. 'Thank you for being prompt, Contessa.'

She didn't want her title to be a barrier. She needed this man on her side. 'I prefer to conduct business on first-name terms. Call me Serafina,' she said, holding her hand out to shake his. 'Thank you for seeing me, Signor Leto.'

'Gianni.'

The photograph from Alessia's article had been a moody shot and hadn't done him justice. He was beautiful enough that he could've been a model. And in the flesh he had more stage presence than any of the movie stars she'd met, including Tom.

His handshake was firm and businesslike, but the touch of his fingers against hers sent a zing all the way through her. It was hard not to look at that beautiful mouth and wonder what it might feel like against her skin.

Serafina shook herself mentally. This wasn't what their meeting was supposed to be about. This was about saving the palazzo and the museum. Nothing to do with attraction. Or sex.

'May I offer you some coffee, Serafina?' he asked. 'Or something cold?'

She needed to focus instead of letting herself dream

about something she knew didn't even exist. 'Thank you, but no.'

He inclined his head. 'Then please have a seat.' He gestured to the chair in front of his desk.

She smiled and sat down.

Despite knowing Serafina Ardizzone's background, Gianni hadn't expected her to be quite so glamorous. Everything from her well-cut suit to her understated make-up screamed class and money. Old money. Old class—the sort that Elena's family had aspired to but hadn't quite managed.

But it was more than that: it was the woman herself.

Serafina was the first woman in years who'd made him feel as if an electric current ran through him when he shook her hand. It made him feel breathless and dizzy. Like a callow teenager. As if his tongue had been glued to the roof of his mouth.

Say something, he told himself. *Act, don't react.*

She was here because she wanted him to do a job for her. And he needed to remember that. Put the business first. It was obvious they should talk about the building. Hoping he sounded a lot calmer than he felt as he sat down again, he drawled, 'I understand you're looking at restoring the palazzo.'

She inclined her head. 'Which I know is going to take time and money.'

At least she was being realistic about some of it. Other parts, not so much. 'It's a long way between Rome and Venice,' he pointed out. Half the country. Five hundred kilometres, give or take. The journey between the two cities took more than three hours, even on a high-speed train.

'So why am I looking at contractors a long way from home?' she asked.

He liked the way she'd picked up on his concerns. 'It makes sense to use local contractors and reduce your carbon footprint. Particularly as Venice has unique challenges and local builders would know those issues and the best solutions in depth.'

'True.' She looked him in the eye. 'But I want the right person for the job, Gianni. Someone who will understand the building and its heritage, and do a sympathetic job.'

'I'd need to see the building for myself and judge the extent of the work before I can give you a quote,' he said. 'Has any work been done on the foundations?'

'I have no idea. There's no paperwork relating to any building work in the last four decades,' she said, 'and my father definitely didn't mention anything happening when he was a child. I assume the foundations are original. Though the wooden piles under Venetian buildings don't tend to rot as timber usually does, because they're covered in mud and then a layer of stone: meaning the oxygen and microbes that do the damage can't actually get to the wood.'

'But there's still *acqua alta*—' the high tides that sent floods sweeping through the city '—which are becoming more frequent every year,' he said. 'And the flooding's salt water. You didn't send me photographs of the side of the palazzo, but I'm guessing the stucco's come away and exposed the brickwork.'

'And there are visible salt deposits and that green line of algae,' she agreed, 'the same as with many other canal-side buildings in the city.'

For someone who claimed to know nothing about architecture, Gianni thought, Serafina was remarkably well-informed. She knew about foundations, salt deposits and what made wood rot. He had a feeling there was more to this than met the eye.

She looked him straight in the eye. 'You restored the town hall in Bardicello.'

The building his father had constructed, where the steel inserts had eventually cracked the concrete and caused part of a wall to collapse. They were lucky nobody had been hurt. But the reputation of Leto Construction had suffered, even though Gianni had fixed the damage. He was still struggling to restore his father's good name.

She clearly knew the worst. Did she plan to use it as leverage? 'And restoring the palazzo would be good publicity for my company, so you think we'll offer to do the job cheaply?' he asked coolly.

'No. It means you'll do the job well because you'll be mindful of your reputation.'

That warmed him; but at the same time it put him on his guard. 'And the rest of it?'

She looked at him, as if calculating something. 'I need to restore the palazzo.'

He already knew that. 'And how do you plan to use the building? Are you looking to make it into apartments or a hotel? Use part of it for some kind of business?' When she said nothing, he said, 'You'll need to make decisions about the restoration before any work starts, and what you plan to do with the palazzo will obviously affect those decisions.'

'At the moment, my mother and I live on the *piano nobile*,' she said.

The first floor. Gianni knew this was where the aristocratic owners had entertained guests and kept their private apartments; some palazzos had a second *piano nobile*. The ground floor of a Venetian palazzo had traditionally been used for business or warehousing, and the servants had been housed in the hidden top floor.

'The house is way too big for the two of us. And I'm not prepared to let the palazzo simply rot away while Mamma and I inhabit a few rooms,' she said. 'I want the building brought back to life. Used, instead of mouldering away.'

'Assuming that most of the rooms are in the same state as those in the photographs you sent me, it's likely to take time and money,' he said. 'There will be mess—a lot of mess—and a lot of noise. I'll be honest with you: your best option would be to sell it to a developer, The sort who has a conscience and wants to do things properly, and will either turn the palazzo into an upmarket hotel, or maybe strip it back and turn it into luxury apartments.'

She looked at him as if he'd offered her a dish of maggots, a mixture of disgust and disdain. 'I can't sell the palazzo. It's entailed.'

'You could rent it out.'

'Right now,' she said, 'it'd probably breach every health and safety regulation going. It's damp and it's crumbling. It needs renovating first. It's my palazzo, it's the fault of my ancestors that it's in the state it's in now, and it's my job to fix it.'

There was a hint of steel and fire in her eyes. He liked that. A lot. Serafina Ardizzone wouldn't back down when something seemed difficult at first glance. She was clearly the sort who'd look at the options and find a way to make things work. She'd push and she'd ask questions, because she wanted to understand the situation and do things properly. Gianni knew he'd enjoy working with someone who was that invested in a job.

Though he damped down the voice in his head that asked if he was more interested in her or in the job. This wasn't about fancying someone out of his league. It was about work.

'Bottom line, the building needs to earn its keep. I plan to rent the ground floor and maybe part of the first floor to a museum.' She spread her hands. 'I also want to use the ballroom on the floor where we live now. As well as exhibitions, we could hold banquets, serving food made from historical recipes; or we could hold musical evenings with the musicians wearing period costume and using period instruments. Or lectures with period refreshments. It'd be easy to fill the seats.'

Eating historical food and listening to a classical concert wasn't the sort of thing Gianni had ever considered doing, but Serafina's enthusiasm was infectious and he was surprised to discover that he was tempted to try both—if she was involved. She was so far away from his own world that she intrigued him. He wanted to know what made her tick; and to see things the way she saw them.

'I'd retain most of the first floor for my family's use, and in time I'd use the second and third floors as accommodation,' she said. 'Possibly for holiday lets, or possibly for longer-term tenancies. But to start with I need the ground floor restored to the point where it could be used by a museum, plus a couple of suites on the first floor that I could use for guests.'

'Restoration in stages,' he said thoughtfully. 'That's doable, provided you warn your guests that there will be noise and mess. But, whatever you plan to do, you need to look at the causes of the dampness first and fix it. Obviously I can't tell you what the causes and the best solutions are without seeing the place, but the options are likely to include tanking—that's putting in a waterproof membrane and concrete to elevate the ground floor above the flood-risk height—or filling the cavities in the wall with special material so the salt water can't seep upwards. Then you need to look at any other areas of the building which are letting in water, and look at the heating and ventilation to deal with condensation.'

'Will that be expensive to fix? And will it take long?'

'It depends what damage there is already,' he said. 'As a rule of thumb, where restoration's concerned, always overestimate the cost by at least fifty per cent. That way you'll avoid the worst of the shocks.'

And now he had to do the bit that Elena's family had always thought vulgar. Mention money. Would this be where she backed away, like they would've done? 'In Venice, everything has to be shipped in. Literally,' he said. 'It's going to cost more than it would in a city where things can be delivered by road. And some of those costs will need to be paid up front.'

'Of course.' She inclined her head. 'Could we perhaps agree staged payments?'

Staged payments? Did she mean that she needed to have the work done first and rent out the ground floor before she'd have enough money to pay his bill? She'd made it clear that she needed the building to pay its way. It seemed that Contessa Serafina Ardizzone, despite her lifestyle—or maybe because of it—didn't have very much in the bank.

'I'd still need a deposit,' he said carefully. 'As would any other contractor.'

'I'm not asking you to do the work for nothing,' she said. 'I'm proposing a business deal.'

Hadn't she done that already, by asking him to quote for a restoration job? He didn't understand what else she could mean.

'You and I,' she said, 'both have…difficulties, shall we say?'

He folded his arms, not liking the sound of this. 'Don't beat around the bush.'

'All right. What happened at Bardicello damaged your company's reputation. A high-profile project like restoring the palazzo will help people to forget that.' She took a deep breath. 'Plus my name will help you. And I have the contacts to get you excellent publicity. Definitely magazines, and possibly television.'

He didn't have a clue where she was going with this. 'What exactly are you suggesting?'

Marry me.

Though Serafina couldn't quite bring herself to say it. She knew her best friend was right: the marriage of convenience was a stupid idea. Who would marry a complete stranger? Of course he'd refuse.

But maybe if he got to know her—if he came to stay at the palazzo, to survey it, he might fall in love with the place. And then she could ask him; and then he might say yes.

'Do you know Venice, Gianni?' she asked instead.

He rolled his eyes. 'Everyone knows Venice. Canals, gondolas, masks, glass.'

It was what the tourists came to see; but there was much more to the city than that. 'When did you last visit the city?'

'I've never been,' he admitted.

'Then you know what everyone *thinks* Venice is, which isn't the same thing at all,' she said. 'Here's my proposal. Come and stay with me for a week. Look at the palazzo and tell me realistically what needs doing, how long it will take and how much it will cost. In return, you get to stay in a palazzo right on the Grand Canal—the best location anyone could ask for. Breakfast on the terrace, where you can watch the boats on the water while you sip your coffee. Mornings strolling around the *calle*, finding hidden treasures at every corner, with someone who can tell you their history and point out little details you might not have noticed. Lunch in a little courtyard filled with flowers, and the sound of birdsong and church bells everywhere instead of traffic. Dinner in a tiny restaurant with amazing food: a place where the locals eat and the menu's what the chef picked up at the market that morning. A glass of wine on the terrace, watching the last streaks of the sunset fade from the sky and the canal turning dark as night, the reflections from the lights in the buildings looking like stars on the water. It's heaven on earth.'

The picture she painted... Gianni could already feel himself falling under the spell of Venice. And under the spell of Serafina herself; he couldn't remember the last time he'd actually noticed the colour of a woman's eyes and the way they changed with the light and her mood.

This was meant to be business, and he was trying to put the past to bed and rebuild his family's good name. Letting himself get side-tracked by the most beautiful woman he'd ever met, a woman whose words spun fairy tales around him and made the world glow, would be the worst thing he could do.

He reframed her proposal into much plainer language. 'You want me to survey the building for nothing, and test market what you're offering your guests?'

Colour tinged her cheeks. 'Not *quite*. I'm suggesting a kind of barter. A survey of the building in return for a week's accommodation, food and entertainment.'

'And the accommodation, food and entertainment is what you plan to offer your guests.'

She shook her head. 'They'll pay for their own lunch and dinner. You won't.'

'If I want to drink vintage champagne and eat lobster at the most expensive restaurant in Venice, that's OK with you?' he asked, guessing that it would be way outside her budget and wanting to see how far he could push her.

'Like a rich tourist, you mean? Then you won't be eating like a local,' she said crisply, 'which is what *I'm* offering.'

She thought on her feet, and she stood up for herself. The more she sparred with him, the more he wanted to get to know her. He wasn't used to being intrigued by someone and it flustered him slightly; at the same time, he found it irresistible.

'What you'll get,' she said, 'is a personal tour guide, good food, decent wine, and accommodation in an amazing location.'

'In a damp, crumbling palazzo,' he reminded her. Wasn't that the whole point? She lived in a house that was falling down. She'd already admitted that in its current state it'd breach every health and safety regulation going.

'Shabby chic is very trendy, is it not?' she asked. 'In my case it's also authentic. Furniture that's been in my family for years, not bought from a flea market and given a fake "distressed" paint job. That's a double win.'

He'd give her bonus point for that. On a sales team, she'd be the outstanding star. She could put the perfect spin on things. No wonder the museum had snapped her up for their board. He'd bet she could talk people into sponsorship deals, or into lending them priceless works of art for an exhibition.

Her work, combined with her best friend, meant that she'd been truthful about having good press contacts. If he worked on her palazzo, he'd get excellent publicity. Something that would definitely make people forget Bardicello. He'd finally be able to restore his family's good name and hold his head up high. Be proud again instead of cautious.

Ah, who was he kidding? It wasn't the job that made him want to say yes. It wasn't even the prospect of working on the kind of building that made his heart sing. It was *her*. This clever, energetic woman who made everything around him feel as if the brightness had been turned up, pulling him out of the shadows.

Which was why he ought to say no.

She obviously didn't have the money to cover the restoration. She'd admitted she needed the house to pay for itself and she'd asked about stage payments. She was even bartering with him rather than paying up front for a survey, which was one of the cheapest items on a restoration job. Did she have any money at all?

His best guess was that she didn't.

From a business point of view, this was going to be an utter disaster. He shouldn't let his attraction to her blinker his common sense.

On the other hand, it was months since he'd taken a break. Probably years, if he was honest with himself; he hadn't been on holiday since his father had died.

A week in Venice, staying in the kind of building that fascinated him and doing the part of the job he loved most: looking at the house, seeing what needed doing, working out how to fix the problems while still staying true to the building's heart. Traditional craftsmanship mixed with modern ideas.

And he'd have his own personal tour guide: a good, solid reason to spend a bit more time with her.

How could he say no?

'All right. It's a deal. Show me your Venice, and I'll do a proper assessment of your house.'

Was it his imagination, or was that relief he could see in those dark, luminous eyes—albeit quickly masked?

'Thank you.' She took her phone out of her bag and flicked into what he assumed was her diary app when she said, 'When's convenient for you?'

It seemed that she was no slouch when it came to closing a deal, either.

Serafina Ardizzone might look like a movie star, but underneath she was an extremely astute businesswoman: one who knew better than to give him time to change his mind.

'I'll check my diary and get back to you,' he said, deliberately baiting her because he wanted to know what she'd do next and where she'd take this.

She glanced at her watch. 'We still have ten minutes left of our meeting. Let's take that window to check your diary. Especially as your laptop is right in front of you.'

Astute businesswoman? No, she was more like a shark pretending to be a mermaid. And he didn't care that he was mixing his metaphors.

The more he saw of Serafina Ardizzone, the more she drew him.

Serafina. Seraph. Angel.

Angels were supposed to be blonde and ethereal, weren't they? Serafina was dark and very, very real. Not in the least bit angelic. That mouth was pure temptation.

How could he possibly resist?

He opened his diary. 'A week.' He was busy. But he could delegate. It would probably be good for him to learn how to delegate, instead of insisting on knowing every single detail of every single project. His father's micro-management had driven him crazy; but here he was, if he was honest, doing exactly the same thing to his team. Gianni didn't want to turn into his father and stifle their creativity, the way his father had stifled him. Serafina Ardizzone had just given him the perfect excuse to loosen the reins a little. Or was he finding the perfect excuse to accept her offer? 'All right. Let's make it Monday.'

'Monday's fine. Will you arrive by train or plane?'

Normally, he'd drive. But Venice had canals rather than roads, so driving wasn't appropriate. 'Train. It's better for the environment than flying.'

She inclined her head. 'I'll meet you at the train station. What time?'

'Morning,' he said. 'I'll let you know the arrival time once I've booked my ticket.'

'Wonderful.' But her smile wasn't pure triumph. He couldn't quite read it, but he thought there might be a tinge of relief. 'Monday morning it is. Do you have any specific dietary requirements?'

'No.'

'And you're OK with fish?' she checked.

'I'm not fussy about food,' he said. Growing up poor meant either you ate what you were given, or you went hungry. He'd never lost the habit, even though nowadays he didn't have to worry about money.

She put a note in her diary. 'I'm sure you're busy. I won't

waste your time by chattering on about nothing.' She stood up and proffered her hand. 'Thank you for your time. I'll see you on Monday.'

Again, when he shook her hand, Gianni's skin tingled. So did his mouth. He was going to have to work on that and get his reaction under control before Monday. 'Monday,' he said, and hoped she hadn't heard the slight croak in his voice.

'*Ciao,*' she said, and gave him a smile that sent his pulse rate up several notches.

And then she sashayed out of his office.

Oh, dear God. What had he let himself in for?

But a smile tugged at the corner of his mouth as he checked what he needed to move and what he needed to delegate.

Serafina kept the bright smile fixed on her face as she thanked the receptionist, but in the lift her knees very nearly sagged.

Gianni Leto had actually agreed to the first part of her plan.

And it was only now that she realised she'd expected him to refuse.

He'd arrive on Monday. Today was Wednesday. That gave her less than a week to prepare.

But preparation was her strong suit. She was about to sit on a train for three hours. Three uninterrupted hours, when she had nothing else to do but focus on Gianni Leto and how to get him to fall in love with Venice and the palazzo. And then maybe she could persuade him to take that one tiny step and marry her, temporarily. That would give her the money to pay him. And then she could rescue both the museum and the palazzo.

She bought a double espresso from one of the kiosks in the station, found her seat, and took a pen and pad from her bag, ready to start making lists. At the planning stage, she preferred the old-fashioned way; there was a direct connection between her hand and her brain, plus later she could see ideas she'd deleted and possible revisit them or tweak them.

But, before she did that, there was something else important she needed to do: persuade her mother to go on holiday for a week. She didn't want her mother to know a thing about her plans for the palazzo until everything was agreed. Francesca took worry to an art form, and Serafina had learned very quickly to copy her father's habit of keeping everything vague, to stop her mother going into catastrophe mode.

Even though Serafina loved her mother dearly, part of her resented the fact that she had to tiptoe round her mother's sensitivities all the time. Weren't you supposed to be able to lean on your parents when things got tough? But, for as long as she could remember, it had been the other way round. She was the one who had to jolly Francesca along. The one who had to find the bright side. The supporter, not the leaner.

She squared her shoulders. That wasn't ever going to change, so it was pointless dwelling on it. Better to use her energy on something positive, the way she always did, instead of wallowing. She'd save the palazzo, save the museum and make sure that her mother didn't have to worry about a thing.

Which meant she needed to keep all the details to herself: though she was realistic enough to know that she wouldn't be able to do any of it without some help.

She took her phone from her bag and called her aunt.

'Serafina! How are you, *piccola*?'

'Very well, thank you. And you, Tia Vittoria?'

'I'm about to head off to aqua aerobics, but I always have time for my favourite niece.'

She was Vittoria's only niece, just as Vittoria was her only aunt, but the affection was real and made Serafina feel warm inside. 'Good. Tia Vittoria, may I ask a huge, huge favour from you?'

'Of course.'

'I have someone coming to see the palazzo next week. To assess it, then tell me what the problems are and what can be done to fix them. And I don't want Mamma worrying herself sick about it.'

'Plus you don't need Cesca in doom-and-gloom mode, talking to your assessor and giving him all the worst-case scenarios,' Vittoria said. 'Which you, *piccola*, are too loyal to say, but she's my little sister so *I* can say it. It can be the brightest, sunniest day, and your mother will still find the clouds and rain.'

It was true; and it was incredibly wearing, trying to make someone see the bright side when their natural inclination was gloom, gloomier and gloomiest. 'Even agreeing with you makes me feel like a really horrible person,' Serafina said, guilt prickling through her veins.

Because you weren't supposed to be mean about your family. You were supposed to love them unconditionally.

Even when you weren't totally sure they loved you back.

No, that wasn't fair. Her mother *did* love her. It just got a bit lost under all the misery.

'You're not horrible at all,' Vittoria said. 'But we need to be practical here and work round the obstacles. Let me know when the survey is, and I'll take Cesca out for a very long lunch and then make her help me find a new dress or something until the assessor's gone.'

'That's lovely of you,' Serafina said. 'But I'm afraid it's not going to be for only a day.'

'The palazzo's that bad?'

'I think it might be,' Serafina admitted. 'But I have a plan.' She told her aunt about the museum's plight, about

the deal she'd reached with Gianni, and how she intended
to raise the money to fix the ground floor.

'Firstly,' Vittoria said, 'a marriage of convenience is a
terrible idea. I know Tom hurt you and the way he cheated
on you stopped you believing in love, but it does exist.'

'I'm not so sure it does, for my family. Look at my parents and my grandparents. They weren't happy together, but
they stuck it out because everyone expected it of them. And
I'm guessing it was the same back in the nineteenth century, and the century before that.' Serafina sighed. 'Maybe
the family curse is real.'

'That curse is a family story to explain away bad be-
haviour,' Vittoria said briskly. 'Your grandparents were
of a different generation—and they were toxic. Your parents should have moved out instead of staying at the palazzo, and your father needed a proper job instead of being
a count in waiting. Living with difficult in-laws and being
dependent on them for money is a recipe for misery. It's no
wonder that things turned out the way they did.'

Serafina knew her aunt had a point. If her father had had
something to fulfil him and a place of his own, he might
not have started gambling to keep himself occupied. And
her mother might have been more like Vittoria, finding
the joy instead of the shadows everywhere she looked. Serafina had been determined not to let herself be dragged
down in the same way, and she'd always managed to find
a positive for every situation.

'And now there's you,' Vittoria said. 'Bright, clever,
beautiful you. You deserve a partner who'll support you
and let you shine, Serafina. A partner who'll love you all
the way back.'

Which, so far, hadn't happened. 'Let's agree to disagree
on that one, Tia Vittoria,' Serafina said. 'I don't want the
headache of a husband.' Except possibly for a convenient
one. 'But the rest of it? Can you help me?'

'If your assessor falls in love with Venice and the palazzo, then I agree he's more likely to help you. He's in the
business of structures rather than their contents; he might
know about grants that you don't,' Vittoria said. 'Of course
I'll help you. I'll call your mother tonight and ask her to
come and stay with me for a week, because I miss my little
sister and I want to spend some time with her.' She paused.
'I'll say want to replant some of the borders and I need her
to help me with the research. We'll need to go and visit several gardens and have lunch out. She'll enjoy that.'

Serafina wasn't sure her mother enjoyed anything other
than finding the gloomy spots, nowadays. A disloyal part
of her thought her mother rather enjoyed having the excuse
of widowhood so she could be ostentatiously miserable. Serafina missed her dad, but she'd buried her grief by keeping herself busy. On the other hand, she needed to know
exactly what they were facing with the restoration so she
could put it in a kinder form for her mother, and that meant
getting Francesca away from the palazzo while Gianni assessed it. 'Thank you. I owe you. Massively.'

'I'm happy to help,' Vittoria said. 'I wish I could do
more. I have some savings; they won't make much of a
dent in restoring that monstrosity of a palazzo, but you're
welcome to them if it will help.'

Serafina swallowed hard. 'That's really kind, but I can't
take your money.'

'Better to have it now, when it can be useful, than wait
until I die—because I intend to live to at least a hundred
and be one of these old women who terrifies the entire village,' Vittoria said. 'And now I must go, *piccola*, or I'll be
late for class.' She chuckled. 'Make sure Cesca packs her
swimming costume. I'll take her with me next week. She'll
be too busy following the moves to worry about anything.'

Once she'd said goodbye to her aunt, Serafina felt much
lighter of heart.

How did you make someone fall in love with a city?

She made of list of places to take Gianni: places where the food was good, or where the buildings were stunning. At this time of year, it was a little quieter; she could take him to see the Doge's Palace and the Basilica when the square wasn't completely teeming with people. And she could take him to lesser-known spots, too; she was pretty sure he'd love the spiral staircase on the outside of the Palazzo Contarini del Bovolo.

La Serenissima in spring.

It was her favourite time of year, when it was warm enough that you didn't need a coat but cool enough that you could walk all day without needing to find a patch of shade to collapse in. Wisteria tumbling from walls, blossom on the trees, and terracotta pots stuffed with greenery and pops of colour to dress windows, bridges and terraces. It was the time of year when she spent the most time painting, loving the beauty of her city and wanting to capture it in watercolours. She wouldn't have to do much; the city would do the work for her and make Gianni fall in love.

She'd just about finished her lists when the train pulled in to Venice. She caught the *vaporetto* to the Rialto, picked up a bouquet of bright pink peonies for her mother from her favourite florist, then walked through the back streets to the back door of the palazzo.

Her footsteps echoed in the hall as she crossed to the stairs.

'I'm going to fix you,' she whispered, stroking the marble newel post. 'You're going to shine again. Especially when the museum moves here. But you need to help me, so I can help you and help the museum. You need to make Gianni Leto fall in love with you, the way I love you.'

And she was definitely going crazy, talking to her house.

She shook herself. Now to face her mother. She took a deep breath, reminded herself to smile, and headed up to the sitting room overlooking the canal. If her mother was reading or doing something, it would be good. If she was staring out of the window, then Serafina would have to try a little harder.

It turned out to be the second.

Steeling herself, Serafina went over to the Louis XVI couch. She couldn't help noticing that the fabric was thread-bare in places and the gilt was chipped. The second that shabby chic fell out of favour they'd be in real trouble.

She greeted Francesca with a hug and kissed both cheeks. 'Mamma. I bought you your favourites.' She handed over the flowers.

Francesca's eyes widened. 'But peonies are really expensive.'

'I bought them because I love you and I thought you'd like them.' Serafina damped down the disappointment. Maybe it wasn't possible to put a sparkle in her mother's eyes or bring her a moment of joy. But she couldn't stop trying, or she'd found herself sucked into the same quicksand of doom and gloom. At least *she* would enjoy the scent and colour of the flowers. 'Shall I put them in water for you?'

'Yes, do that.' Some of her disappointment must've shown in her face, because Francesca added, 'I'm sorry I snapped, *bella*. My hip aches today.'

It was an excuse, and both of them knew it. 'Have a rest, Mamma. I'll go and make dinner. Or I can order something in, if you like.'

Francesca sighed. 'This house. I *hate* this house. It's mouldering away. The only good thing about it is the view.'

At least her mother could see *one* good thing about the palazzo. Serafina held on to that. 'The house will be fine when we've fixed it up.'

'Will it? This house is unlucky. And we have no money to fix it up because your father gambled away everything we had. And we can't sell it because of the lawyers.' Francesca shook her head mournfully. 'I don't know what we're going to do.'

Serafina didn't dare tell her mother about the museum. It would send Francesca into total catastrophe mode. 'Leave it to me, Mamma. Try not to worry,' Serafina said. 'I'll make you some coffee and sort out dinner.'

And she really hoped that Gianni would help her find some real answers to her situation, next week.

CHAPTER THREE

GIANNI CHOSE THE high-speed direct train from Rome to Venice, to avoid changing trains and giving himself time to work without interruptions. But when the train stopped at Padova, half an hour from Venice, he found himself staring out of the window, thinking about Serafina.

Part of him thought this whole trip was insane. If she didn't have the money to do the work, what was the point of him even going to assess the house?

On the other hand, how could he resist the temptation to assess a centuries-old building that hadn't been touched within living memory? It was the kind of job he loved most—and that was why he'd fallen out with his father. Gianni's father had been keen on ultra-modern designs and loved concrete; whereas Gianni preferred more old-fashioned designs, and liked to see how modern materials could be used seamlessly with traditional ones. Their clashes had left Gianni frustrated that his dad refused to see his point of view or even consider a different way of doing things; it convinced him that his dad didn't respect him or think him good enough to take over from him when he was ready to retire.

And now he'd never get his dad's approval.

His dad definitely wouldn't have approved of this new job.

Though even considering this job had nothing to do with

a secret rebellion or a yearning to prove himself. If he was honest, Serafina Ardizzone herself was the real lure to the Venetian project. In the short time he'd spent with her, he'd realised that she was bright, full of energy and sparkle, and it made him wonder why on earth Tom Burford had let her walk out of his life. Gianni had no intention of looking at the gossip pages and soaking up all the speculation; he'd seen a story saying that her engagement to the film star had ended a few months ago, and the reasons behind it were none of his business. But, if Serafina had been engaged to him, he knew he wouldn't have let her go so easily. He would've done his best to fix whatever the problem was.

Right now, beneath that sparkle, he had a feeling Serafina wasn't happy. Not just because she, like him, was grieving for a lost parent. There was something vulnerable about her. Was she shouldering the burden of the palazzo alone? What about her mum? Did she have any family or friends on her side, people who could advise her or be a sounding board? He was lucky in that his sister Flora was always there for him, and so was their mum; but did Serafina have anyone?

And why was he even letting himself think about Serafina in any terms other than that of client? Even if she was single, Gianni had no plans to get involved with anyone. He was busy with his job and repairing his family's reputation. He didn't have the time or the space in his life for a relationship—or the inclination, after the way Elena had broken their engagement mere days after there had been a suggestion of a problem in his business. Her family hadn't thought him good enough for her, and she hadn't loved him enough to disagree with them. He wasn't giving another posh woman the chance to use him and dump him; he'd rather put his energies into his business.

Yet he still couldn't concentrate on his paperwork.

And he knew it was because he'd be seeing Serafina.

Almost as if she knew he was thinking of her, and she was thinking of him too, his phone pinged with a text message and her name flashed up on the screen.

When you get off the train, walk down the steps at the entrance. I'll be waiting for you in front of the lamp-post. S

Gianni gave up all pretence of working after that; instead, he packed away his laptop and enjoyed the scenery. Crossing the causeway over the lagoon on a train felt distinctly odd; yet the views were stunning. He could see the city in the distance, the buildings packed close together and lit by the sun with a kind of haze round them. La Serenissima: The Most Serene, rising from the sea like a mirage. Venice really was otherworldly, like no place he'd ever visited before.

Once the train had come to a halt, he gathered his luggage together, headed for the entrance to the station and walked down the steps. In front of the station was a green lamp-post with three old-fashioned lanterns; and in front of the lamp-post was Serafina, leaning casually against it with one foot tucked behind the other, as if she was preparing to step forward.

She looked like a nineteen-fifties film star, wearing a brightly patterned fuchsia-pink scarf tied round her hair, navy capri pants, a navy-and-white-striped top, a white shirt with the sleeves rolled up to act as a light jacket, deck shoes to match her scarf, and a pair of designer sunglasses. And she was holding a placard that said 'Gianni Leto'. It was completely unnecessary, given that they'd already met and knew what each other looked like, but he couldn't help smiling. Being met like this made him feel as if he were special. If he were one of her guests, he'd be thrilled to bits by the welcome.

Should he kiss her on the cheek?

But, technically speaking, he was here as her consultant rather than a friend. Plus, for all he knew, his attraction to her was completely one-sided. Feeling slightly wrong-footed, and determined to seem businesslike, he held out a hand to shake hers. 'Good to see you again, Serafina. Thank you for meeting me.'

'You're welcome, Gianni.' Her smile was bright and made him feel warm from the inside out. 'How was your journey?'

'Good, thanks.'

Gianni discovered that the handshake was a mistake. Just as last time, the feel of her skin against his sent adrenalin prickling down his spine, unsettling him. 'Are we taking the water bus?' he asked, needing to distract himself from his reaction to Serafina.

'It's your first time in Venice. No,' she said, leading him away from the yellow sign for the *vaporetto* stop and towards a pier. 'For your very first trip in Venice, you need to travel by water taxi. The *motoscafi* aren't allowed on the Grand Canal during peak hours, apart from access, but at least this way you'll get to see a bit more of the city than you would on a *vaporetto*.' She smiled. 'I would've collected you and driven you myself, but sadly our boat gave up the ghost a couple of years ago and it costs too much to repair. Though, if we had repaired it, I would've persuaded my father to convert it to an electric engine. They're much better for the people—and the buildings.'

She was conscious of the environment, then. That sat well with him.

'I'll show you the Grand Canal properly at some point during the week,' she said. 'And I assume, given what you do, that you'll want to see the famous buildings. I hope you don't mind being up early, because that for me is when the city's at her best.'

'It's fine by me,' he said. 'And yes, I'd love to see the buildings. The Palazzo Ducale in particular.'

'I guessed you might. I've got us timed tickets for to-morrow, to skip the queue,' she said.

The water taxi driver took Gianni's luggage and helped them both on board. Once the boat had gone under the pe-destrian bridge by the train station, their driver turned off the Grand Canal onto a narrower, quieter waterway.

'I'm not even going to talk to you from now until we're back at the house,' Serafina said. 'Sit back and enjoy the view—and let Venice introduce herself to you. She's at her best in the little hidden corners.'

Gianni felt like a celebrity, travelling down the tur-quoise waters of the canal in a private boat. Every so often, the sunlight caught the water and made it sparkle; and all around him were tall buildings with narrow windows, beautiful doorways and metal grilles. When a bridge—a mixture of stone, brick, wood and iron—crossed the canal, underneath every single one he could see silvery reflec-tions from the water rippling across the stone.

Even though the builder in him winced inwardly at the damage the water had done to the structure of the build-ings, at the same he couldn't help being enchanted by the chipped and faded stucco, and the timeless elegance of the architecture. How many people had passed this way over the years, nurturing secret hopes and dreams and falling under the spell of the city?

He heard a nearby church clock strike the quarter-hour, and then another and another, echoing away into the dis-tance: and then it struck him how quiet it was here. No cars, no furious horn-beeping or engines revving or screech of tyres as someone braked. This was another world.

The driver expertly took them through the maze of ca-nals, and then they were back on the Grand Canal itself and Gianni realised they must be near to the palazzo. When the boat pulled up by a narrow pontoon that was clearly a private entrance, he recognised Ca' d'Ardizzone from the photographs Serafina had sent him. Close up, he could see the damage to the stucco on the front of the palazzo and the unevenness of the colour.

What would it be like inside? Had her photographs shown the damage as it truly was, or minimised it?

The driver helped them both out of the boat, sketched a salute to Serafina, and drove off.

'Welcome to Ca' d'Ardizzone, Gianni,' she said.

'Thank you.' He inclined his head. 'How much do I owe you for the water taxi?'

'Nothing. It's my pleasure.'

Pleasure.

Why did that word suddenly make him feel hot all over?

This was ridiculous. He was here on business. Well, *mainly* business. Which meant he needed to get himself back into professional mode instead of mooning over her. 'Thank you,' he said again.

She opened the door and ushered him in.

'Centuries ago, my family imported wines and spices,' she said. 'There's a second water gate on the side of the palazzo, and that's the one the merchants would have used. But this one—though we don't tend to use it much nowadays—would have been for guests.'

The entrance hall was enormous, running from the front to the back of the building; it clearly followed the classical floor plan of a Venetian palazzo, with a *portego*, or large entrance hall, having all the rooms leading off it. The floor was Venetian terrazzo, crushed marble set in lime and then ground and polished to a shine; the plain wooden ceilings were high; and there was a grand staircase with marble newel posts and delicate wrought-iron balustrades leading up to the next floor.

It was stunning.

'And this is the area you're planning to rent to a museum?' he asked.

'Yes. It's perfect for exhibitions. Look at the light,' she said.

He had to agree. Superficially, the room was perfect. Close up, the imperfections would show and reveal the damage—he could definitely smell damp, and he suspected there was crumbling plaster behind that wall-covering—but he could see the potential.

'I'll give you a super-quick tour before lunch, but let me show you to your room first, so you can freshen up. I'm afraid we don't have en-suite bathrooms,' she added apologetically, 'but there is a bathroom next door to your room.'

'That sounds good. I'll follow you up,' he said.

Portraits in gold frames hung on the wall next to the staircase, following the line of the stairs upwards. Her ancestors, he presumed. All of them looked stern and gave off a faint air of disapproval, or maybe that was simply the way they'd been posed.

At the top of stairs was another enormous hall.

'The kitchen's through there,' she said, indicating the first room, 'and I'm going to sort out some coffee.' She waved her hand towards the side of the house facing the canal. 'Ballroom, dining room, drawing room, sitting room, library. The bedrooms are all at the back of the house, mainly because it's a bit less humid there. The kitchen's at the back, too.' She led him past several doorways. 'This is your room. I hope you'll find it comfortable, but let me know if there's anything you need.' She smiled. 'There are fresh towels on the bed. Come and find me in the kitchen when you're ready.'

The room was a good size, with parquet flooring and a thick rug in shades of red, blue and gold. The wide bed had a gilt and dark blue velvet headboard, the Louis XVI settee was also gilt and dark blue velvet, and there was a mirror with an ornate gilt frame above the gilt and cream dressing table. A matching ottoman with a blue-velvet-upholstered top stood next to the dressing table and the cream and gilt wardrobe. The wallpaper was faded in places, and by the window was an area of water-staining. In winter, Gianni thought, this room would smell as damp as the downstairs hall had. On closer inspection, the upholstery was faded and slightly threadbare in places, and the gilt and paint were definitely distressed—albeit from age, rather than a designer's judicious sandpapering. Shabby chic, as Serafina had called it. Designers would pay a fortune for that effect; but Gianni could imagine how the room must have looked when everything was still new. Opulent and comfortable at the same time.

He took one of the towels from the bed and went to explore the bathroom. A quick inspection showed him terrazzo flooring, some tiling on the walls that had cracked in places and at the very least needed new grouting and sealant, and it looked as if the brass taps were at least a century old. When he tried the cold water tap, it worked without a problem. Perhaps the plumbing had been put in order relatively recently; though, in a house that was more than five hundred years old, 'recently' could mean any time in the last fifty years. He wondered if the electric wiring had even been looked at since it was first installed. From the colour of the socket next to the bed, he had a feeling it hadn't.

When she'd first said that the house would breach all health and safety conditions, he'd thought she might be exaggerating. But now he was pretty sure she'd been stating the truth.

He splashed his face, dried it, and went to find Serafina in the kitchen.

The room was a strange mixture of ancient and new: a terrazzo floor, several vintage dressers and shelving, an antique marble-topped table and chairs at the far end of the room, and then a very modern fridge, cooker and washing machine.

'Perfect timing,' she said, holding a mug of coffee aloft. 'Do you take milk or sugar?'

'No milk and half a sugar, please,' he said.

She finished preparing his drink and handed it to him. 'Mamma and I tend to eat in here, rather than in the dining room, if there are fewer than six of us. Or on the terrace, if the weather's nice. Come and have the super-quick guided tour. Bring your coffee.'

He sipped it gratefully—relieved to find that the coffee was good and he wasn't going to have to be polite about it—and followed her back into the hall.

'This is the ballroom. Apparently my great-grandparents were fond of parties and used it quite a lot, though I can't remember the last time a party was held here. Probably when I was very small.'

The floor was parquet in here, rather than terrazzo; Gianni assumed that the dust sheets were draping over sofas and small tables, which were probably in the same shabby condition as the furniture in his bedroom. The furniture was all set against the walls; he'd need to move it to check the condition of the walls behind it. Mirrors reflected the light from the huge windows and were strategically placed to catch the light from the glass chandeliers, making the room feel beautifully spacious and airy. Large glass doors led to the balcony; he could imagine the room being full of people dancing, drinking champagne and chattering, then going onto the balcony for a breath of fresh air.

'The dining room,' Serafina said at the next door. 'Though, as I said earlier, we don't use it that often.'

Again, the furniture was dust-sheeted: what he assumed was a very large table and chairs sat in the middle, with console tables and cabinets at the sides. There were plenty of pictures in gilt frames on the walls, and he wondered why she hadn't sold some of them to pay for the building work. Or maybe they, like the palazzo itself, were entailed and couldn't be sold.

'Drawing room. Which we don't use,' she said. 'I'm afraid the dust-sheeting is a bit ugly, but it saves a lot of cleaning.'

It must be hard, he thought, showing someone round your home—a place where your family had lived for centuries—and knowing that person was about to find every single fault with it, even if you'd actually asked them to do an honest assessment. And every fault would cost money and time to fix. It would be daunting even if you were used to building work; and he could see that she was trying to hide her worries behind that over-bright voice. Part of him wanted to give her a hug and tell her that it would be all right; but, apart from the fact that it wouldn't be appropriate to hug her, he didn't believe in giving false promises.

The next room was the sitting room. 'Now, we *do* use this,' she said. 'It would be a crime to waste the view.'

Again there were large glass doors which led to a balcony; he went over to admire the view of the Grand Canal. 'You're right. It's fabulous,' he said.

The sofas here were made comfortable with cushions and throws, which he suspected covered up threadbare materials; there was also a flat-screen television and an ancient-looking piano. 'Do you play?' he asked.

'A little,' she said.

Which could mean anything from picking out a tune very haltingly with one finger through to being concert pianist standard. He didn't know Serafina well enough yet to know if she was over-modest or straightforward.

'The library,' she said, taking him to the next room. 'It used to be my father's den. Now it's my workspace.'

The desk overlooked the canal and was perfectly clear

except for a laptop; the walls were lined with bookshelves; and there were a couple of large leather armchairs that looked very uncomfortable. He couldn't imagine her curled up in one, lost in a book.

Once they were back in the main hall, she gestured to the side of the house that didn't overlook the canal. 'Six bedrooms and three bathrooms, all pretty much like the ones you're using. The next floor up has a similar layout, but all the furniture's dust-sheeted, to save cleaning,' she said. 'It's where my grandparents used to live. They had bedrooms at opposite ends of the floor, and separate sitting rooms and dining rooms.'

Which sounded as if they were either hugely old-fashioned or loathed each other. Or was that the way the upper classes lived? 'Do you remember that?' he asked.

'Not really. They died about twenty-five years ago, when I was still very young,' Serafina said. 'My father didn't speak much about them. Mamma doesn't say much, either.'

Which reminded him of his earlier concern. 'Does your mother mind me staying here?'

She smiled. 'Mamma's staying with her sister this week.'

Which didn't answer his question, and it made him wonder: did her mother even know he was here? And, if not, why had Serafina kept his visit from her? Was it anything like the way Elena had kept their relationship a secret from her family, at first? But he couldn't think how to ask without it sounding belligerent. He wanted to work with her, not fight with her.

'The top floor is more of the same,' she said. 'Originally they were the servants' rooms. They've been shut off or used as store rooms for as long as I can remember.' She shrugged. 'And now I'm the custodian of the palazzo. I don't want to let it moulder away. I want it to be used. To *shine*.'

Exactly how he'd feel about the place, in her shoes. He

could see past the shabbiness to the bones of the house, and they were beautiful. The proportions were perfect. 'I get that,' he said. 'But you need to do this with your eyes open. There isn't a quick, cheap fix.' He looked her in the eyes. 'Well, there is: you can paper over the cracks. But if you don't solve the underlying problems they'll just get worse—and it'll cost more in the long run.'

'Cost.' Her face went tight for a moment. Then she glanced at her watch. 'Shall we have some lunch?'

Clearly she needed some time to come to terms with reality. He wouldn't push her too hard, too fast. He had a whole week to help her face reality. 'That would be great. What can I do to help?'

'Go and sit on the balcony, and enjoy the view,' she directed. 'Would you like some wine?'

'Water's fine, thanks,' he said. He wanted to work with a clear head.

'The doors in the sitting room open out onto the balcony. I'll bring everything through. It's going to be very simple, I'm afraid, but I'll take you to an *osteria* on the other side of the canal for dinner tonight, so you get to experience proper Venetian food.' There was a hint of mischief in her eyes as she added, 'Unless you insist on eating at a place with Michelin stars, though I can't guarantee they'll offer you lobster.'

He couldn't help smiling back, remembering that conversation and how he'd tried to push her. 'Proper Venetian food sounds good.'

The balcony ran across the whole front of the house; there were terracotta pots squeezed in between the balusters, filled with herbs and geraniums. At one side there was a metal bistro table with a glass top, and four chairs; she'd already placed cushions on the seats and set the table with cutlery, crockery, glasses and linen napkins. And the view was unparalleled: the turquoise waters of the Grand

Canal, lined with palazzos and churches. Rather than sitting down, he leaned his forearms on the balcony and looked out. Everywhere he looked, there were domes and interesting windows and architectural details. He could quite see why Venice turned so many people's heads. The city was beautiful.

Like Serafina. Which was exhilarating and terrifying at the same time. She was the first woman who'd made him feel this pull of attraction since Elena: which meant that maybe at long last he was putting all the heartbreak behind him. On the other hand, Elena's family hadn't thought he was good enough for them, and they weren't even proper aristocrats—unlike Serafina. A titled woman's family would no doubt look down even further on him.

He was going to have to put a lid on his attraction to her and keep things strictly professional.

Having a stranger in her house was harder than Serafina had expected.

OK, this week had been her idea, and she'd thought it was a good one at the time. But she'd forgotten how gorgeous Gianni Leto was. How the touch of his palm against hers made her skin tingle and made her catch her breath. How beautiful his mouth was.

She couldn't afford to let herself fall for him. Even though the sensible side of her knew that the family curse was a ridiculous superstition, if she looked back at her love-life she'd fallen for one Mr Wrong after another. Men who hadn't felt as deeply for her as she'd felt about them. And then, there had been Mr Completely Disastrously Wrong: Tom Burford, the movie star who'd swept her off her feet and made her believe that he'd really loved her for herself. Except he'd been acting, because he'd wanted her aristocratic connections rather than her. He'd carried on having flings with whoever took his fancy, and she'd only found out because she'd flown out on a surprise visit and found him in bed with someone else.

It had been the final disillusionment that had stopped her believing in love.

Falling for Gianni Leto would be a huge mistake. She needed him to fall in love with the palazzo and with Venice, yet at the same time she had to keep her heart intact. She'd be bright and charming, the way she'd always been at work, pointing out all the positives and dealing quietly with the negatives. And she'd definitely have to ignore the way her blood felt as if it fizzed through her veins whenever Gianni smiled at her.

Focus, she told herself. She sliced the bread, put it in a wicker basket and put the basket on a tray, along with a platter of cheese and a dish of sliced tomatoes sprinkled with fresh basil. She added a jug of iced water with slices of lime, then carried the lot out to the balcony.

He was standing with his arms resting on the stone, looking out to the canal, and she itched to sketch him. Which was strange, because her pen-and-ink drawings and watercolours were all landscapes, slices of canal and buildings or a close-up of a detail that interested her. She didn't usually bother sketching people. Why him? What was so different about him?

It wasn't a question she'd let herself dwell on. The answer was potentially way too distracting. Instead, she took a deep breath and set the tray down on the table.

He turned to face her, and that smile made her heart feel as if it had done a backflip. 'This is a lovely spot.'

'It's good for eating, or reading, or just watching the world go by.' And sketching, when she had time. Not that he needed to know about that. It wasn't relevant. 'Please help yourself. The bread's from the bakery round the corner, and they're very good.'

'Thank you.' He waited until she'd sat down before taking his seat. Old-fashioned manners: she liked that.

'Right,' she said brightly. 'About this week. Obviously you need time to assess the palazzo; but I thought during the week I could show you some of the famous buildings in the city, and maybe some of the less famous ones. There isn't any ballet or opera on this week, but there are plenty of string quartet concerts. I could get tickets for one evening, if you'd like to go.'

'That's kind of you to offer,' he said, 'but classical music's not my sort of thing.'

Which meant he wouldn't be enthused about her idea of holding small concerts of classical Venetian music in her ballroom, then. 'Sorry. Most of the music venues tend to be classical,' she said, 'or jazz. But there are plenty of other things we can do. And I'd like to take you to see one palazzo that's been restored, so you can see for yourself what this house might have looked like in its heyday.'

'Do you have any old photographs?' he asked. 'Something that might show the interiors?'

'There are probably some in the old albums.' She bit her lip. 'Sorry, I should've thought to look through them earlier.'

'No problem.' He looked at her. 'I'm guessing you've been thrown into this in the deep end.'

'Not *exactly*. I'm part of a long line of people who didn't pay enough attention to what was happening right under their noses, I'm afraid. I kind of got what I deserve. Particularly as an art historian—I should've known better,' she said. 'Though I admit I'm a bit worried about the assessment and how bad the damage actually is. And how long it will take to fix.' She knew she'd have to tell him about the time constraints, and probably sooner rather than later, but she didn't want him to take a negative view of the situation before he'd even started. She wanted to start with what the damage was, how long it would take—and then, if necessary, tackle how it could be sped up in time to rehouse the museum. 'Is there anything I can do to help? Hold one end of a tape measure for you or something?'

Gianni didn't have the heart to tell her that he normally used a laser measure, particularly as she'd been honest with him about the fact her family hadn't paid enough attention to the house over the years. 'I'm happy for you to be alongside me as I work. I can show you what I'm looking at as we go, and you can ask questions about anything that isn't clear. I believe in transparency for my clients; and you in turn can tell me everything you know about the palazzo. That way we're both working with the best information possible.'

'Thank you,' she said. 'I'll try not to get under your feet or start micromanaging, though you might need to tell me to shut up.'

He couldn't help laughing. 'I wish all my clients took that attitude. And, by the way, this bread is excellent.'

'You're welcome.'

She smiled at him, a genuine smile rather than the professional one he suspected she'd been using with him so far, and his pulse sped up. When she smiled like that, it made him feel as if the sun had just come out after a long, dull, rainy day. And he wanted more of that feeling.

After lunch, he insisted on helping her wash up. Then he collected his damp meter, laser measure, clipboard and camera from his room.

'No computer?' she asked when he joined her back in the kitchen.

'Not at this stage. I think better with a pen than with a keyboard—it's something to do with the connection between the hand and the brain,' he said, 'and photographs help.'

'It's the same for me at the museum,' she said.

'What does an art historian do?' he asked. 'Do you write about art?'

'Sometimes. The museum where I work specialises in women's art, and I organise exhibitions and write the catalogue and the notes that go with the exhibits. Sometimes I give a talk or do the occasional guided tour, and as a board member I persuade people to give us grants or lend us beautiful things.'

That was where her professional smile came from, then. Was she going to try to persuade him into something, the way she persuaded people at work?

Then again, she already had. He'd agreed to do the assessment in exchange for a week's break at the palazzo, with her as his tour guide.

'Let's start with the ground floor and work upwards,' he said.

He walked round the ground floor and sketched the floor plan first, marking in doors and windows as he went, then went back to each room in turn to measure the dimensions.

'I feel very stupid,' she said, 'not thinking that you'd have a laser measure.'

For a second, he thought he could see the sheen of tears in her eyes. Had someone made her feel stupid, in the past? Or was she just worried sick about exactly how much work the palazzo needed—and how she was going to finance that?

Weirdly, he found himself wanting to protect her. Which was crazy. Apart from the fact that he'd already worked out she was very capable, he couldn't snap his fingers and make all the problems vanish.

But maybe working with him would help to distract her from her worries, just for a little while. For long enough to get her equilibrium back. He could at least do that for her. 'A metal ruler has its place,' he said. 'But a laser measure's accurate. And, short of us having to use a ladder, it's the easiest way to measure the height of the walls as well.' He marked the measurements on his floor plan as he made them. 'You know you asked if you can help? I'm going to take a few moisture readings, and it'd be great if you could write them down for me.' Wanting to put her at her ease, he smiled at her. 'You can be in charge of the clipboard.'

'That sounds good.'

He sketched out a plan of the wall and labelled the points where he planned to measure. 'I'll call them out in order, if you wouldn't mind writing next to the labels?'

His fingers accidentally brushed hers when he handed her the pen and the clipboard, and again that zing of awareness went down his spine. So much for trying to distract her; it felt more as if *she* was distracting *him*.

Gianni's touch sent adrenalin fizzing through Serafina's veins, which was ridiculous. For a second, her thoughts were scattered; and then she realised he was waiting for a response to his question.

'Sure. Next to the labels. Got it.'

'I'm hoping that an art historian's handwriting isn't like a medic's.'

His words defused the tension, to her relief. 'No. Mine's legible.'

'Good.'

He was methodical about where he took the measurements, and she wrote down the numbers he called out. 'Are they good or bad?' she asked when he finished.

'Mixed,' he said. 'I need to take some photographs before we do the next room.'

His voice was neutral and she couldn't tell anything from his expression. 'That sounds faintly ominous.'

'It's practical,' he said. 'I've been looking at how other buildings in the city deal with *acqua alta*. There's one in particular I want to visit, because they let the water come in through a metal gate and channel it out.' He smiled at her. 'It's a museum now. Hopefully you'll know someone there who will allow me to poke about and ask questions.'

She relaxed again. 'I probably do. Or we'll know people in common, at least. It should be fine.'

'Does this level flood?'

'Not really,' she said. 'We're a bit higher up here than in St Mark's. I know they had terrible floods when my dad was a child and he told me he could remember it being flooded up to the third step, but there's been nothing like since then.'

'That's useful. Thank you.' He took the clipboard back from her, and made a note.

But the photographs were worrying. Particularly when he looked at the surfaces behind the wall-coverings that had peeled away. Was her palazzo rotting from the ground up? Could it be saved at all? Was he going to tell her that this was all a waste of time?

Once they'd finished the ground floor, they headed up the stairs.

'These are all your great-whatever-grandfathers?' he asked, indicating the portraits.

'Yes. There's one of my father and my grandfather in my office. They're in date order, the newest portraits at the bottom—though you probably already guessed that from the way they're dressed.'

'None of them are smiling,' he said. 'Or is that a convention in art?'

'Partly convention, because a portrait was formal and smiling was a breach of etiquette—back in the eighteenth century it meant you were poor, drunk, or lewd,' she explained. 'But mostly it was practical. If you sit for a portrait, you have to hold the same position for hours. And it's impossible to maintain a smile for that long. You end up with pretty much a rictus grin, and that would detract from whatever the person commissioning the portrait wanted to get across—whether that was power, wealth, learning or virtue. You might get a bit of a smirk, like Mona Lisa's, but that's about it.'

'I had no idea,' he said.

'But you have a point. They don't look happy.' She thought again of the family curse. Despite her aunt's explanation for her parents and her grandparents, there had been a whole line of unhappy Ardizzones and it showed in every single portrait. The only one who had looked even slightly happy was Marianna, in her miniature: and Marianna had had the saddest ending.

They went through the rooms in the *piano nobile* with the same thoroughness; it took time, because Gianni needed to move the furniture to check the walls behind them. 'I'd be happier if I could move the pictures as well, to see what's behind them.'

'I had to do that to inventory them for inheritance tax purposes,' she said. 'There isn't any mould or any sign of peeling wallpaper.'

Unlike by the windows; the worst of it was hidden by floor-length drapes, but she knew there were problems. And the expression on his face when he'd checked the window frames told her that they'd need at the very least repairing, if not full replacement.

'Are you sure your mother won't mind me assessing her room?' Gianni asked, stopping by the doorway.

'My mother...' Serafina winced. 'Let's just say she worries. If she knew you were a guest, she'd make you very welcome.' Or as welcome as she could; they'd had so few visitors over the last few years, apart from Vittoria, that Francesca was out of practice. 'If she had any idea you were assessing the house, she'd panic. I want to spare her all the worrying, so I haven't told her, and that's why she's staying with Aunt Vittoria this week. But if she did know about the assessment, then of course she'd understand why you need to see her room and she'd be fine about it.'

Serafina was clearly very protective of her mother and had taken the kind way out. Gianni liked that—and he was also relieved that it wasn't because she was ashamed of the stuff that was going on between them under the surface, the way he'd eventually realised Elena had been. Though he still felt faintly uncomfortable about invading Contessa Francesca's private space.

'I'll make us some more coffee,' Serafina said, when they got to her own room.

Yeah. Assessing her private space, in front of her, would've felt very odd. Gianni compartmentalised his thoughts, switched into professional mode, and did the measuring and checking.

When he'd finished, he went to join her in the kitchen.

'Let's have a break before the next floor,' she suggested. 'Shall we go and sit on the balcony again?'

'That'd be nice.'

She put some ring-shaped cookies on a plate, and ushered him out to the balcony. 'Help yourself,' she said, indicating the cookies.

He took one. Buttery and lemony, rich and tart at the same time. He could easily scoff the lot. 'These are amazing,' he said. 'I assume they're from the same bakery as the bread?'

'No. I made them this morning from my best friend's *nonna*'s recipe.' She smiled at him. 'I was thinking what you said about the portraits. I do have one with a slight smile, as it happens. And, because I'm a terrible nerd when it comes to art, I'd rather like to show it to you. Excuse me a moment.' She disappeared back into the sitting room, and returned with a box, which contained something wrapped in paper. 'Acid-free paper, for protection,' she explained, and unwrapped the artwork before handing it to him.

It was a miniature of a woman in a rose-coloured silk dress, her fair hair in an updo. The woman was smiling; it wasn't a broad smile, like you'd see in modern photographs, but the smile definitely reached her eyes.

'This is my Great-however-many-times-Aunt Marianna,' Serafina said. 'I think it's actually my favourite piece of art in the palazzo. The style owes a lot to Rosalba Carriera, though sadly it isn't one of hers.'

'I assume Rosalba Carriera is a famous painter, but I'm afraid I've never heard of her,' Gianni admitted.

'She was an eighteenth-century Venetian painter. I studied her as part of my Master's course,' Serafina said. 'We have some of her work at the museum.'

There was one thing he didn't understand. 'If you love this painting, why keep it wrapped up and out of sight? Why not keep it on show?'

'Because this is a watercolour, and watercolours fade easily. It's why you'll often see miniatures displayed in a case covered with a curtain in a museum, to protect them from the light but still give people access to them,' she said. 'Carriera started out decorating snuff boxes, then moved over to painting miniatures. At the time, miniatures were painted on vellum, but she experimented and found that ivory worked better. Her portraits are beautiful. She used white chalk over her pastels, to make things more luminous.'

Right then, Gianni thought, Serafina looked luminous; talking about art made her light up. And that brightness made the whole room feel as if it had lit up. He wanted to get to know this woman better. A lot better. And he was starting to see a connection between them in their shared love of architecture—his in general, and hers for the palazzo.

She took her phone from the pocket of her capri pants and brought up some images. 'Look at these. They're gorgeous.' She smiled ruefully. 'Though I'd better shut up. I can drone on for hours about Rosalba Carriera.'

Gianni thought that he could listen to Serafina talk for hours. She had a beautiful voice. If she were reading the dullest list of statistics, she'd still manage to hold his attention completely. She'd said that she sometimes gave lectures; he'd bet that everyone was spellbound by her.

'You look like your great-aunt, though obviously your hair's much darker,' he said, handing the portrait back.

'Her hair was probably the same colour as mine, underneath the powder. It was the fashion to powder your hair, back then,' Serafina said. 'Sadly, she didn't have a happy ending. She fell in love with a local man, and her parents forbade her to see him because they wanted her to marry someone else. She planned to elope with him, but while she was trying to creep out of the house she tripped on the stairs, fell down them and broke her neck.'

'That's really sad,' Gianni said.

'Isn't it?' Serafina wrapped up the miniature again.

'What made you become an art historian?' he asked, wanting to know what drove her.

'Wherever you go in Venice, you see art,' she said. 'When I was small, I wanted to know more about the pictures and the statues. Who made them, how they lived, why they chose those particular themes. Especially when I learned that a painting is more than a pretty picture of someone; the way they're posed, the way they're dressed and the items in the painting tell you more about that person. If there's a Renaissance portrait of a woman and she's wearing pearls, the person commissioning that portrait wants you to know she's pure and chaste, because that's what pearls symbolise, and also very rich, because pearls were rare and very expensive. Marianna's wearing rubies in her portrait—a choker, earrings, a brooch on her bodice and two smaller ones on her shoulders. Rubies are associated with purity, wealth, wisdom and calming wrath. Assuming her father was the one who had the miniature painted, any potential husband would take one look at it and know exactly what her character was like.'

He wouldn't have had a clue, and he loved the fact that Serafina could fill in all the details for him but without making him feel as if she were lecturing or as if he were stupid. 'Does your family still own the rubies?'

Serafina shook her head. 'Apparently they went missing after she died. They're probably somewhere at the bottom of the canal, buried under a great deal of mud; or maybe someone melted down the jewellery and reset the stones. Nobody knows.'

'There are a lot of paintings in the palazzo,' he said. 'Have you thought about—?' He stopped, realising how rude and intrusive the question was.

'Selling them to finance the house repairs?' she asked.

'Yes. Though I assume they're entailed, like the house,' he said.

'They're not, but unfortunately the ones that would have raised a lot of money are copies. The rest are portraits of my family, painted by artists who followed a trend rather than set one. The amount they'd raise at auction, after tax, wouldn't make up for the effort of trying to sell them.' She shrugged, as if to say that it was a pity but she'd have to live with the situation. 'I'll just put Marianna away safely.'

'Sure. And we can get started on the next floor.' He drained his coffee. 'I'll wash up.'

'You're a guest. You don't need to wash up.'

'I'm not quite a guest. I'm here to assess the palazzo,' he corrected. 'And it won't kill me to wash up some cups.'

'Then thank you,' she said. 'I'll see you in the kitchen.'

By the time they were halfway through the rooms on

next floor—rooms that clearly hadn't been used for a long while, and smelled musty—they were both covered in dust. Gianni just about managed to resist the urge to wipe a smudge off Serafina's cheek.

She glanced at her watch. 'I guess it's a bit naive of me. I didn't think the assessment would take this long.'

'It does if you do it properly,' he said.

'I've got a table booked at one of my favourite places, and I had kind of planned for us to go out at six, to show you a bit of the area,' she said.

'We can do that,' he said. 'Let's stop now and continue later.'

'Wonderful,' she said. 'Though I think we could both do with a shower before we go out.' There was distinct colour in her face when she added, 'The plumbing can be a bit temperamental and doesn't always like it if more than one shower runs at a time. I'll let you shower first.'

Gianni had a moment when he imagined them sharing a shower, and it made him feel hot all over. Desire licked down his spine as he imagined her with wet hair slicked back, laughing up at him. How soft her skin would feel as he lathered it and then, as the water washed the suds away, how her eyes would darken with need, and she'd reach up to…

Oh, for pity's sake. Since when he did start fantasising about a woman he hardly knew—a potential client, too? 'Thanks,' he muttered. To stop himself adding something completely inappropriate, he made himself think about damp proofing methods.

She glanced at her watch. 'I was thinking we could have an aperitif and *cichéti*, then take a stroll around San Polo before dinner. Is that OK with you?'

'*Cichéti?*' he asked.

'Little snacks to go with your drink,' she said. 'The Venetian version of *mezze*, or perhaps tapas, but don't ever say that to a bar owner.'

'Noted,' he said, smiling back. 'What's the dress code?'

'Smart casual,' she said. 'See you on the balcony when you're ready?'

'OK. I'll knock on your door when I've finished in the shower, so you're not hanging around waiting for me.'

'That's kind, but actually I'll be in the drawing room, seeing if I can find those photos you asked about,' she said. 'Can you come and give me a yell there?'

'Sure.'

She smiled her thanks at him, and again Gianni had that weird sensation as if his heart was doing a somersault. It unsettled him to the point where, once he'd scrubbed the dust from his skin and his hair, he switched the shower to cold to put some common sense back in his head.

This week was meant to be about work. He shouldn't let himself blur the boundaries—no matter how attractive he found Serafina Ardizzone.

CHAPTER FOUR

WHILE GIANNI WAS SHOWERING, Serafina went into the drawing room and checked the cupboard where all the photographs were kept. She fished out the earliest albums; hopefully there would be something in there showing the interiors of the palazzo.

For exterior views, she knew of a couple of paintings that included Ca' d'Ardizzone. If she was very lucky, there might also be something in Ruskin's early daguerreotypes of Venice; or perhaps there would be some old photographs in an internet archive somewhere. Still sitting on the floor, she flicked into her phone and did a quick search. The first two archives had nothing, but she found a whole series of colour photographs from the end of the nineteenth century, which she bookmarked to check later.

There was a rap on the door, and she looked up.

'Shower's all yours,' he said.

Gianni was fully dressed, in a casual shirt and chinos, but his hair was still damp and mussed from being towelled; and he looked so incredibly sexy that Serafina's pulse kicked up a notch.

'How did you get on with the photographs?' he asked.

'I've found our earliest family albums, but because I was checking for images on external archives I haven't started looking through them,' she said. 'Maybe we can do that together later.'

'Sounds good,' he said.

'See you in twenty minutes. Help yourself to coffee or something cold. Everything's in a sensible place in the kitchen,' she said, and left the albums on the table in the sitting room before heading for her own bathroom.

She showered swiftly, wrapped her hair in a towel while she changed into a pretty summer dress and added the lightest touch of make-up—mascara and lipstick—then plaited her still-damp hair to keep it out of the way. She added canvas shoes that were easy to walk in, and she was ready.

Gianni was sitting on the balcony, finishing a coffee and looking out at the view. His smile made her heart feel as if she'd done a backflip. 'How do you ever get anything done, living here?' he asked. 'I'd spend all my time looking at the view.'

'When I'm working from home, I use a timer, otherwise I'd do exactly that,' she said with a rueful smile. 'Let's go and grab something to eat.'

She wouldn't let him wash up his mug before they left the palazzo, simply locking up after them and ushering him out towards the Rialto bridge.

'You can see why people photograph it so much,' he said. 'It's beautiful. The proportions are perfect.'

She smiled. 'I knew you'd like it.'

'And this leads to the market?'

'Yes. I was planning to take you there early on Wednesday morning, when you can see it at its best.'

'Look at this,' he marvelled as they walked up the steps. 'You can actually see where people's hands have brushed against the bridge and polished it over the years.'

At that moment, his hand brushed against hers. And she had to fight against the instinct to let her fingers tangle with his. This wasn't a date. She wanted Gianni to fall in love with the palazzo and the city, not with her. Because love for a place was permanent and reliable, whereas falling in love with a person wasn't. She'd fallen for Tom the moment she'd met him at a glitzy party held at the museum where she worked, and clearly she'd confused the man with the characters he'd played on screen: they were noble and brave and unselfish, whereas Tom had turned out to be a liar and a selfish cheat. He'd made her feel loved and cherished, but it had all been an act. When she'd walked into his flat and discovered her fiancé mid-shag with an actress who'd hoped to get a part in his next movie, it had broken her faith in her judgement. How could she have fallen for someone who'd use his position to prey on others? For a man who let his libido rule everything? For a man who'd professed to love her and hadn't meant a single word?

OK, so Gianni didn't seem like that. But how could she trust herself to see him clearly, when her judgement in men was so bad?

So instead, she made herself tell Gianni stories about the bridge and the area, pointing out the church where her favourite painting in the city was, before leading him through an alleyway.

'I promised you real Venice,' she said. 'Would you prefer an Aperol spritz or wine?'

'I'll have whatever you're having,' he said.

She smiled, and swiftly ordered a plate of snacks to share and two glasses of dry white wine. 'It's an *ombra*,' she explained when the wine arrived.

'A shadow?' He looked mystified.

'Centuries ago, the wine seller in St Mark's Square used to move his cart around to keep his wine in the shadow of the bell tower. Or so the story goes; gradually "meeting in the shadow of the bell tower" started to mean meeting someone for a glass of wine. Over the years, that got shortened to "shadow", meaning the wine itself, or a spritz.' She raised her glass. *'Salute.'*

He chinked his glass against hers. *'Salute.'*

His eyes were really beautiful. Dark and soulful. Serafina found herself leaning slightly towards him, and it made her panic: she hadn't reacted to anyone like this before, not even Tom. She couldn't risk falling for this man the way she'd fallen for Tom, only to be let down again. How could she be sure that his integrity in his business life would be matched in his private life? To distract herself from how attractive she found him, she told Gianni about the food. 'I've ordered things you're unlikely to find outside Venice. This is *sarde in saor,* sardines in a sweet and sour sauce. It was originally invented for sailors, as a way of preserving fish for long journeys and also adding a bit of vitamin C through the onions to prevent scurvy—and obviously the spices in the sauce are a nod to the city's trading history.'

'Are you sure you studied history of art and not social history?' he asked.

'I was born in Venice. You grow up with the stories,' she said, but inwardly she was pleased by the compliment. 'And *baccalà mantecato:* creamed dried cod, whipped into a mousse and served on grilled polenta.' She smiled. 'And fried stuffed zucchini flowers, which I know you have in Rome, but I happen to like them. Plus white asparagus wrapped in pancetta, and a slightly different bruschetta.'

She had the tourist patter off to a fine art, Gianni thought. And he loved the way she lit up when she spoke about her city and its customs. 'This all looks great,' he said.

'It tastes even better than it looks,' she said.

Which made him think of her mouth and wonder how it would taste...

He wasn't looking for a relationship. But flirting—

something that he could stop before it went too far—might be fun.

'If you close your eyes,' he said, 'it heightens your other senses. How about I do that, and you test me on what I can actually taste?'

There was a tiny flush on her cheeks, and he guessed that she was thinking the same thing. Closed eyes. Tasting. *Kissing.*

Would she back away? Or would she flirt back?

Eventually she nodded. '*Sarde* first.'

He closed his eyes and concentrated on the flavour. 'The fish is good. The sauce: I can taste the sweetness of honey—' as sweet as he thought her mouth might be '—and sultanas and the sourness of vinegar. Pine nuts. Coriander?' He opened his eyes and kept his gaze fixed on hers.

'The only thing you missed was cloves,' she said. 'You're a foodie?'

'Sometimes. I'm guilty of not noticing what I eat, when I'm working,' he admitted. 'A sandwich is—well, just a sandwich.'

'Not in Venice, it isn't.' She smiled. 'I'll introduce you to *tramezzini* tomorrow.' She ate her share of the sardines. 'Which one do you want to try next?'

He picked the cod, which turned out to be garlicky and much nicer than he'd expected.

The bar was growing more crowded, and they had to stand closer together. By the time they'd reached the last of their *cichéti*, he'd ended up with a protective arm around her, and he was very aware of the warmth of her body against his.

'Last one,' she said.

'Bread, tomato and pesto—but there's something different. I can't work out what.' He opened his eyes. 'Tell me.'

'Nettles,' she said.

'Seriously?'

'Seriously.'

'Venice is full of surprises,' he said. One of them being her.

'There's still so much to see,' she said, and he had a feeling she wasn't only talking about her city.

'It's getting busy in here.' She glanced at her watch. 'Our table will be ready in half an hour. Let me show you round San Polo.'

Gianni would've been quite happy to stay where they were, close together, but he could see a tiny bit of wariness in her face. Not wanting to push her too far out of her comfort zone, he agreed. As they strolled through the now-closed fish market, she pointed out the carvings on the columns, the churches in the various squares, and buildings with grand facades.

The *osteria* she took him to was small and simply furnished, and the menu was chalked up on the board. Bruschetta for antipasti, risotto for the first course, shrimps with grilled vegetables and polenta for second course, and semifreddo for dessert. There were no choices; clearly the chef was cooking what had been picked up at the market that morning.

It turned out to be the best food he'd ever eaten.

'Told you,' she said. 'The best food is cooked simply and done well.'

'I knew the seafood would be good in Venice,' he said, 'but these shrimps are incredible.' Simply served with olive oil and a squeeze of lemon juice, they were sublime.

'This is Venice at her best,' Serafina said softly, and he had to agree.

The blue hour, the few minutes after the sun had set and when everything was hazy, was one of Serafina's favourite times. On the way back to the palazzo, Gianni seemed entranced by the changing colour of the water in the canal and the way the light reflected on it. Just as she'd hoped he would be.

'Let's have a glass of wine on the balcony,' she said when they got to the palazzo. 'I know I keep dragging you out there, but the view…' She spread her hands. 'It's my favourite in the whole world.'

'I think even if it was dull and raining, it'd be stunning,' he said. 'Every time I look out, something different catches my eye. A roof or a door or a window or a dome.'

'And it changes with the light,' she said.

'"The reflections from the lights in the buildings look like stars on the water. Heaven on earth",' he quoted when they took their wine outside and settled on the balcony. 'That's what you told me back in Rome.'

'And now you can see it for yourself,' she said.

He inclined his head in acknowledgement. 'At the time, I thought you were being a bit too poetic. But you were right. The lights reflected in the canal really do look like stars.'

It sounded as if he was starting to fall in love with her city.

Tomorrow, she'd show him buildings to take his breath away and make him fall in love even more deeply; but for now she wanted to get to know him better. Find out what made him tick.

Once they were settled on the balcony with a glass of wine, she turned to him. 'Did you always know you were going to be a builder?'

'Like my dad, you mean?' he asked. 'Probably. I used to follow him around all the time. I had a set of wooden building bricks, and he taught me how to make arches and bridges that would bear the weight of my toy cars or my little sister's toy horses. I pestered him to let me help him at work, until finally he gave in and let me help him mix mortar on a Saturday morning. I wasn't even ten when I built my first wall. He taught me to keep my tools clean and always be polite to the client.' He smiled. 'He was right. You catch more flies with honey than you do with vinegar.'

It was obvious that he'd loved his father deeply, the same way that she'd loved hers. Though Serafina hoped that Gianni had been spared her own experience of learning that the father she'd adored was very far from perfect. 'And you joined him in the family business?'

'There wasn't a family business when I was very young,' Gianni said. 'He worked for someone else. But then the construction market went through a bad patch, and he was made redundant. He was out of work for quite a while. He swore he'd never rely on someone else again and he started working for himself. He did little jobs and repairs at first, and then people asked him to build their extensions, and then houses—and then he was employing his own team, tendering for commercial projects.' He looked at her. 'He said you always knew when people had saved up for a job, because they treated you well and appreciated what you did, always made you a drink and let you use their toilets.'

Serafina had a nasty feeling where he was going with this. 'And rich people didn't?'

'If you're doing a job for someone rich, you soon learn to take your own hot drink with you and find out where the nearest public toilet is,' Gianni said dryly.

She flinched inwardly. Was that how her dad had treated anyone who'd done a job for them?

Then again, her family was no longer rich.

And the very first thing she'd done when Gianni had walked through her door was to offer him a hot drink.

Did he know how poor she was? She suspected he'd checked her out on the internet, just as she'd checked him out. Which meant he'd know about Tom. And a journalist

somewhere would no doubt have dug up at least some of
the dirt on her father.

'For the record,' he said softly, 'not everyone fits their
boxes.'

She wasn't even sure what her box was, any more. 'Were
you close to your dad?'

'I loved him very much,' he said. 'Though we didn't see
things the same way. We didn't agree on the way forward
for the business. He liked modern architecture and concrete, especially after building the town hall at Bardicello
changed our lives. Though I always hated that building.'
His eyes were shadowed when he added, 'And it broke him
when it went wrong. It's what caused his heart attack. The
one that killed him.'

Just as her own father's bad news had caused his heart
attack. She and Gianni weren't so far apart, then. Both had
loved their father dearly; both had lost him to a heart attack after bad news. 'I'm so sorry,' she said. 'It's hard when
you lose your dad. As if a bit of you has been broken off.'

He nodded. 'And it's the stuff you didn't have time to
sort out that hurts the most.'

'All the things you wish you'd said—the things you wish
they'd said,' she agreed.

His eyes darkened. 'And you have to come to terms
with the regrets, the way you feel you disappointed them,
because you can't change anything.'

He, too, felt like the child who'd let their parent down?
She reached across and squeezed his hand briefly. 'You're
the first person I've met who really understands that.'

'Same with you,' he said. 'I mean, my sister gets it, but
she didn't clash with our dad the way I did.' He looked at
her. 'Though I least I have her. There's just you.'

'Just me,' she said. 'But I'm getting there.' She hoped.
'What actually happened at Bardicello?' she asked. 'I
thought concrete was supposed to last for centuries—look

at all the undersea ruins divers have found. Or is that why they were ruins?'

'Concrete does last for centuries,' he said. 'And not only in ruins. I assume you know the Pantheon?'

'It's my second favourite building in Rome, after the Colosseum,' she said.

'My dad took me to see it when I was tiny, and he told me it was made of concrete. It's still the world's largest unreinforced concrete dome. And that,' he said, 'is the key word. *Unreinforced*. If the Romans had reinforced their dome with steel, the structure would've collapsed a long time ago.'

'Why is reinforcement a problem?'

'Steel's made from iron, so it rusts. A hundred years ago, everyone thought reinforced concrete was the answer to everything. Steel adds strength, meaning you can have thinner structures which look more attractive, plus they're cheaper and faster to build. Concrete's alkaline, which should inhibit rust, and steel and concrete have similar thermal expansion profiles so there's less chance of cracking.' He paused. 'That's the theory. The buildings were meant to last for a thousand years.'

'And in practice?'

'The steel corrodes. You can't see it deteriorating until it's too late and the concrete's damaged. It's part of the reason I don't use reinforced concrete: the corrosion and the fact that there's a huge carbon footprint.' He grimaced. 'Most of my fights with my dad were over concrete. It kind of got worse after my degree. He thinks—thought—architects were dreamers and pen-pushers.'

'Your degree's in architecture?' she asked.

'No. Building engineering. I knew how things worked; I wanted to know *why*,' he said. 'My dad didn't see the point of studying. He thought I should concentrate on the practical side of building instead of mooning about over the theory.'

It made Serafina realise how lucky she'd been; her family had been happy for her to study whatever she wanted, and had made no protest about her studying for her first degree in Rome rather than in Venice. Gianni had clearly had to fight to get what he wanted.

His next words confirmed it. 'We had endless rows over it, and I was pretty near to walking out of the family firm. In the end, Mamma and Flora—my sister—made us both see reason. We compromised that I'd do the degree alongside my job.'

He'd admitted earlier that there were clashes between himself and his dad, but this was ridiculous. 'Studying and working full-time in tandem? That's a pretty heavy workload.'

He shrugged. 'It was a compromise that meant we both got our own way. But it also meant I argued with him more. Whenever I tried to persuade him to take the company in a different direction, he said I was becoming a pen-pusher instead of a builder.'

That had clearly hurt; unable to stop herself, she squeezed his hand again. 'It's always good to look at things from another angle.'

'I just wish...'

'He'd understood you more? Confided in you? Let you shoulder some of the burden?' The things she'd wished for from her own father.

'Yeah. It's hard to separate the guilt, the anger and the regrets from the love. And I *miss* him,' he said. 'It's been two years; but, even now, there are things I see or hear that I'd love to share with him, and it hurts like hell that I can't.'

'Me, too,' she said. 'Are you close to your mum and your sister?'

He nodded. 'Flora and I run the company together. She

handles finance and the office, and I handle the construction side. We trust each other's judgement.'

Would she have to convince Flora, too, before Gianni could restore the palazzo? 'Sorry. If I'd realised, I would have invited your sister to visit, too. And your mother. I apologise.' She grimaced. 'I didn't do my research thoroughly enough.'

'You didn't need to invite them. Flora trusts my professional judgment. And finances aren't the only thing to influence whether we take on a project.' He gave her a rueful smile. 'Mamma and Flora have been nagging me for months to take time off. When I told them I was coming to Venice, they were all for it. Apparently I have to take a selfie outside a mask shop, on a gondola, and in a glass-blowing place and send them to them—as proof that I'm not spending all my time measuring things, taking samples and clambering about in attics or squinting at joinery.'

'I'll take the photos for you,' she said with a smile.

'You don't mind me changing your list of things you wanted to show me?'

'They were on it anyway,' she said. 'Though there's a lot more to Venice than masks, gondolas and glass.'

'Noted,' he said. 'But I need to see the touristy bits because I also want to buy a present for my niece.' He smiled. 'Sofia's four.'

'How about a teddy bear with a bridal veil made from Burano lace?' she suggested.

'Possibly yes to a teddy, but maybe not the lace. Our Sofia's not a girly girl,' Gianni said. 'According to Flora, that's her Tio Gi's fault, for teaching her how to make sand wet enough to build with and buying her a toy toolkit for her third birthday instead of a doll's house.' He grinned. 'But if you're going to build a sandcastle, you don't want it to fall down before you've even filled the second bucket of sand. And, the way I see it, if her passion is for building, it's my job as her uncle to support that. Girls can be builders as well as boys.'

Clearly Gianni was very much loved by his family, and Serafina felt a twinge of envy. Her father had loved her, but not enough to trust her with the true state of the family finances; and her mother was so wrapped up in doom and gloom that Serafina trod on eggshells around her most of the time. The only people to nag her about relaxing more was were her aunt Vittoria and her best friend.

'A teddy bear with a gondolier outfit, then,' she said.

'A girl gondolier?'

'Gondoliera,' Serafina said. 'Though there are less than a handful of them.'

'Why?' He looked at her. 'You told me you can drive a boat. Women can drive cars. Why can't a woman be a gondolier? Do you need extra strength to manoeuvre a gondola, or something?'

'I think it's mainly tradition,' Serafina said. 'Fathers tend to hand the business down to their sons. There's a course, and a potential gondolier has to pass exams on local knowledge as well as proving they can manoeuvre a boat. There are less than half a dozen new gondoliers each year.'

'There's still no reason why women can't be gondoliers.'

Serafina liked the way he saw things. If she was honest with herself, she liked *him.* 'I agree. A job appointment should be based on your ability and skills, and nothing else.'

'Absolutely.' He lifted his glass in a silent toast. 'What are the plans for tomorrow?'

'I know you need to do more assessment in the house, but I want to take you to San Marco for breakfast in the oldest coffee house in the world, and then visit the Palazzo Ducale. I think you'll enjoy it.' She'd enjoy it, too.

'I look forward to it,' he said.

She kept the rest of their conversation light until they'd finished the wine.

'I need to catch up on a few emails, if you don't mind.'

'Of course.'

'I'll see you in the morning, then,' he said.

'We'll leave at eight, if that's OK,' she said. 'Feel free to make yourself coffee if you're up earlier.'

'Thank you.' He smiled. 'Goodnight, Serafina. And thank you for a lovely dinner.'

CHAPTER FIVE

GIANNI SLEPT WELL, and was awake ridiculously early. He showered, dressed, and went into the kitchen to make himself a coffee. He thought about making one for Serafina, but he was wary of knocking on her bedroom door. They didn't know each other well enough for him to be comfortable doing that, plus strictly speaking she was a potential client. He'd seen too many examples of people mixing business with pleasure and ending up in a mess.

While he waited for the coffee machine to finish making his coffee, he looked at his surroundings.

This didn't feel like a home.

His mother's kitchen had Sofia's drawings held on to the fridge with magnets, a calendar with reminders and a grocery list. Flora's kitchen was the same. Even his own was decorated with drawings his niece had made for him, with *Ti amo Tio Gi* written across the top in her wobbly handwriting. This kitchen was like that of a show home, with nothing personal on view. No photographs, no postcards, no notes of any description.

No, not a show home, he amended. A museum.

And Contessa Serafina Ardizzone was the last of her line, held here like a pinned butterfly in a frame.

She clearly loved the palazzo, but to him it felt like a mausoleum. All the disapproving portraits, the dust-sheeted furniture, the rooms that had been shut off for decades. The mustiness.

She'd told him that her mother worried. He rather thought that the palazzo would make his own very capable, no-nonsense and bustling mother start to worry, too. The place was oppressive. A burden.

Would it squash Serafina beneath its weight?

He found the tin of sugar and added half a spoonful to his cup, set his mug on the kitchen table, then fetched the file he'd started yesterday and started working through the figures. He was making notes when Serafina walked into the kitchen.

'Good morning,' she said.

She was wearing jeans today, he noticed. Faded ones which hugged her curves, teamed with a strappy top and canvas shoes. She'd taken her hair out of the plait and it fell in waves to her shoulders; shockingly, he found himself wanting to twirl the ends round his fingers.

'Good morning,' he said. 'I did think about making you some coffee when I made mine, but I didn't want to…' He struggled to find the right word. 'Intrude.'

'Coffee is never an intrusion,' she said with a bright smile. 'Did you sleep well?'

'Yes, thanks,' he said, 'though it felt very odd this morning, not hearing any traffic noise.'

'After growing up here, it took me almost a month to get used to the traffic noise when I was a student in Rome— and it was always strange for a few days when I came home,' she said. 'Are you nearly ready for breakfast?'

'Sure.' He closed the file. 'I'll just put this away.'

'I'll grab something to cover my shoulders,' she said.

It was still early enough that not many people were about; Serafina led him through narrow alleyways and across bridges, stopping to point out buildings she thought he'd like along the way.

'We can come back to the shops later,' she said. 'There's a good toy shop nearby.'

'I'm in your hands,' he said.

Then she led him through an archway and stopped talking, letting him drink in his surroundings. He'd seen photographs, but he hadn't been prepared for the sheer grandeur of St Mark's Square in person. There had been little squares on the way here, but he'd got used to narrow passageways and canals everywhere, every bit of space used to the full. Even the gardens were vertical, here.

And now suddenly there was space.

A huge rectangular space, with buildings with elegant arcades and columns bounding three sides of it. On the fourth side, he recognised the iconic view of St Mark's Basilica with its onion-shaped domes, the glittering gold mosaics in its arches and the loggia with the four bronze horses. Soaring up into the sky was the slender brick *campanile* with its green triangular roof; and then he could see the Doge's Palace with its graceful arcades, gothic quatrefoils and pink and white walls.

'That's stunning,' he said, enthralled.

She looked pleased. 'Isn't it just? Up close, the carvings on the columns are fabulous. I hoped you'd like this.'

'I do. A lot,' he said. He itched to explore. More than that, he itched to explore—with her right by his side.

She shepherded him towards one of the cafés; tables were set up outside. 'Would you prefer to sit inside or out here?'

'Out here, if you don't mind,' he said. 'That's a view not to be missed.'

The waiter seated them and brought the menu; they ordered coffee and pastries, then sat back and enjoyed the sunshine, watching the square come to life. The coffee was good, as were the pastries.

'Shall I take a picture for your mother?' she asked.

'To prove to her that I'm idling, not working? Thanks, that'd be kind.' He flicked into his phone's camera app and handed it to her.

'Smile,' she directed, and took a snap before handing the phone back.

He took a snap of the basilica and sent both photos to his mother and his sister, along with a message.

Having breakfast in St Mark's Square. Nice view.

They didn't need to know that the nicer view was Serafina Ardizzone.

Within seconds the replies came back, telling him to relax and have fun. He laughed. 'I'm under strict orders to enjoy myself.' It was hard not to, when the sun was shining and he was having breakfast with someone he was starting to like very much indeed.

'Venetian architecture and Venetian food are excellent. Of course you're going to enjoy yourself,' she said.

He filled in the third excellent Venetian thing for himself: the company of a certain *contessa*.

'Is it a trick of the light, or are two of the columns actually a different colour?' he asked, gesturing to the Doge's Palace.

'Two of them are pink. It's where the Doge stood during official ceremonies, where death sentences were announced and where aristocrats were executed and their bodies displayed as a warning not to plot against the state,' she explained.

'Gory,' he said. 'But, given the gladiators and prisoners in the Colosseum, I can hardly claim the moral high ground.'

'That's my favourite building in Rome,' she said.

'Mine's the Pantheon,' he said. 'Because of the dome.' He smiled. 'I wrote a paper on domes as part of my degree. It was a good excuse to climb inside St Peter's in the Vatican and Brunelleschi's Duomo in Florence.' He looked speculatively at her. 'Can you climb inside any of the domes at St Mark's?'

'Unfortunately not,' she said, 'but the mosaics mean they're pretty spectacular viewing. We could go in for quick look before we go to the Doge's Palace, if you like.'

'That'd be good,' he said. 'Thank you.' He excused himself to go to the bathroom, intending to quietly pay for their breakfast, but discovered that she'd already beaten him to it.

'Thank you for breakfast,' he said when he returned to the square. 'I had planned to treat you.'

She smiled. 'My pleasure. You can buy me lunch. And we're having *tramezzini*.'

'Fine by me,' he said. 'Come and show me your favourite bit of the Basilica.'

'That's the mosaic floor,' she said promptly. 'It's like a sea—not only because of the colour, but because it's actually wavy.'

'Was it designed that way?' he asked, intrigued.

'No. The ground beneath has moved over the centuries. I know it's damage that probably ought to be fixed, but it adds to the atmosphere. Oh, and don't miss the peacock mosaic. That's glorious.'

Once they entered the Basilica, they observed the notices and walked round in silence; it felt more like a sultan's palace than a church, with the glittering gold tesserae covering every surface. Gianni looked up at the ceiling of the domes, the way the tiny windows shed little shafts of light onto the mosaics; they were stunning, but they didn't move him half as much as the woman beside him. In the silence, it felt as if it were just the two of them walking through the church, an oddly intimate feeling among the crowds. When she pointed out the wavy floor and the peacock, he could see the delight in her eyes, and he enjoyed the fact that his personal tour guide was sharing something of herself with him: as well as the fact that she seemed to share his love of architecture.

'Why the peacock in particular?' he asked when they were back in the square.

'I think it's the colours of the feathers,' she said. 'Those gorgeous shades of blue and green, with a hint of gold. Kind of like the different colours in the lagoon at different times of day. Family legend says one of my ancestors used to have a tame peacock and it used to strut around on the ground floor.'

Gianni had never seen a peacock outside a zoo, let alone known anyone who kept a peacock as a pet. It was another reminder that Serafina was from a very different world to his own. And yet, when they'd talked about their fathers, they'd been coming from the same place.

'Depending on what happens with the restoration,' she said, 'I might redecorate some of the bedrooms using those colours.'

'They'd look good in a bathroom, too,' he mused. 'A band of glass mosaic tiles. Especially if you decide to add en-suite bathrooms to the bedrooms you redecorate.'

'I like that idea. Glass, like the tesserae in the Basilica.' She smiled. 'Are you quite sure you're not really an architect at heart?'

'No. I'm a building engineer,' he said. 'I'm the one who turns the dream into a reality. And not all architects are good when it comes to reality. My dad loved Frank Lloyd Wright's designs, but those cantilevers...' He shook his head. 'For them to work, the builders had to do a bit of finessing.'

'You said you wrote a paper on domes. Have you ever built one?'

'No. Maybe one day,' he said.

'If you could build anything you like,' she asked, 'what would it be?'

Could he tell her? Would she think he was crazy? Or was she open-minded enough to get what had fascinated him, this last year?

'I've been reading interesting things about acoustics,' he said.

'So you'd want to build a concert hall with a dome?' she guessed.

'No. A living space,' he said. 'Because sounds in a building affect the way you feel and the way you react to things. Think of the way an echoing corridor can make you feel uncomfortable, or a bathroom can make your singing sound better.'

'And a dome can do that?'

'Curved ceilings can,' he said. 'Studies show that particular sound frequency affects brain activity. Build your room the right shape, and it can help you concentrate, or calm down.'

'You can actually do that with space?' she asked, looking intrigued. 'When I'm working on an exhibition, I look at the light in a space and the way people will move round it, so I can arrange the art to show it off properly. I never considered sound. Could the shape of the exhibition space and the way it reflects sound enhance people's enjoyment of what they're seeing?'

'That's maybe stretching it a little,' he said, 'but it's an interesting idea.'

'I'd love to see research on that. Can you give me any links to papers?' she asked. 'So I can see where it might fit in with my ground floor?'

She clearly didn't think he was weird or nerdy, the way Elena had when he'd talked about the theory of building. Serafina seemed to be as interested by the ideas as he was, and it made him feel warm inside. Gianni never felt in tune with someone else like this before; given that they were from such different backgrounds, she was the last person he'd expected to understand what made him tick. 'When we get back to the palazzo,' he promised. 'I have notes on my laptop. I'll show you what I've been reading.'

He loved the architecture of the entrance to the Doge's Palace, and he enjoyed listening to Serafina telling him about the art, including the largest oil painting in the world in the Chamber of the Great Council.

'Is Tintoretto your favourite artist?' he asked.

'No. That's either Carriera or Titian,' she said. 'I can take you to see my favourite painting in Venice, later in the week. If you want to, that is,' she added swiftly.

'As long as it's not modern art,' he said. 'I'm really not keen on the kind of blobs and squiggles anyone can make if they fling paint at a canvas.'

She laughed. 'As an art historian, I should perhaps stick up for abstract art. The point of it is about how it makes you feel, not how it looks.'

'Maybe I'm uncultured, because it irritates me,' he said. 'But this sort of stuff…' He gestured to the painting. 'There's so much in it. All the little details and meanings. You make it come to life when you tell me the stories behind it. I really like that.'

'It's a delight showing someone who actually gets it,' she said.

Maybe Serafina's ex—despite being an actor—hadn't shared her love of art and hadn't been interested enough to find out what mattered to her, Gianni thought. He was glad she hadn't actually married the man; he hated to think of her moving from a palazzo that threatened to stifle her to a lifestyle that would *definitely* have stifled her.

Gianni Leto was full of surprises, Serafina thought. She'd never considered how the acoustics of buildings could af-

fect people, apart from noise making it hard to concentrate.
He'd made her see space in a different way.

And he seemed to understand how she felt about art. Unlike Tom, he wasn't bored by the paintings and only interested in their monetary value. He'd asked questions about
little details that Tom would never have noticed; and he'd
approached the art in a very different way, asking about the
way canvases were constructed and how they were built to
fit a particular space. And he listened to her answers instead of glazing over. The intensity of his gaze made her
spine tingle with pleasure.

Once they'd finished at the Doge's Palace, she took him
shopping.

'Sofia will love this,' he said, picking up a teddy bear
dressed as a gondolier in one of the shops. 'And I'd like to
get some glass for my mother and my sister.'

'Wait until we go to Murano,' she advised. 'You can see
the glass being blown as well.'

'More photo opportunities to prove I'm being idle,' he
said with a grin. 'Bring it on.'

She enjoyed showing him her favourite places, including
the bookshop where the books were kept in a gondola and
bathtubs, meaning they'd float and not be damaged when
the high tides flooded the city. And she enjoyed introduc-
ing him to *tramezzini*, the overfilled triangular sandwiches
that were the city's speciality.

They spent most of the afternoon in a restored palazzo, so Gianni could see how Ca' d'Ardizzone might have
looked in the eighteenth century.

'This is the place I was hoping to visit,' he said, looking pleased. 'I know they're lower down here than in your
part of the city, but I want to see how they deal with the
water, close up.'

He took plenty of photographs on the ground floor, particularly of the water gate; and he spent time talking to the

curators, borrowing a tape measure from them. 'You asked me if you could do anything to help,' he reminded her, and waved the tape measure at her.

She'd never visited a museum and taken its measurements before. But she understood why he needed the information; watching him work and seeing the concentration on his face fascinated her.

She knew he was in charge of Leto Construction now, but would he still get a chance to do the hands-on work he clearly loved? The way he'd spoken about working with his dad when he was young: she could imagine him now, working on her house, his hands sure and capable. And from there it was an easy step to imagining his hands touching her, that little pleat of concentration on his brow as he traced the curve of her face with his fingertips, then drew the pad of his thumb across her lower lip...

Oh, for pity's sake. This wasn't about her and Gianni. It was about her palazzo.

But she couldn't push the thought out of her head. She was really aware of him and the way he moved; when his fingers accidentally brushed against hers it felt as if she'd been galvanised.

He'd clearly made a hit with the curators, because when he returned the tape measure they gave him the phone number of the restoration team's office.

'Thank you,' he said. When he and Serafina went up to the next floor, to see the restored rooms, he turned to her. 'Is there a good chocolate shop nearby? Because they've been very helpful and I want to show my appreciation.'

She liked the fact that he wasn't the kind of man who took someone for granted. He was sure of himself without being arrogant, and he listened as much as he talked. If her situation was different, she'd be tempted to start dating him.

But right now her life was a mess, and she couldn't let

herself be distracted from her goal. She needed to save the palazzo and save the museum.

'Yes. There's one round the corner,' she said.

'Good.' He studied each room in the restored rooms, taking detailed notes and photographs as they went round. 'I'm going to compare this to your palazzo, later,' he said. 'This has given me an excellent idea of how it would've looked. Though obviously there are differences: you have no frescoes or decorative plasterwork on the walls or ceilings. And the wallpaper here doesn't have damp stains or peel away.'

He certainly wasn't pulling his punches, she thought. She appreciated his honesty; but it didn't sound as if he was anywhere near falling in love with the house, the way she'd hoped he would. She obviously needed to work harder.

'Do you think the staining on the wallpaper is from rising damp, or from something else?' she asked.

'I need to look at the outside of the palazzo to check a few things,' he said, 'but at the moment I think on the ground floor the damp patches might be from a structural problem, and on the *piano nobile* it's a combination of water coming in through rotten parts in the windows and condensation caused by poor ventilation. I looked where the wall-coverings had come away and some of the plaster's crumbling, too. But it's all fixable.'

In one way, that was reassuring; in another, it wasn't, because he hadn't mentioned how much fixing the problems would cost in terms of time and money.

He glanced at his watch. 'We probably should get back. I'd like to finish assessing the second floor today.'

That was the whole reason why he was here; but Serafina had been enjoying showing him her city, and she felt oddly flat at the idea of stopping. And she was cross with herself when she realised that it wasn't so much showing off her beloved Venice that she'd enjoyed; it had been spending time with Gianni that had made her feel so bright. 'Of course,' she said politely.

He bought chocolates to thank the curators; they went all fluttery over him, and Serafina didn't want to examine quite why that irritated her. But she was definitely feeling a bit out of sorts by the time they got back to her palazzo.

'I want to look at the outside,' he said when she unlocked the back door. 'Can I get access to the outside of the building through the second water gate?'

'I'll need to find the key,' she said.

'I'll continue working on the second floor,' he said. 'Come and get me when you've found the key.'

Serafina found five possible keys, but none of them would turn in the lock. 'I can't even remember the last time we used that door. It's probably seized up. Should I get some oil for the lock?' she asked Gianni.

'No. That's a myth, because what happens is that dust sticks to the oil and makes it worse. You need a dry lubricant,' he said. It was obvious that she didn't have a clue what he meant, because he smiled and said, 'We'll improvise.' He took a multi-tool from his pocket and whittled a pencil, leaving a long length of lead, and shoved it into the lock.

'Isn't that going to make it worse?' she asked, when the lead broke.

'Not once I've jiggled the key enough to grind it up. Dry lubricant is powdered graphite, and that's what we'll end up with,' he said.

It took a few goes, but eventually he was able to open the lock and inspect the wall outside.

'And this is what I thought I'd find,' he said, showing her the crumbling brickwork; there were cracks in the mortar. 'When the levels rise in the canal, the water comes through here. Bricks are porous. Rainwater's fine, but salt water tends to cause damage, particularly when the water goes upwards. You might need to replace some of the bricks as well as the mortar. And you need lime mortar, because it's porous.'

'But you just said being porous is the problem.'

'Not for mortar, because it means the water evaporates easily. Modern cement mortar traps moisture; the water can't escape through the mortar, so it moves to the surface of the bricks. As soon as there's frost, the water freezes, and the brick starts crumbling. That's what you can see here.'

'I think I'm beginning to see why my ancestors ignored the problems,' she said with a sigh. 'It's a lot easier than worrying about whether you can fix them.'

'It's all fixable,' he said.

'But you're going to give me a huge list of things that need doing, aren't you?'

'That,' he said, 'was the whole point of my visit, was it not? You needed an honest list of what the problems are—and that includes the things you'll need a specialist to look at.'

'Specialist?' She felt her eyes widen.

'For the electrics and the plumbing, which I'm not qualified to assess,' he said. 'But, once you have your list, you can put the tasks in priority order and work through them.'

'Which I guess is a bit like setting up an exhibition,' she said.

'It's the same with any project. Rome wasn't built in a day, and neither was Venice. Or even this house. You have to break it down and do some critical path analysis,' he said. 'List what needs to be done, how long it takes, and what tasks impact on others. Nothing's impossible. You need to find the right way to approach it, and break it down into smaller steps where you can.'

He made it sound really easy. And she'd coordinated plenty of projects over the years. She knew she was good at organising.

So why did this suddenly feel horribly daunting?

Probably because it didn't only affect her, any more. It affected the future of the museum, too.

'I need coffee,' she muttered. And preferably her body-weight in *bussolai*.

He rested his hand briefly on her shoulder. 'Breathe,' he said softly. 'You're perfectly capable of sorting this out.'

She wasn't sure what warmed her most: his faith in her, or the touch of his hand through the cotton shirt she'd used as a jacket. Not many people in her life had really believed in her: her best friend, her aunt, her boss, and sometimes her dad. Support from such an unexpected source made her heart skip a beat. Gianni seemed to see who she was, beneath the title and the glitz: the person who did actually *do* the hard work, even when it was a struggle. And that bolstering really helped with the ridiculous wobble in her confidence.

'If I can be cheeky,' he added, 'I'd love a coffee, please. I need to do some measuring and take some photographs out here. I'll lock up when I'm done.'

In other words, he didn't want her under his feet, getting in the way and distracting him with a gazillion questions. And hadn't she promised not to micromanage? 'I'll sort the coffee,' she said.

Once she'd delivered a mug of coffee to him, she took the photograph albums and a pad of sticky notes out to the balcony, and went through them, marking the useful pages.

Eventually he came out to join her. 'OK. That's three floors and the outside done. Just the top floor and any attic space to go. I'm assuming you do have a ladder to get up to the attic space so I can check the inside of the roof?'

'Somewhere,' she said. She hadn't been up there for years. 'It's most probably in the room with the trap door. I'll check before we go out tonight. If I can't find it, I'll borrow one.' She bit her lip. 'How bad is it?'

'Apart from the things I've already told you about, you have a bit of a condensation problem. I'd recommend having an extractor fan fitted in the kitchen and bathrooms. In the meantime, keep the door closed and the window open to stop the condensation spreading to the rest of the palazzo, especially when you dry clothes,' he said. 'You've done the right thing, keeping the doors closed for the rooms you've shut off; but you also need to ventilate them properly. And you'll need to make a decision about the wall-covering: whether you conserve some of it on a feature wall, repair the damaged bits, or take it all down. Obviously that depends,' he said, 'on what you intend to do with the rooms.'

'Shabby chic isn't going to cut it,' she said with a sigh.

'You might be able to get away with the furniture,' he said. 'But definitely not the plumbing, the electrics or the bits that need repair. That wall-covering's going to have to come off anyway, so the electrics can be replaced—though that's also good for you, because you can make sure you have enough sockets.' He glanced at the albums on the table next to her. 'From those sticky notes, do I take it you found something?'

'I did.' She opened the first page. 'You wanted early photographs. These are my great-great-great-grandparents in the ballroom at the end of the eighteen-hundreds. My great-great-great-grandfather's here in the library, and here in the family gondola. And these are my great-great-great-grandparents in the drawing room giving dinner parties.' She gave him a wry smile. 'That might have been the real Canaletto, back then.' But had the partying been a way of dealing with all the tensions in her great-great-great-grandparents' marriage, just as her mother's doom-and-gloom and her father's gambling had been their way of dealing with it?

'This is fascinating,' he said sitting next to her and looking at the albums with her. 'This would be before electricity was installed—and definitely before your heating was put in.'

'I'm guessing the radiators need updating. I have to bleed them a lot,' she said.

'I'm not surprised. Your plumbing needs work, too.'

'Is *anything* about the house OK?' she asked, wincing inwardly as she heard the plaintiveness in her tone.

She sounded so forlorn. Gianni wanted to wrap his arms round her and tell her everything was going to be all right—that he'd make it all right—but how could he? It wasn't his place to hold her. But he could at least reassure her from a professional point of view. 'The structure of the palazzo is reasonable, given its age,' he said. 'Yes, there are problems, but they can be fixed. Though now is your chance to be radical. to make it the home you want it to be.'

'What would you do with it, if it was yours?' she asked.

'To make it pay for itself and be used? I'd turn the top two floors into apartments,' he said, 'and rent them out; then it would be full of people instead of silence. I'd remodel this floor for personal use, with good en-suite bathrooms and decent heating, add extra plug sockets during the rewiring so you have enough to suit a modern lifestyle, and partition some of the rooms to maximise their use. I'd definitely get rid of the wall-covering.' He saw her flinch, and said gently, 'Donate it to a museum, because it's not doing you any favours here. It's damaged, and reproducing what you have here is going to be costly and take a lot of time. If it was mine, I'd replaster the walls and add a bit of plaster detail—doing it the same way they would've done at the time the palazzo was built—and then paint it.'

She looked aghast. 'That means you'd lose the history.'

'A compromise. I'd bring it back to life. Make it a proper home.' And he could see it: a comfortable, bright space. Though he wasn't entirely sure whether the brightness was because of the palazzo itself or because of the woman who stood before him. He spread his hands. 'You did ask. If you want to live in a museum on all four floors, sticking with the choices of the people who came before you, that's your call. But for me a home reflects the people who live in it. It's where they can be themselves.'

She didn't look convinced.

Well, he'd started now. He might as well push it a bit more. 'Your library. Your office. Do you ever sit in those big leather chairs and read or listen to music?'

'No,' she admitted.

'Then maybe,' he said, 'you need to go through the furniture. Sell the stuff you don't use or don't love, or donate it to a museum, and bring in stuff that works for you. Being the custodian of a place doesn't mean you can't ever change things. It means you can add your own layer to the history.'

She looked thoughtful. 'I'd never considered that.'

'It's something to add in to your renovation plans,' he said. 'Spend a while thinking about what *you* want.'

'Maybe.' She glanced at her watch. 'It's too late to climb the stairs today, but I'd like to show you a tower on the way to dinner.'

'Dinner which I'm paying for,' he said swiftly, 'given that you bought me dinner last night.'

'You're my guest. We'll argue later,' she said.

They wouldn't argue, because Gianni knew a quick way to circumvent any disputes. Though he appreciated the fact that, unlike his ex, Serafina didn't expect him to pick up all the bills simply because he was rich. 'I need to dust off and change,' he said. 'I'll be quick.'

'Me, too,' she said.

When he emerged from his room, she was wearing another of those pretty, floaty summer dresses. He wondered if she had any idea how stunning she was. Though it wasn't only her looks that attracted him. It was Serafina herself: her energy, her brightness.

She took him through a maze of alleyways. 'This is Scala Contarini del Bovolo. It's at its best in the evening light.'

'I can see why they called it a snail shell, having the spiral visible on the outside as well as the inside,' he said. 'I like it very much.'

'Maybe we can climb it later in the week,' she said. 'It's unusual in being one of the high places in Venice where you can't actually see any water from the top.'

'Though the tower isn't quite as tall as it looks,' he said.

She looked surprised. 'How do you mean?'

'They're using an architectural trick,' he said. 'Every layer you go up, the loggias decrease in size.'

'I've lived in Venice all my life—apart from my three years in Rome—and I never realised that,' she said.

'Just as I'm sure you could show me things in Rome I didn't know about,' he said with a smile.

When she took him to another *osteria,* not far from St Mark's Square, Gianni took the precaution of handing his credit card over at the beginning of the evening, to make quite sure he picked up the bill without having to argue with her.

They ate scallops first, served with good bread to mop up the garlicky juices, and a bone-dry white wine. He enjoyed the meal, but even more he enjoyed Serafina's company. For someone who'd lived a public life, as the former girlfriend of a movie star, he thought she was a very private person, giving little away about herself. The nearest she'd come to opening up was where art or her house were concerned.

She was talking about her balcony when she said, 'It's a good place to paint.' And then she looked shocked, as if she hadn't meant to let that slip out.

'You're an artist as well as an art historian?' he asked, intrigued.

'Not really. I paint just for me. For fun.'

'What sort of thing do you paint? People, animals, landscapes?' Then he remembered her comments about modern art. 'Or is it the sort of abstract stuff I insulted?'

She smiled, then. 'No, it's realist rather than abstract—and I paint Venice. The canal. Water and sky and light.' She wrinkled her nose. 'And my house. Little details. I did a pen and ink sketch that Alessia thinks would make a perfect label.'

'Label?'

'She has this mad idea that I should turn the house into a gin palazzo and use the downstairs as a warehouse and distillery.'

'A gin palazzo.' He grinned. 'Oh, I love that. It's inspired.'

'It's not practical. You can't just buy a still and make some gin. You have to work out your recipe and test the botanicals, trial and error, until you get the right blend. Plus commercial production means expensive equipment and employing a good distiller.'

'It sounds as if you've looked into it.'

'Not quite. Alessia wrote a feature on gin, and she made me go with her to help her taste-test stuff,' she explained.

He smiled. 'Tough job, but someone had to do it?'

She smiled back. 'Exactly. When I was saying that I need the house to pay its way, she came up with the idea of making craft gin.'

'It might be worth costing it out properly,' he said. 'On the upside, you wouldn't have to worry about guests being upset by the mess and noise of the restoration of the other floors. And it might make you more money than the museum can pay you.'

'I thought about it,' she said. 'But the ground floor is definitely going to be an exhibition space.'

'Why?'

She shook her head. 'I can't discuss that.'

'Can't or won't?'

'Can't.' She raked her hand through her hair. 'Right now, all I can tell you is that I have a suitable space and I know an organisation that could use it.'

He appreciated the fact that she wouldn't break a confidence. And he wasn't going to push her on it. Instead, he took the conversation back to something light, talking about movies and Rome, things they had in common. She persuaded him to try the tiramisu, which she said was the best in the city. And they lingered over coffee, just talking.

It wasn't a proper date, but in a weird way it felt like one. Serafina was the first woman since Elena had dumped him to make him actually want a relationship. He knew he'd used work as an excuse, claiming he was too busy to date. It was true; but he also hadn't wanted to risk dating someone, only to find that again he'd picked someone who valued him for his bank balance and didn't see him for who he really was.

He was beginning to think that maybe Serafina was different. Like him, she was shouldering responsibilities; like him, she was struggling to cope with the loss of a parent. And, like him, she kept herself at a slight distance from other people, not quite trusting relationships.

Maybe they could help each other move past the things that held them back.

If he was prepared to take the risk, would she? Or was he deluding himself?

On the way back to palazzo, they walked through St Mark's Square again. It was very different at night, and brighter than he'd expected. Moonlight spilled over the stone paving; there was a lantern in every archway on every floor of the elegant buildings, making it seem magical. The front of the Basilica, too, was lit up, and the golden mosaics sparkled.

There were musicians playing outside one of the cafés—not the endless Vivaldi that Gianni had been expecting, but a show tune he recognised. 'Somewhere' from *West Side Story*: a film he knew well, because it was one of his mother's favourites.

Although there weren't that many people around, a few couples were dancing in the square.

On impulse, he held out his hand to her. 'Dance with me?'

She stared at him as if he'd grown two heads. 'Dance?'

'Sorry. Stupid tourist idea,' he muttered.

'It's not a stupid idea at all. It's been a while since I've danced,' she said.

And the last time she'd danced, he thought, had been with a movie star. How could a mere builder begin to compare—even if he did happen to be the head of a large firm? Plus he couldn't even remember the last time he'd danced.

'Thank you for asking. Yes, I'll dance with you,' she said, and took a step towards him.

Gianni was glad he'd asked her, but regretted it at the same time: because being this close to her really made him aware of her. The way she felt in his arms, the sweet floral scent she wore, the warmth and softness of her skin.

Dancing together for the first time should've been slightly awkward; weirdly, it felt as if they'd done this before. He drew her closer and she rested her cheek against his shoulder When he closed his eyes, he felt as if it could have been only the two of them in the whole wide world. Nothing but them and the music and the moonlight.

Her arms tightened round him.

Somehow they both moved, and they were cheek to cheek.

Another tiny shift, and the corners of their mouths were touching.

He couldn't resist brushing his mouth against hers: a light, sweet touch, exploring rather than demanding. When she kissed him back, tentative and shy, it felt as if fireworks were going off in his head: starbursts of gold and silver.

The next thing he knew, they were kissing properly.

In public.

In the middle of an enormous square with complete strangers around them.

This was something he would normally never do; but something about her made him want this. And more. He wanted to carry her back to her palazzo, carry her up the stairs to his bed, make that mausoleum echo with laughter and joy.

He broke the kiss and stared at her.

Her eyes were huge, mingled desire and joy and worry skittering over her expression. And he could guess why. He'd kissed her. OK, she'd kissed him back, but he'd been the one to cross the line—and he shouldn't have pushed her.

'I'm sorry,' he said, taking a step back. 'I shouldn't...' He shook his head. 'It's no excuse, but this...' He gestured to the square. And the little orchestra seemed to be reading his mind, because now they were playing a jazz tune his grandmother loved: 'You and the Night and the Music'.

He'd never understood that before.

He did now.

'You and the night and the music,' he said helplessly.

'It...we both made a mistake,' she said.

And there were shadows in his eyes that broke his heart. Shadows he rather thought her ex might have put there, because although he hadn't known her for long he was pretty sure she wasn't the sort to cause the problems in a relationship.

'We'll...' She swallowed hard. 'We'll pretend it didn't happen.'

Pretend he hadn't seen fireworks in his head when she'd kissed him back?

Then again, maybe she was right to call a halt. He hadn't been good enough for Elena's family, so how could he possibly be good enough for a *contessa* whose family stretched back centuries and who had the gilt-framed portraits marching up her staircase to prove it? He'd be setting himself up for a fall—again—if he kept up this stupid idea about dating Serafina. Hadn't he learned his lesson that posh women were trouble?

'Of course,' he said.

They walked back to the palazzo in silence. He didn't have a clue what to say; in the end he said nothing, afraid of making the tension between them worse.

The city was quiet apart from the swish of the waves and the gondolas bobbing at their stands. For a moment, Gianni longed for Rome—noisy, uncomplicated Rome with all the cars rushing round. But if he wasn't here, he wouldn't be with Serafina. And it unsettled him that he wanted to be with her more than he wanted to be at home. How had that happened?

'I need to check my emails and sort out some things for work,' he said as she unlocked the back door. It wasn't strictly true, but it was easier to give a polite fib.

'Sure. See you tomorrow,' she said. 'I hope you don't mind leaving the house at seven? I've planned to take you to the Rialto, and we can have breakfast out.'

'See you tomorrow,' he said. 'Is it OK if I grab a glass of water?'

'Please, treat the house as your home,' she said. 'If you want a drink or a snack, raid the fridge or the larder.'

The stilted conversation felt all wrong, after the way she'd felt in his arms, but he couldn't for the life of him think how to fix this, how to tell her about the weird thoughts spinning through his head. Instead, he took refuge in small talk. 'Thank you. Can I get you anything?'

'No, I'm fine, thanks,' she said, and gave him a super-bright smile.

Cursing himself for being an idiot, Gianni sorted out a glass of water, then went to his room and checked his emails. His team had kept him briefed on what was going on. Some of the project managers had taken decisions without checking with him first, and were clearly enjoying their chance to shine. Good. That was the direction he'd wanted to take the firm in. He wrote supportive replies, then tried to concentrate on working on the report for the palazzo; but he couldn't get Serafina out of his head. Serafina and the shadows in her eyes. Serafina, who'd made the world vanish with a kiss.

He needed to work out what the barriers were between them—and how he could overcome them.

Serafina went to the library, cross with herself. She should at the very least have offered Gianni somewhere to work. There was a dressing table in his room with a stool, but that wasn't good enough for working. Though she could hardly go and knock on his door right now, could she?

The door to his bedroom.

Her mouth tingled.

No.

Focus, she told herself fiercely. Tomorrow morning, she'd offer him the sitting room or the kitchen table or her library, whichever he'd like most.

She checked her emails. One from Alessia in Florence, where she was interviewing a subject and taking a couple of days out, asking her how things were. One from her aunt, attaching a rare photograph of her mother actually smiling—and how much that lightened Serafina's heart. One from Maddalena, asking how it was going with her assessor and with the new exhibition catalogue, and if there was anything she could do.

She started to reply, but all the words felt jumbled in her head. That kiss had thrown her. It was the first time anyone had kissed her like that in the last year.

And the way Gianni made her feel was like nothing she'd ever experienced before. Dancing with him, she'd felt as if she was floating in the square, and the kiss had increased the floatiness. It had been as if they were dancing under a sky of shooting stars.

When he'd stopped kissing her, she'd realised she was risking making a fool of herself.

She couldn't afford to let anything get in the way of fixing the palazzo and saving the museum. She needed to get things back on an even keel between herself and Gianni, which meant that the attraction she felt towards him would definitely have to be squashed.

Then she looked down at the lined pad next to her laptop and discovered she'd sketched him, without even realising that she'd taken the lid off the gel pen.

Oh, for pity's sake.

This had to stop.

She couldn't afford to take a risk. Relationships didn't work out, in her family. She'd thought she was the one who'd break the cycle, but she'd fallen for a cheat and a liar. Gianni had integrity; but there was simply too much at stake. If she started seeing him and it went wrong, it would mean he wouldn't help her with the palazzo. And that would be disastrous for the museum as well as for the palazzo.

So she'd just have to keep her feelings under control and treat this whole thing as business.

CHAPTER SIX

GIANNI WOKE TO a silent house, turned over in the unfamiliar bed and thought of Serafina.

How was he going to face her this morning?

He knew he shouldn't have kissed her.

Though she *had* kissed him back.

She'd said it was a mistake and they'd agreed it shouldn't have happened; but that had been last night. Today, he still felt out of sorts and fidgety. How would she be with him today? Bright and breezy? Or shy and awkward?

He could ask the same question of himself. How, just how, was he going to face her?

Given how badly things had ended with Elena, he knew this could end up in a huge mess, too. Maybe he should simply tell her he was sorry but he couldn't help her.

Then again, he'd started to fall in love with the palazzo. The idea of turning it from this dust-sheeted, damp and silent place into one that was full of life and people was all too tempting.

And it meant he'd be spending more time with Serafina. Getting to know her. Letting her get to know him. And maybe, just maybe, that mistake they'd made tonight would change into something else. Something they both wanted.

He couldn't hear any sounds of her moving about, so he judged it would be safe to make himself a coffee. Caffeinated-up, he might have a better idea of how to approach her this morning. After he'd showered, he made himself a mug of instant coffee and went to sit on the balcony: but when he opened the doors he discovered that she was already there, with an empty coffee mug and a sketch pad in front of her. Meaning that she must have been up much earlier than he had.

She looked at him, her dark eyes huge.

This was awkwardness piling upon awkwardness.

'Good morning. About last n—' he began.

At exactly the same time she said, 'Good morning. About last night.'

He stopped. 'Um—you first?'

'I was going to say the same thing,' she said, colour slashing across her cheekbones.

OK. He'd be brave. 'I'm sorry. I crossed a line. I don't want things to be awkward.'

'Me, too,' she said. 'To all of it.'

'Let's put it down to…'

'Propinquity?' she suggested.

'I was going to say the atmosphere.'

'That, too. The music. And Venice at night is…' She spread her hands.

Enchanted. Romantic. A place that could make him forget who he was. 'Yeah.'

'Is that coffee cold enough to chug down?' she asked.

'It will be if I add some cold water. Why?'

'As you're up, we might as well hit the Rialto,' she said. 'I'll buy the makings of dinner at the market. We can grab breakfast at a *pasticceria*. And I think the market right now would be a good photo for your mum.'

'I'll go fix my coffee,' he said.

He added enough cold water to be able to drink it straight down, then let her lead the way to the Rialto.

The market was nothing like the quiet courtyards they'd

walked through on Monday. In the early morning, it was full of people. Stallholders in the fish market were using watering cans to water their wares, keeping the fish cool and making them glisten invitingly in the light: everything from soft-shelled crabs to slices of fresh tuna, lobsters to sole. Fishermen were bringing their catch straight from their boats to the tables, to be prepared for customers. Fruit and vegetables were piled high on the stalls in the other part of the market, everything from radicchio to artichokes to tiny wild strawberries, velvet-skinned peaches and fresh herbs. People were talking, bargaining, laughing; old ladies with their shopping trolleys and old men were catching up with their friends, all mingled together with young parents with babies in slings, students, and clearly local people picking up the makings of dinner before going to work.

It was noisy and chaotic, and Gianni loved it. 'It reminds me of the Campo de' Fiori.'

'Venice is *way* better than Rome,' she retorted.

'In your dreams,' he scoffed. 'It was the Roman Empire that ruled the world, not the Venetian one.'

And, just like that, the awkwardness between them had gone, replaced by the camaraderie they'd built before that kiss. He enjoyed watching her haggle for fish, picking out choice pieces. 'I'm cooking fish stew for dinner tonight,' she told him. 'Oh, wait—here's a good spot for a photo for your mum.'

He handed his phone to her, and she took a photograph of him with one of the fish stalls in the background.

'Thanks,' he said.

'Right. I need fennel and thyme,' she said.

Once they'd bought everything on her list—a list, he noticed, that was entirely in her head—they headed over to one of the small bars surrounding the market, ordering coffee and pastries which they ate standing at the bar.

'We'll drop this lot off before we go exploring,' she said.

She showed him a couple of statues on the way; and then, to his surprise, instead of going via the bridge, she took him to the edge of the canal to join a queue.

'We'll cross by *traghetto*,' she said. 'It's a bit like a large gondola, except you stand up for the crossing.'

He eyed the water. 'Stand up?' Was that even safe? Weren't you supposed to sit down on a boat?

And then he could see for himself: a boat was coming towards the quay, with a man standing at each end with large paddles to row the craft across the canal, and the dozen or so people in the centre were all standing up.

Once the passengers had disembarked, the people in their queue began to board.

'Is this what it's like, being in a gondola?' he asked quietly.

'Sort of. Actually, even though this is a touristy thing, I don't think I'm going to take a photo of this for your mum, because you look a bit worried,' she said.

'I'm not used to travelling on the water,' he said. 'Standing up feels…' He wrinkled his nose. 'I guess the first time you went on the Metro in Rome it must've felt as weird for you as this does for me.'

She laughed. 'Just a bit. I'm not used to the underground. We don't have catacombs in Venice, and there aren't even many crypts.'

'Because they flood?' he guessed.

'Exactly.'

Gianni was glad that she chatted to him all the way across the river, and even more glad when they were able to disembark. He hadn't enjoyed the way the gondola had felt as if it were bouncing on the surface of the canal whenever a larger craft went past.

'I had planned a proper gondola trip this evening,' she said. 'Will you be OK, or would you rather skip it?'

'If we're sitting down, I'll be fine,' he said. 'It was only when other boats passed us and made the *traghetto* bob up and down. I could imagine losing my balance, knocking into the other passengers like a domino and making them fall overboard.'

She laughed. 'You were perfectly safe. You're more likely to fall when you're climbing up inside a dome or on a roof somewhere.'

He wasn't convinced but said politely, 'I guess.'

Once Serafina had bought bread from the little bakery round the corner from the palazzo and put the fish in the fridge, she took Gianni out to explore Dorsoduro.

'It's the highest part of the city,' she told him. 'It's very pretty. And there's a shop I think you'll like—at least, your mum will,' she added with a smile.

'No lecture about Venice being more than just masks?' he teased.

'Because then you'll start telling me there's more to Rome than the Colosseum,' she teased back.

When they rounded a corner, a figure wearing a plague doctor mask loomed by the shop doorway.

'Masks. Another to tick off my list,' he said. He duly posed next to the figure so she could take a snap for his mother.

Then she made the mistake of catching his gaze.

She could imagine being at a masked ball with him. Dancing, the way they'd danced in the square last night. And kissing...

Oh, help.

Now her brain was scrambled.

What had she been talking about?

Masks. They were at a mask shop. Of course she was talking about masks. 'I think your mother's going to protest if you send her a snap of you posing outside a shop, but not one of you wearing a mask.'

'Let's go and try one on,' he said.

He put on a Harlequin mask with its distinctive diamond pattern in red and black and gold; and he looked breathtakingly handsome. At a ball, he'd definitely sweep her off her feet. They'd agreed to pretend last night never happened, but she couldn't put it out of her head.

The way she'd felt when he'd kissed her.

That feeling of floating on air, dissolving into a spiral of desire.

'Now you,' he said.

'Um…'

'Can I pick for you?' he asked.

She nodded and he chose a Columbina mask in deep blue, adorned with a peacock feather.

'It suits you,' he said, and traced her jawline with the tip of his finger. She felt her lips part, inviting him closer.

This was crazy.

It could never work between them. They lived miles apart, they came from different worlds, and they wanted different things. Plus she was an Ardizzone, doomed by an ancient curse that had never let any of her family have a happy relationship.

'Let me take a photo for your mother,' she said, hoping that he wouldn't hear the crack in her voice.

When she'd taken the snap, he said, 'And now one for yours. Smile.'

She let him take the photograph, because it was easier than explaining why she could never send a picture like that to her mother. Though maybe her aunt or Alessia might like it.

'Are all the masks tied by ribbons?' he asked.

'It's more practical,' she said. 'You can buy ones with a baton so you can hold the mask up to your face—or there's the Moretta mask, traditionally worn by women.' She gestured to the plain black oval face masks. 'They don't quite hide your face; but you hold them in place by biting a button, meaning your voice can't give away your identity.'

'That,' he said, 'sounds utterly ridiculous. You couldn't eat, you couldn't drink, and what if you had a sneezing fit?'

'Agreed. They weren't practical.'

Unlike a certain building engineer.

He bought a Columbina mask with bright red feathers for his niece, and she continued showing him round Dorsoduro.

'I read this was the academic area of Venice,' he said. 'Your museum's near here, isn't it?'

'Yes, but it's not open right now,' she said swiftly. Although part of her wanted to take him to see it, part of her was antsy. There was a fair bit of the kind of modern art she knew he didn't like at the museum; she wanted him only to see things about Venice he'd definitely love rather than something that might make him feel lukewarm about the palazzo restoration. She distracted him from asking her when it would be open by taking him to see a workshop where they repaired gondolas. Thankfully he was interested enough in the construction to drop the subject.

Why was Serafina so keen to keep him away from the museum where she worked? Gianni wondered. Unless *that* was the museum that needed the space at her palazzo. But he had a feeling that, if he asked, she'd stonewall him.

Later that afternoon, back at the palazzo, he assessed the rest of the top floor and wrote up his notes while she made a fish stew.

'How was it?' she asked when he came back into the kitchen.

Her eyes were full of hope. He hated to wreck that; yet, at the same time, he couldn't lie. 'We've got the same window problem, with damp in the plaster where the woodwork has rotted and let water in. And two of the rooms have water damage to the ceiling; either the guttering's failed or there's a problem with your roof.'

He could see her shoulders hunching, absorbing yet another blow, and it made him feel horrible. 'I need to check the attic.'

She nodded. 'I'm calling in a favour from a friend. We can pick up the ladder tomorrow.'

'OK,' he said. And then, because he wanted to stop her worrying about what he might find, he said, 'Something smells amazing.'

'Thank you. I'm going to start the polenta now. Half an hour until dinner OK with you?'

'Fine,' he said. 'I'm a bit…um…dusty. Do you need a hand with anything, or do you mind if I take a shower?'

'It's fine,' she said. 'I'll see you for dinner.'

The stew and polenta tasted as good as they smelled. But he couldn't take his eyes off her.

When they'd danced together, she'd kissed him back. They were both single. They were from different worlds, yes, but he didn't think she'd be bothered about his poor background; there was none of the snobbery that he'd encountered from Elena's family. He couldn't think of one good reason why they couldn't see where this took them.

But he knew she'd been hurt. Of course she'd be wary. How was he going to persuade her to take a chance on him? Then again, part of him was scared to take a chance on her. He didn't have a clue how to pick his way through the minefield.

She kept the conversation light and sparkly, telling him snippets of the history of Venice and gondolas: all stuff he found interesting. But he was aware that she was wearing a mask: that she was acting the role of hostess.

No, that wasn't fair. She was a good hostess. She was genuinely making him welcome in her home. But she was definitely hiding herself. He couldn't help wondering why—and wondering exactly what she was hiding.

'And now you'll get to see the Grand Canal properly,' she said. 'By gondola.'

'We'll have the guy in a straw boater and stripy jumper singing "O Sole Mio"?' he asked.

'Apart from the fact that's a Neapolitan song, not a Venetian one, the gondoliers concentrate on rowing,' she said. 'Besides, you said you weren't keen on classical music, and the *bacarolles* sung on a gondola are mostly inspired by opera.'

That was true: but part of him felt disappointed. A gondola ride at sunset without someone singing? It didn't feel right.

As if his disappointment showed on his face, she said, 'Actually, I did hire someone to serenade us because I wanted you to have the—well, "Venetian" experience.' She added quote marks with her fingers.

'Even if it means songs from Naples?' he teased.

'Even if.'

She took him down to a gondola stand and introduced him to Franco, their gondolier, and Roberto, who was already seated in the gondola and holding a guitar.

He settled back against the surprisingly comfortable seat next to Serafina, and Franco rowed them along the canal.

'Shall I get *that* one over with, first?' Roberto asked with a grin, and proceeded to sing 'O Sole Mio'; tourists stood watching them on the banks, applauding as they went past.

Serafina took a few seconds of video footage on her phone, of both Roberto and Gianni. 'So your mum knows you did this the traditional way,' she said. 'I'll send it to you later.'

Gianni smiled in acknowledgement. 'Thanks.'

Franco rowed them under the Bridge of Sighs, then took them through a narrow maze of canals. As the light began to fade, Roberto switched to playing a mixture of ballads and short classical pieces Gianni didn't recognise but discovered he actually liked. He found himself relaxing, enjoying the views and the music and the changing colours in the sky.

When they went round a narrow corner, there was a slight jolt and somehow Gianni ended up with his arm round Serafina, steadying her on the seat.

Their eyes met, and colour stole into her face. He could feel his own cheeks heating, too.

He wanted her. Really, really wanted her. Part of him remembered how it had felt to dance with her in St Mark's Square and wanted to draw her closer; but part of him panicked, remembering how much he'd hurt after Elena had dumped him.

Panic won, and he withdrew his arm. 'Safer than being on a roof, right?' he said dryly.

But this wasn't a physical danger, one he knew how to minimise. It was an emotional danger, and he didn't know where to start guarding himself against that. Particularly when Franco steered them back onto the Grand Canal and they had a wonderful view of the sun setting as they sailed under the Rialto, the colours in the sky turning the turquoise waters pink, too.

How easy it would be to kiss her again.

To fall in love with her.

And then would he get his heart broken all over again?

Back at the gondola stand, they said goodbye to Franco and Roberto.

'Thank you,' he said politely to Serafina. 'That was a real treat.'

'You're very welcome. I'm glad you enjoyed it,' she said.

He was tempted to ask her to have a drink with him. To walk hand in hand with him under the darkening skies, watching the lights turn to stars in the canal. To kiss him in the moonlight.

But then things would start to get complicated.

'I'm sorry to be rude,' he said, 'but I need to deal with a couple of things for work.' It wasn't strictly true—they were things that could wait until he was back in Rome next week—and he berated himself for being cowardly enough to use work as an excuse. But with work he knew where he was; with Serafina, his head was all over the place.

'Of course. And I have an exhibition catalogue to finish writing,' she said politely, and took him back to the palazzo. 'You're very welcome to use the sitting room or the library, if you need space to work.'

'Thanks, but it's fine,' he said, and shut himself away in his room.

Two days.

Serafina had two days left to make him fall in love with Venice and the palazzo.

Tonight, when the gondola had jolted her into his arms, she'd wondered. Surely the sunset and the gorgeous music and the stunning views would do it?

But she'd seen the precise moment he'd shuttered his feelings away.

Clearly someone had hurt him. Badly. Though she could hardly ask him what had happened. It was none of her business and nothing to do with working on the palazzo.

Plus her own attempts at compartmentalising her feelings weren't working. The more time she spent with him, the more she liked him. The more attractive she found him. The more she wanted to take a risk with him.

And to think this had all started with her idea of offering him a marriage of convenience. She knew now that definitely wasn't going to work. But was there a way of them seeing how things went between them, without either of them getting hurt?

The following morning, she took him to Murano to see glass being blown, and to take a photo of him for his mother. In the shop, he bought a stunning bowl for his sister and a vase for his mother. 'I can't resist this,' he said, picking up a starfish-shaped necklace in shades of teal and aqua. 'Sofia will love it, along with her gondolier teddy and her mask.'

'The glass here is pretty amazing,' she said. 'And some of the furnaces date back to medieval times.'

Once they'd had a look round the museum, she took him to the Basilica of St Mary and St Donatus. 'You have to see the dragon bones,' she said.

'Dragon bones?' he repeated, raising an eyebrow.

'The story goes back to the twelfth century. St Donatus slew a dragon who'd poisoned a well, and allegedly these are the bones of the dragon. One of the doges stole them and brought them here. They're probably the ribs of a whale,' she admitted with a smile, 'but it's a nice story. Plus the mosaic pavement here is gorgeous.'

He spotted the peacocks. 'Your favourites.'

She nodded, pleased that he'd remembered.

They wandered along the canal and cut through to a courtyard that opened up to a little square containing the most enormous glass star, in shades of blue and green and white.

'That's stunning,' he said.

'The Cometa di Vetro,' she said. 'Better still, it lights up at night. Another photo for your mother, I think.' This time, she took it on her phone. And she couldn't resist taking a close-up of him, too. Although the glass sculpture was beautiful, it was the man in front of them who took her breath away. And just for a moment she wished they were both tourists, enjoying the views and wandering around hand in hand, completely carefree.

She'd gone back into super-bright tour guide mode, Gianni thought. And he wanted the woman back. The woman who'd shown him so much over the last few days and was hiding herself again.

'It's a pity we don't have enough time to go to Burano today,' she said. 'The houses are painted all different colours: some are incredibly bright, so the canal side looks like a rainbow, and others are ice-cream shades. It looks so pretty, reflecting in the water.'

But nothing like as pretty as the woman walking by his side in a summery dress, a floppy hat and a smile that made his heart feel as if it had done a backflip, Gianni thought.

His hand brushed against hers as they walked along, and his skin tingled at the contact. The second time it happened, he couldn't resist entwining his fingers with hers. When she didn't pull away, it made him feel weirdly settled. As if he'd been looking for something for so long, and he'd finally found it.

He sneaked a glance at her, but her expression was unreadable.

It was complicated. He still didn't have a clue where this thing between them was going. But for now he wanted to just *be* and not think about anything other than walking hand in hand with a woman he really liked.

And maybe it was the same for her because, although she didn't comment on the fact that they were holding hands, her fingers tightened slightly round his.

He had to drop her hand when they came across a tour group and needed to squeeze by; but then the moment was broken and it felt too awkward to take her hand again. Particularly when she glanced at her watch and said, 'We need to get back to pick up the ladder.'

'Of course,' he said.

Back to business.

Which was sensible.

'Last bit,' he said when they got back to the palazzo with the ladder.

'Do you want me to come and hold a torch for you?' she asked.

'If you have time, that'd be good,' he said.

It turned out that there was a leak in the roof, which was why two of the rooms had been affected by damp. 'Again, it's fixable,' he said. 'And the good news is that most of the roof structure is sound, with the exception of the cracked tiles that let in the water, and some of the wood underneath it.' But he documented everything thoroughly, taking measurements and photographs.

And then, to stop himself doing something stupid—like kissing her—he shut himself away again to work on his report, while she cooked dinner.

They ate on the balcony, and Serafina kept the conversation light and easy, though inwardly she felt nothing of the kind. Today in Murano, when she and Gianni had held hands, she'd felt as if he really was falling in love with her city. And she thought that he understood how she felt about the palazzo: but she needed to be sure. She had one more day to make sure he'd completely fallen in love with Venice and the palazzo. And she'd already brought out all the big guns: the Palazzo Ducale, Ca d'Oro, St Mark's in the evening, the view of the sunset over the Grand Canal, the glass-blowing.

She was running out of time.

So was the museum.

The next day, she took him to a quieter part of the city to see Tintoretto's house and told him about Tintoretto's daughter having to dress as a boy to do her artist's training. 'Women weren't allowed to do figure work because it meant drawing from nudes,' she explained. 'Gradually it changed, so aristocratic women and nuns could work on illustrated manuscripts or needlework. And eventually women could paint people. It's important to tell their stories.'

'You really love your job, don't you?' he asked softly.

'I love my job, I love my city, and I love my palazzo,' she said. 'Not necessarily in that order. They're all kind of mixed up together.' Which was why the restoration was so important to her.

'You still haven't taken me to see your museum,' he said.

Because she worried there was too much at stake. What if his dislike of modern art put him off the idea of helping her? 'There's a lot of modern art you wouldn't enjoy,' she prevaricated. 'And I want you to see the bits of Venice I think you'll enjoy most. Come and see the Three Moors and their camel.' She distracted him with tales of the three statues and Sior Antonio Rioba with his metal nose, then took him down another little alley to show him an archway she thought he'd like.

But the grey skies had been darkening all morning, and raindrops started to spatter round them. What began as a light shower soon turned into something much heavier, and she took his hand. 'This way. I know where we can get some shelter.'

Gianni ran through the little *calle* with Serafina, and they ended up ducking through an archway into a *sotoportego*— one of the tunnels that went underneath a building and connected two streets.

Either everyone else had found shelter elsewhere, or they'd stayed indoors rather than venturing out when the rain started, because the *sotoportego* was deserted. He could hear the rain pattering down on the cobbles of the street; the air felt warm and damp.

He was still holding Serafina's hand. Just like he had in Murano—except it felt as if there was some electrical charge surrounding them, and all of a sudden he could hardly breathe. He was incredibly aware of her. The colour of her eyes. The curve of her mouth. Her scent. The feel of her skin against his.

She swayed towards him, and he was lost. He wrapped his free arm round her and drew her closer. The next thing he knew, he was kissing her. Their arms were wrapped tightly round each other; she was so close that he could feel her heart beating against his, and he was sure that she could feel the drumming of his own heart.

Time felt as if it had stopped. He couldn't even hear the rain any more, beating away time with every droplet. There was only the here and now. The warmth of her body against his. The way her mouth moved against his, offering and taking at the same time.

When he broke the kiss, he felt dizzy. Serafina's eyes looked huge in the shadows; her mouth was slightly swollen and reddened, and his own felt in the same state.

She breathed his name, and he tucked a loose tendril of hair behind her ear. Then somehow the pad of his thumb seemed to have a life of its own and it was tracing her jawline, her lower lip. Her mouth parted, and he desperately wanted to kiss her again.

'Serafina. I want you,' he whispered.

'I want you, too,' she whispered back. 'The palazzo's three minutes away from here at a run.'

Where he could kiss her in private, for as long as they both wanted, and they wouldn't have to stop.

The rain was drumming down hard again, almost in time with his heart.

He took her hand. 'Let's go.'

They ran through the rain together, neither of them caring that they were getting soaked.

And then they were at the back door of the palazzo, the street entrance. She opened the door; the second it closed behind them, they were kissing again.

He swept her up in his arms and carried her up the stairs. Her arms were wrapped round his neck and both of them were laughing; and he kissed her on every step up to the first floor, heedless of her disapproving ancestors looking down from the walls.

He carried her along the corridor to his bedroom, still kissing her; then finally set her down on her feet when he was standing next to his bed.

'Gianni.' She stroked her face, and his heart felt as if it had done a somersault. He'd never wanted anyone so much in his life.

'Are you sure about this?' he asked softly.

She answered him with a kiss that started out sweet and ended up scorching.

He'd been drawn to her since the moment they'd met. He'd wanted her since he'd danced in St Mark's Square with her. Since he'd held hands with her on Murano. And he couldn't resist her any more.

CHAPTER SEVEN

GIANNI LETO WAS the first man Serafina had made love with since Tom. The first man she'd kissed since Tom. The first man she'd really *noticed* since Tom.

Apart from their initial meeting in Rome, they'd barely known each other a week.

And yet she felt more in tune with him than she had with the man who'd asked her to marry him and then broken her heart.

The first time she and Gianni had made love, it had been frantic, because they'd both needed to slake their thirst for each other.

Then he'd taken time to explore her. He'd taken her breath away, and she'd had the pleasure of watching him come apart under her touch, too.

And now she was lying in Gianni's arms, her head against his shoulder and her arm wrapped round his waist, holding him close. Right then, she was warm and comfortable and drowsy, and she wanted to stay here for ever.

He dropped a kiss on top of her head. 'What now?' he asked, his voice soft, but the words were enough to break the spell in her head.

'I don't know,' she said.

'You live in Venice. I live in Rome. Long-distance rela—' He stopped, and his arms tightened round her.

'Sorry. I know you've already been there and worn the T-shirt.'

Serafina and Tom hadn't even lived in the same continent, let alone the same country or the same city. She agreed with Gianni that long-distance relationships didn't work. Then again, relationships didn't work for her family, full stop. Plus he'd said that he was focusing on his business. She needed to focus on fixing the palazzo.

This thing between them didn't stand a chance: but she didn't want him to say it first. She didn't want to let herself get hurt again. Which left her with no choice but to say, 'I'm not looking for a relationship. I don't have the space in my life.' It wasn't completely true, but maybe if she told herself often enough she might start to believe it.

'Same here,' he said.

'What just happened…' She leaned her forehead against him for a moment. 'I think it was us getting something out of our systems. And now we need to go back to how things were. A business relationship.'

'Contractor and client,' he agreed.

Because even friendship wouldn't be enough. Not now they'd made love. Not now she knew how he could make her feel.

And, much as she wanted to stay exactly where she was, she knew it would be a mistake and she'd end up eating her heart out for something she couldn't have. Better to leave now. While she could still pretend to be cool and calm and every centimetre a *contessa*. 'You have a report to finish writing,' she said, 'and I'm supposed to be working on an exhibition catalogue. Maybe we ought to…um… get up and do some work.' Which would buy her time to regroup and get her head back into sensible mode. 'Maybe we can talk again in a couple of hours.' She glanced at her watch. 'Over dinner. I'll buy you that lobster you wanted, in a posh restaurant.' It would wipe out her finances for the rest of the month, but she'd stopped caring.

'OK,' he said. 'But the lobster's on me.'

'My idea, my bill,' she corrected. 'Would you mind… um…closing your eyes?'

He smiled. 'Shy, considering what we just did?'

'I know. But I'm not brave, Gianni. I can't get up and saunter out of your room, naked.' Even if, strictly speaking, the room belonged to her and there was nobody else in the palazzo to see them. 'That's not who I am.'

He nodded. 'OK. Eyes closed. I'll open them again when I hear the door shut.'

She knew he meant it. Gianni Leto didn't say things he didn't mean. Unlike Tom, he was straightforward and honest. 'Thank you. Help yourself to whatever you want from the kitchen.' As soon as his eyes were closed, she slid out of bed, wrapped her clothes round her, and bolted.

Gianni kept his eyes closed even after the door had shut.

By sleeping together, he and Serafina had made everything much more complicated.

The problem was, now they'd spent an afternoon in bed together, it wasn't enough for him. He wanted more from her. He wanted everything.

But he knew he couldn't have it. How could he and Serafina have a future? They'd both agreed that long-distance relationships didn't work. No way would she move from Venice, away from the job she loved and the house she loved; and he didn't want to move from Rome, hours away from his family. There wasn't a middle ground.

Even if they could find a way round that, there were all the other barriers. They were from different worlds. Serafina had gold-framed portraits in a line up the staircase to illustrate her family tree; Gianni knew his ancestors back to his great-grandparents, and that was it. He was wealthy now, but his family was firmly rooted in a lower class than hers. Although he didn't think she was like Elena's family, he still had their words in their head, saying he wasn't good enough for them: and if he hadn't been good enough for them, how could he possibly think he was good enough for the family of a *contessa*? Money didn't change a thing.

Plus she'd explicitly said she didn't want a relationship; there was no point in trying to find a way to make it work.

From now on, he and Serafina were strictly business.

He wanted for long enough to make sure he wouldn't bump into her in the corridor, then took a shower before settling down with his laptop to finalise his report.

Serafina deleted the paragraph for the third time.

'For pity's sake, just *focus*,' she told herself crossly.

Daydreaming over Gianni Leto wasn't going to solve anything.

Making love with him had been a mistake. Instead of getting him out of her head, it had only succeeded in making her think about him even more.

How stupid this was. If he'd wanted her, he would've argued with her when she'd suggested taking their relationship back to a purely professional one. He hadn't. Obviously for him this had been getting it out of his system—and for him it had worked.

He didn't feel the same way she did.

And she didn't have time to brood about it. Right now she needed to sort out her work and sort out her finances, to get the palazzo fixed.

Though, given that Gianni had said he wasn't looking for a relationship, would he agree to her idea of a marriage of convenience? Only for a year?

She was still thinking about it when her phone shrilled. She glanced at the screen: her mother. No doubt she was double-checking the arrangements for her return home on Sunday. For the fourth time.

Forcing herself to sound a lot brighter than she actually felt, she answered the phone. 'Hello, Mamma. How are you?'

'I… Oh, Serafina.' Francesca burst into tears. 'I'm so sorry.'

'Mamma? What's wrong?' Dread flooded through her. Oh, no. Please don't let anything have happened to Tia Vittoria.

'I know I'm supposed to come back on Sunday afternoon, but I can't bear the idea of coming back to that house. All the damp and the lumpy beds and the shabbiness. It's a *tomb*.' Francesca sobbed again. 'I hate Venice. I *hate* that house. Without that place round our necks, maybe your father and I would have been happy. I know you're trying to fix things, but I don't think anyone can fix things where that place is concerned. And I can't live there any more. I just *can't*.'

Relief that Vittoria was all right was quickly replaced by dismay. If her mother wanted to move from the palazzo, then she would need somewhere to live. She'd also need an income. How on earth was Serafina going to find enough money to support two households—particularly as the palazzo was going to eat up every penny she had and then some?

Why, why, *why* hadn't her father been sensible enough to get his financial affairs in order and sort out a pension, to make sure Francesca had enough to live on if he died first? Why hadn't her mother nagged him into it, back in the days before his gambling addiction had taken such a hold? Why hadn't she realised that her parents were completely hopeless when it came to money, and acted sooner?

What was she going to do?

'Serafina?'

The last thing Serafina needed now was an outpouring of doom and gloom. 'I'm here, Mamma. Sorry. I was thinking something through.' Panicking, but her mother didn't need to know that.

'I know we can't afford it, but I just…' Francesca's voice hitched.

'Mamma—it's OK. I know Venice has a lot of unhappy memories for you.' Serafina took a deep breath. 'Don't worry about the money.' That was her job. It was always going to be her job, but it felt as if someone had piled yet another weight on her shoulders. The lightness of spirit she'd felt in Gianni's arms had vanished, replaced by dread. 'We'll find you somewhere nice, somewhere near Tia Vittoria if that's what you'd like, and I'll make sure the bills are paid and you have enough money for a comfortable life.' She'd do it, even if she had to work three jobs and exist on less than four hours sleep a night.

'I'm sorry. I know I'm letting you down, leaving you all alone,' Francesca said.

'You're not letting me down at all, Mamma,' Serafina lied. 'I take it you're staying with Tia Vittoria for a bit longer?'

'Yes.'

At least she had a breathing space before she had to start paying rent. The tension in her shoulders eased a tiny bit. 'Do you need me to bring you anything from here? Or can it wait a few more days while—' she scrabbled frantically for a plausible excuse '—while I sort something out at the museum?'

'A few more days is fine. Vittoria and I are going shopping tomorrow.'

If Francesca put whatever she bought on credit, that would give Serafina a few more days to work out how to find the money to pay for it. She'd have a quiet word with her aunt later to fill her in on the situation. 'That's good.

Have a lovely time, Mamma. Sorry to be rude, but I need to go. Love you.'

When she ended the call, she stared at the table, unseeing.

Somehow, she had to find a way to pay for the restoration of the ground floor of the palazzo—and have the work done in the next three months so she could save the museum. And on top of that she needed to find her mother a house where she'd be comfortable but the finances were manageable.

The bank had refused her a loan, but Serafina knew that going to a loan shark for money wasn't the answer. Interest rates meant that the debt would spiral quickly.

Walking away wasn't an option. If she let the palazzo rot, then whoever inherited it would have the burden dumped on them—whether that was a distant cousin or her own child. That wasn't fair. It wasn't fair to the house, either.

She had to do something. Find someone who was willing to lend her money until the palazzo was back on its feet and the museum was safe.

But her brain felt completely empty. She didn't have a clue where she could go from here.

Right at that moment, she'd never felt more alone, and a wave of hopelessness swamped her. Giving in to it, she put her face in her hands and sobbed.

As Gianni walked through the hallway to the kitchen to make himself a coffee, he could hear someone crying.

Big, hiccupping sobs.

It sounded as if Serafina was breaking her heart.

Even though they'd agreed to keep things strictly professional between them, he couldn't pretend he hadn't heard her crying. Though he also wasn't going to walk unannounced into her study. Not without a prop.

He made coffee and raided the cupboard for biscuits, put the lot on a tray, then rapped on the door of her study. 'Serafina?'

'Sorry, I'm a bit busy,' she called back.

No, she wasn't. And he'd despise himself if he walked away, knowing that she was upset. 'I heard you crying,' he said. 'I thought you could do with coffee and biscuits. I'm coming in.'

When he opened the door, she looked away from him and rubbed at her face; but when she turned back she couldn't disguise the puffiness of her eyes.

Something was obviously very, very wrong.

He wasn't conceited enough to think it was because they'd called a halt to what was happening between them. It was more likely to do with the palazzo.

'Here. You don't have to talk. Not yet, anyway. Just eat one of these.'

She gave him a watery smile. 'Thank you. That's kind.'

He set the tray on her desk and sat in one of the armchairs—which turned out to be even less comfortable than it looked.

When it was finally obvious to him that she wasn't going to talk without a prompt, he said gently, 'Sometimes, it helps to talk to someone who's not involved.' He knew that wasn't strictly true of their situation; part of him *was* involved since he'd met her and come to Venice.

She looked at him, as if weighing up whether she could trust him. 'This stays between you and me?'

'It stays between you and me. I promise. And I don't break my promises,' he reassured her.

Her continued silence told her that either she didn't quite trust him, or that someone had let her down badly in the past.

But she'd trusted him with herself—something that he

thought was more precious than whatever was holding her back right now.

He was about to break the silence when she took a deep breath. 'OK. Thank you.' She scrubbed at her face again. 'I don't even know where to start.'

'The beginning?' he suggested.

She gave him a very wan smile. 'I'm not quite sure where the beginning is.'

'Then start wherever you like,' he said.

'The palazzo, I guess.' She blew out a breath. 'Way, way back, my family were merchants. They did well for themselves. One of them married into the nobility and ended up with the palazzo—and then they found they had a status to maintain. They liked to entertain. And over the years the trade and the money dried up. Things were sold to pay for entertaining, instead of the money being used to fix problems with the house. I had no idea how bad it was until...' She swallowed hard. 'Until my dad died.'

'Yeah. I know how that feels. It changes everything,' he said. 'And you always look back and wonder if you could've done something to stop that heart attack happening, even though the sensible bit of you knows you couldn't and it was never your fault in the first place.'

She bit her lip. 'Sorry. I didn't mean to bring back bad memories for you.'

'It's fine,' he said. 'What I meant is that I probably understand more than someone who hadn't lost their dad to a heart attack.'

'Did your dad make mistakes?' she asked.

'The citizens of Bardicello would say so. Their town hall was a pretty big one,' he said. 'We were lucky nobody was hurt.' He looked at her. 'What was your dad's mistake?'

'He knew the house needed work and we didn't have the money to fix it.' She took a deep breath. 'He'd always enjoyed playing cards—and he'd always won.'

Lucky at cards, unlucky in love. The phrase slid into Gianni's head from out of nowhere.

'What I didn't know was that he didn't only play cards with his friends for relatively low stakes over a bottle of grappa, for fun. He played online. With a high credit limit, one he kept increasing. He had a few wins that encouraged him—but then he hit a losing streak.' She shook her head. 'He kept telling himself he'd get his lucky break and win it all back, and more. And he kept going.'

Then she stopped, as if she couldn't bear to go on.

'But the lucky break never came?' Gianni asked softly.

'It was a spiral. The more he lost, the more he gambled in an attempt to win it back, and the more he lost. That last loss was the really big one, the one that brought on the heart attack. And I didn't even know he was gambling like that. I was his daughter, I was living here, and I didn't know how bad things were. How could I have been that oblivious?'

'Addicts tend to be good at hiding things,' he said. 'Did your mum know?'

'To some extent, yes, but neither of us knew how bad it was until I started sorting out the estate. I still owe some of the inheritance tax, and I can't even use the art on the walls to pay it off because everything that *might* have been worth something is actually a copy. That's why the house will have to pay its way.' She looked away. 'Yeah, I know. Poor little rich girl. Doesn't your heart bleed for me?'

The savagery in her voice made him wince. 'Poor little rich girl? That's not who you are, Serafina. You're not expecting other people to bail you out,' he said. 'You're trying to sort out the problems yourself.'

'Even so. My mother hates this house. She says it's like a tomb.'

Her mother had a point, he thought. The palazzo did feel like a mausoleum.

'I promised to fix it and make things better...and I

haven't even managed to start it. I've let her down. And she called me just now to say she doesn't want to come back to Venice. She wants to stay near Verona, where she grew up. Near her sister.'

And did Serafina's mother have an income? Or would Serafina need to support her mother, too? he wondered.

'And I've let the museum down,' she continued.

'The museum you work for? Is that the one you wanted to have the ground floor?'

She nodded. 'I'm sorry. I should've been more open with you about that, but it isn't really my place to discuss it because I'm not the director.' She blew out a breath. 'Will you promise me this goes no further than you?'

'I promise,' he said.

'The lease on our building is up for renewal. Beppe, the guy who owns our building, wants to quadruple the cost of the lease.'

Gianni frowned. 'Surely that's illegal?'

'It ought to be,' she said, 'but Madi—the museum director—got a lawyer friend to look at it. It seems Beppe can do whatever he likes. There weren't any clauses protecting our lease when he bought the building. Either we have to increase our running costs hugely, which isn't an option, or we have three months to move the museum somewhere else with an affordable rent. The ground floor of the palazzo would be the perfect place. Except it needs bringing up to all the safety standards, first. The museum can't afford to pay for the renovations to the space, and I can't afford it, either.' She closed her eyes. 'I've let everyone down. We can loan the exhibits to other museums; at least they'll be stored in the right conditions. But it means the collection's going to be scattered after years and years of building it up.'

'It's not your fault, Serafina. You can't blame yourself for the business decision of someone who—'

'—wants to gut the building and turn it into an upmarket hotel,' she finished, her lip curling.

'I can see now,' he said dryly, 'why you looked so angry in Rome when I suggested selling your palazzo to a developer.'

She nodded. 'Developers aren't my favourite people. Though, even without the entailment, I wouldn't have sold the palazzo. But now I'm in a place where, however I look at it, I've let my mother down, I've let the museum down, and I've let the palazzo down. The only thing that I can think of that might work...' She shook her head. 'No. I can't ask you.'

Was she going to ask him for a loan, perhaps? Maybe he could help her. 'Try me,' he said.

She looked at him, her dark eyes luminous. 'Marry me?'

'What?' It was the last thing he'd expected. He couldn't see how marrying her would have anything to do with the restoration or her financial problems.

'I mean a marriage of convenience,' she clarified.

He still didn't get it.

When he said nothing, she said, 'We're both single. There aren't any complications for either of us. We stay married for a year. You'll get the social cachet of my name and good publicity for your business, and I'll get the funds to start the restoration of the palazzo.'

'How exactly does marrying me get you funds? Or are you straight out saying that you want to marry me for my money?' he drawled, trying to disguise the sting of hurt. Even Elena's family hadn't been that bold.

'It's not *your* money I want,' she said. 'It's the magazine's.'

'What magazine?'

'*Celebrity Life.* If we give them an exclusive on our wedding photos, they'll pay us a fee. Enough to make a start on the renovations.'

Gianni could hardly believe he was hearing this.

He wasn't sure what annoyed him most: the idea of marrying for money, the way she'd talked about giving him social cachet, or the fact she could come out with this outlandish proposal when they'd just spent the afternoon in bed together *and* they'd both said they weren't looking for a relationship.

'No,' he said.

She spread her hands. 'See? I told you I couldn't ask you.'

'Where did you get that ridiculous idea from in the first place?'

She looked away. 'It was the deal I had when Tom… Well. It doesn't matter, because the wedding didn't happen.'

Gianni had always thought himself a reasonable judge of character, but he'd failed with Elena—and, worse, it seemed he hadn't learned from that and he'd made exactly the same mistake with Serafina. It made him feel sick to discover that she was as much of a snob with her eye on the money as Elena had been, deep down. Anger bubbled through him and he couldn't help lashing out. 'I'm not surprised he changed his mind about marrying you, if you'd set up a deal like that.'

She flinched. 'It wasn't *my* deal. It was Tom's publicist's. I'd planned to donate my half of the money to a good cause.'

'Like fixing up your palazzo?'

'No, actually. I was going to give it to a women's refuge. One that had helped a friend.' She narrowed her eyes at him. 'And, for your information, Tom wasn't the one who called off the wedding. I was.'

Now he felt guilty. Maybe he'd got her wrong, after all.

But he couldn't quite apologise, not when she'd asked him to marry her for money.

He'd grown up knowing what a good marriage was. Yes, his family had been poor, but his parents had loved each other and they'd loved their children. No way was he settling for anything less. Marriage might be a business deal for a countess, but it wasn't that for him. 'Marriage should be for love.'

'I don't believe in love,' she said. 'It's a fairy tale.'

He couldn't help sniping. 'And you're Cinderella, are you, Contessa?'

'No. I simply have a bit of a cash flow problem.' She sighed and raked her hand through her hair. 'I didn't intend to insult you, Gianni. But I was trying to think of how I could raise the money to start restoring the palazzo. The magazine had offered us money for the wedding photos. Tom, being the Hollywood star, was the obvious draw; but I had a quiet word with the magazine and it seems their readers like—well, royal stuff.'

At least she squirmed when she said it. Not that it was much consolation to him.

'And it seems a Venetian *contessa* counts as "royal stuff". They offered me a deal. Obviously not as much money as they would've paid if I'd still been marrying a movie star, but enough to fund the first bit of the restoration. And then I'd have the rent coming in from the museum—even though I'd rather them not have to pay me any rent at all—and that would pay for renovating the top two floors to rent out as accommodation. At a fair rent. And then the money coming in from the accommodation would pay for renovating my floor, and once that was all done I could drop the museum's rent to a peppercorn.'

She was putting herself last again, he noticed. And he could see the logic behind her reasoning, even if he didn't approve of it. 'A marriage of convenience is a bad idea,' he said. 'I believe in marrying for love, the way my parents did.'

She looked away. 'Love doesn't work where my family is concerned.'

'Why not?'

'Because of the curse.'

This was the first he'd heard of it. 'What curse?'

'Remember I showed you Marianna's portrait?' As his nod, she continued, 'When Marianna died, her lover cursed our family and said that no Ardizzone would ever have a happy marriage. Yes, I know that all sounds completely ridiculous and melodramatic: but, if I look at my family history, there's a long line of unhappy marriages. My grandparents loathed each other. My parents weren't happy—when I look at it now, I realise my dad's gambling made my mum more anxious, and the more doom-and-gloom she got the more he turned to gambling, and it was a vicious spiral. And I'm pretty sure it's been like that for all the generations before them.'

'What about you?'

Her eyes were bleak. 'I thought I was the one who'd break the curse. I met Tom at a glitzy party when he made a movie here—our museum was the venue—and we hit it off instantly. He asked me out, and pretty much swept me off my feet. I honestly thought he was The One. When he asked me to marry him, I said yes. But then I flew out to LA a couple of weeks later to surprise him.' Her eyes darkened. 'When I let myself in to his flat, I found him in bed with someone else.'

He knew she'd been engaged, but he'd had no idea that the guy had cheated on her.

Before Gianni could even process that, Serafina continued, 'It turned out she wasn't even the first. He'd been cheating on me even before he asked me to marry him. The curse of the Ardizzones held true.' She blew out a breath. 'If you don't marry for love, then you don't have unrealistic expectations and it's not going to go wrong.'

He thought about it.

But Elena hadn't really loved him. Not enough to stand

by him when things became difficult after the building collapse at Bardicello: she'd broken off their engagement within days. Maybe he'd had unrealistic expectations; but he thought that the lack of love was what would have wrecked their marriage if they'd actually got that far.

'My parents married for love,' he said. 'And they still loved each other on the day my dad died.'

'Maybe they were just lucky,' she said.

'My sister and her husband love each other, too,' he said. 'So, no. I don't think my parents were lucky. They worked at it.'

Her eyes narrowed. 'Are you saying that my family gave up on their marriages? That they used the curse as an excuse?'

'It's one possibility,' he said. 'And I think that's a more likely explanation than a curse.'

At that, all the fight went out of her. 'Probably,' she said. 'Though, curse or no curse, it doesn't change my situation now. Even if you agreed to let me make stage payments, I'd still need the money from the magazine to pay for the first lot of renovations until the ground floor was properly useable and the rent from the museum came onstream.'

'Was that the plan when you contacted me? I was single, so you thought you could ask me to marry you, have my picture plastered all over a celeb magazine and then take the money?'

'Yes. No. I mean, I did think it, at first,' she admitted. 'But my best friend said it was a stupid idea. My aunt did, too. I came to see you because I thought you'd do a good job—and because I thought you might know more than I do on the building side of things and could advise me who to contract to try and get a grant. I know the system from a heritage point of view, for exhibits, but not for the buildings.'

He was still digesting this. 'You were going to ask me

to marry you—before you'd even *met* me? Is that why you asked me to spend a week here?'

'No. I wanted you to see the place for yourself and do an honest assessment,' she said. 'And in return I was offering you a week's accommodation in an amazing location. A *quid pro quo*. Though I admit, I hoped that when I showed you Venice—*my* Venice, full of buildings and art and lovely things—you'd fall in love with city and see the potential of the palazzo, and that would persuade you to help me. And then maybe I could ask you about the— well, the magazine.'

Had she wanted him to fall in love with her, as well as with the city and the palazzo? Because he knew he was close to it. Crazily close.

Was that why she'd slept with him? Because she was using him, the same way Elena had?

Or did Serafina feel that same pull of attraction that he did, but she wouldn't let herself believe in it because all her forebears had been married unhappily and her own engagement had ended in misery?

Maybe it was a mixture of the two.

But, the more he thought about it, the more Gianni felt that it had been a set-up, all along.

To a point, her plan had worked. He'd fallen in love with Venice. He wanted to work on the palazzo and bring it back to life. And he was more than halfway to falling in love with Serafina.

But it was still a set-up, and that was more than he could stomach. 'A marriage of convenience.' Even Elena hadn't offered him that. Or had she, but she hadn't spelled it out the way Serafina had?

'I'm sorry,' Serafina said. 'It wasn't meant as an insult. And I know it's a stupid idea. Born out of despera—' She stopped. 'Sorry. I'm digging myself a deeper hole. And you've been so nice.'

'Nice' wasn't how he was feeling right now. At all. 'Two years ago,' he said, 'I was engaged.'

She looked at him.

'Elena was from…not the aristocracy, like you, but from "a good family".' He punctuated it with air quotes. 'One who wasn't happy that she was marrying a man whose father worked his way up from nothing, in a trade. But having money kind of made up for my lack of social respectability.'

She narrowed her eyes at him. 'That's appalling snobbery.'

'But weren't you just offering me the same? Your name, to make me respectable?' Which made her as bad as Elena, in his view.

She was silent for a moment, clearly thinking about what she'd said. 'Respectable in the eyes of people who were judging you unfairly. It never occurred to me how insulting that was, and I apologise.'

He could see that she meant it. 'Apology accepted,' he said.

'The way I saw it, I was trying to see what I could offer you in return for your help. Good publicity and the Ardizzone name seemed a reasonable way of doing it. I honestly didn't intend to make you feel as if you were…' She shook her head. 'You're not beneath *anyone*, Gianni. You're the CEO of a construction company—yes, it was your father's company, but you worked your way up right from when you were small and helped him mix mortar on a Saturday morning. And you studied for your degree at the same time as putting in a full day's work. There aren't many people who could do that. You deserve recognition for what you've achieved, not dismissiveness.'

Her eyes were full of fire, and he realised with shock that it was all for him.

'I apologise for being intrusive, but I don't understand. What happened to your engagement?' she asked.

'Bardicello,' he said with a shrug. 'Elena's family didn't want to be associated with it. They didn't want their name tainted with the scandal.'

She frowned. 'But if Elena loved you, why didn't she stand up to her family? Why didn't she stand beside you? None of it was your fault.'

Because he hadn't been enough for Elena. She hadn't wanted to fight for him. Rather than say that, he focused on what else Serafina had said. 'I thought you didn't believe in love?'

'For me, I don't. But for other people…' She spread her hands.

In Elena's shoes, would Serafina have stood by him? He rather thought the answer was yes. This time he was honest, even though it hurt to say it. 'She didn't love me enough,' he said.

'I'm sorry. You deserved better.'

Said the woman who'd walked in on her ex being unfaithful to her, not long after they'd got engaged. 'So did you.' He looked her in the eye. 'But I still believe love exists.'

'For you, maybe. Not for my family.'

'Curses,' he said, 'are not real.'

'But families tend to follow patterns,' she said.

'That's true,' he acknowledged. 'But you're already breaking one pattern in your family. You're doing something about the palazzo instead of ignoring the problems and letting it decay further. Why not break the pattern of unhappy relationships, too?'

'I'm trying to do something about the palazzo, but I'm failing,' she said. 'What I have is a building that needs fixing before I can make it earn its keep, debts that are increasing daily, and I'm letting down my mother and I'm letting down the museum.' She shook her head. 'I can't see any way forward. I'm *stuck*.'

Not only with the palazzo, he thought, but with an unrealistic view of love. But he'd have to deal with one thing at a time. The palazzo was definitely easier to deal with than emotions were. 'And the bank won't lend you anything?'

'They were my first port of call.' She rolled her eyes at him. 'Obviously I didn't totter in, bat my eyelashes at them and ask them for money. I gave them a business plan. Before Madi told me about the museum's lease, originally I was going to resign from the museum and get a paid job to support my mother and pay the bills, and I'd offer holiday accommodation to tourists.' She spread her hands. 'The bank said no.'

'Hang on. Backtrack a second. The museum doesn't pay you?'

'Technically I'm a volunteer—not simply the board stuff, but the day-to-day work I do there as well,' she said. 'If you want to make lots of money, you don't work in the heritage sector. I thought I had family money to support me, and if the museum didn't pay me then it meant they could offer a paid position to someone who wanted to work in heritage but needed a salary.'

He noticed she'd said she'd *thought* she had family money. Clearly that wasn't the case.

'What happened to the family money?'

'We have a trust fund. My dad was the trustee. He moved some of the investments to beat the market, except the market beat him. And then he borrowed some of the funds to try and make the money back,' she said grimly. 'Mamma and I have been living on my savings for the last six months.'

'Your dad embezzled the trust fund?'

She frowned. 'No. He didn't *steal* it. He always intended to pay it back.'

Gianni was truly shocked. Then again, gambling was

an addiction, and addicts didn't tend to have the clearest view of their actions.

Serafina's financial situation was worse than he'd guessed, though at least she'd finally been honest with him. She didn't have the money to begin the repairs, but she had a strong sense of responsibility—to her family and to the museum—and it was clear that she was trying to find a way to rescue everyone and everything.

He could walk away. Go back to Rome and pretend he'd never met her or seen this place.

Or he could act on his instincts. The voice in his heart that urged him to step in and help her, because she needed someone on her side—and he knew what that felt like, thanks to Bardicello and the way he'd had to struggle afterwards to persuade clients that their firm could still be trusted. He'd ended up keeping an online diary of the restoration, with video and photographs, and that had helped to restore their confidence. But for a while he'd felt very, very alone.

'So we have a little under three months to get the ground floor fixed,' he said.

She stared at him, hope lighting her expression. 'Does this mean you've changed your mind and you'll marry me?'

'No. I still don't believe in a marriage of convenience,' he said. 'If I ever marry, it'll be for love. I won't accept anything less—and neither should you. Patterns can be broken. You don't have to be defined by your parents, or your grandparents, or that long line of miserable portraits in your hallway. They're part of you, yes, but there's more to you than that.'

She inclined her head in acknowledgement. 'But how does that get my palazzo fixed? Do you know somewhere that will offer me a grant, or a loan?'

'Me,' he said quietly.

Her eyes widened. 'But I can't expect that from you. Not after...' She flushed. 'After the way I've treated you.'

'You love this house,' he said. 'You want to make it shine again. And you're trying to help the museum. You said that if you can get the ground floor fixed, the rent paid by the museum will pay for the upper floors to be repaired and converted to accommodation, and then renting those floors out will finance the repairs to your floor.' He looked at her. 'Do you have the figures to back that up?'

'I do.' She got out of her chair and gestured to him to take a seat. 'Let me show you.'

She brushed against him as she switched out of the word processing program and into the spreadsheet. He could feel the warmth of her skin, smell the light floral perfume she wore, and suddenly it was a struggle to think straight, because he was sideswiped by the memories of making love with her.

'Gianni?'

He pulled himself together and looked at the figures she'd put together.

'I assume the rent the museum will be paying is the same as they're paying now?'

'Proportionally less, because the space is smaller. But it works,' she said.

'But they don't pay you a salary. Without an income you're going to be in trouble.'

'Madi says she's going to try and get me a salary. I don't need much,' she said. 'Enough to support my mother, wherever she decides to live, and cover my food and the basic bills for the palazzo. It'll be six months before I start needing to heat the place again, and the bills are a bit more manageable over the summer.'

Elena would've complained about not being able to buy new clothes and shoes, he thought. Serafina had completely ignored those aspects. And she'd thought of her mother before anything else. His first instincts about her had been right, after all—even if she had made that stupid suggestion about a marriage of convenience.

'I know you have to pay some of the costs upfront— the materials and the labour—but if there's a way you can hold off for three months before I need to start paying you back, then I'll repay every single cent. With interest,' Serafina said. 'And I'm pretty sure everyone at the museum will muck in and help with the restoration in their spare time, including me.'

'Are any of them trained construction workers?' he asked.

'No, but not every single task in a restoration needs someone who's trained, does it? There's fetching and carrying, preparation work and painting walls—the kind of things people do when they redecorate their own homes,' she said. 'Or whatever your team directs us to do.'

'Extra help with that sort of thing will help to cut the time and the costs,' he said.

'When you do site visits, you're very welcome to stay here,' she said.

Site visits. What if he stayed and oversaw the restoration personally? Then he'd be working side by side with her every single day...

It was way, way too tempting.

And it would be much too easy to fall back into bed with her. Fall all the way in love with her. End up torn between Venice and Rome.

'And any of your crew's welcome to stay here, too,' she said.

Because it would cut the costs of the project? Or because it meant they'd have other people in the palazzo to act as a buffer between them? Did she feel the same way that he did, this weird mixture of longing and need warring with a determination to be sensible?

'I'll probably hire in local people for the crew,' he said, 'but thank you for the offer.'

'And your mother and your sister are very welcome to stay, and—'

'I get it,' he cut in. 'Now, let me go and get my laptop and we'll go through the notes I've made about the building, so we can work out our business strategy.'

'OK.'

But then her stomach growled. 'Sorry. I guess I'm hungry.' She grimaced. 'Sorry again. I promised you lobster tonight.'

Lobster she couldn't afford, and he knew she was too proud to let him pay. Plus, given how upset she'd been, he guessed she wouldn't feel like going out. He'd let her keep her dignity. 'I'm not really in the mood for going out,' he said, and the relief in her face told him he'd made the right choice.

'I could order a pizza,' she suggested.

He raised an eyebrow. 'Remember where I come from.'

That made her smile. 'Yeah. I admit, the pizza in Venice isn't as good as Rome. But at least it's quick.'

'By the time it's been delivered, I could have cooked pasta, served up two bowls, and we could've eaten it,' he pointed out.

She blinked. 'You cook?'

'Have all the men in your life been that hopeless?' He shook his head. 'My mother would've shooed every single one of them into her kitchen and made them repeat the dish until they'd got it right.'

She smiled at that, and he knew he'd managed to ease some of the misery she felt.

'I assume you have pasta, cheese and eggs in your kitchen?'

'Yes,' she said.

'Then I'll make us carbonara, and we'll eat on your balcony. If you want to go and freshen up, we'll be eating in ten minutes.'

CHAPTER EIGHT

IT FELT STRANGE to have someone else taking charge—particularly here at the palazzo, Serafina thought. But at the same time it was wonderful to feel that not all the burdens of the world were entirely on her shoulders.

Why had she assumed that Gianni couldn't cook? He was the kind of man who could do absolutely anything he put his mind to.

And again she felt guilty for suggesting a marriage of convenience. Of course he'd want the real deal: something she couldn't give him. He must've thought her as much of a snob as his ex's family.

Well, she'd prove to him she wasn't like that.

She'd do whatever any of his team asked her to do at the palazzo during a working day, and then finish her museum work in the evenings.

In the bathroom mirror, she could see what a mess she looked, her eyes puffy and her cheeks tear-stained. But at least now she had hope. There wasn't that crushing feeling of being alone and not being able to hold everything up, any more.

She washed her face and tied her hair back, then headed for the kitchen. 'Can I do anything to help?'

'Nope.' Gianni, looking perfectly at ease in front of the stove, smiled. 'You have two minutes until it's cooked.'

'Right. I'll set the table, then,' she said, grabbing cutlery from the drawer. 'Wine?'

'Water for me, please,' he said, 'because after dinner we're working on figures.'

She filled a jug with water, picked up two glasses, and had just finished setting the table on the balcony when he bought out two steaming bowls of carbonara.

'This is really good,' she said after the first mouthful.

'Don't sound so surprised,' he said dryly.

'It wasn't meant to be insulting,' she said. 'I was trying to be appreciative. It's lovely not to be the one doing all the cooking. I assume from what you said earlier that your mum taught you?'

'She says everyone should be able to make some basic food. Even my dad could cook a good arrabbiata,' he said.

Serafina thought of her own father. He would never have dreamed of standing in front of a stove. Neither would her mother. They'd had a housekeeper until Serafina came back from Rome; when the housekeeper had retired, Serafina had stepped in to do the cooking on the days when her parents didn't eat out.

Maybe if they'd done more of the everyday things, life might've been a bit easier for them.

Not that it would make any difference now.

Gianni kept the conversation light until they'd finished eating. Then he fetched his laptop and went through his notes. The more he showed her, the worse it looked.

'Thank you for being thorough,' she said. 'Bottom line: can we fix the ground floor in three months, or not?'

'Everything's possible,' he said. 'My dad taught me that. There might have to be some compromises, but it's possible. I need to find a local workforce—but that's something I do in every job, because if local people are involved in a project they'll tend to support it.'

'Good point,' she said.

'If your colleagues at the museum can join the team to do some of the non-skilled jobs, as you suggested, that would be helpful.' He looked at her. 'Your director—I know it's super-short notice, but if she could meet us tonight or tomorrow, then we could go through what we need to do and make a proper project plan. Then I can go back to Rome tomorrow, sort out whatever I need to do there, and we'll start work next week. I'll oversee the restoration myself.'

'And the costs?'

'Your figures stack up,' he said. 'Once the museum's moved in here and they're paying rent, that can start to pay for the next stage of renovations.'

'But what about the costs of the first stage?'

'You asked for a three-month delay before you start paying, plus I can get Flora to look into grants. We'll work something out,' he said. 'I know you'll pay me back.'

'Thank you doesn't seem enough,' she said.

He shrugged. 'It's enough.'

'Though I want a proper contract drawn up to make it clear I'm paying you back. With interest at the current bank base rate plus one per cent.'

'I'll get a contract sorted out next week,' he said.

'I still can't believe you're doing this. Especially as you hardly know me, and I pretty much insulted you earlier.'

'Everyone deserves a second chance,' he said. 'My dad taught me that. And what goes around, comes around. Be kind, and when you need kindness someone will be kind to you. You're already trying to do something good for other people. Fixing problems that you've inherited. I think you could use a friend.'

The problem was, friendship wasn't what she wanted from Gianni Leto. Though, with that stupid marriage of convenience proposal, she'd ruined the chance of their relationship turning into anything else.

'I could indeed. To friendship,' she said, raising her glass of water.

'And to the success of the palazzo,' he said, chinking his glass against hers. 'Call your boss and see when she's free.'

Maddalena was free that evening; she came over and walked through the ground floor with them.

'The light's wonderful. You were right, Serafina. It's the perfect space for the museum,' she said.

'As it is, or do you want partitions put up to make smaller rooms and give you more display space?' Gianni asked.

'Partitions would be good. And a small space for a gift shop and a café,' Maddalena said. 'We'll also need bathrooms and wheelchair access.'

In Serafina's kitchen, they sat down and worked out exactly what they needed.

'I'll talk to an architect friend tonight,' Gianni said. 'He owes me a favour, so that's not going to be an additional cost. I'll give him your list and the measurements, and hopefully he can help us make this space work the way you need it but without making too many changes to the heritage.'

'We might be able to get a grant towards some of the costs,' Maddalena said, 'though you know how slowly administrative things work. Serafina, because you're charging us less rent than we're paying now—'

'Because the space is smaller—it's in proportion per square metre, and I'll make sure you have the figures to make it all transparent for the rest of the board,' Serafina cut in.

Maddalena gave a nod of acknowledgement. 'It means we can afford to change your position to a salaried one, from the first day we move here.'

And that in turn would mean that Serafina could afford to rent somewhere comfortable for her mother. 'Thank you,' she said.

Maddalena stayed for a glass of wine on the balcony; when Serafina saw her out, she said, 'I like him. He's one of the good guys—not to mention being gorgeous.'

Serafina felt a blush steal into her face.

'And it's obvious he likes you,' Maddalena said.

'We're friends. Or becoming friends,' Serafina amended.

'Think about it,' Maddalena advised. 'Not all gorgeous men are as self-absorbed and selfish as a certain actor we won't name. He'd be good for you—and he'd also be lucky to have you.'

'This isn't about anything other than the palazzo,' Serafina said.

'Hmm.' Maddalena gave her a hug.

'I like your boss,' Gianni said when Serafina came back to the balcony. 'She tells it like it is.'

Serafina nodded. 'Indeed.'

'I've spoken to Stefano—my architect friend. He's going to get us some preliminary drawings for Monday. Flora's going to look up grants and see what she can do. And I've changed my train ticket to first thing tomorrow.'

'You did all that while I was saying goodbye to Madi?' Serafina stared at him. 'Was I ages, or can you do six million things at once?'

'There's no point in waiting unnecessarily,' he said.

So it really was going to happen.

She realised she'd spoken aloud when he said, 'Yes. Team Ca' d'Ardizzone for the win.'

'It's been a horrible few months. I didn't think there was any hope on the other side,' she admitted.

'I've been there,' he said. 'With Bardicello. I know how it feels. We had customers cancelling on us all over the place, and I had to prove to them that we were reliable. I put a video diary of the restoration on our website, and that helped a lot. But for a while I thought we were going to lose Dad's business, and I wasn't doing enough to fix it.'

Impulsively, she reached across the table to squeeze his hand—then wished she hadn't when desire licked up her spine.

This afternoon wasn't to be repeated.

She was in Gianni's debt.

And, until she was out of it again and could meet him as his equal, she needed to keep things strictly business between them.

Back in Rome, Gianni got the grilling he expected from his sister.

'You've known her a week, you're fixing her palazzo and you're not even charging her?' Flora put her hands on her hips and glared at him. 'You had sex with her, didn't you?'

He winced. 'That makes it sound bad.'

'It *is* bad. And utterly crazy.'

'And not quite accurate,' he said. 'She's going to pay me every single cent of the renovation costs. I'm simply giving her staged payments. The first one will start in three months, when the museum starts paying rent.'

'What if she doesn't pay you back?'

'She will,' Gianni said. 'Apart from anything else, it'll be in our contract. At her insistence.'

'Poor little rich girl.' Flora shook her head. 'I don't like this, Gi. She sounds like another Elena.'

'No. She's nothing like Elena. Elena would've walked away from this and let someone else deal with the problems. Serafina's taking responsibility and sorting them out herself—even though she inherited the problems rather than creating them,' Gianni said. 'She says you're welcome to come and stay at any time—you, Rico, Sofia and Mamma.'

'I suppose at least she made you relax a bit and have fun, judging from those photos,' Flora said.

He remembered dancing with her. Kissing her in the rain. Making love with her.

Flora coughed. 'You're blushing, Gi.'

'No, I'm not.' Though his face felt hot.

'You're smitten. Which doesn't bode well for this job,' Flora said, narrowing her eyes. 'It's always a mistake to let emotions get in the way of your business judgement.'

'Flora, look at the facts. I'm going to work on a palazzo nobody's touched for decades—in part, maybe for centuries,' Gianni said. 'With structural challenges I studied at university but never had the chance to put into practice. It's a dream job.'

'You still haven't sold it to me. It might be a dream job, but in the real world it could be a nightmare.'

'Let me show you.' He opened his laptop and brought up the spreadsheet.

Flora read through it carefully. 'Everything I'd want to see is there. And it looks sensible,' she said at last. 'But I'm still going to double-check your figures before we draw up a contract. And I need you to promise me that you won't lift a finger on the place, hire a team or order any materials until that contract is signed.'

'Flora, we kind of have a ticking clock.' He explained the museum's situation.

'You just said "we", not "she",' Flora said gently. 'Be careful, Gi. It sounds as if your heart's involved more than your head. I don't want to see you hurt again, the way Elena hurt you.'

'Serafina won't hurt me.'

'I hope not.' Flora bit her lip. 'I worry about you.'

'I'm fine. You don't have to worry.' Gianni gave her a hug. 'But I appreciate you having my back.'

How could you miss someone after a single day? Serafina wondered. But she kept herself busy on the Sunday, packing things her mother wanted and taking them to Verona so she could spend the day with her mother and her aunt. Vittoria suggested that Francesca should stay with her for a couple more months before starting to look for a house; and Serafina was thrilled to see that her mother seemed a lot happier away from the palazzo.

'I feel guilty for abandoning you,' Francesca said.

'You haven't abandoned me, Mamma,' Serafina reassured her. 'I'm sorting the palazzo out. Once it's restored, you might feel differently about it. You'll always have a home there. But what I want most is to see you happy. Verona's not far from Venice. We can still see lots of each other.'

Though when she was back in the palazzo, that evening, it felt as if she was rattling round. There were too many echoes from the past.

But she was going to change things. Make Ca' d'Ardizzone a happy place again. With Gianni's help.

On Monday afternoon, Gianni sent Serafina an email with a contract for her to check with her lawyers, along with a schedule of works, saying that he'd be back in Venice on Thursday morning. She called her solicitor and arranged a meeting for them both to sign the contract with the solicitor as a witness on Thursday.

In the meantime, Serafina spent her days working in the museum, helping to sorting out the plan to pack and move the exhibits, and her evenings packing up as much as she could on the ground floor of the palazzo ready for the restoration to start.

On Thursday, she was awake ridiculously early, filled with adrenalin. Today she'd be seeing Gianni again. She'd managed to get into professional mode by the time she met him at the train station, although her heart felt as if it had done a backflip when she caught sight of him walking out of the station entrance.

'Good to see you,' he said, shaking her hand.

'You too,' she said, trying to suppress the urge to throw her arms round him and kiss him. He was clearly keeping a professional distance; she'd do the same.

They caught the *vaporetto* back to the palazzo to drop off his suitcase.

'You're in the same room as last time, if that's OK,' she said.

'That's great.'

'And you need somewhere to work. It's up to you whether you'd rather have the dining room or the study.'

'The dining room's fine,' he said. 'It'll save you having to move—plus it means I have a big table to spread out on.'

It was only then she realised she'd hoped that he'd suggest sharing her study.

Which was ridiculous.

He was here to do a job. Sharing a study would be too distracting.

'You've already done a lot of packing,' he said when she let them into the palazzo.

And cleaning; even though the building work would create a lot of mess, she wanted the place clean before they started. 'You can hardly start work if there's clutter everywhere. The boxes are all numbered, and I have a master list of what's in each one.'

He looked approving. 'I've interviewed people over video calls, and I was hoping to meet up with the people I want on the crew here tomorrow, if that works for you.'

'You're the project manager,' she said. 'You're in charge of arranging things.' She fished in her bag and brought out a door key. 'And you need this, so you don't have to worry about whether I'm here or at the museum.'

'Thank you. For the back door, I assume?' he checked.

'Yes. And I'm getting the key to the side water gate copied for you to give you access for deliveries.'

Once the contracts had been signed, time seemed to

move at a rapid pace. The next thing Serafina knew, the ground floor was full of builders and electricians and plumbers; walls and floors were being stripped back to bare bones; the air was full of dust; and there was the sound of hammers and drills everywhere, mingled with people talking and laughing and radios playing.

How long had it been since there were this many people in the house?

It was noisy and messy. Her mother would've hated it. But she loved it. She enjoyed the way the builders all greeted her in the morning, the way they smiled at her when she brought them mugs of coffee and plates of biscuits, and their patience as they taught her new skills so she could be a part of the restoration, too.

Gianni was right in the middle of things, doing physical work as well as directing his team, and every time she glanced at him she was more and more aware of him. In faded jeans and a T-shirt that showed off his muscular shoulders to perfection, he was utterly gorgeous.

But she couldn't let herself act on that attraction. Not while she was in his debt for the palazzo restoration. She'd simply have to suppress the memories of dancing with him in the twilight, kissing him in the rain, and making love with him in the bedroom next to hers.

So she smiled, she worked hard, and she kept things as professional as she could.

Serafina was definitely keeping him at a distance. Gianni had thought that taking the palazzo out of the equation might make things easier between them, but it had actually made things more complicated. Now they had a formal business relationship, it had put another barrier between them. She was working ridiculously hard, too, disappearing into her library straight after dinner to keep up with her museum work as well as helping the renovation team during the day.

How was he going to persuade her to let him close?

He managed to distract himself by checking through the schedule and working out what needed to be done next, when Robi, the site manager, came over. 'Gi, we've found something a bit unusual by the water gate. I wanted to check it with you before we carry on.'

Gianni followed him over to the water gate; some of the team had been working on the jetty, taking out the damaged bricks and mortar work.

'From outside, we found a cupboard behind the wall,' Robi said, 'but there's no sign of it on the inside of the house. You can see it for yourself.' He indicated the spot. 'It's flat plasterwork.'

Gianni looked at it, frowning. 'That's where I had high damp readings inside. I assumed water had come in through the cracked mortar and damaged brickwork and soaked into the plaster. But, as there's a cupboard there, maybe the water came through the doorway and someone blocked it up.'

'Instead of sorting it out properly by replacing the bricks and the mortar and making the outside waterproof.' Robi rolled his eyes. 'There's a space underneath the cupboard with a wrapped bundle. It looks old. We thought you ought to see it before we take it out.'

Gianni followed him out onto the jetty, took the proffered torch and checked the hollow space beneath the former cupboard. As Robi had described, there was a wrapped bundle. 'Good call, Robi.' He took his phone from his pocket and took a quick snap of the bundle, using a flash to get a better picture. 'I think Serafina needs to see this. I'll go and get her.'

'Come in,' Serafina called at the rap on the library door.

'Got a minute? The site manager's found something interesting,' Gianni said. 'Did you know there was a cupboard by the water gate—the merchants' gate, not the front one?'

She frowned. 'I've never seen one there.'

'We've been taking out the damaged bricks and mortar, and the team found the cupboard—from the outside. There's a space beneath the floorboards of the cupboard and there's a bundle of something beneath it.'

'Have you taken it out and opened it?'

He shook his head. 'I thought you ought to see it, first. I've taken a photograph.' He showed her on his phone. 'It looks to me as if someone put it there deliberately.'

Serafina took a pair of cotton gloves from her desk drawer. At his surprised glance, she explained, 'It might not be anything important—but, if it's a book or a diary, the gloves will at least protect it from the oils on my fingertips. Just in case it's something important, if I give you my camera, can you document it as we go?'

'Of course,' he said.

She followed him down to the water gate. 'There's no sign of a cupboard on this side of the wall.'

'From the outside, you can see that the door's this side,' he said. 'The opening's been plastered over. It could be that the cupboard was damp and it was shut off, so nobody made the mistake of storing anything in it.'

'That sounds about right, where my family's concerned,' she said grimly. 'Though my dad never mentioned a hidden cupboard. It must've been shut off for at least sixty years.'

She peered into the recess from the jetty.

'Can you reach it?' Gianni asked.

'Just about.'

'OK. Stop there while I take a picture—and now I'm switching to my phone to film you.'

She brought the bundle out into the light.

'It's about the right size, weight and shape for a book. It looks as if it's been wrapped in leather,' she said. 'Maybe to try and keep the contents waterproof. If it's a diary, that would make sense. Let's go and take a proper look inside.'

Everyone stopped work and gathered round the table in the middle of the hall. Gianni had her camera in one hand and was videoing her on his phone with the other.

It took a while, but finally she managed to remove the leather covering. Rather than the book she'd been expecting, it was a small, plain wooden casket with a brass lock. When she tried to open the lid, it refused to move. 'It's locked,' she said. And there was no key within the bundle.

'I'll go and see if the key's dropped out into the wall,' Robi said.

'What do you think's inside?' Gianni asked.

'Given the size, maybe papers or jewellery.' And then she caught her breath. A locked box, hidden under the floorboards of a cupboard by the water gate. As if someone had been planning a getaway and had stashed money or documents or… Her heart skipped a beat. Was this the proof of the family legend? Could this be Marianna's rubies?

Robi came back, shaking his head. 'Sorry. There's no key or anything in the cupboard or under it,' he said.

'Do you have any keys that might fit the lock?' Gianni asked.

'There are probably lots of old keys in the boxes on the fourth floor,' Serafina admitted, 'but finding one that fits is going to be like finding a needle in a haystack. Madi will probably know a specialist locksmith who can open it.' She wrinkled her nose. 'Though we might have to send it away.'

'In your shoes,' Gianni said, 'I'd want to know what's in that box as soon as possible—and I'd want to be there when it's opened.'

'My brother's a locksmith,' one of the construction workers said. 'If he can't open it, he'll know someone who can.'

'Could you ask him, please?' Serafina asked.

'Sure.' He took his phone out of his pocket and headed for a quieter area of the hall.

'What are you thinking?' Gianni asked when everyone had gone back to work.

'Why would you hide a locked box near a doorway?' she asked.

'It depends what's inside it. If it's money, then whoever put it there might have been planning some kind of secret escape.'

'Like eloping,' she said.

He looked at her. 'Marianna was going to elope. Do you think it's hers?'

'I'm trying not to get my hopes up,' she said. 'The box might be empty.'

'Rattle it,' he said.

She did, and there was definitely the sound of something moving.

'It could be coins,' he said.

'Or something else that could be turned into money.'

'Jewellery,' he said immediately.

She nodded. 'When Marianna's rubies went missing, everyone assumed they ended up at the bottom of the canal. But supposing she knew about the loose floorboard in the cupboard, and she'd hidden the box underneath it, intending to take her rubies with her to sell when she and her lover were far enough away?'

'Wouldn't she have worn her jewellery rather than hiding it?' Gianni asked.

'It'd be safer in a box,' Serafina said. 'Especially if she was trying to travel incognito. Say she'd borrowed a dress from one of her servants. Expensive jewellery pinned to a cheap dress would make people suspicious. Anyone who saw it might've thought she'd stolen it and they'd get a reward if they took her to the authorities, or they might've tried to steal it from her. Whereas if they were in a box like this, she could hide them safely in her dress.'

'If they are Marianna's rubies,' Gianni said, 'would they be worth a lot?'

'I studied fine art, not jewellery,' Serafina said. 'Your guess is as good as mine. But eighteenth-century jewellery is pretty rare. If they're the ones in Marianna's portrait, and they were found in this house and the plasterwork dates back far enough, it'd be provenance enough.'

The locksmith was there within the hour. Over a mug of coffee in Serafina's kitchen, he looked at the box. 'It's a simple tumbler lock. I'm pretty sure I can open it without damaging the box. If there's a problem, I'll stop, and we can look at your options.'

'Thank you,' she said.

'Nobody's seen what's inside this for decades, then?' the locksmith asked.

'Depending on what's in it, maybe for centuries,' Serafina said.

'It's a privilege to work on something like this,' he said. 'And it's a lot more interesting than my usual work of opening a door because someone's locked themselves out or a key's stuck.'

Serafina worked on her laptop while the locksmith worked on the lock.

Finally, he put his tools down. 'It's open. And, as it's your box, I think you should be the one to open it.'

'Gianni will want to see this, too,' she said. 'And your brother and the rest of the crew.'

They took the box downstairs, and Gianni called everyone round.

Serafina was aware of her heart beating faster—and not because of what she might find in the box. If they were Marianna's rubies, then she'd have the money to fund the restoration. Which meant that she and Gianni would be equals. And maybe, just maybe, they could have a future together.

The hinges of the box creaked as she opened it.

Inside, it was lined with black velvet.

Nestled in the velvet were a ruby choker, three bow-shaped brooches and a pair of earrings. Jewellery that she recognised instantly. 'They're the ones from Marianna's portrait,' she whispered.

The family rubies.

Everything that was once thought lost. And they had been in the house the whole time. Hidden, for hundreds of years.

Serafina's head swam, and she sat down. 'Poor Marianna.' Her eyes prickled with tears. 'All her hopes and dreams were in this box. A future with the man she loved. If only she hadn't tripped on the stairs.' She shook her head. 'That's so *sad.*'

Gianni squeezed her hand. 'I'm sorry.'

She blew out a breath. 'I need to tell my mother.'

'Of course. We'll all give you some space,' he said. 'Let me know if you need anything.'

'Thanks.' She closed the box, thanked the locksmith, and took the rubies up to her study before talking to her mother, her boss and her best friend.

Later that day, Maddalena came over with Enzo, a friend who worked at one of the other local museums and who specialised in jewellery. He handled the rubies carefully, checking them with a loupe. 'They're definitely eighteenth-century,' he said. 'Later jewellers could mimic the rose-cut, but if you look through the loupe you can see the tool-marks. They were cut by hand, not machine. It's why the stones aren't all identical.'

Serafina looked at the jewellery, seeing exactly what he meant, then handed the loupe to Gianni.

'The fastenings are all exactly what I'd expect from

the early eighteenth century, and the stones are backed in gold rather than being openwork.' Enzo turned the largest brooch over to show them. 'Madi says you have provenance.'

'We found a cupboard in the wall when we were working on the restoration,' Gianni said. 'It had been blocked up from the inside of the house. The jewellery box was in a gap underneath the floor of the cupboard.' He showed the expert the photographs of the box in the wall.

'I didn't even know that cupboard existed. I've no idea how long the box has been there, though there's a family story that my great-however-many-times-aunt was trying to elope, three hundred years or so ago, except she fell down the stairs and broke her neck,' Serafina explained. 'I have a miniature of her.' She produced the portrait.

'That's incredible,' Enzo said, staring at the miniature and then the jewels. 'This is either the exact jewellery from the portrait, or an extremely good copy. Though I'd say these were original. And they're in incredible condition because they've been untouched for centuries. No damage, no repairs. I've never handled anything quite like this in all the years I've worked in a museum.'

'Can I ask a horrible question?' Serafina took a deep breath. 'Obviously I'd much rather lend these to a museum where they could be on show, along with Marianna's portrait—but, as you already know from Madi, the palazzo's currently being restored.'

'And restoration costs money,' Enzo said, catching on instantly. 'If you put them in an auction, what they'd fetch would depend on the day, but I can give you a ballpark estimate of their worth.' He named a sum that, had she not been sitting down, would've made Serafina fall over. 'It goes without saying, you need to keep them in a safe until you decide what to do with them.'

'We don't actually have a safe,' Serafina said. 'The family jewellery is all paste.'

'Except this,' Enzo said.

'The bank will be closed now. Do you want me to store the rubies in the museum's vault for you tonight?' Maddalena asked.

'Yes, please,' Serafina said gratefully.

'Let's go now,' Maddalena suggested.

'I'll leave you to it,' Gianni said. 'I have building works to oversee.'

'I…' Serafina knew she needed to say something. But all the words had gone out of her head. This was as much of a shock as learning that all the family money had gone and she was in debt. Now, she'd be able to repay the debt and pay Gianni on time. 'Thank you, Gianni. Without you…'

Gianni lifted one shoulder in a half-shrug and left.

'I'll come to the museum with you,' Enzo said. 'And I can give you the names of some good auction houses. The story of your great-aunt and how you found the rubies is going to raise a lot of interest. And I'll need to talk to our director. It's possible we might be able to make you an offer for the stones and the portrait, so they can stay in Venice.'

Serafina's head was whirring all the way to the museum. Marianna's story had been the start of the downfall of Ca' d'Ardizzone. Maybe finding the rubies meant that the curse was lifted—and her relationship with Gianni stood a chance. She could pay for the repairs herself, instead of borrowing the money for the first stage from him. Meet him as his equal. She had her self-respect back.

And maybe, for the first time in centuries, an Ardizzone could be truly happy.

CHAPTER NINE

SERAFINA HADN'T ASKED him to go with her to the museum.

To Gianni, that felt like a bad sign.

On the one hand, maybe she'd see finding Marianna's rubies as a sign that the curse was lifted from her family.

On the other, selling the rubies meant that she'd be able to afford to pay for the renovations herself. She wouldn't need his help any more. And, even though he tried to tell himself that she wasn't like Elena's family and of course she wasn't going to back off from him, deep down he was scared that she'd see things differently now. That's she'd see the huge gap between their backgrounds and walk away.

By the time the stragglers on his team had left for the day, he still hadn't heard a thing from her.

She'd pushed him away. Shut him out.

How stupid he'd been to think that there was a chance things could work out between them.

His sister had been right, after all. He'd let his heart rule his head. Again.

Maybe it would be better to back off completely and leave one of his team in charge.

His stomach growled. He made himself a sandwich; but the food was tasteless.

By the time Serafina finally came back, he was in a foul mood.

'Sorry I was such a long time,' she said. 'Enzo had a lot of information for me. And the press officer at the museum wanted to talk to me to put a draft press release together. The story of Marianna and the rubies is going to help put the museum on the map when it moves here.'

'Uh-huh.' Though she still could've called. Or texted. Or *something*. The silence was what had upset him most.

She frowned. 'Are you all right?'

'Perfectly, thank you.'

She grimaced. 'Sorry. I should've called you to let you know I'd be a while.'

The fact that she hadn't stung more than he'd expected. 'I'm not your keeper,' he said. 'You don't have to tell me anything.'

She narrowed her eyes at him. 'That's uncalled for.'

He knew that, but he couldn't stop himself sniping. 'You're back to being *rich* little rich girl, then.'

She folded her arms. 'Looks like it. Surely that's a good thing, because it means you don't have to wait for me to pay your bills?'

Yes. And no. How could he tell her what was in his head? Especially when everything felt as if it had changed, and not for the better? That he thought she was rejecting him? And it brought back the way he'd felt when Elena had dumped him: that he wasn't good enough for her.

His silence made her narrow her eyes at him even more. 'Hang on. Are you angry because you're not my knight on a white charger any more?'

'No.' But she had a point, and it irritated him. He wasn't sure who he was more angry with—her, or himself.

'Oh, for pity's sake. *Men*.' She shook her head. 'I'm going to make dinner. Are you joining me?'

'I've already eaten.'

She lifted her chin. 'Right.'

He knew he was being rude. He could at least have a drink

with her while she ate. But he didn't trust himself not to say something even more stupid. 'I have work to do. Excuse me.'

He thought she muttered something as she headed for the kitchen, but he wasn't going to ask her to repeat it. He knew pride was standing in his way; but he didn't want her to reject him, so it was better to avoid her until they'd both cooled down a bit. Wasn't it?

Except, the next morning, the tension between them felt worse. They barely spoke over breakfast. She went to the museum instead of working on the restoration, the way she usually did. And she avoided him in the evening on the grounds that she had a lot of admin to do and dinner was going to be a sandwich at her desk.

'I don't mind cooking for both of us,' he said, wanting to break the stalemate between them.

'I'm fine with a sandwich,' she said coolly.

She couldn't even accept a simple dinner from him?

If she wasn't going to meet him halfway, then they really weren't going to stand a chance.

Maybe absence would make the heart grow fonder. Or at least give him a chance to get his head straight and he could protect his heart. 'I'm going back to Rome tomorrow,' he said. 'I'm not sure when I'll be back. If you need anything, ask Robi.'

'OK,' she said.

She wasn't even going to wish him a safe journey?

Fine.

He booked the first train ticket he could get, left her a note the next morning with the keys to the back door and the water gate, suggesting that she could pass them on to Robi, the site manager, and headed back to Rome without seeing her.

Serafina stared at the note. Gianni hadn't even bothered to say goodbye in person. He'd simply left that cool little note next to the keys she'd given him.

Finding Marianna's rubies hadn't broken the Ardizzone curse, after all. She was as miserable now as she'd been when she'd broken up with Tom.

But at least she could fix the other problems in her life now. Her mother, the palazzo and the museum.

It would have to be enough.

She continued working with the restoration team during the day and doing her museum work in the evening. Although she knew that Gianni had been in contact with Robi every single day, for an update on the restoration, he hadn't left any message for her. She almost called him, several times, but each time she ended the call before it had even connected. She didn't have a clue what to say to him or how to get him to talk to her.

Weirdly, even though the palazzo was full of people, it felt emptier than the days she'd spent there alone. And she knew why: because Gianni wasn't there.

At the beginning of the following week, Enzo had a meeting with her and the director of his own museum, and they made her a formal offer for the rubies. Although she knew she'd probably get more money if she put Marianna's jewellery up for auction, she wanted it to stay in Venice, so she accepted the offer.

As soon as the money came through, she paid a chunk off the taxes she owed, sent money to her mother, and did a bank transfer to Leto Construction.

Now the ball was in Gianni's court. He'd either talk to her or keep his distance: and his reaction would tell her how he really felt about her.

'Gi, there's something you need to see. Log in to the business bank account.' Flora leaned against her brother's desk.

Frowning, he did as she asked. There was a deposit from 'S Ardizzone'. A sum which covered everything up to the end of the first stage of renovations.

There was only one reason she could've afforded to pay him. 'She must have sold the rubies,' he said. And he damped down the hurt that she hadn't even bothered telling him what she was doing. She'd shut him out completely.

'You need to talk to her,' Flora said.

He shook his head. 'You were right in the first place. She doesn't need me any more.'

'If I were in her shoes,' Flora said, 'I'd hate having to ask for help. I'd hate having to be in someone's debt. Especially if it was someone I liked a lot.'

He said nothing.

Flora sighed. 'Gi, you're being stubborn. Obviously she likes you. Think about it. I know what happened with her ex. It was all over the gossip columns. That'd break anyone's ability to trust.'

He understood that. But he still hated the fact that Serafina had shut him out. He'd thought they were becoming a team, but she hadn't included him.

'I know Elena hurt you, but at least she didn't cheat on you. Imagine how hard it was for Serafina, walking in on her fiancé with someone else.'

He lifted one shoulder.

'Are you seriously going to let what happened with Elena wreck this for you, too?' Flora shook her head in exasperation.

'I thought you didn't like Serafina?'

'I didn't like the fact that you were bankrolling her,' Flora corrected. 'Yes, I worried at first that maybe you'd fallen for another Elena, but the fact she's paid you back like this tells me that she's not. That she's genuine. And you've got a chip on your shoulder, little brother. Just because she's posh, it doesn't mean she's going to hurt you.' She shook her head, looking exasperated. 'I'm half tempted to go and see Serafina myself, bring her back to Rome and bang your heads together. Sofia's got more sense than the pair of you combined.'

What was he meant to say to that?

Flora rolled her eyes. 'Stop being so stubborn. You miss her, don't you? And don't you *dare* do the strong-and-silent thing on me. Admitting your feelings is not a weakness.'

He sighed. 'Yes.' He hadn't been able to settle back in Rome. Home didn't feel like home any more, because she wasn't there.

'And I bet she misses you, too,' Flora said.

And that was his big fear. 'What if she doesn't?'

'She asked you for a three-month payment holiday, but she's paid the lot in one lump. That's a gesture, Gi. A big one. It means "Talk to me".'

'How do you know?'

'Because it's what I'd do in her shoes if I wanted you to talk to me.' Flora's voice gentled. 'And you've been like a bear with a sore head ever since you came back to Rome. Even Sofia says that Tio Gi is growly.'

He winced. 'Sorry.'

'Go and see her,' Flora said. 'You can't have a conversation like this on a phone or even a video call. It needs to be face-to-face.'

'I'm fine.'

Flora sighed and gave him a hug. 'At least think about it.'

'Uh-huh.'

'See you later, Growly.' But she looked sad rather than teasing.

Gianni fully intended to bury himself in paperwork.

Except he couldn't concentrate.

All he could think about was Serafina.

Was paying upfront a challenge, like Flora thought it was? Or was it Serafina's way of saying thank you and goodbye?

He picked up his phone and tapped on her name. And then he cut the call before it connected.

His sister had a point.

This ought to be a face-to-face conversation.

And there was a train to Venice in thirty minutes. He'd just about make it if he left the office now.

He went into his sister's office. 'I'm going to Venice.'

'Good.' She patted his shoulder. 'You know it makes sense.'

He missed the train.

The next one was a slow one.

He paced the platform until the next fast train arrived.

And then, once he'd boarded, the doubts came back. What if she wasn't there? She might have gone to see her mother. Or gone anywhere.

He should at least have phoned. Or maybe made an appointment with her.

Cross with himself, he called Maddalena. 'It's Gianni Leto. Do you happen to know where...?' What did he call her? The Contessa? Serafina?

'Serafina is?' Maddalena filled in. 'Yes. Right now, she's sitting at her desk in the office next door to mine. I'll transf—'

'No, please don't do that,' he cut in hastily.

Maddalena coughed. 'I'm not in the business of playing games, Signor Leto.'

'I'm not playing games. I'm on the train to Venice and I want to be sure she's there.'

'Wouldn't it have been better to check *before* you got on the train?'

He knew he deserved every bit of the 'How stupid are you?' tone. 'I wasn't completely sure she'd speak to me. We...um...had a slight falling-out before I left.'

'If you hurt her,' Maddalena said, her voice dangerously calm, 'I'll come after you and cut out your heart with my letter-opener. Which is blunt, so it will take a long and painful time.'

'I'm not going to hurt her,' Gianni said. 'But if you can keep her at the office until I get there, I'd appreciate it.'

For a moment, he thought she was going to refuse. But then she sighed. 'All right. I'll keep her here.'

The rest of the journey felt as if it took for ever, but at last the train crossed the causeway and he could see the city rising out of the sea.

He caught the *vaporetto* to the Accademia, then got out his phone to make sure he was heading in the right direction through the narrow alleyways to the Museum of Women's Art. On the way, he passed a florist's.

Should he take Serafina flowers?

He owed her a lot more than flowers. He owed her honesty.

But flowers might help break the ice a little.

Then he realised he didn't have a clue what her favourite flowers were. Roses felt too cliched. But then he saw a bucket full of sunflowers, and they made him think of her. How he felt when he was with her: as if the world was bright and shiny and new.

He bought a large bunch, then found his way to the museum. The receptionist was one of the people who'd given up her spare time to work on the palazzo; recognising him, she smiled. 'Are you here to see Serafina?'

'If she's in her office, yes.'

'I'll just c—'

'Please don't,' he said. 'I want to surprise her.'

The receptionist looked at the flowers. 'OK. I'll buzz you through.'

She directed him through the back to the museum offices, and he rapped on Serafina's open door.

'Come i—' She lifted her head and stopped mid-sentence when she saw him.

'I brought you these,' he said, lifting the sunflowers.

She made no move to take them. 'Why?'

'Because...' He blew out a breath and closed the door behind him. 'Because I don't know what to say to you. I've spent three hours on a train, trying to plan what to say, and nothing sounds right. And I saw these on the way here, and I thought you'd like them, and they remind me of you because they're like sunshine, and I thought they might break the ice, and—' He stopped and groaned. 'I'm babbling like an idiot.'

'You are.' But she was smiling. 'Thank you. They're lovely.'

'We need to talk,' he said.

'Not here. Let's go for a walk,' she said. 'I'll put these in water in the kitchen and let Madi know I'm going out.'

He nodded and waited in the doorway to her office while she went to the kitchen.

'Madi, I'm leaving my desk for a bit,' she said.

'My fault,' Gianni said, leaning round the doorway.

Maddalena smiled, waved her letter-opener at him and did an elaborate wink.

'What was that about?' Serafina asked as she led Gianni out of the museum.

'She was reminding me of our conversation this morning, when I asked her to keep you here. She said if I hurt you, she'll cut out my heart with her letter-opener.'

Serafina grinned. 'And she would. She's scary, our Madi.'

'She is,' he said.

He waited until they'd left the museum and found an empty bench on the wide pavement overlooking the canal before speaking again.

'I'm sorry,' he said. 'I've been very stupid.'

He waited for her to agree. Or at least say something. Eventually, she sighed. 'You're not the only one.'

Relief flooded through him. At least she recognised they were both at fault. 'Thank you for the stage payment. Which I note is a couple of months earlier than we agreed.'

'Because I sold the rubies to Enzo's museum. I'm loaning him Marianna's portrait, on condition we get to display the rubies for the first six months when our museum opens at the palazzo.'

'That sounds good.' Except it wasn't the rubies or Marianna he wanted to know about. It was Serafina. 'How are you?'

'Perfectly fine, thank you. And you?'

He could be polite back; or he could be the first to admit the truth.

'Miserable,' he said.

He held her gaze. Would she admit how she felt, too? Or would she push him away?

Her shoulders drooped. 'Me, too.'

'I missed you,' he said softly.

'Did you? Because you left without even saying goodbye.'

'Because I was angry and hurt,' he said. 'As well as thoroughly in the wrong. What you said about me wanting to be a knight on a white charger—that was all true.'

'And I pushed you away because I panicked,' she said. 'Relationships don't work, in my family.'

'I know. The curse. But haven't you broken it, now? You found the rubies, you're telling Marianna's story to the world, and you're rescuing the palazzo.' He looked at her. 'And you sent me the money.'

'I didn't want to be beholden to you,' she said. 'I wanted to fix things myself. So I can meet you as your equal.'

He frowned. 'My *equal*? Hang on. You're a *contessa*. That makes you way, way above my station.'

She scoffed. 'Who cares?'

'I wasn't good enough for Elena's family. And you're

really posh. What makes me good enough for yours?'
he asked.

'You're good enough because you're you,' she said simply, and took his hand. 'I'm not Elena, and you're not Tom.'

He squeezed her hand. 'I'd never cheat on you.'

'And I'd never look down on you.'

'What, exactly,' he asked, 'are we both worrying about?'

'That it's going to go wrong and we'll get hurt,' she said.

'If we talk, if we're honest with each other—there might
be times when we fall out and start fighting, but if we trust
each other instead of trying to second-guess each other
we'll get through the sticky spots,' he said. 'It's *not* talking that makes things go wrong.'

'The palazzo's felt empty without you,' she said.

He coughed. 'Are you telling me our crew stopped working when I went back to Rome?'

'No. Just it *felt* empty,' she said.

'Rome doesn't feel like home any more,' he said.

She was silent for such a long time that he didn't think
she was going to answer. But then her voice cracked slightly
as she asked, 'Could Venice be home?'

'I think,' he said, 'home might be where you are.'

Her eyes glittered with tears. 'That's the nicest thing
anyone's ever said to me.'

'I mean it. I want to be with you, Serafina. I want to
make a future with you. Make a family with you.' He
looked at her. 'But that all rather depends on what you
want.'

'I want to be with you, too,' she said. 'A future and a
family sounds perfect.' She paused. 'I'm sorry I panicked
and pushed you away.'

'I'm sorry I pushed you away, too,' he said.

'We're both in the wrong,' she said.

'Then let's make it right,' Gianni said. He cupped her
cheek with his hand. 'When you asked me to come here,

you showed me *your* Venice. But it wasn't the city I fell in love with. It was you. And I was furious when you asked me to marry you, because I didn't want a marriage of convenience. I don't want to walk away from you after a year. I don't want to walk away from you, ever. I want you for a lifetime. I love you.'

'I love you, too,' she said.

He brushed his mouth lightly against hers. 'Will you marry me—not for the palazzo, but for me?'

'Yes.'

'Then let's seal the deal,' he said, and kissed her.

EPILOGUE

Two years later

GIANNI STEERED HIS wife out of the front door. 'Stop worrying. Marianna's going to be fine.'

'I guess having six babysitters for our first night out without our daughter might seem a bit over the top,' Serafina said.

He shook his head. 'Best compromise ever,' he said. 'Neither of our mums wanted to miss out on being her first babysitter. Neither did your Tia Vittoria or my sister.'

'And Lessi and Madi staked their claim as her godmothers,' Serafina said. 'You're right. Best compromise ever.'

'Plus it means,' he said, 'we get time on our own.'

'Are you sure you don't want that lobster in a Michelin-starred restaurant? It's been two years, now, and I still haven't made good on that promise,' Serafina reminded him.

He grinned. 'I've got a much better idea. *Cichéti*, catch of the day in our favourite *osteria*, and then dancing in the moonlight in St Mark's Square.' He spun her into his arms for a kiss. 'And then I'm going to kiss you and tell you how much I love you on every single bridge on the way home.'

She laughed. 'That sounds perfect. And, with six babysitters, we can take the long way home…'

* * * * *

COMING SOON!

MILLS & BOON®

Coming soon

FINDING FOREVER ON THEIR ISLAND PARADISE
Therese Beharrie

'Everything about this feels real. Too real,' he said with a frown.

A piece of her hair fluttered over her forehead. He focused on that. The slight curl of it; the tiniest fuzz around its edges. Slowly, he lifted his hand, gripped the strands in his index finger and thumb, and gently put it back behind her head. It promptly flew to the front again. He smiled.

'When you say things like that…when you do things like this…' She nodded her head so he'd know she was talking about his actions with her hair. 'You take my breath away.' Her hands gripped the front of his t-shirt. 'I don't like feeling vulnerable either. The last time a man made me feel that way, I almost lost…' Her voice faded. Her fingers tightened.

'I don't want you to lose anything,' he whispered.

'I know.' Her gaze met his. 'Maybe that's why I feel like I'm gaining something with you instead.'

His heart filled. Overflowed. With what, he didn't know. Wasn't sure he wanted to find out. But he knew that honesty had brought them here. Vulnerability. Things he'd viewed as enemies since they'd done nothing but hurt him when he'd tried them with his family.

But now they'd brought him this closeness with Morgan.

Literally and figuratively; both seemed of the utmost importance. Although literal took precedence now that he could see the faint dusting of freckles on her right cheek. There was nothing on her left, and it fascinated him. As did the sparkle in her eyes. Every time he looked at them he came up with a better description for their colour. Today, they looked mahogany. Full, deep, rich; the colour would make the most beautiful piece of furniture. A desk, he thought. He'd make a desk of this exact colour so that he could be reminded of her eyes, of her, whenever he sat down to work.

'What are you thinking about?' she asked quietly.

His eyes dipped to her lips. They were somewhere between pink and red, reminding him of a tart fruit, and their creases formed a pattern he wanted to memorise. An impossible task. An illogical task. He wanted to take it on nevertheless.

'I'm thinking I'd...I'd like to kiss you.'

She smiled. 'What are you waiting for?'

Continue reading
FINDING FOREVER ON THEIR ISLAND PARADISE
Therese Beharrie

Available next month
www.millsandboon.co.uk

JOIN US ON SOCIAL MEDIA!

Stay up to date with our latest releases, author news and gossip, special offers and discounts, and all the behind-the-scenes action from Mills & Boon...

 millsandboon

 millsandboonuk

 millsandboon

It might just be true love...

MILLS & BOON
MEDICAL
Pulse-Racing Passion

Set your pulse racing with dedicated, delectable doctors in the high-pressure world of medicine, where emotions run high and passion, comfort and love are the best medicine.